HA
HUSBAND
& HIS
CURIOUS
WIFE

HELEN E. FIELD

BOOK TWO OF THE DE'ATH FAMILY ANTICS

THE HAPLESS HUSBAND & HIS CURIOUS WIFE

First published in the UK in 2021 by In Jest

In Jest

Go to www.helenefield.com to sign up and subscribe to Helen's infrequent but exclusive and interesting emails about her books as well as updates and advanced notice of new releases.

Paperback ISBN: 978-1-8382692-4-1
epub eBook ISBN: 978-1-8382692-5-8

Cover design and typeset by Spiffing Covers

Helen E Field's Other Books:

The Mystery Shopper & The Hot Tub:
Book One in The De'Ath Family Antics Series

Contents

Author's Biography

Helen Field is a business woman, writer, publisher of greetings cards, funny poet, speaker, traveller and author of *The Hapless Husband & His Curious Wife* and also *The Mystery Shopper & The Hot Tub* – both books in the De'Ath Family Antics Series.

She was born and brought up in Waltham Abbey in Essex and currently lives in a small village in North West Essex, so it would be fair to say she has earned her 'Essex girl' badge!

Helen has had a varied and interesting career in retail and hospitality in UK, Europe and the USA, including setting up and running her own restaurant and she ran her own training consultancy to the hospitality industry. One element of her business was designing and implementing mystery shopper programmes all over the UK for some of the most well-known organisations. With inside knowledge of the industry and armed with thousands of funny mystery shopping incidents, she was inspired to write her debut novel, *The Mystery Shopper & The Hot Tub.*

After more than twenty years, Helen has changed direction and is now focussed on her writing. She is fortunate enough to be able to do this while travelling around the world with her husband.

She is married to Nic, has three amazing grown-up children and an African Grey Parrot.

AUTHOR'S NOTE

For international readers, who may not be familiar with UK regional dialects and colloquial language, it is worth explaining that Essex is a home county very close to London. Over the years, many Londoners moved out to Essex and their language and accent followed – sometimes referred to now as Estuary English. It is spoken to this day in the county. You may also find the occasional strange word or phrase in some of the dialogue, with which you are unfamiliar. To assist and for your interest, you will see occasional footnotes where the meaning of words or phrases may not be clear. Cockney rhyming slang, which originated in the East End of London in the 1840s, was a means by which market traders, hawkers and possibly criminals would hide what they were saying from passers-by and the authorities. It is also still used to this day and my characters use it from time to time in their speech. (See www.cockneyrhymingslang.co.uk/ for further information.)

For my late in-laws, Fay and Gordon Bennett, who partly inspired a couple of characters in the series.

1

Having a Domestic

Brooke bobbed about amongst the bubbles, frowning and fidgeting wildly, before peering down inside Tuesday's bikini. Her discomfort eventually compelled her to thrust her hand down inside the left cup and underneath her breast, lifting it up and around, before locating and removing a small piece of Lego. She tutted and threw it on the grass. Continuing to hold her left breast in her right hand for a minute, she inspected it at close quarters, screwing up her face. 'Ugh! Where did you come from? Pesky little buggers!' With the speed and precision of an assassin, she pincered two fingernails together and whipped out three or four hairs that had made an unwelcome appearance on her otherwise hairless body.

'Are you doing what I think you're doing?' Dean shouted from inside the conservatory, clearly disgusted.

'Well there ain't no nipple fairy coming to get rid of 'em during the night, you know! Someone's gotta do it!' she said, calmly finishing off the right breast.

'You'll end up like a prune if you're not careful,' Dean warned as he strolled out onto the patio and perched on the edge of the hot tub in his suit. He could not help but recall the hideous, torturous birth of Paige almost two years ago and the high blood pressure situation that arose for Brooke as a result, never mind the unmentionable minor damage to her lady parts. 'How long have you been in there?'

Here he goes again!

Ever since that memorable birthday last September when the hot tub had been delivered, she'd pampered herself in it almost daily; she'd already had her money's worth. Brooke went on the defensive and pulled a face, mocking Dean's nagging. 'Only about half an hour; since I put Paige to bed.'

'You know you shouldn't stay in there much longer. It's not just your blood pressure I'm worried about. Did you know you can get Legionnaire's disease and something called hot tub rash? Apparently, "the average bather's got around one gram of faeces in their gluteal fold which then ends up in the water". He poured a bag of crisps into his mouth until it overflowed. 'Saw that on LADbible the other day.'

Brooke's mind wandered back to earlier in the week when Dull Dave and Porno Gazza had been over for a 'mates' session. They'd been competing to see whose farts most resembled the water bubbles created by the jets. She grimaced at the mere thought of what they might've left behind.

Better check the chemicals tomorrow.

'You're such a bloody hypochondriac, Dean. I'm fine. I'm getting out now anyway.' As she stepped out and her stunning athletic figure towered over him, she rested her hands on his shoulders so she didn't slip.

'Mind those plates of meat[1]!' Dean joked. Brooke gave him a playful slap on his head. He grabbed the towelling dressing gown off the chair. She'd bought it from The White Company at great expense, specifically for using when she got out the hot

1. Feet.

tub, along with seven new bikinis – Primark, of course – one for every day of the week. Tuesday was leopard print's turn. Dean helped her on with the gown and wrapped her tightly from behind, around her waist, affectionately rubbing her dry and nuzzling his nose into her damp ringlets.

Mmm, you smell like the rosemary bush.

He noticed a magazine on the chair where her dressing gown had been. *National Geographic* was opened at an article entitled 'Harbin International Ice and Snow Sculpture Festival in China'. He picked it up and laughed.

'What's this? Where d'ya get this from?'

Brooke snatched it out of his hand, rather too quickly if the truth be known. 'The library,' she lied, thinking of the pile of *National Geographics* that she'd found at Lady Townsend's. He snatched it back and cursorily flicked through to another page Brooke had earmarked for reading; 'Importing Antiquities from SARs of China'.

'Don't tell me you wanna go to China for our next holiday?' He guffawed, put his fingers up to his eyes and pulled them out to the side; his wife's increasing worldliness unwittingly threatening the very essence of who he was and his own ignorance manifesting itself.

Brooke rolled her eyes.

So bloody uncultured.

'It's interesting! What's it to you, anyway? I can read what I like,' she replied defensively.

'Course you can, love. C'mon, let's get you in before you get cold.' He ruffled her hair as one would a mischievous boy who had to come in for tea.

Brooke stomped upstairs and sat on their bed, niggled. She

wasn't sure why, until she thought about Dean's reaction to her reading material. In fact, now she thought about it she'd become increasingly irritated at Dean's reaction to the few things she was trying to do differently in her life. She thought about her employer and unofficial mentor, the elderly, elegant and classy Lady Townsend. She'd learned so much from her since she'd defied Dean's wishes and secretly taken a cleaning job at her large, grand, historic country house called Purses, nearby, almost a year ago.

A smile crept across her face.

Her Latin book was a permanent fixture in her handbag these days. She'd mastered her newfound method of getting in and out of a car and it made her feel positively duchess-like. She'd refined her demeanour and she'd even managed to persuade Dean to start opening the car door for her. An eclectic collection of publications from *Antiques Monthly* and *Country Homes & Interiors* to *The Smithsonian* and *The Economist*, had been successfully squirreled away in her underwear drawer, somewhere Dean was unlikely to go. She'd struggled with *The Economist*. She didn't understand half of it but she'd soldiered on, trying to learn about the GDP of Russia and wondering why it mattered. There didn't appear to be any sort of theme to her choice of literature. Whatever took her fancy, she'd stealthily slip into her handbag and take home from Purses at the end of the day, although she was sure Lady Townsend wouldn't have objected, even if she'd known about her 'petty thieving'. Brooke was more afraid that she might laugh at her. To claim Brooke was like a sponge would be an understatement. She was beginning to see that there was so much more to life than she currently made of it. Places to see, people to meet, things to do and things to know. Never had she felt so restless.

She frowned and pondered how on earth she was going to tell Dean that she'd been working for the past nine months, if indeed she could bring herself to tell him at all. She'd tried to pluck up the courage several times, but when it came to it, she just couldn't go through with it. She adored him so much that she couldn't bear to upset him. She knew he'd think it'd be too physical with her blood pressure issues. In addition, he'd still got this old-fashioned view about wanting to be the breadwinner and 'head of the house'. He'd proudly tell his friends that she didn't have to work; she believed *that* stemmed from his mother. When she and Dean married, he'd sworn blind to her that he'd always take care of her and their children – not like his father. The problem was, the longer she lied, the harder it would be to tell the truth.

She pulled on her pink sheep pyjamas, followed by her pink llama cleaning slippers. She'd regrettably used them for sweeping the kitchen floor once too often, plus they were actually a tad too small for her, so her big toe peeped out, revealing her exquisitely manicured toenail. Before going downstairs, she popped her head around Paige's bedroom door and watched for a few moments. Silence. Oh, what joy! Asleep.

Thank god!

Dean was splayed out on the sofa, beer in hand, watching *Top Gear*. Brooke brought two large pizzas and curly fries in from the kitchen and they ate on their laps while watching TV. The pizzas were so big, she had to place them on large chopping boards. Dean liked to hold one end of the curly fry in his mouth and pull it out slowly at the other end to see how straight he could get it before it broke.

'Dean, what the hell are you doing?'

'Nothing, why?'

'You're meant to eat 'em not play with 'em.'

He stopped playing but then complained about the unevenness of the pizza toppings over the base. 'What make of pizza is this? Look at these toppings. They're all shoved in one place. That's not how they're meant to be.'

'I can't remember, but it all goes down the same way. I wouldn't worry about it.'

He proceeded to reposition them all so that they were equidistant from each other before tucking in. 'But it's not good, is it?' Dean replied, miffed. With that, he retrieved the pizza packaging from the bin and brought it into the living room, frowning at the picture.

'Look at that. My pizza doesn't look anything like that.' Dean pointed at the evenly spaced chilli peppers and thrust the box into Brooke's face.

'Dean, just get it down your Gregory[2] or it'll get cold.' She continued eating, unperturbed by the uneven distribution of vegetables.

Dean turned the packaging over and started reading until he came across the customer helpline number. He stabbed the box with his finger.

'Right. I'm calling them after tea.'

Brooke rolled her eyes. Never had she met anyone as particular as her husband. They finished their pizzas, Dean licked his fingers and then rang Iceland's customer helpline.

'Iceland Customer Helpline, Jean speaking, how may I help you?'

---

2. Gregory Peck – Neck. Stop complaining, get on with it and get it down your throat.

'I wanna complain about my pizza.'

'I'm sorry, sir, can you tell me which pizza you have and what precisely is wrong with it?'

'It's the spicy meat feast and the toppings are unevenly spaced over the base. There're six bits of red chilli and they're all shoved down one end. They should be approximately eight centimetres apart if each slice is gonna have one on; same for the chunks of beef.'

Brooke looked over to him with an emotionless face and shook her head. She could only hear one half of the conversation of course, but it was clear that Jean from Iceland thought he was an eccentric. The call went on for twelve minutes. Topics of discussion included the average diameter of a red chilli pepper, the cooking time of frozen beef mince and the advantages of red onion versus Mediterranean onion.

Finally, the call finished and Dean re-joined Brooke, who was waving her size 8s at him – the unwritten sign that meant she wanted them massaged. He had an air of smugness about him as he removed her slippers.

'Honestly, Dean, I don't know anyone else on the planet who actually phones those helplines. It's a bloody monthly event for you.'

'Well, it was worth it. She apologised and said we'd get a voucher as a gesture of goodwill and that she'd pass my comments to their food development team.'

Brooke looked decidedly unimpressed and went back to reading *National Geographic*.

'Dean, have a guess how big the biggest ice sculpture ever in the world was?'

'What?! I dunno.' *Top Gear* was rather more gripping to

Dean than random pointless facts about weird pastimes of the Chinese.

'Go on – just have a guess.'

'How about four metres high?' he said without taking his eyes off Jeremy Clarkson's leaderboard.

Brooke laughed, and, with the excitement of a small child, replied, 'No. Way off. It was 250m wide and 8.5m high! Imagine going to see that. You could walk inside it.'

'You could ski along it in your bare feet!' Dean roared laughing at his own joke. He was most fortunate to have married a woman with a sense of humour. A more sensitive soul might have been reduced to tears.

'Haha!' Brooke lifted her foot and swiped him on the cheek with her sole. A play fight ensued with squeals that could be heard at the end of Elephant Close. When it was over, Brooke's demeanour changed and her face turned serious as she swivelled around to face to Dean.

C'mon, girl, you can do it, this is as good a time as any.

'What? Why are you looking at me like that?' Dean suddenly pushed himself upright on the sofa.

Here goes.

'Dean, what would you say if I said I wanted to get a job?' Mmm. Not exactly truthful, but it would at least provoke a conversation.

'No, Brooke. We've talked about this before. It's still too risky with your blood pressure and your...you know...' he said, nodding towards her lower lady parts. 'Remember what the doc said about pregnancy-induced hypertension carrying on way after you've had a kid and that your...little lady friend down there needs at least a year to recover.'

Brooke bristled, tempted to immediately go on the defensive, as was her tendency, but she managed to keep her cool. 'I know, babe, but that was a while ago now and Paige is less demanding than she used to be and…' She twiddled with her ringlets. 'I'm getting a bit bored, to be honest.' She looked straight into his eyes in hopeful anticipation.

'You? Bored? Don't make me laugh! All them trips to Lakeside, chinwags with Dawn and cosy little chats with your new mate Lady Townsend in the library?!'

God, I can't believe he still thinks I met her in the library.

Brooke froze at the mention of her name. 'But what if it was just a really easy little part-time job?'

'Like what?'

'Oh, I dunno, I haven't thought that much about it,' she lied. It had occupied her thoughts for at least six months.

Dean stopped massaging Brooke's feet, gently placed them on the floor and moved closer to her, putting his arm around her shoulders and giving her a squeeze.

'Brooke, you do know that I worship the ground you stand on, don't you?' Brooke nodded, but, inside, knew that a caveat was coming before trying to persuade her against it. Again. 'Well, *I* was thinking that, maybe…we might want to start trying for baby number two?'

Brooke herself had considered this a while ago, but the longer she worked for Lady Townsend, the more interesting she found it and the less she'd felt she was ready. Those thoughts flooded back.

I'm just not sure. There's so much I want to do first.

'Well of course *I* want another baby, it's just that… I thought I might enjoy a bit of freedom before going through all that again?' She said it tentatively, glancing briefly at Dean's face. It came out as a question. A veiled request for permission to say no.

'Blimey, I thought you'd leap at the suggestion! I don't get you sometimes, Brooke.'

Oh crikey, this is definitely not going to plan.

'I'm not saying no, I just need some time to think about it.'

Dean was taken aback, if not a little upset. Since his promotion at TrussInUs he'd been thinking about little else. 'You know you don't have to work, babe. I know things were tight before my promotion, but it's OK now. We can survive just fine without you having to work. If you're a bit short of cash, just tell me and I'll give you some more.' It was common knowledge that Dean was proud of being able to 'keep' his wife.

He just doesn't get it.

'Yeah, but it's not just about the money, Dean. Like I said, I'm a bit bored and would quite like to do something apart from shopping in Lakeside and to earn some money of my own.'

Dean looked genuinely perplexed. He failed to comprehend why his wife would possibly choose going to work over a life at home doing whatever she wanted. 'Well what kind of things? You mean going shopping somewhere different to Lakeside? Like Bluewater? Clubbing with the girls? The Ideal Home Exhibition? That sort of thing?'

'Do you realise how sexist you sound? No! I dunno; going to the theatre or doing some charity work or something.'

'You what?' Dean said incredulously. 'Since when've you been interested in the theatre? You've never even been to a theatre!'

'I know! That's precisely my point! Why not? Why 'aven't

we been?' Brooke's voice was getting louder and she made that palms-up gesture.

Dean was speechless. ''cause we're not interested in it, that's why not. What's got into you, Brooke? Where's all this stuff coming from?' He scratched his head as if trying to work out a tricky problem. Suddenly he looked up.

'It's that Lady Townsend woman, isn't it? Ever since you met her, you've been... I dunno...just different, that's all.'

'What? No!' Brooke lied – again.

'It is, isn't it? It's her. What's she been saying to you?'

'Nothing, Dean! She's lovely. You leave her out of this. We just chat in the library, that's all. She reads to Paige and we natter sometimes.' Oh dear, what a whopper!

I need to stop this conversation right now.

Dean looked suspicious and stomped off to get another beer.

'Let's just forget I said anything, OK?' Brooke said sharply.

Dean went back to *Top Gear*, Brooke went back to The Harbin Ice Festival and they sat in silence for the remainder of the evening.

2

LGBT, Pret and Debrett's

'Syrian refugees, black, Asian, disabled, transexuals, bisexuals, gay, jailbirds, Rastafarians, Muslims, pregnant women, Gypsies, old people, Jews – I want the lot.'

Dave strutted up and down his office at the TrussInUs Call Centre as he was talking; hands in pockets and occasionally glancing up at the ceiling as if giving dictation to a secretary.

'Why?' Dean asked.

'Well, Dean. I've been enlightened. Last week I attended a very interesting networking evening at the local Chamber of Commerce and there was this speaker there talking about workplace diversity and something called 'unconscious bias'.' Dave used his fingers to put imaginary quote marks around the words. 'I'd never even heard of it. Bloody fascinating, it was. Really made me think. Did *you* know there was forty-six different sexual identities?'

'What d'ya mean?' Dean screwed up his face.

'Well, people apparently identify in loads of different ways, not just your usual BLT crowd.' He waved his hand about impatiently. 'You know who I mean. There's other types – like pomosexuals, for example. That's when people "reject sexuality labels or don't identify with any of them".' His face was a picture of satisfaction that he'd remembered such an important piece of information.

'How can they do that? They've gotta be something. Surely. You know. Either a man or a woman...or gay?'

'Dean. Let me ask you something. Are you sexist, or racist?'

'No! Course not.' A fleeting thought crossed his mind about his difficult conversation with Brooke the previous evening about her not working and her hurtful accusation that he was sexist.

That's different though. I'm just worried about her.

'Dean, how would you feel if I told you I wanted to become a woman?' Dave's face was deadpan.

Dean cracked up laughing. A vision of Dave as a sort of Ru Paul drag queen character sprang to mind. Seeing Dave's reaction to his howling, he stopped pretty sharpish.

'You see. I rest my case. You assumed I was joking. But what if I wasn't, Dean? What if I was one of the blokes in the office who came to you and said that? Said that he needed help and that he was worried the business wouldn't understand? Would you just take the piss?'

'Well... I'd just think he was 'aving a laugh, to be honest,' Dean said innocently.

'You see. Unconscious bias. It's everywhere. You don't even realise how offensive you're being.' Dean looked wounded as Dave threw a bunch of handouts onto his desk and motioned to Dean to pick them up.

'Dean, I want you to read these notes from the speaker and implement a new company wide diversity policy. Since your promotion to Operations Manager, you've done very well but I don't want you to get too comfortable.' Dave loosened his tie, sat down in his large leather chair and leaned forward, looking

Dean straight in the eye.

'I need to keep challenging you, Dean, and I think this is exactly the project you need. I want TrussInUs to be the most diverse business in our field. When we open the next call centre later this year, we're gonna need over twenty staff for it and I want you to make sure that our new recruits represent the whole of British society.' He sat back and smiled at the mere thought of it.

'What, you mean, like...one of each?' Dean thought for a moment. 'We've got an Irishman. Patrick's Irish, does that count?'

'I'll leave the details up to you, Dean, but there's a Chamber of Commerce Gala Dinner at the end of July. There's an award for the company who's shown "an outstanding commitment to ensuring a diverse workforce". I wanna win it, Dean. And I'm holding you responsible.' He smiled again.

Dean frowned and scratched his head, at a loss as to how to respond. He glanced out of the office window into the call centre and scanned his current team.

God, he's right. Shit! They're all white! And they're nearly all blokes.

He was unable to fathom any religious or sexual persuasions just by looking at them. The virtually all-male situation had been thanks to Dean's predecessor; a ghastly male chauvinist called Brian, with a penchant for ladies of colour and an inability to control his wandering hands. Dave walked around the desk and hovered over Dean. 'I want updates at our weekly meeting, Dean. Can you please add Diversity as a new regular agenda item. Now, any questions? If not, I must get going. Got a Freemasonary meeting tonight.'

'What if I manage to find them, but their CVs aren't great or someone else meets the job spec better, or they're lacking in essential skills? We still need them to be able to do the actual job.'

'Of secondary importance, Dean. Secondary importance. Diversity is the number one priority.'

Dean stared at the handouts and was silent for a minute before getting up out of his chair and declaring, 'Right. OK, well in that case, no questions. See you next week.' They both walked out the office, Dean flicking over the handouts as he went, preoccupied.

As he reached his desk, his phone rang. It was Angie from Sonny Global Mystery Shopping. Dean's little side hustle was his way of getting some time away from his demanding wife and screaming baby. 'Me time', he called it. If Brooke knew he was doing it, there's no doubt she'd insist on accompanying him, so it was his little secret.

'Angie! *HI!* I thought I must've done something wrong. I haven't heard from you in ages.'

'I know, I know, but no you haven't done anything wrong; we just haven't had any suitable visits for you.'

Dean wondered what she meant by that. What did they consider unsuitable? The Dorchester? The Ivy? McDonald's? He ignored his own thoughts. 'So, what can I do for you?'

'Well, we've got a lunchtime visit which needs doing in Pret A Manger in Bank. That's not far from you, is it?'

'No that's doable. I like Pret as it goes.'

'Great. It's short, easy and quick; if the shop scores 100% – which a lot of them do, then you give them a M.O.T. card.'

'What's that?'

'It stands for moment of truth. You have to go back into the store and ask for the manager. You then give them the card, they take it to the till, take fifty quid out and share it however they want with the team. They tell the staff in the shop there and then that they've achieved 100% on the mystery shop, so it can be quite fun.'

'Blimey, I've never seen that and I've been eating at Pret for years. That's pretty impressive as it goes.'

'That's Pret for you! Anyway, I'll send the documents over now. Anytime over the next seven days'd be good. Give us a ring if you've got any queries.'

'OK, Angie, thanks a lot, bye.'

Dean was pleased and felt reassured that he'd not been side-lined. He realised that this would, however, be another visit with no payment. It's not that he minded doing these mystery shops gratis, as he quite enjoyed them; it's just that it wasn't what he'd envisaged when he first signed up. He shook his head and tutted to himself at his own stupid delusion.

He looked around at his team and observed them working for a few minutes. They were indeed a motley crew and managing them had been the hardest part of Dean's job since he'd been promoted. They practically terrorised him, taking advantage of his good nature and knowing more about their rights at work than he did; one or two were positively militant. He listened in to a few calls and cringed at the way Patrick spoke to a customer.

'That's right, Mrs Johns… I know it's bloody stupid … I feel like an eejit even askin' you, but turn it on and off again and see if it starts. Make sure you hold onto the tin with one hand or the beans might come flying out and splat all over yer kitchen wall to be sure! And we wouldn't be wantin' that, now would we?'

TrussInUs was a call centre giving technical advice to elderly and disabled customers who'd bought medical aids and equipment. The never-ending stream of phone calls they received kept staff on their toes.

Considering the average age of their customer was around eighty, they often needed significant support and the agents had to talk very slowly and clearly in order to be fully understood. Many were cloth-eared. When one added the complication of explaining sometimes very technical devices such as bath or stair lifts, conversations could get quite heated.

TrussInUs was expanding because they were taking on a new range of mobility scooters made primarily from recyclable parts and materials and the team were going to need intensive training about them and how to deal with the inevitable customer enquiries and complaints that would come.

For no particular reason Dean started thinking about Brooke; his shoulders drooped and he sighed heavily. She seemed so discontented and yet they'd moved up so much in the world, what with his promotion and pay rise, company car and hot tub; what was there to be unhappy about? In what way was he being unreasonable? Surely she must love being at home and not having to work? He thought back to when his father walked out on his mother and how they'd had so little; his poor mother was barely able to cope with him and his five sisters and she'd become ill. Brooke's blood pressure problems meant Dean was never going to let Brooke suffer like that. As far as Dean was concerned, if she didn't have to work, then that would protect her health.

Hi babe. Love ya loads. Hope u r ok xxx

***

Meanwhile at Purses, Brooke was perched precariously on top of the ladder in the beautiful wood-panelled library, searching for a specific book for Lady Townsend. *Horse Racing's Strangest Tales* by Andrew Ward. She finally discovered it next to *Debrett's Guide to Form* on the top shelf. She frowned, not understanding what the title meant, so brought it down with her, along with the horse book and another tome which caught her eye, *Sotheby's Catalogue: Silver, Gold Boxes, Ceramics 2012, London.*

It was time for a tea break, so she took the books to the kitchen and made herself a cup of Twining's English Breakfast. Her love of PG Tips had gradually been replaced with Twining's since she'd been working for Lady Townsend. Now she didn't buy anything else at home, much to Dean's annoyance. *Debrett's Guide to Form,* with its red and gold glossy hardback cover, lay on the huge pine table; elegant, inviting and important. Brooke browsed the contents page with interest and casually turned to the chapter on 'Social Graces – Polite Actions'. Every so often she laughed out loud at what she read:

Entrances and Exits. *Avoid turning your back on a room. When entering, close the door behind you while remaining face on and moving forwards into the room. On exiting, try to reverse through the door so that the last impression you give isn't of your back.*

Brooke frowned and tried to imagine what that would actually look like.

Bloody daft! You'd knock your arse into the door handle!

She sat for a while flicking through the pages with increasing incredulity and amusement when, without warning, Hugo, Lady

Townsend's Executive Assistant, walked in. Brooke had thought he was out with Lady Townsend at a trustees' meeting. She immediately stood up. 'Just having my break.' Her face turned red as Hugo caught sight of the book she'd been reading.

'Ah! *Debrett's*. Interesting choice of reading material, Brooke?' He smiled warmly, clearly anticipating some form of response.

Brooke felt decidedly embarrassed, although she didn't understand why.

Why shouldn't I read it?

'I thought you were at a trustees' meeting with Mrs Townsend?' She picked up the horse-racing book. 'I found the book she was looking for and came across that *Debrett* one next to it.' Brooke pointed at it. 'It looked interesting, but it's dead weird!' She pulled one of her funny faces.

Hugo laughed. 'Well, you might find it weird, but it's the "bible of polite society" for anyone needing to know about social, business or cultural etiquette. In Mrs Townsend's world, it's all just par for the course.'

'And *your* world!' she exclaimed and sighed. 'Don't make out like you're not part of it!' She prodded him affectionately in the chest and then stroked the cover. 'Well, I definitely won't be needing it then.'

Hugo continued to smile warmly at her, maintaining an intense form of eye contact, which he was prone to do with her on occasion. He thought for a moment before speaking. 'You know, you shouldn't assume such a thing. You may've only worked here for nine months or so, but it's long enough to know how active and interesting Mrs Townsend's life is. You never know what the old girl might ask you to do.'

'What, like take me to another one of those posh old men's private clubs?' Her mind wandered back to almost a year ago to her surreal visit to Brooks's in London with Mrs Townsend. 'Anyway, she's got *you*! A ready-made posh boy!' She and Hugo had developed a good friendship since Brooke had started working at Purses and they frequently indulged in good-natured banter, each poking fun at the other's background.

'Well she might not have this posh boy for much longer. Portia wants us to buy a house in London.'

Brooke bristled at the mention of Portia's name. She was Hugo's girlfriend and she and Brooke had never met, but Brooke had taken an inexplicable and immediate dislike to her as soon as Hugo described her. She too was from a wealthy family and had been to Cheltenham Ladies College, followed by Cambridge, where she'd studied Philosophy. She was now working for a large management consultancy in London. Hugo had shown Brooke a photo of her. She was very petite, with pitch-black, short hair and pale skin. Brooke had felt like a juggernaut in a skirt in comparison.

I bet she's got tiny feet.

'Oh no! I'd be well upset if you left. Who else could I rib around here?!' She found herself twisting her ringlets in her fingers feeling genuinely sorrowful at the prospect of working at Purses without Hugo around.

'Well, it won't be for a while yet, if it happens at all. In the meantime, I wouldn't laugh at *Debrett's* if I were you; I'd get used to it! You never know when you might need it. It could change your life!' With that, he took the horse racing book, winked at her and left. After he'd disappeared, she sat down again and stared into space thinking. She opened the book again, this time it fell open at ***Table manners*** – *challenging foods.* She looked down the inventory of foods and was alarmed to see apples on the list.

How can an apple be challenging to eat?! Surely you just bite it until it's gone, for god's sake!

She read *Debrett's* instructions. '*At the dinner table, apples should be cut into quarters and the core removed from each piece. Then use fingers to eat the quarters.*'

Why would you do that? What a waste of time! Just get your chops round it and tuck in!

She moved on to *Serving Tea* and was amused to discover that one should '*Use the teaspoon to stir the tea (without clinking) and then place it back on the saucer. Cups are held by the handle – being careful not to raise the little finger – and placed back on the saucer between sips. Saucers remain on the table and are never raised when the cup is lifted up.*'

Who in god's name writes this stuff?!

Brooke laughed loudly and shut the book, but stared for a while at the red and gold cover wondering whether this book could, realistically, help her change her life.

3

Mystery Visit to Pret and Brooke's Hinterland

Is the shop clean and tidy with no rubbish on the floor or overflowing out of the bins?

Dean walked around the shop and cast his eye over the whole place. He was concerned he looked like some sort of environmental health inspector.

Were the fridges and display stands full or being constantly replenished by staff?

Dean returned to the shop front and stood for a while, surreptitiously watching the staff coming and going. One girl caught his eye and smiled; Dean looked away embarrassed and worried that he appeared suspicious.

He rummaged around the fridges checking things were in order and that staff were moving older stock to the front and putting newer stock at the back, much to the annoyance of real customers who wanted to get in and out as quickly as possible.

He selected an egg and cress sandwich and a piece of his favourite carrot cake; moist, tasty and the perfect size. He made his way to one of the queues for coffee.

Ensure you note the name of the person who served you – all servers wear their name on a badge on their cap.

Dean waited until the person in front of him had walked away and he moved to the front. He immediately found himself looking intently at the woman's head, unable to see a badge.

'Good morning, what can I get you?' she was bright and breezy with a big smile and not English. Dean observed her hair was white blond and her skin tanned and pure.

She's gotta be Swedish.No English girls ever look like that.

'Erm… I'll have a cappuccino, please.'

'Eat in or takeaway?'

'Eat in, please.' Dean put his food on the counter and added a bag of crisps.

Did they offer you a receipt?

'That'll be £8.50, please. Would you like a receipt?'

He took the till receipt and folded it up so the corners exactly met and slid it inside his wallet. As she disappeared to collect his drink, he peered at her from a number of different angles to try and get a peek at the side of her head, where he thought he'd caught sight of something. But she kept moving so fast and the woman in the queue next to him was giving him strange looks. A minute or so went by as he waited for his drink, still desperately trying to catch the side of her head.

Suddenly there was a window of opportunity when she dropped something and had to bend down. He quickly bent slightly forward to look at the badge, only to realise he couldn't read the name. He whipped on his glasses and leaned forward again, but it was too late. She was on her way up.

'Perv,' mumbled the woman in the queue next to him as she threw him another look; one that easily matched Brooke's worst. It bothered Dean that this woman clearly thought he was looking at the server's backside. He stood facing her with his mouth opening and closing like a fish, desperate to explain but helpless in the face of mystery shopping rules. He'd no choice but to sit down with his lunch and hope he'd get another chance to take a look at the server's head.

He found a free table and sat down with his round metal tray and several paper napkins. He took a sip of his coffee and decided that it wasn't as hot as it could be.

Was your beverage hot and to your liking? If not, did staff put it right for you?

Aha! I'll go back up and ask for it to be heated up.

Dean left his stuff on the table and took his coffee to the counter, holding back a bit until the Swede's counter became free.

'Sorry, but could you possibly heat this coffee up, it's not that hot?'

She looked genuinely worried, apologised and immediately took the cup, said she'd sort it and bring it over to him. Dean was surprised, but sat down as told and examined his sandwich, checking closely to see if they'd spread the filling right up to every edge as he liked it and with the cress sprinkled evenly over the top. Within a minute or two the server returned. As she placed his coffee down she also placed a chocolate bar on the tray.

Ingrid. Her name is Ingrid.

'That's from us to say sorry for your cold coffee.'

'Oh you didn't have to do that, it's fine honestly. Thanks!' Dean smiled, suitably impressed.

Was the food fresh, tasty and well presented?

He scoffed down his sandwich and crisps quickly, but took his time over his carrot cake. He always ate carrot cake at Pret. Everyone who knew Dean would agree he was a creature of habit in his eating, as in most things in his life. He very carefully removed the cake from its cellophane wrap and inspected it. Then he gently peeled back the protective layer on top of the icing. Frustratingly for Dean, a bit came off with the paper. He took small bites at a time, savouring every mouthful between gulps of cappuccino.

Yes the food and drink were great.

He decided to ring Brooke, just for a chat, as he had a few minutes to spare. Her phone rang and rang, but no reply.

Where is that girl? What the hell is she doing? Why does she never pick up these days?

Brooke felt her phone vibrate in her pocket. She was listening impatiently but politely to Mrs Townsend talking about some up-and-coming auction, while all Brooke wanted to do was get on with her polishing. At the same time, she could feel her phone buzzing, worrying that if it was Dean, he would be cross if she didn't pick up. He'd become increasingly suspicious at her tardy replies to his messages or her simply not picking up when he rang during the day. Her use of the 'I'm at the library' excuse seemed to be wearing a bit thin. What could she possibly be doing? She didn't go anywhere…did she? Poor chap, if only he knew!

Dean looked around the shop and was trying to find fault but couldn't. As soon as he'd finished lunch, he scrutinised the lavatory. It was spotless and fully stocked with everything, despite being busy over the preceding twenty minutes.

Would you come back to this Pret store and would you recommend it to a friend?

Absolutely. Yes.

Dean sat back for a few moments and looked around one more time before leaving. This questionnaire was very short, simple and quick to complete. He'd been instructed to do it immediately outside the shop in case they got full marks and he had to go back in again.

Dean sat on a bench close by and quickly filled out the card. They'd got 100%. This meant he had to go back in and give the manager the M.O.T. card. He was pleased for them but was running rather short of time and could've done without the faff. But Dean, being the conscientious chap that he was, dutifully walked back in and bumped straight into Karen Diamond coming out; she was an ex of Dean's and an old school friend of Brooke's.

'Hey, Dean!' She gave him a big hug and a kiss and looked particularly happy to see him.

'Hi, Karen! How are you? Haven't seen you in ages.'

'I know. I'm fine, thanks. How's Brooke and little Paige?'

'Well not so little any more – she's not far off two now'

'Blimey, time flies. What you doing over this part of the world? Your office is in Holborn, isn't it?'

'Yeah, but I had to come over this way for a meeting.' It slipped out. So easily. He'd become a liar extraordinaire since keeping his regular mystery shopping secret from Brooke.

'Actually, I've just gotta do something quickly; hang on a minute and I'll be right back. I'll meet you outside.' He walked back into the shop, abandoning Karen outside the door.

Dean walked over to a man who was clearly the manager.

'Excuse me, but are you the manager?'

'Yes, sir, how can I help you?'

'I'm the mystery shopper and you've just scored 100% on your visit. Here's your M.O.T. card.' Dean followed word for word what he was told to say. Before he had a chance to even move, the manager held up the card and shouted at full volume.

'WE JUST GOT 100% IN OUR MYSTERY SHOP!!! WELL

DONE, TEAM!!!' The whole shop burst into spontaneous applause – staff and customers. Whooping, cheering and clapping all round. Angie had always made it very clear that Dean was meant to tell no one about his mystery shopping.

Oh my god, shut up, shut up!

Dean smiled awkwardly and put up his hand meekly and discreetly as if to say 'No worries, please don't make a fuss!' as he looked anxiously towards Karen who was peering bemused through the window and intrigued by the excitement inside. He swiftly headed towards the front door, desperate to remain incognito. This was impossible as most customers had clearly witnessed Dean hand over the card and the subsequent response from the manager. They seemed to be holding up their hands and directing their clapping at him.

'What was going on in there? What did you do? I could hear the noise out here!' asked Karen straining to see what was going on inside the shop.

'I didn't do anything,' Dean replied ever so slightly too quickly for someone who was entirely innocent. 'I think the manager got over excited about something.' Dean tried to sound casual, quickly changed the subject and led Karen away from the shop towards Bank station. 'I need to get back to work, Karen, I'm running late, do you wanna walk with me to the tube?' He was in a hurry now, but didn't want to seem rude, so they chatted until they got to the stairs leading down into the 'hell hole' as Dean called it. He gave her a hug and said it was nice to see her after all this time. 'Pop in next time you're round our way' was exactly what he said, in that casual manner that means you don't actually ever expect them to.

In fact, he would never have made the offer at all had he

known about the fight that Brooke and Karen had had a couple of years back on the pavement outside The Sugar Hut. Karen had swung at Brooke, who'd made a snidey comment about her boyfriend's eyebrow-plucking habit. Brooke had fallen to the floor, but picked herself up and, unfortunately, in a rather drunken moment of madness, had tried to hit Karen back. Karen had ducked and Brooke had punched 'Lights Out Lenny' the bouncer instead. He'd decided that Brooke wasn't 'the kind of clients we like here at The Sugar Hut' and so she'd gone home humiliated. They'd not exactly been friends since then. Brooke had never mentioned the incident to Dean, who'd once declared his disgust at women who got into fights.

***

Brooke continued to listen superficially to Lady Townsend, but worried she was getting behind with polishing the silver and so surreptitiously looked at her watch. Of course, Lady Townsend never missed a trick and instantly asked 'Do you need to be somewhere, dear? You seem concerned about the time.'

Even after all these months working with her and getting to know her, the awe and respect she felt for the elderly, elegant and impressive Lady Townsend meant Brooke still behaved around her as though she were royalty sometimes. She'd still from time to time refer to her as Lady Townsend, which always resulted in a horrified 'No! Please don't call me that!' after which Brooke would chastise herself, saying, 'Sorry, Mrs Townsend' accompanied by a sort of sycophantic semi-bow.

Brooke explained she still had the silver to polish before she left for the day and she was running out of time. Lady Townsend waved her hand dismissively and indicated to Brooke she wanted her to sit down.

'Come, sit, sit. You know sometimes, Brooke, I just want to talk to you!'

'What d'ya wanna talk to *me* for?' Brooke asked, confused.

Lady Townsend sat staring at Brooke, making her feel quite uncomfortable. In her immaculate Max Mara trousers, John Smedley cashmere sweater and Bally flat pumps, she was the picture of understated elegance, contrasting strikingly with Brooke's ripped jeans, long-sleeved Zara t-shirt and Nike sneakers.

'What've I done wrong? Why are you staring at me like that?' Brooke eventually asked, raising her eyebrows and frowning.

'Brooke, do you still like working here?'

'Course I do! It's…it's like, well…amazing! Why d'you ask?' Her voice was one of concern and surprise all rolled into one.

Lady Townsend smiled. 'Well, I wasn't sure. You've been here nearly a year now and I wondered if you're at all interested in any of the other activities that I get involved in? You appear to stick solely to your housekeeping duties.'

Brooke's stomach dropped and, once again, the warm glow of her cheeks, already flush with exquisitely applied blusher and contouring, turned her face a rather unflattering strawberry colour. 'Oh my god, Mrs Townsend, you must be joking! I'm totally fascinated by your life. You should see the books I read from your library! I can't get enough of them. And I'm still working away at me Latin.' She dived into her handbag, pulled out the Latin book and waved it in the air proudly. 'But why would you be wasting your time talking to *me* about all this stuff! All those people that you know; I've watched 'em and they all talk a certain way. They're so clever they make me feel stupid.' Brooke's tone was one of inadequacy and hopelessness. 'I can't exactly hold a conversation about any of it, can I? I can tell you who won *Big Brother* and how much a pack of knickers from Primark costs, but what do I know about art and horses and charities? Sweet FA! That's what! It's embarrassing. I feel so useless, even though I do try. I've never read so much in my life since I've been working here!'

Lady Townsend tutted and shook her head. 'Brooke, I've told you before, you underestimate yourself. I absolutely love having you at the house. You are so refreshingly down to earth I can't tell you and I'm delighted to hear you've been borrowing books from the library. I'm most fortunate to have such a wonderful collection.' She was silent again for a moment and rubbed her chin gently while her eyes bored into Brooke's, as if deciding something extremely important about her. 'Brooke, tell me something, have you ever been to an auction?'

Brooke burst out laughing. 'You're kidding me! Why would anyone like me have ever gone to an auction? Mind you, I did find this catalogue from Sotheby's up on one of your book shelves. That was pretty interesting as it goes. The one about silver and ceramics, from 2012. I love all that stuff.'

Lady Townsend's face brightened as she recalled her bidding that day. 'Oh yes that one. I bought a few lovely pieces at that auction.' She paused and looked at Brooke affectionately as she stared up at her; it was almost a maternal moment and a strange but pleasing feeling for the childless Lady Townsend.

'Hugo was meant to be coming with me to an auction on Wednesday next week, but has asked to have the day off to go house-hunting with Portia.'

Brooke rolled her eyes, but Lady Townsend ignored it and carried on, 'So, I was wondering if you'd like to come with me instead?'

Brooke gasped and clapped her hands excitedly like a child. 'Oh my god, Mrs Townsend, are you serious? That'd be awesome! Would it be like, a normal work day, if you know what I mean?'

'If you mean, am I going to pay you, then yes of course. It'll be quite an experience and possibly a long day for you, but we do need to increase your hinterland.'

'If you say so, Mrs T.' Brooke's eyes widened; she'd no idea what she meant, but quickly visualised herself in one of the sale rooms she'd seen in the Sotheby's catalogue and her mind turned instantly to what she'd wear.

I can't wear my LK Bennett dress again. She'll think I haven't got anything else. I could wear my Louboutins though! Perfect! At last, a chance to wear them!

Her mind raced when thinking about the comment 'it'll be a long day'. She couldn't imagine how bidding for a Limoges pill box or a pair of Georgian candlesticks could possibly be considered a long day.

'Do you know what hinterland means, Brooke?' Lady Townsend could've warmed her hands on Brooke's cheeks.

'No, actually, I don't.' She shook her head and looked at the floor.

'Look it up.'

'What, now?'

'Yes, now.'

Brooke pulled her phone out and typed in the word hinterland: 'an area lying beyond what is visible or known'.

She frowned, trying to understand what Lady Townsend was attempting to say to her.

'One feels a certain…responsibility to help you broaden your horizons, Brooke. I fear your life has been…how shall I say…somewhat limited and I have the time and ability to help you change that…for the better.'

Brooke's automatic internal response was to feel defensive, but that quickly changed as she became more reflective.

Broaden my horizons. Mmm.

Brooke thought back on her life. She was twenty-five years old, married with a toddler, and had lived in the same tiny house in Brentwood for four years. She'd left school at sixteen, worked for Clinique in John Lewis and as an administrative assistant and PA for a year before having Paige. She'd been misguidedly persuaded by Dean into being a stay-at-home mum ever since. She had no hobbies, played no sport, only went shopping (mostly of the window variety), out to the pub and the occasional nice restaurant for a special occasion. That was it. That was her life. At least it was until she took the cleaning job at Purses anyway, and even that was difficult because of having to keep it secret from Dean.

'Only if you want them broadened, of course!' Lady Townsend smiled.

Brooke laughed. 'Sounds painful, but who wouldn't want their horizons broadened? Especially by you, Mrs T?!'

They laughed together.

'Right, that's settled then. Broadening your horizons it is. So, lesson number one. You need to stop saying "Oh my god!"'.

Brooke's mouth dropped open as she watched Lady Townsend imitate her hand and facial expressions, as well as her Essex accent, but couldn't deny it was very accurate and very funny.

'It's very lazy, Brooke, and very…well…Essex. Something like "well I never" or "how wonderful" might be better phrases to use. Mmm?' She raised her eyebrows and looked Brooke straight in the eye waiting for some sort of indication that she understood. Brooke nodded obediently.

'Secondly, always look up the meaning of any word you don't understand. It'll add to your vocabulary and that in turn will enable you to feel more confident and comfortable when speaking with a broader social circle of people.'

Brooke thought about this for a minute before saying, 'Yeah, but if I start banging on about increasing my hinterland to Dean, he'll think I've gone barmy. He wonders what's happened to me as it is. He says I've changed over the past few months.'

Lady Townsend smiled, looked sympathetically at Brooke and rubbed her affectionately on the back. Brooke had previously told her what Dean was like, although she'd failed to mention that he didn't actually know she worked for Lady Townsend. One could sense her wondering if she was going to be responsible for unwittingly starting a marital revolt. For the moment she kept quiet.

'Let's have some afternoon tea.' Lady Townsend motioned to the cake stand on the table and invited her to take a scone with jam and clotted cream and a cup of tea.

Just as Brooke went to put her phone away, Dean messaged her.

Fancy a KFC for tea 2nite? Will pick up on way home.

Brooke sighed.

OK.

4

Diversity Challenge.

For days, Dean had been working himself up into a tizzy thinking about the enormity of his diversity challenge ahead. Whatever way he looked at it, he couldn't see his way through the nightmare; and the pressure of winning the award was like carrying lead weights around with him all day long. He concluded that he'd tell Brooke what Dave had tasked him with and talk it through with her. She was usually splendid at working through problems. Since his promotion she'd already advised him on how to deal with menopausal women, staff who were always ill on a Monday and Friday and customers with Alzheimer's. Although whether she'd forgiven him for his pushing back about her wanting to work, was yet to be seen. She'd dished out the silent treatment for a week now; it rarely went on longer than that.

He stared out the train window on the way home thinking about it, when his daydreaming was interrupted by a call from Angie at Sonny Global. She had another visit for him.

'It's to a branch of the gym chain SweatUBet. There's about twelve of them in the Southeast. Do you know it?' she asked at her usual machine gun speed.

'No, never 'eard of 'em, but then I'm not exactly a gym rat, to be honest, Angie. Not sure I'm the right person for this particular assignment.'

'Mmm. Well, considering one of the things they want to assess is how well they treat potential members who don't currently go to a gym, you'll probably be exactly the right person to assess it.'

'Maybe,' he replied non-commitally. 'Where's the branch and what's involved?' Dean asked in his notoriously cautious way.

'It's in Billericay. Basically, you have to phone to enquire about membership and make sure they invite you for a show-round. They have to take you through a sales process that's been set out by the owners and at the end of it you have to sign up for membership. Obviously, we reimburse you. Then you've gotta go back for the induction and assess how well they do it. Finally, you've gotta go to a Boxercise class.' Angie crossed her fingers, scrunched up her face and shut her eyes tightly.

'Blimey, that's quite a commitment.' Dean responded.

'Yeah, I know. It's not easy to find assessors willing to do it, never mind people who live near Billericay. That's why we'll pay seventy-five quid for this visit.'

Dean thought about it. He had a lot on at work and ummed and ahhed, much to Angie's annoyance.

'I've got another very nice visit coming up soon. How about I give you that one as a thank you for you doing this for us?' Angie was having to use all her wile and charm to get this wretched visit allocated.

'Well what's that one?' Dean asked, a bit more encouraged.

'The Royal Opera House in Covent Garden. That's next month.'

Dean burst out laughing. 'You must be joking. I don't know anything about opera!' A fellow commuter looked up from his

Angling Times and glanced at Dean, clearly intrigued at what this rather unkempt chap was having to do, that involved needing to know about opera.

'Neither do most people who go! It doesn't matter. It's a great night out and it includes dinner in their Balconies restaurant as well. Very fancy! The client's extremely demanding and you do produce the best reports of any assessor we've got, so I'd actually be very relieved if you did it. It's for two people, so a great chance for your wife to dress up.'

Mmm. Well she wouldn't be coming.

'Well as long as I don't have to wear one of them poncy dinner suits.'

'No, but smartish definitely. Great. So, you'll do the SweatUBet one for us then?' She was pushing him hard because, unbeknown to Dean, Angie was desperate. She'd tried three times to get an assessor to do this visit; not only did she have no assessors in Billericay but the prospect of someone having their carefully nurtured facial features damaged in the Boxercise class was putting people off.

'OK then, send the details across and I'll let you know when I've done it.'

'Brilliant, you're a star, Dean. Thanks. Speak soon. Bye.' Angie breathed a sigh of relief and punched her fist in the air when she got off the phone. 'Yess!'

'Don't say you actually managed to allocate the SweatUBet visit?' asked one of Angie's team.

'Yep. You all owe me a fiver each. I'm gonna be rich!' The team had made a bet that she wouldn't be able to find an assessor before the day was out. Oh how they misunderstood Angie's skills!

Diversity Challenge.

Almost as soon as he'd finished the call, Dean wished he hadn't agreed to SweatUBet. His brain had run out of RAM and he wasn't sure it would cope with any more. On the other hand, the Royal Opera House would be something different. Quite so!

Who the hell can I take to that one? That's gonna need some careful thought.

***

Dean walked into the hallway with a face like West Ham had just lost 3–nil to Arsenal. He took a deep breath and acted for the seventh day running as though they'd not had cross words.

Paige toddled up to the door and fell flat on her face. Brooke instantly whipped out a Chupa Chups and thrust it into Paige's mouth to stem the screams. She'd had a box of forty-eight delivered that morning, so, for the first time in a week, she wasn't having to ration her.

'What's the matter, babe? You look like a right barrel of laughs.' Brooke went to give Dean a kiss. She'd decided he'd been in the dog house long enough and that her strategy now would be to pretend they'd never even had the 'getting a job' conversation. She'd just have to keep working in secret until a more pressing need to tell him arose.

Dean breathed a sigh of relief, threw his man-bag onto the floor, kissed her forcefully on the lips and then slapped her bottom. That poor bottom had had more than its fair share of slaps over the years; round, pert and curvy, it was the perfect specimen of a female posterior. Dean made his way to the sofa, plonked the KFC down on the coffee table and watch Paige crawl up and sit next to him, sucking noisily on her lollipop.

He put his head into his hands and blurted out, 'Brooke, do you know what a pomosexual is?'

Brooke laughed and then tried to recollect her Latin, but decided in this context pomosexual definitely had nothing to do with fruit. 'No. Sounds like a made-up word to me. Why? What does it mean?'

As they conversed, they tucked into their twelve-piece dipping-feast sharing bucket, occasionally popping something into Paige's mouth. Dean copied Dave's expression and mannerisms and replied, 'A pomosexual is when someone "rejects sexuality labels or doesn't identify with any of them".'

Definitely nothing to do with apples then.

'Huh? That doesn't make any sense. They've gotta be something – a bloke or a woman or gay!'

'That's exactly what I said. But apparently not.'

'Bloody daft! What's the point of that?'

'God knows, but I've gotta have one of 'em in the business within the next few months!'

'Huh? What d'ya mean? Why? Who says?' Brooke retorted dismissively.

Dean went on to explain at length the challenge he'd been set by Dave; how he was expected to bring diversity into their workforce where there was currently none and within a matter of months to win the award.

'We've gotta be the "variety box" of workforces. And I've gotta stop being unconsciously bias apparently.' Dean kicked off his shoes. 'You wouldn't get us a beer, babe?'

Brooke went to the kitchen and thought about the phrase.

Unconscious bias. Mmm?

Lady Townsend's words came to mind. Always look up

words you don't know.

'I think you'll find unconscious bias is *the underlying attitude and stereotype that a person unconsciously attributes to another person or group of people that affect how they understand and engage with a person or group.*'

Dean listened with mouth gaping and eyes wide open. 'How the hell d'you know that?' Dean shouted aghast through a mouthful of fried chicken.

Brooke wandered back in and handed him his beer. She laughed. 'It's called a dictionary! So, what made him accuse you of that?' Brooke asked, a tad worried about Dean's apparent faux pas in his relatively new position. She demanded a run-down of his day every evening when he got in from work, ready to give advice and suggestions if she thought he was doing anything wrong. She wanted to ensure that he'd always be seen in the best possible light by his boss. 'Behind every successful man there is a woman,' she'd frequently say. In the absence of seemingly not being permitted to be successful herself, that's how she liked to think of herself. Dean said he'd laughed at the prospect of Dave or one of the men in the office coming to him to say they wanted a sex change.

'Well I'd have laughed too. I wouldn't worry about it, babe.'

'That's gonna be easier said than done. I've been thinking about it for days. You should read these notes he gave me from this event he went to.' Dean gave them to Brooke to take a look at. 'They're bleedin' mad! If I recruited one of each of these different groups, it'd cause a bloody riot! Can you imagine Patrick sitting next to a Muslim girl? He'd be cracking jokes all day long about what she's got in her rucksack and what she's hiding under her scarf thing.'

'Hijab.' Gosh that felt good!

'Yeah that. And her buggering off every few hours to pray? Where would she do that, for Christ's sakes? We 'aven't even got room for the amount of meetings we have, never mind a dedicated room for praying in! What would everyone think? We 'ave a revolt every time someone even goes for a fag break! And I definitely can't afford to employ a woman if she's pregnant, I need her to be at work, not at those poxy ante-natal classes and on year-long maternity leave. We'd never make any money.'

'Oi! That's against the law, Dean De'Ath. You can't discriminate against women – especially pregnant ones!' Brooke was rather taken aback at Dean's antiquated thinking. She knew he was rather old fashioned and protective towards *her*, but they'd never discussed how he viewed his female colleagues and it'd never occurred to her to enquire. She was rather shocked, but it got her thinking about Dean's whole approach to women and feminism.

'And transexuals? I mean, can you seriously imagine some bloke who's had his bits either cut off or rearranged to make him look like a woman, coming into our office and thinking that wearing a Monsoon dress will change the fact that he's a bloke? We wouldn't be able to concentrate. And what toilet would they use? It'd be a nightmare! And as for pomosexuals, where would I even go about finding one to recruit? Is there a *Pomosexual Life Weekly*? Then I could be accused of sexual discrimination against heterosexuals for not advertising the role in a mainstream paper. I'm tellin' you, Brooke, you can't win. It's gonna be a fucking nightmare. Mark my words.'

Brooke giggled. 'No swearing in front of Paige, Dean, remember? Well, I'm sure if you try to get the biggest, you know, "variety" you can, that'll do.'

Dean looked doubtful and took a glug of his beer. 'Disability's a big one too. I'll have to find someone who doesn't need a wheelchair and has got the use of both legs and arms just to be able to get up to our floor, 'cause the bloody lift's always out of order. Working our phone system – that needs both hands, and listening to customers requires good hearing, so they can't be deaf, looking at the screen needs eyesight so they can't be blind. So, I don't know what kind of disability options I've got left?'

Brooke considered this for a few moments before offering, 'How about a diabetic?'

'Ooh that's a good shout! Yeah, your dad's diabetic and he's always worked. Does he have any problems?'

'Well, he does if he doesn't control what he eats and if he forgets to inject himself.' Brooke looked thoughtful. 'In an ideal world, you do need a reliable diabetic really. They can definitely go a bit ditsy if they're not careful. They have to inject themselves, but Dad does it in the front of his cab; the passengers don't even know he's doing it!'

Dean nodded thoughtfully.

'Stacey's Jewish, so I can ask her about the best place to find some Jewish people.'

'Stacey?! Jewish?! Bloody 'ell, I never knew that!'

'Well, she doesn't exactly follow it, only when her mum and dad get a bit aggy about them Friday night meals they have. You know that one? What's it called? They like her to turn up to that if she's around.'

What is the name of that meal they have?

Although strictly speaking, this wasn't a 'looking up a word' situation, it was more of a 'I don't even know the word I want' situation, so it was a bit different, she felt sure Mrs Townsend would expect her to find out the correct word. So, for the third time in one day she looked something up on the internet in order to expand her hinterland, rather than see how fast a dress from New Look could be delivered.

Oh yeah, Shabbat – that's it. Now I remember. All that candle-lighting and hand-washing malarkey Stacey used to go on about.

'Shabbat!' she shouted joyously as she cleared up the bucket and stray chips into the kitchen. Brooke felt a warm glow of satisfaction.

Dean ignored her and began to wonder what the best way of going about this mammoth task he'd been given was. He opened up Excel on his laptop and looked up to the ceiling for help; it had always been his friend, but this evening it gave him no inspiration for his diversity challenge chart.

He ended up typing a list of all the different racial groups, religions, sexual identities and other minority groups he could find on the internet, down one side. That went on to over one hundred lines, before he suddenly stopped.

Hang on a minute, if I'm only going to need to recruit twenty-three people, I can't have one of each. That just ain't gonna work. Maybe I can do a two in one? Like a disabled Gypsy or a gay Jew or something?

He tapped his pencil on his teeth.

I'll have to find out which groups have got the highest proportion percentage wise in the population as a whole and pick the top twenty-three. There's no way I'm gonna manage to get everyone in.

He bit his lip, unsure if this was really the right way to be going about it. They didn't have an HR department in TrussInUs. Jules took on that responsibility, but she wasn't qualified and

Dean felt she was pretty ruthless and wouldn't give him the time of day to discuss such a 'problem.' This is the same woman who refused to give Patrick time off to go to Ireland for his mother's funeral. No, this was one of those jobs he was going to have to work out how to do himself.

Brooke called out to him to put Paige to bed with a bedtime story, so he shut his laptop and fulfilled his fatherly duties.

***

'I'm in the hot tub!' Brooke shouted from the patio when she heard him come down the stairs.

She'd changed into her favourite yellow spotted bikini, the one for Wednesdays, poured herself a glass of Chardonnay and relaxed back into the hot water. Oh, how she adored her hot tub! Dean behaved like a proud peacock whenever anyone commented on it, explaining how he'd bought it for Brooke's birthday. It made him appear the family provider he so craved to be! Dean stood in the lounge and for a few minutes watched his wife sipping from a wine glass as large as a grapefruit and tossing her ringlets over the side of the hot tub.

God, you're beautiful.

Mikey next door was also watching and drooling over Dean's wife, from his upstairs bedroom, yearning to be sliding about in there with her. His wife was about as sexy as Angela Merkel.

A few minutes later Dean pranced out from the lounge in a pair of threadbare SpongeBob underpants singing 'Itsy Bitsy Teeny Weeny Yellow Polka Dot Bikini'. Brooke laughed, but reprimanded him.

'What are you doing in those disgusting things, anyway?

They're so...common. Where are those nice Paul Smith swimming shorts I bought you for Christmas?'

'I can't wear them in there. I read on the care label that the chemicals in hot tubs make them fade. These old friends don't matter.' He pinged the waistband of his pants.

'Only you'd read the bloody care label before wearing a pair of swimming shorts!'

Dean climbed in and sat opposite Brooke, who immediately placed her feet on his lap. Her immaculately groomed toes were so close to his face he started to nibble them and suck the big toe on her right foot. She giggled and squirmed, pretending it tickled her and demanding he stop. When he refused, she suddenly plunged herself under the water, lunged over to him and pulled his pants down. Screeching and cackling followed, disturbing the silence in Elephant Close. When it'd finally subsided, Dean held her hands and gazed meaningfully into Brooke's eyes.

'Brooke...about what we were talking about last week, I just wanted to say...'

Brooke looked meaningfully at him, shook her head and put her finger to his lips.

OK, so she wants to forget all about it. That's fine by me.

He stood up and pulled her up. He so wanted to scoop her out of the hot tub and carry her in his arms up to bed, but at nearly six feet and eleven stone, he could only ever be reminded of the time he once tried it and jolted his back, leading to a grim few hours in A&E, so he gave her a piggy back instead. Not quite the same, but the sentiment was there.

'Let's have an early night, shall we?' Dean asked with a cheeky glint in his eye.

5

Brooke's First Auction

The following week, Lady Townsend asked Brooke to meet her at the auction, which was being held the following day. She'd given Brooke the address and asked her to meet her at the entrance at just before 10am, when the sale would start. Brooke had incorrectly assumed it would be in London and so had been expecting to go by train. Once upon a time she'd have feigned a breakdown to avoid driving because she was so ashamed of their ancient car. But since Dean's promotion had come with a company car, she now possessed a splendid banana yellow Seat Leon (aka Flora), so was happy to drive.

On the morning of the auction, Brooke was barely able to hold back her excitement and had agonised for days over what to wear. The only thing she'd decided for sure was that those Louboutin's were coming out – by hook or by crook!

She'd been to TK Maxx at the weekend and delved around the Gold Label designer section, selecting a brightly coloured, patterned Moschino shift dress and a navy, cropped Vivienne Westwood jacket. She'd wanted to look sophisticated, but also to show her fun side and this seemed to fit the bill perfectly. She was most fortunate to have secured it at all and certainly had to be more than assertive with another woman eyeing up the same dress.

Snooze you lose!

Predictably, she looked positively fabulous. Oh, how she was going to show those who mattered, that she could fit in very nicely, thank you very much! She observed herself from all angles and smiled a knowing smile. After spending some time convincing herself that these were necessary purchases and that they'd contribute to Lady Townsend's strategic plan to help her increase her hinterland, she checked the prices. £95 for the dress and £40 for the jacket.

Bargain at twice the price!

She'd pre-warned Dawn, her rather rough and portly childminder, friend and alibi, that she'd need to drop Paige off at 8.30am on the day of the auction. Dawn's mouth almost hit the floor when she saw Brooke. 'Bloody hell, Brooke, where are you going? You look like you should be on a catwalk!'

'Can you believe it, but Mrs Townsend's invited me to an auction! Hugo can't be there so she asked me to go instead. She thought I'd enjoy it! Hahaha! I can't wait; I'm so excited! You should see these auction houses, Dawn. Amazing places!'

Paige, dressed much to her mother's despair in a Spiderman outfit she'd been forced to buy in a charity shop, wriggled free of her mother's hand, ran into Dawn's and straight over to the pretend kitchen in the corner.

'Blimey, well I hope she's paying you.' Dawn paused for a moment and became serious. Dawn didn't do serious as a rule, so it had to be taken...well...seriously, when she did. She continued, 'I don't suppose you've told Dean?'

'Course I haven't. You know I can't. After the other night, it's gonna be even more difficult. To be honest I dunno what to do. I'm in a bit deep, but he made it obvious he definitely doesn't want me to get a job. He's obsessed with my blood pressure. It's quite sweet in one way, but, god, I dunno how I'm ever gonna get myself out of all this.'

'Well I guarantee it's gonna come back and bite you in the bum, Brooke. I'd hate either of you to get hurt.'

'I know. Anyway, I gotta go, Dawn. See you later. I'll let you know when I'm leaving and I'll be about an hour or so after that.' She blew a kiss to Paige who blew one back before returning to her plastic pizza slices.

Brooke departed, put the postcode into the satnav and played her favourite tracks by The Pussycat Dolls as she drove, singing throughout the journey and dancing about in her seat.

Every so often she'd check her seat belt wasn't creasing her outfit, as well as pull down the driver's mirror to check her make-up, quite oblivious to the drivers overtaking her and making rude gestures at her slight but frequent swerving across lanes.

She came off the M11, onto the A11 and then took the A1304, a long straight road all the way into Newmarket, flicking her head from side to side as she drove, not wanting to miss anything along the route. More swerving. She hadn't expected to be coming to anywhere so small and countrified. Soon she came to a statue of a rearing horse on the first roundabout she came to and continued over into the High Street. She'd imagined Newmarket to be a large town or city, but it became clear as she drove through the High Street that this must be quite a small, niche auction house.

Within a few minutes, the sat nav was directing her around a few very fancy houses in residential roads and up into a car park. She sat in her car looking around her for a moment before turning her engine off, unable to compute what she was seeing. She checked the postcode. This was definitely correct. She watched for a few minutes as a multitude of men in the oddest country clothes and wellingtons roamed around – with horses in tow. There were horses everywhere.

The bloody sat nav's probably taken me to the wrong car park or something.

She had no choice but to get out and ask someone. She took one more glance at her make-up and topped up her lipstick before exiting the car in the way Mrs Townsend had taught her. The path was rather uneven, so she tottered up to the first man she saw who wasn't encumbered by a horse.

''scuse me, but can you tell me where the entrance to the auction is? I've got a feeling I'm in the wrong place?' She showed him the piece of paper upon which Lady Townsend had written the name, address and postcode.

The gentleman, in tweeds, flat cap and boots, stared at her as though she were an alien from Mars, took the piece of paper, not taking his eyes off her for a moment. He glanced down at it, pulled a strange face and said, 'Yep, this is it alright. Tattersall's.'

Brooke looked around her with an increasing feeling of anxiety, still convinced she must have to go to another building or to a different part of this site, whatever it was.

'So, where's the entrance? To the actual auction, I mean.'

He smiled in that way that suggested he knew something that she didn't and pointed over to a round building 100m away with horses appearing to be walked in and out of what looked like a huge double door. She couldn't see Mrs Townsend, but slowly made her way over to the entrance, painfully aware of the strange looks she was getting from everyone she passed and no one was making any bones about it. Although she was used to that – her Amazonian figure and stunning good looks always turned heads – this felt different; a similar, uneasy feeling she'd experienced when she'd arrived at Brooks's Club. She began to get very bad vibes as she tottered in her Louboutins near to a group of young women dressed in jeans, Barbour jackets and wellies, who openly sniggered at her.

Stuck up bitches.

As she got closer to the entrance, all she could see were horses and more men who all looked exactly the same. Suddenly, she caught sight of Mrs Townsend just inside. She too was wearing tweeds and Wellington boots. At once, Brooke felt sick. That familiar feeling of red fire licking up her face and sweat beginning to develop in all manner of places. Something was wrong. Very wrong.

'Mrs Townsend!' Brooke called out loudly but nervously, and waved.

Mrs Townsend turned around and her face fell as she set eyes on Brooke. She dashed over immediately. 'Good heavens, Brooke, why on earth are you dressed like that?!'

'I thought we were going to an auction! I wanted to look smart and…appropriate.' Brooke cried out.

'We *are* at an auction. A *horse* auction! What on earth did you think Tattersall's was?' Lady Townsend was visibly aghast.

'I dunno, I thought it was another one of them fancy auction houses like Sotheby's or Christie's!' Brooke burst into tears. The humiliation was too much to bear.

Lady Townsend put her arm around Brooke and led her away out of the auctioneer's ring and whispered close to her ear, 'It's *those* fancy auction houses, dear, not *them* fancy auction houses.'

Brooke was dumbfounded. 'Whatever!' She was not in the mood for a grammar lesson and wanted to bolt back to her car and go home.

Lady Townsend hurt for her. 'Brooke, I'm so sorry, I assumed you'd know. Tattersall's is one of the biggest, best and certainly most famous race horse auction houses in the world. But it's my fault entirely. I should've been more explicit when I talked about an auction. I've come here to buy a racehorse!'

'Oh…my…' Brooke stopped in her tracks, pulled herself up, wiped away her tears, took a deep breath and rephrased. 'Well I never, how very interesting.'

Lady Townsend smiled. 'That's my girl! Now, why don't we go to my car. I have a couple of spare pairs of wellingtons in the back and another jacket you can slip on, so you don't look quite so…glamorous.'

'I can't, Mrs T. I feel so stupid. All those people were staring at me and those women over there were actually laughing at me. I just wanna go home.' She motioned with her head over to where the group of smirking young women were still gossiping.

'Nonsense. Ignore them. You've more taste in your little finger than they have between them. Little hussies! You'll be fine once we dress you down a bit.' With that, Brooke was marched, in full view of what felt like England's entire equestrian community, to Mrs Townsend's clapped-out Ford Fiesta and given an old green quilted Barbour jacket. Brooke took one look at the wellington boots and her lips started to quiver again.

'They aren't gonna fit, Mrs T. I'm a size 8.' The tears welled up as Mrs Townsend confirmed they were in fact a size 3.

Then, quite without warning, a gentleman in the distance

shouted over to them, waving and smiling away. 'Letitia! Letitia!'

As he came lolloping over, Brooke recognised him. It was Lord D'Arcy! He was beaming, revealing his overly large teeth that rather reminded Brooke of piano keys.

'Oh my and we have young Brooke as well! How utterly delightful! How the devil are you, sweetheart?' He didn't seem to notice her rather unusual mode of attire at all. Without any qualms, he pulled her towards him and gave her a kiss on both cheeks. He then held her by her shoulders and examined her as he would a son who'd been away at Eton for the term. His jolly demeanour and genuine pleasure at seeing her lifted her spirits enormously and she was finally able to smile. Lord D'Arcy had thought Brooke a 'fine filly' with 'good fetlocks on her' ever since he was first introduced to her at Brooks's.

'Salve[3], Geoffrey! Nice to see you too.'

'Oh very good, Brooke, very good!' Lord D'Arcy looked ecstatic at Brooke's brave stab at speaking Latin with him. 'Letitia. Forgive my appalling manners.' He bent over to kiss Lady Townsend on the cheek. She smiled warmly as she turned her cheek and allowed him to do so – just the once.

'Geoffrey. We have a bit of a situation. Brooke here didn't realise we were coming to a horse auction – my fault entirely – she thought it was a Sotheby's-type auction, so she's not dressed appropriately and feels rather conspicuous in front of all these people.'

'Well I think you look marvellous, my dear. Ignore the buggers, I say!' he roared loudly, laughing.

'No, Geoffrey, she can't do that. Do you happen to have a spare pair of wellingtons? Brooke has rather… Well, what I

3. Hello.

mean is she can't quite squeeze into mine.'

Lord D'Arcy grabbed Brooke by the hand and told Letitia that they'd meet her inside the auction ring in a few minutes. Without further ado, he pulled Brooke along to his Land Rover, reiterating how lovely it was to see her again. Brooke didn't know whether to laugh or cry. His nonchalant attitude towards her appearance and the way he simply took charge was rather charming and reassuring. Somehow, she felt protected at that moment, when a few minutes before she'd felt so vulnerable and exposed to ridicule. Once more she found herself in a totally surreal situation.

Boots were found – albeit in a size 10. Lord D'Arcy also found a rather resplendent fedora which he thought might make her feel a little less conspicuous. He placed it on her head at a jaunty angle and pecked her on the cheek, declaring that she looked splendid. She felt completely ridiculous, but Geoffrey insisted that it didn't matter one jot and that she should enjoy herself and learn.

'So why are you here, Geoffrey? Don't tell me you're gonna buy a racehorse too?'

He laughed. 'Well, in a manner of speaking, I'm going to buy a piece of a racehorse.'

Brooke's face was a picture. 'I don't like the sound of that. What d'ya mean? Like a leg or something?'

'Well, you could put it that way. I'm in a syndicate with Letitia and another couple of friends of ours.'

'What, you mean like the lottery? Loads of people buy tickets as a group and agree to split the winnings?'

'That's exactly it. Except we buy a racehorse – not a lottery ticket. And when the horse wins a race the financial prize is split between the syndicate.'

'Oh…my…g… I mean, how interesting, I didn't know anything like that even existed.' Brooke was very pleased with herself and the speed at which she had rephrased what she wanted to say.

'We need to get a move on because the horse we're interested in is coming up shortly.' He once more grabbed her hand, not giving two hoots about what Brooke was wearing, who saw them or what people might've been saying. It was so refreshing to her. In her world, everyone was always judging everyone else and it was hard to be accepted just as you were. She grinned.

Brooke had a multitude of questions as to how it all worked and quite forgot about her attire as Geoffrey dragged her behind him while she attempted to squeeze her toes together to stop the wellingtons from slipping off. This was a most unique experience for her; footwear that was too big!

How do they know what horse to buy? Can anyone be part of a syndicate? Who does the bidding? How do they know the horse is a winner? Where does it go after you win the auction? Can you go and watch it race?

Before she knew it, she was more interested in what was going on, than what other people were thinking about her, as she was pulled into the ringside seating by Lord D'Arcy. They sat next to Letitia who'd been joined by another gentleman – Henry Pilkington, the bloodstock agent – who turned out to be the chap who'd bid and buy the horse on their behalf. Lady Townsend made the introductions and, for the first time ever, Brooke recognised that Mrs Townsend was following the *Debrett's* Guide to Introductions to the letter. Henry looked Brooke up and down as though he was witnessing a first, grunted something inaudible and looked back into the ring. The other two friends in the syndicate were not apparently going to be in attendance and had left the purchase entirely up to Lord D'Arcy, Letitia and Henry. The place filled up and at 10.05am, the first horse was brought into the arena. Brooke could only watch on in bewilderment as the auctioneer set to. She didn't understand anything that was going on. Nor did she understand what the auctioneer was saying, who the people were that were bidding or, indeed, how much they were bidding. This was, to her, truly like landing on another planet. But a planet that did far more than pique her interest! The one thing she absolutely did understand is when a horse had been sold. BANG! Down came the hammer – or rather gavel – as Mrs Townsend had explained. Then mumblings and murmurings went on for several minutes before the next horse – or lot – as Geoffrey taught her, was brought into the ring.

Brooke's mouth remained resolutely wide open as she strained to understand the auctioneer, fascinated by the speed at which he spoke, in awe of the people who were bidding and intrigued at the apparent knowledge of those around her. Horses went for anything from a couple of thousand and one went for over one hundred thousand guineas and caused quite a stir.

What even is a guinea?

She couldn't deny that it was incredibly exciting. The first horse the syndicate had been interested in had been withdrawn from the auction earlier on that morning due to injury, but at about 10.30am their second prospect came into the ring. Its name? *Turn The Paige*. Brooke laughed out loud and wondered whether this was a fatalistic sign as she thought momentarily about her daughter. She felt inexplicably enraptured, as though she were actually a part of it, even though she quite clearly wasn't. She remarked at the coincidence that Paige was her daughter's name and what a beautiful browny-black colour it was.

'Bay,' responded Lady Townsend in the way a teacher would when correcting a pupil. 'A horse with red-brown colouring and some black points is called "Bay".'

Bay. Bay. I must remember that.

'Can I ask how much the syndicate's gonna pay for it?' Brooke enquired of the grumpy bloodstock agent.

'Not worth more than between 30 and 32,000 guineas, max, I'd say,' Henry replied without moving his head from its position facing the ring. 'The price of a horse is always quoted in guineas at Tatts; that's a pound and a shilling or a pound and five pence in today's money.'

Brooke screwed up her nose but decided against asking why. She fell back into her seat, as the reality of these people's lives really hit her.

Bloody hell, that's nine grand for a leg each! Only the leg! And it's loose change to them!

What ya doing, babe?

The message pinged through from Dean. Brooke shrieked inwardly and was momentarily brought back down to earth with the most almighty thud.

Not much. Out and about.

Good god, if only he knew.

Love ya! CU2nite.

Love ya too! xxx

The bidding on Turn The Paige went up and up and up.

Even Brooke – as ignorant as it was possible to be – realised there must be something special about this horse as there were at least eight people bidding on it. It was certainly lively and seemed to thoroughly enjoy being paraded around, showing off at any opportunity, which made Brooke laugh. She thought it had a cheeky determination.

'Is it a girl or a boy horse?' Brooke enquired innocently, aware that all eyes and all concentration was on the bidding, tension in the air. She felt foolish having even asked the question, realising how ignorant she was showing herself to be.

'It's a filly,' explained Geoffrey quickly, 'or a female horse of three years old. I think this one's rather unique.'

The auctioneer was down to three bidders, including Lady Townsend's syndicate.

God, this is crazy! Sooo exciting!

She hadn't had an adrenalin rush like this since she spent over £500 on her Louboutins in Selfridges! It gushed through her body and her heart pounded loudly – at least to her! Not thinking that bidding on a silver Victoria tea caddy, or similar, would ever be cause for medical concern, she hadn't brought her mobile blood pressure device with her either!

It got to 32,500 guineas and Henry shook his head at Lady Townsend and Geoffrey. Brooke was most upset; Henry was clearly advising that the horse was not worth that much money and the syndicate should pull out of the bidding. Brooke started thinking about the money she'd earned and saved and was unable to spend without Dean being suspicious. Maybe she could launder some of it this way?! Despite not knowing anything about horses, let alone racehorses, Brooke suddenly blurted out, unable to contain her excitement. 'Geoffrey, please buy him...

I mean her! I can be another member of the syndicate. I'd love to be! I can put in another £3500. Pleeeeze?!' Brooke gabbled at high speed and put her hands together, like a child begging for something from their parents.

Geoffrey laughed loudly, rubbed his hands gleefully and after a very brief conflab with Letitia turned to her and asked, 'Are you absolutely sure? We need to be quick!'

Lady Townsend also looked at her straight in the eye with a very serious demeanour and said, 'Brooke, this is a huge undertaking. Are you absolutely sure you want to do this?'

Brooke thought intently for at least half a second before confirming, 'If this doesn't increase me hinterland, Mrs T, I don't know what will!'

Lord D'Arcy instructed Henry to go higher. The bidding went on for several more minutes and as the auctioneer was clearly looking at Henry Pilkington and one other bidder, it went to G33,000, then G34,500 then to G36,000 when the other bidder dropped out.

BANG! The gavel descended.

'SOLD to Henry Pilkington for G36,000.'

Brooke rose to her feet, punched both arms and fists up in the air and screamed out, 'Yesssss! We did it!'

'Brooke, dear, please sit down, you're making a spectacle of yourself,' Lady Townsend implored quietly, pulling Brooke's Barbour. Nearby punters found it most amusing and one could see their perplexed faces as they watched Brooke's excitement, as well as her Moschino dress lift rather too high for modesty, but not quite enough for Lord D'Arcy's liking!

'Sorry, Mrs T. I'm just so excited. I can't believe what I've just done!'

The next lot was brought out and the bidding continued.

'Well done, sweetheart! You are now the proud part-owner of a racehorse!' cried Lord D'Arcy.

Brooke was physically shaking, unable to get a grip on what she'd actually committed to; laughing and crying all at once.

Oh my god, what have I done? What have I done?!

'Which bit do I own? Can I have the tail?' she asked jokingly.

'Of course you can, sweetheart, whichever part you want. We just need to inform our friends that our syndicate went up to five.' Lord D'Arcy took pleasure in the pure and innocent joy that he and Letitia had facilitated.

Although the contract was actually with Henry Pilkington who paid straight away, Lady Townsend asked the sales team to explain the contract to Brooke, who listened with such intensity as though her life depended on it. Brooke asked Lady Townsend and Lord D'Arcy if she could pay her share later as she only had the money in cash back at home.

Lord D'Arcy waved his hand dismissively and told her not to worry, that he would pay her share to the agent and she could pay Lord D'Arcy back. In the back of his mind, he was thinking it would be another opportunity for Brooke to pay him a little visit to Ingatestone Hall, his ancestral historic country pile (which was open to the public and in which he still lived as 18th Baron D'Arcy, but in a private wing.) He did so enjoy her company. Lady Townsend was rather quiet and not as excited as Brooke thought she should be, given what'd just happened.

'Are you alright, Mrs T? You've gone all quiet. Have I made a mistake?' Brooke hadn't seen Lady Townsend like this before and it worried her.

She smiled. 'Let's hope not, dear. I don't want you to get into trouble with your husband. What will he have to say about it?'

Brooke looked quite indignant. 'Oh god, *he* won't know anything about it! This is my little secret. It's my money. I earned it. I can spend it how I like. If she wins any races, *then* I might tell him!'

They both laughed, but inside Lady Townsend was beginning to feel a tad uneasy.

What had she started?

6

Lunch At The Jockey Club Rooms

'We must celebrate!' Lord D'Arcy declared. 'Letitia, Brooke? Are you both up for lunch at The Jockey Club Rooms?'

Brooke had never heard of the place, but assumed it was another exclusive club for old men. She was thrilled at the prospect, because underneath this hideous outerwear, she was keen to show off her real outfit. But what about Paige? It was already coming up for 1pm. Lunch was bound to go on for a couple of hours at least and then she had to navigate the M25 at the start of rush hour. She was torn. For approximately three seconds.

'That'd be bril... That would be lovely, Geoffrey. Thank you,' Brooke replied rather too quickly. Lady Townsend declined the offer explaining she had to get back for a meeting, but encouraged Brooke to go without her and enjoy the experience. Brooke was disappointed, if not slightly concerned at being left alone with Geoffrey. She very much enjoyed chatting with him, but it meant she didn't have her trusted mentor to guide her and ensure she didn't make an idiot of herself in yet another new environment.

Geoffrey was clearly ravished at the thought, and, before Brooke knew it, he'd said his goodbyes to Letitia and was dragging Brooke off to his car. They detoured to collect her shoes from her car and drove two minutes to the Jockey Club Rooms in the High Street.

What a weird place to have it – fancy putting an ancient old building in the middle of all these shops!

They pulled up to the black iron gates, which slowly opened automatically. As they were pulling into the car park, up ahead a gentleman was stepping out of a black Bentley in Chambers car park.

'Who's the geezer with the tea towel on his head?' Brooke enquired, straining hard to look through the windscreen.

'That geezer, my dear, is Sheikh Mohammed Bin Halam. He's a crown prince and owns some of the most successful racehorses in the world. He's a member here. And that so-called "tea towel" is called a ghutra.'

'Oh, right. So you mean he comes all the way from… Israel or wherever, to come and buy his horses here?'

'Saudi Arabia, Brooke.' Lord D'Arcy became very serious. 'Don't make that mistake again.' Brooke shrunk to her five-year-old self.

Oh god, what have I said?

'I'm sorry, Geoffrey. I'm not fit to be let loose in your world, am I? What did I say wrong this time?' She tried to joke, but was feeling as though she'd just been put in the naughty corner.

'Poppycock! You're learning, that's all. Arabs (Saudi Arabia) and Jews (Israel) are arch enemies. Now, let's go in. Maybe I can introduce you.'

Why are they arch enemies?

'You mean you actually know this bloke?' Brooke did not think it possible to be any more amazed than she already was.

'I've known him for over twenty years. Our sons were in the

same class at Eton.'

Course they were. Should've guessed.

Brooke quickly removed Mrs Townsend's Barbour and slipped on her Louboutins, bringing her up to Geoffrey's height as she stood up.

'Golly, you *are* a tall girl, aren't you?' Geoffrey remarked, looking her up and down as though she were a special species of giraffe worthy of more attention. She smoothed out her dress and jacket, tilted her head and chin up slightly and tossed her long mane over her shoulders. She minced towards the elegant white wooden doors, with Geoffrey guiding her with his hand in the small of her back. They were met at the entrance by Christopher, the general manager.

'How good to see you again, Lord D'Arcy. It's been a while. Are you wishing to have lunch today?' He smiled warmly at Brooke and gave a slight nod of the head. She smiled back. He made her feel welcome and at ease.

'This is my guest, Mrs De'Ath. Please may we have my usual table by the window, Christopher?'

'Of course. Please, follow me.' Christopher engaged in small talk as he escorted them through the club. Brooke kept stopping to look at the paintings and other strange objects to be found on tables, sideboards and in cases on the walls. Christopher graciously gave comprehensive explanations when she asked a question.

She was drawn to the painting of Eclipse – the most famous horse in racing history – and, underneath in a case, the whip used by and donated to the club by King Charles II. Christopher explained that all thoroughbred horses racing in the world today can stem their lineage back to Eclipse. Apparently, after he died, vets opened him up to see how he ran so fast and discovered a heart weighing fourteen pounds! Twice that of any normal horse! Brooke was utterly fascinated.

They finally arrived at the restaurant and Christopher seated them at the large bay window overlooking the immaculately cut lawn and trimmed hedges. The room flickered with sunlight and the silver cruets, cutlery and glassware on the tables sparkled whenever the sun rays touched the edges.

'If you haven't been here for ages, how come he remembers your name?' Brooke asked suspiciously.

'Brooke, Christopher knows all the members here. There are over 200 of them and he knows all their names,' replied Lord D'Arcy.

'What?! That's impossible. No one can remember that many names.'

'Ah, well, you don't know Christopher. He and all his staff do.'

'Bloody hell!' Brooke said and immediately put her hand to her mouth to apologise. 'I mean…well I never!'

Lord D'Arcy laughed heartily at her commendable attempt to speak with more decorum. As he was recovering from his laughing fit, Sheikh Mohammed walked into the room looking like a ship in full sail, his voluminous white kandura flapping behind him. He spied Lord D'Arcy immediately and walked at pace over to his table.

'Geoffrey, my friend, how good to see you. It's been too long!' he boomed from the other side of the dining room. As he got closer, he extended his right hand towards Geoffrey.

'As-salamu alaykum,' said the sheikh.

'Alaikum assalaam,' Lord D'Arcy replied and shook hands

warmly with him.

What the hell does that mean?

'Very good to see you too, Your Excellency. I hope you're well,' he continued.

Brooke hadn't the faintest idea of the etiquette in this particular situation, so chose panic and stood to attention, as though she were about to be inspected. Her mouth dropped open, her head remained still and her eyes moved from one man to the other. Oh how she wished she'd been more diligent in her reading of the section on foreign royalty in *Debrett's*!

'And who is this beautiful young lady you have brought with you today?' asked the sheikh, looking at Brooke intently and making her feel like a prostitute being given the once-over.

I've heard about what blokes from that part of the world get up to when they meet Western girls.

Brooke's face was one of sheer terror.

No, please don't introduce me, please don't.

'This is my friend, Brooke De'Ath. She's unexpectedly joined our syndicate today. We just purchased a lovely filly this morning.'

He called me his friend!

'Ah, so you are interested in horse racing? You must come and visit my stud farm in Dubai when you next come over.'

Yeah right. On my annual trip for some winter sun.

Brooke thought she could get away without an actual response so merely smiled at him and giggled. Lord D'Arcy gave her a sideways stern look of expectation. She quickly came to the conclusion she was expected to say something.

She'd read nothing in *Debrett's* about how to address a sheikh. She decided to follow Geoffrey's lead, but remained as if she was tied into a straitjacket.

'Nice to meet you, Your Excellency,' she managed to blurt out.

God, is this actually happening to me?

She curtsied and thrust her hand out towards the sheikh at the same time. The move resembled a tribal dance and again Lord D'Arcy gave her another stern look that seemed to indicate a big, fat, silent 'No!'. She somehow managed to wither upwards from her curtsey and withdrew her hand as fast as she'd thrust it out. The sheikh roared laughing at the whole debacle.

'Don't you worry, my dear. If you want to shake my hand you are more than welcome.' He smiled and put his hand out and she looked over to Geoffrey for permission. He nodded discreetly and she shook the sheikh's hand – exactly as Mrs Townsend had taught her – and crushed his bones.

'Aaagh!' he wailed, followed by further roaring laughter as he rubbed the injured hand with the other.

'She has a firm grip on her, this one! Maybe she can come and work for me, Geoffrey? I could do with a strong woman about the place!'

I bet you could, and not to do the cleaning.

The two men laughed amiably, as Brooke stood by, excluded from their little private joke, hands now behind her back and her head bowed.

What's so funny?

She didn't like it, being at the receiving end of such misogyny, so decided to take a risk. 'Are you staying at The Jockey Club Rooms, Your Excellency?' Brooke enquired with fake sincerity, as she knew full well the answer.

'I am indeed, Ms De'Ath – or may I call you Brooke? I'm

staying in The King's Suite.'

Like I need to know. If you think you're getting into my knickers, you've got another thing coming.

'But you're only a crown prince, how come you're allowed to stay in The King's Suite?'

The sheikh and Geoffrey roared out laughing again.

'Oh, my dear, you are funny! Perhaps you would like to join me for dinner later?'

Oh gawd! Not expecting that! Think, think!

'Err…that's most kind. But err… I'm afraid I er…'

Gotta collect Paige!

'I have a previous engagement. Maybe another time?'

The sheikh looked genuinely disappointed. 'I won't forget that promise, young lady!' he continued. 'And I'm a man who always gets what he wants!'

Well not from this Essex girl you ain't.

Geoffrey and the sheikh said goodbye and he sailed off to join his lunch guests. Geoffrey motioned for Brooke to sit back down and pulled her chair out for her. She sat slowly, as though she'd forgotten how to do it, her eyes transfixed on the sheikh.

'What does that "assam alkum" thing mean that he said to you and you said to him?' Brooke's curiosity, which had so attracted Lord D'Arcy, came to the fore.

'It means "May peace be upon you" and I replied, "And peace be upon you".' Geoffrey replied matter-of-factly.

'How do you know that stuff? I mean, I don't know anyone who would know that!' Brooke cried out, frustrated, yet in awe of this man's seemingly unending knowledge of the world.

'I've been to Saudi Arabia many times over the years on business. I've some property interests out there. The sheikh's quite a character when you get to know him, you know.' remarked Geoffrey. 'Well done, Brooke, you handled him well.'

'I can't believe I've just met a crown prince and nearly broke his hand. Sorry about that, Geoffrey, and the curtsey thing, I didn't know what to do. I did the same thing when I first met Mrs Townsend. I'm so stupid.'

Geoffrey's eyes twinkled as he gazed at her. 'It's fine, Brooke. Well. Lucky you! Now you have an invitation to Dubai!'

'Yeah and pigs might fly! I don't think he's after my horse racing knowledge somehow!' Now it was Brooke's turn to burst out laughing.

'Oh trust me, that's no joke. He meant it. The Saudis are an incredibly hospitable bunch. As far as he's concerned, if you're a friend of mine, you're a friend of his. You'd be treated like royalty.'

Brooke laughed some more, checked her watch and picked up the menu. 'C'mon, Geoffrey, we need to get a move on. I've gotta pick Paige up at four.'

The menu was daunting. She blew out through pursed lips as she read it all.

Jus? Chicken Rillette? Coquilles St Jacque? Gazpacho? Oh god, I dunno. Foie gras?! I fancy some mac 'n' cheese.

'I definitely don't want that foie gras stuff. I know what they do to 'em. I looked it up… I mean those poor ducks,' she stated firmly.

Geoffrey smiled at her refreshing straight forward manner. He seemed to have the same knack as Lady Townsend and observed Brooke's menu discomfort and he'd no wish for that, so he made recommendations which Brooke gladly went with. After all, this is the man that'd successfully persuaded her she'd like cold rice pudding at Brooks's.

Geoffrey ordered and they enjoyed a splendid lunch of potted shrimps followed by sole meunière with artichoke puree, washed down with a superb glass of Sancerre. Throughout, Brooke fired so many questions at Geoffrey about the syndicate, to the point where his comprehensive answers meant he'd barely touched his food when she'd finished hers. He took that opportunity to ask her a question and then stuff his own mouth full of food, forcing her to do some of the talking. He'd a way of making her feel comfortable in this environment, as though she'd every right to be there and that he found her conversation interesting. Which he genuinely did. He nodded in all the right places, maintained strong eye contact and made various noises indicating he was in agreement or that he understood what she was saying.

At the end of the main course, Brooke looked at her watch again and suddenly remembered that Geoffrey would have to drive her back to Tattersall's to collect her car.

I'm an idiot, I should've driven here myself and saved some time.

'I'm so sorry, Geoffrey, but we've gotta go. I've gotta pick my car up, don't forget.'

Lord D'Arcy graciously understood and they made ready to leave; it looked to Brooke as though Geoffrey didn't even need to sign a bill or pay for the meal. They got to his Land Rover, he walked round to her side and 'helped' her in.

He's such a gentleman.

She practiced her ladylike way of getting into the car, much to Geoffrey's disappointment, whose eyes were clearly on her honed thighs. How he'd wished for a glimpse a little further up!

He'd forgotten what Lady D'Arcy's legs looked like. She wore support tights all year round and in bed at night changed into compression stockings for DVT. Most unattractive.

They arrived back at Tattersall's, which was deserted by this time and Geoffrey parked right next to Brooke's car. They sat awkwardly for a moment before Geoffrey leaned over, pecked her on the cheek and thanked her for a thoroughly enjoyable lunch before getting out and opening her side. Before she was able to get into Flora, he clutched her by her waist, pulled her towards him and gave her another kiss on both cheeks. She stiffened slightly as memories came flooding back of his making – what had become known between her and Dawn as – 'the hot tub pass'.

Oh not this again, please!

'Brooke, thank you once again for a delightful lunch. I hope this means I'll be seeing a bit more of you now that you've joined our syndicate. There'll be lots to discuss and we'll soon be finding out when Turn The Paige can race, but I'll have to discuss that with Mark Fairbairn, who's her trainer over at Portland Lodge in Bury Road.'

God I hope that's not why he let me join the syndicate!

'I should be thanking you for lunch, Geoffrey. It was lovely. Shame we didn't have time for pudding! I fancied that chocolate tart. Not that I could've eaten it, to be fair. I'm absolutely stuffed!' She rubbed her belly. 'Look, I've got a food baby! I still can't believe what I've done today. Girls like me don't have days like this!' Brooke put her hands to her head as the reality of the past five hours began to sink in.

'I'll bet you can't wait to tell your husband, mm? Dean, isn't it? He's going to get a bit of a shock, eh? Sends his wife out cleaning and she comes back part-owner of a racehorse!' Lord D'Arcy roared in that way that only he could.

The cleaning comment cut her to the quick, although she was sure he hadn't intended to be cruel. Brooke's thoughts suddenly turned to Dean. She took her phone out of her jacket. Earlier she'd turned it down so she wouldn't be distracted during the bidding, but, in all the excitement, had forgotten to turn the volume back up again. Six missed messages from Dean. Oh dear, that was rather careless!

'Oh hell, sorry, Geoffrey, gotta scarper. Thanks again and say hello to the sheikh from me if you see him again. Tell him yes, next time I'm in Dubai I'll look him up!' Brooke winked and laughed.

Geoffrey stood in the car park, a lone figure in his tweeds and flat cap, waving and beaming at Brooke as she wheelspan out the exit. He remained there for several minutes debating whether to go back to The Jockey Club Rooms to have a drink with the sheikh. He just wasn't quite ready to go home to Lady D'Arcy's flower-arranging group quite yet.

Meanwhile, Brooke had to whistle and ride, speaking to Dean as she drove along. 'Hi, babe, it's only me. Sorry I missed your calls. What's up?'

'Where are you, Brooke? Why haven't you picked up? I've rung six times!'

'I know, I've just seen, sorry. I was in the library with Paige and Lady Townsend was in there today and…she invited me for lunch.' She gulped. 'It seemed a bit mean to say no, so I dropped Paige off at Dawn's and went out for lunch.' Brooke took a deep breath. Now that was positively BAFTA-winning! Her performances were getting better and better!

'Oh.' Dean sounded somewhat deflated. 'Why didn't you take Paige?' he asked, a tad suspiciously.

Think, think.

'Well…she was a bit irritable…and I thought she might need a kip,' Brooke replied, this time crossing the fingers on both hands.

'Where'd ya go, then?' Dean enquired in an overly casual manner. Brooke hadn't expected such questioning.

Shit shit shit!

'Oh, only… The Nag's Head.'

Christ, he'll be asking me what I ate next!

'What did you have to eat? Anything nice?' Dean asked innocently.

Brooke was truly under the cosh now. It took every ounce of the information retrieval skills she possessed, to recall the last time she'd been to The Nag's Head and seen their menu. She shook and thought her voice trembled a little as she blurted out, 'Just a prawn sarnie. I wasn't that hungry.'

'Is that all? Blimey, you'd have thought she'd manage a better dinner than that! Must be one of them poor aristocrats!' Dean responded. Brooke found herself wanting to defend Lady Townsend, but thought better of it.

'It's lunch, Dean. Not dinner,' Brooke said irritably. 'So, what did you want? Is everything OK?' Brooke was glad to get off the subject of her imaginary lunch with Lady Townsend.

'Yeah, all I wanted to know was if you fancied going out for tea tonight? Pizza Hut have got a 2 for 1 deal but they said we needed to book 'cause they're gonna be busy. We can take Paige and you can fill your boots with pizza to make up for your pathetic dinner,' Dean replied.

'Can't we can go another time?' Brooke was relieved that's all it was. 'And, Dean, it's lunch not dinner.'

'Whatever!' Dean retorted, rather confused and rattled at Brooke's sudden habit of correcting him. 'No, I booked it. When I didn't hear back from you I took an executive decision that we'd go anyway. I'll be home early so it's not too late for Paige.'

NOOOOO!

'What time'll you be back?' she asked as casually as her state of mind would allow.

'About five, I'm gonna leave the office early.'

A full-on meltdown was on the cards. Could she hold her nerve? Was she able to come up with something feasible? What if there was traffic on the M25? Maybe she could faint or have a minor accident? She was only meant to be in Brentwood and here she was, twenty-five miles away near Stansted airport on the M11.

'Oh right. Well, I've just left the pub, but I'm...having my nails done...and I've gotta pick up a few bits at Tesco as well before I get Paige. I should be back before you...but just in case...' She held her breath anticipating a complaint about having her nails done twice in one month.

'Alright, babe, no worries, see you later. Love ya!'

Brooke pressed the red button on her phone. She was physically shaking as she continued down the M11; she kicked off her Louboutins and pressed her paddle-like foot firmly down on the accelerator, reaching 90mph alarmingly quickly.

She examined her nails. Perfect. Not a chip in sight. Most fortunate!

Oh and, by the way, I met a sheikh, lunched at The Jockey Club Rooms and bought a bit of a racehorse!

At that moment it was as if someone had snapped her out of a hypnotic state. The ordinariness of this journey she was now making, the tedium of the scenery and dullness of the sky; it all hit her like the most vicious slap in the face. There followed a scream as good as any that her daughter could muster, only Brooke's was followed by hysterical laughter until the tears ran down her cheeks.

'I OWN A GODAMN RACEHORSE!!'

...well the tail anyway!

***

After breaking the speed limit for forty-five minutes, back in Brentwood, Paige was collected and Dawn updated and suitably thunderstruck at Brooke's latest antics. Her response was predictable. 'You did WHAT?! Bought a fucking racehorse?!'

'Shh, Dawn. No swearing in front of Paige. Well, a part of one anyway,' Brooke replied nervously.

'I don't believe you. Why? You don't know anything about horses. You've gone bloody mad! What's Dean gonna say?' Dawn wasn't interested in hearing about The Jockey Club Rooms, lunch with Lord D'Arcy or the sheikh.

'He won't know anything about it. It's my money, remember. I can spend it on whatever I like. I've saved everything I've earned since the hot tub malarkey and it's a good way of spending it without Dean noticing.' Brooke's mood was one of defiance with a hint of defensiveness.

Dawn could only shake her head in disbelief. 'That's...that's like money laundering, but within the family!'

***

A couple of hours later, Brooke was forced to eat a Meat Feast pizza that her belly fought against, in Pizza Hut in the High Street. She looked around her at the brown sticky tables, the disinterested waiting staff and the coarse customers scoffing on their four cheeses deep pan.

Dean munched his way enthusiastically through his large BBQ Americano with extra chillies and jalapenos, oil dripping down his chin. He'd stuffed his paper napkin into his shirt to catch the worst of it. Brooke stared at him, no longer even with that despairing look she saved for such moments, but with something nearer pity.

'How's your pizza? You don't seem that keen.' Dean asked with his mouth full.

'It's fine. I'm not that hungry.' Brooke pushed her plate away, half her pizza remaining on the plate. Dean leaned over, grabbed a slice and shovelled it into his mouth.

'Don't wanna waste it, eh? We could ask for a doggy bag.' Some of the pizza fell out of his mouth as he was talking. Paige picked it up off the table and put it in her mouth.

Brooke closed her eyes for a moment, folded her arms and stared out the window in silence.

7

SweatUBet

After returning home from work one evening a few days later, Dean waited for Brooke to disappear for a few minutes before reading through the visit brief that Angie had sent him, one more time, before his phone call to SweatUBet. His assessment was about to begin. He practised it in his head a few times before picking up the phone. The most important thing, Angie had told him, was that they invited him to go to the gym for a 'show-round'.

'Oh hi, I was wondering if you could tell me a bit about your gym and possibly becoming a member?' Dean spoke in his best telephone voice.

'Right. Yeah, well, we've got all the usual equipment you'd find in a gym and we run a bunch of classes. Oh yeah and we've got a cafe and a bar,' came the monotone reply.

Dean waited patiently to be offered a show-round. Nothing.

Mmm.

You must give the staff every opportunity to display the standard we want assessed.

He tried another tactic. 'OK. Er…how big is the gym?'

'Well, it's pretty big. We've got six running machines,' the chap replied, evidently already bored at being asked such tiresome questions.

'What are the changing rooms and showers like?' Dean was sure this would provoke an invitation to go to the gym and have a look around. Sadly, it was not to be. He thought for a moment and decided to give it one more go.

'What *kind* of members do you have? I mean…is it mixed and what sort of age?' Dean enquired with a seemingly deeper meaning.

The chap at the other end of the phone pulled the phone away from his ear for a moment and stared into the mouthpiece with a look resembling disgust.

'Oh right, yeah, see what you're getting at. We've got men *and* women – and some pretty hot ones at that. It's about sixty per cent women and forty per cent men, so if you're looking for some…er…socialising, it's pretty good.'

Dean rolled his eyes and sighed.

Well I'm gonna have to mark that down as a 'No' – no invite for a show-round.

'Could I possibly come and have a look around?'

'Yeah sure, come in any time.'

'Don't I need to book?'

'Nah, mate. Just turn up.'

'Who am I speaking to please?'

'Peregrine.'

Stunned silence. Dean could hear the slapping sound of chewing gum down the mouthpiece and Pharell William's 'Happy' pumping away in the background.

'Sorry?' Dean was compelled to check he'd heard correctly. It was essential that he gave the names of all the staff he interacted with in his report. Normally this was easy, as one simply looked for their name badge, but on the telephone one had to get it right.

'Peregrine Childs-Sheenan,' he replied flatly, with no hint of jest.

Dean cupped his hand over his mouth; it was as much as he could do to stop himself laughing. He just didn't sound like a Peregrine. Mind you, Dean had never met a Peregrine, so he really couldn't judge.

'Peregrine Childs-Sheenan?'

He's gotta be takin' the piss.

'Yeah.' Peregrine sniffed.

'OK, Peregrine, I'll check my diary and I'll probably try a bit later this week sometime after work.'

'Alright, mate. See ya then. Bye'

Mate?! You don't call a prospective customer mate!

Peregrine put the phone down. Dean burst out laughing, unable to fathom how such an oik with the intelligence of an amoeba could possibly have been cursed (or blessed) with such a name. Without warning and making Dean jump up like someone had lit a match under his backside, Brooke appeared behind him on the sofa.

'What are you laughing at?' she asked.

'Jesus, Brooke, I wish you wouldn't do that! Creeping up on me like that. I thought you were in the shower.' Dean sounded cross; irrationally so to Brooke's mind.

Hell, did she overhear any of that? That's all I need.

'Keep your hair on[4]! I *was* in the shower, then I came *out* the shower and downstairs; what's your problem?' she went into her both-hands-on-both-hips mode of talking, which was never a good sign.

4. Don't panic.

'Nothing, sorry, you just spooked me. I didn't hear you,' Dean responded with a touch of defensiveness in his voice.

'Well as long as you're not organising to see your lover,' Brooke said with a deadpan face as she leaned over the back of the sofa and placed her cheek next to his. He scowled when he saw that face. He was never quite sure how to take it. 'Who's *Peregrine* and why are you seeing them after work?'

A rush of adrenalin surged through Dean's body. He'd been caught off guard.

Think! Think!

'Um…well…he – or she – is my first potential pomosexual; I think I've found one!' Oh dear, the outrageous untruth sort of tumbled out in a moment of sheer desperation!

'You're kidding me?' Brooke's mouth dropped open and she came round and sat next to Dean on the sofa.

Oh shit, shit, shit! What have I done? Think, think!

'What do they look like?' Brooke asked, innocently imagining an exotic, untouchable lifeform of some description. Dean took a deep breath.

In for a penny in for a pound.

'Dunno, that's why I'm meeting them next week. I've gotta interview them.'

'Blimey! Where d'ya find him – her – whatever?' Brooke's face was a picture of fascination.

Knowing that he was going to have to go back to SweatUBet at least a couple more times, Dean tried to make things a little easier on himself. 'He's currently working in a gym in Billericay.' He was in it deep now. 'Martin knows him from the snooker hall and said he was looking for another job.' What a whopper! Well poor, unsuspecting Martin (Dean's rather coarse best chum) was going to be most interested to hear that he associated with pomosexuals.

'Bloody hell, who knew they had pomosexuals in Billericay?' exclaimed Brooke, truly astonished at such a revelation.

'Well, they might not be rampant. He might be the only one for all I know. But yeah, I'm thinking of them for the admin assistant's role in the new call centre when it opens. You know, give 'em a job where they'll be in constant touch with all areas of the business – to help break down discrimination barriers. That's what Dave's notes said.'

'Yeah right. Well, I can't wait to meet them.' Brooke said, adding to Dean's already stressed heart. She went into the kitchen trying to imagine what a pomosexual called Peregrine would look like and whether they'd help advance Dean's career. 'Fancy a beer, babe?'

'Thanks, love,' Dean replied, hands shaking and beads of sweat waiting to pop out above his top lip.

I think I'm gonna need it.

***

On the Friday of that week Dean, already perspiring, pulled up to SweatUBet on his moped. He'd been unable to get rid of it as he'd hoped, after he'd got his company car. Brooke had insisted that she have the new car, her argument being that Dean would only leave it at the station all day and then simply drive it home again, whereas she'd use it extensively during the day. So, Edna was disposed of. They actually ended up having to pay seventy-five pounds for someone to tow her away. They were both so glad to see the back of that car that Brooke extravagantly purchased a bottle of Möet to celebrate.

Dean looked at the gym from the outside. There were giant photographs plastered on the windows, of male and female models with abs like David Gandy and quads like Jourdan Dunn, allegedly working out at SweatUBet. The gym itself had the misfortune of being nestled between a McDonald's on one side and a KFC on the other. What hope for all those gym rats, with such temptation visible every time they walked out of the place!

Dean strolled into the lobby where there was a small area selling various items of gym apparel. A rather striking set of zebra-print leggings and matching crop top caught his eye, as did a men's fluorescent-green t-shirt and matching shorts, which required sunglasses to look at. Various towels and drinks bottles languished on the hooks, covered in dust and grubby marks.

Mmm. I wonder when someone last bought from that lot.

A young man leaned back with his legs splayed wide open behind the reception desk, his eyes superglued to his mobile. He was sporting what looked to be a staff uniform of red polo shirt with the SweatUBet logo (which, along with a bright mop of ginger hair, rather amplified his very ruddy acne-ridden complexion), a pair of navy-blue joggers, stained where they shouldn't be and not-so-white trainers. His face had adopted the sort of zombie look that teenagers develop when playing *Call of Duty* on their PlayStations. Or 'COD face' as Brooke used to call it.

Dean sauntered up to the desk and waited for the young man to get off his phone. He waited and waited. Eventually Dean coughed and the chap looked up and merely raised his eyebrows, silently saying, 'What do you want?'

'I just wondered if I could possibly have a look round the gym? I rang up the other day to say I'm thinking of joining. Spoke to someone called Peregrine?' Dean looked at the chap with a questioning expression as though he was pretty damn sure he'd got the name wrong.

'Yeah, that's me. 'ang on a minute and I'll get someone over.' The chap slid off his stool and strolled nonchalantly over to Kelly, one of the young female instructors, and had a word. Dean followed him with his eyes.

So, this is the man I've claimed is a pomosexual to Brooke and that I'll apparently be interviewing for a role in the new call centre. Gordon Bennett[5]*!*

Kelly looked over to Dean and grinned. She left the gym floor and came over to him.

'So. You wanna join SweatUBet? Do a bit of "socialising", I understand?" she said with a smile, a wink and hand quote marks around the word 'socialising'. She looked him up and down, causing him to feel rather exposed and vulnerable.

'I never said that! I wanna have a look round and see what I think before I decide to join,' Dean said stiffly.

Did the instructor who showed you round, ask your name, use it throughout and engage in small talk beforehand?

Mmm. Not really, no. She was straight in there.

'D'ya belong to a gym at the moment or have you ever belonged to one?'

Oh good, she's meant to ask that.

'Nah. I'm not a gym person, me,' Dean said without thinking as he looked around. Kelly tilted her head to one side.

5. An exclamation of anger, surprise, frustration and incredulity.

'So...why d'ya wanna join now?' she ventured.

Dean realised his answer must have made him sound a bit thick, so he quickly said, 'Oh it's the wife. She thinks I've put on a bit of weight.' He patted his stomach and grinned.

'Oh. We've got a few of them types 'ere. You won't be alone. They all go to the bar after their workouts! Follow me and I'll show you round.' With that, Kelly walked ahead in a casual manner, rather like an insolent gang member and 'showed' Dean the gym while standing in the doorway. By way of a single arm movement sweeping across all the equipment, she actually declared the somewhat obvious 'this is the gym'.

Dean was rather stumped. He'd expected a little more detail as per the visit brief. Kelly folded her arms and leaned against the doorway, clearly not planning on actually venturing inside the gym area.

Did the instructor show you all the equipment in the gym and enthuse about what each could do for the relevant part of the body?

Dean thought she might need a bit of encouragement and asked, 'So what does that machine over there do?' He was pointing to a stair-climber over the other side, which was impossible to see properly from where they were standing.

'That's good for yer glutes and gives you a pert bum.' She remained steadfastly where she was. Still leaning. No eye contact.

'What about that one over there?' He pointed to an alarming-looking piece of medieval torture equipment.

'That's a cable crossover machine. Good for working the upper body,' she replied and yawned, not looking at him and while waving at someone she knew on one of the running machines.

Well, she's not exactly enthusing. Ask the instructor something out of the ordinary but relevant to test how well they handle your enquiry.

Dean had been thinking about what he'd ask, while reading over his visit brief and had decided he'd kill two birds with one stone and conduct some research at the same time as fulfilling his brief.

'So, out of interest, do you have any instructors or members who don't identify as either male or female?' Dean asked casually.

Kelly all at once unfolded her arms and turned round to face Dean with a look of suspicion. 'Umm. Well definitely no instructors. I dunno about members.' She stood thoughtfully for a moment, pondering the question. 'No. I mean, I dunno. I mean how would I know? How would anyone know?' Kelly's eyes quickly glanced down at Dean's crotch and back up to his face. Her eyes squinted slightly. 'No one's ever asked before.'

'Just wondered,' Dean said casually, as though it was the most normal of enquiries.

Mmm, interesting.

Kelly motioned for Dean to follow her to the dance studios where the classes took place. They crept inside and observed as a Zumba class was in progress. Dean's face was a picture as his eyes rested on each female participant for a few seconds before moving onto the next one. He was overcome with exhaustion simply looking at them. He couldn't ever recall seeing such a range of female body shapes in one place – especially their bottoms – fat, flat, round, saggy. He smiled.

Not a patch on Brooke's. God, that looks knackering. Those women haven't got enough to do if they've got enough energy to prance about like that at the end of a working day.

'Looks tough,' admitted Dean, nodding his head.

'That's the beginners' class. There's an intermediate and advanced class as well,' Kelly responded with a wry smile. Dean's eyes widened in horror. 'There's classes for blokes too. We've got a very popular Boxercise class on Tuesday and Thursday evenings.'

Ah, good! She's actually mentioned something she's meant to!

Kelly led Dean out of the studio and took him to another one next door.

'This is our pole-dancing class,' she said as she pushed the door open and let him in. Anyone would've thought he was hiding from the police, if his reaction was anything to go by. He rammed himself up against the wall at the back, with his arms stiff and firmly by his sides as he looked on in astonishment – a sort of rabbit in the headlights look, but worse – at a woman upside down, with her legs wrapped around the pole and her hands dangling down toward the floor. She smiled and waved at Dean, who gasped and feared for her head should she fall. The woman must have been in her sixties if she was a day. All her parts were drooping in the wrong direction; a most disconcerting sight for the poor chap.

Babe, where r u? Was expecting u about an hour ago??

Dean jumped a little, startled at Brooke's contacting him when he wasn't expecting it.

Sorry, luv. Just interviewing the pomo! Be back soon!

Dean felt a little conspicuous, if not downright voyeuristic, and so asked to leave. Kelly laughed. As they came up to another set of doors, Kelly asked, 'Do you wanna see the showers and changing rooms?' in a voice that sounded like she hoped not.

'I need the loo anyway, so I'll just pop in myself if that's OK,' Dean suggested. She said she'd go outside for a 'fag break'. Dean shot inside and was met with a group of naked Arnold Schwarzenegger wannabes.

Where are their towels?

The men stood legs apart and slightly thrust their groins towards him.

Oh right, now I see.

He physically shrank as he walked past them. They all stopped talking and followed him with their eyes, a little reminiscent of the time he'd unwittingly walked into an IRA pub in Kilburn. Dean glanced around briefly and became increasingly aware of the smell and the numerous old towels lying around and pairs of trainers everywhere, ammonia emanating from them all. It felt damp and unhygienic, causing Dean to shudder and escape as quickly as possible. His OCD kicked in, compelling him to get vigorous with his hand wipes. He could only imagine how many verrucas were picked up there. Kelly spied him coming out of the changing rooms, threw her cigarette butt on the floor, stamped it out with her foot and strolled over to Dean. It was at this point he also observed a roll of belly fat over her leggings and so she wasn't the best role model for healthy living in Billericay.

They then jogged up the small flight of stairs to the cafe and bar – RefuelU.

In the cafe, did the instructor offer you a non-alcoholic beverage, sit with you and encourage you to become a member in a professional manner?

'Wanna drink?' Kelly asked.

Mmm, not exactly professional.

Dean asked for a coke and while Kelly was at the bar he picked up the menu; alarmed to see burger and chips, fried chicken and chips and fish 'n' chips to name but a few of the meals on offer. He was no expert on the idiosyncratic eating habits of gym rats, but he was sure they didn't include chips. Where was the rabbit food?

Not exactly healthy eating.

Dean looked over to the bar where Kelly was chatting with a member; clearly someone she knew. It was all ''allo, babe, 'ow's yer Mum?' The barman grinned as he carried on drying a beer glass and said something to Kelly out the side of his mouth. Raucous laughter followed as they both looked over at Dean, who shifted around uneasily in his chair.

What are they laughing at?

After talking to everyone but him it seemed, Kelly finally came back to the table with Dean's coke. 'So, are you gonna join or what?' she blurted out. Considering Kelly was so entirely devoid of charm, Dean thought she was most audacious. He sniffed, took a sip of his coke, looked around the bar at the tattooed, steroid-laden men and equally tattooed, fully made-up girls with enhanced mammary glands who were drinking prosecco. They flirted with the Arnie wannabes, who were more interested in preening themselves in the mirror behind the bar than seducing the pretty girls in front of them. Oh, the foolishness of men!

'Not sure,' he said dismissively. 'How much is it?'

Kelly ran off without warning and brought some paperwork back a minute or two later.

'As a special offer, there's no joining fee and only twenny-five quid a month.' Kelly gave a pen to Dean. 'You need to fill the form in and sign here and here and you're all done.' She stabbed the document in the relevant places.

Did the instructor use skilful sales tactics to get you to join?

Er, no.

Did they ask you a series of questions to which you had to answer 'Yes'?

Nope.

Was the instructor genuinely interested in how your fitness needs would be met by SweatUBet?

Nope.

Dean didn't think he'd ever come across a place so unprofessional. He was quite sure that Peregrine and Kelly didn't care about him one jot; they were eager to get him to sign the paperwork and get rid of him and that was it. He was unsure what else he could do to give them the best opportunity to score better in this mystery visit. At the moment they'd only hit two standards out of thirty on the visit questionnaire. Shocking! What would Angie say? What would the owners of SweatUBet say, more to the point? But he'd run out of ideas and time, so reluctantly took the pen, completed the paperwork and signed on the dotted line.

Did they summarise the benefits of the package deal you signed?

Nope.

Did the instructor offer to let you keep the SweatUBet branded pen with which you signed the paperwork?

'So now we just need to book you in for your induction. You can keep the pen.'

Alle bloody lujah.

A date for the induction was sorted, Kelly took the paperwork, said thanks and goodbye and left Dean to finish his coke on his own.

Well, if that's how they sell the place, god knows what the induction will be like.

***

No sooner had Dean arrived through the door than Brooke was shouting out, 'How did your interview with Peregrine the pomo go?'

Oh christ, let me get in the bloody door.

'Yeah, it was alright; a bit tricky. We sat in the gym cafe but his colleagues and bosses kept walking past while I was interviewing him on his break,' Dean lied with a weariness in his voice. He'd started to feel ashamed at how easy he was beginning to find lying. Paige, not yet in bed, toddled over to him for a cuddle. He picked her up, kissed her tenderly, then she put her thumb in her mouth and lay her head on his chest.

'What did he look like? Was he – you know – unusual? Like, sort of half-man half-womanish?' Brooke had already made up her mind that he was going to present rather like those androgenous models one sees in *Vogue*.

'Like a normal bloke, actually,' Dean said in the hope of stemming what he knew would otherwise be an endless stream of questions about him.

Brooke was most disappointed. 'Oh. So are you gonna offer him the job then?'

Dean bounced Paige on his lap and declared that he hadn't made up his mind yet because he hadn't been able to interview him properly. He would have to go back again to conduct a second interview. Brooke was taken aback that he was prepared to go to such lengths. She reminded him that Peregrine was only one of the many groups he had to have represented in the new call centre team. He couldn't spend this much time recruiting one person, surely? Dean told her not to worry her pretty little head about it – he'd sort it out one way or another. With that, he asked about her day; at which point, she turned away and walked into the kitchen. Paige wriggled free of her father and followed her mother, falling over on the way but bouncing back like a jack-in-the-box. Brooke's heart raced; she felt herself go slightly red and she had to be steady when she spoke so as not to give away the wobble in her voice.

'I'm having a glass of wine, d'ya fancy a beer?'

Brooke'd been trying to come up with new excuses to feed Dean as to what she'd been doing that would explain why she often didn't pick up her phone. She needed to allay any suspicions he might have about her whereabouts during the day. She'd got into a comfortable rhythm on a Monday, Wednesday and Friday of taking Paige to Dawn's and picking her up while she worked at Purses. Her entire routine was carried out like a military operation. In fact, she'd named it Operation One Out All Out (OOAO)

Brooke had never revealed to Lady Townsend that Dean didn't know she came to work at Purses three times a week. She'd have been mortified! The longer it went on, the harder it became for Brooke to tell her. But she didn't want to think about it. It was the one area in her life where she became the proverbial ostrich, burying her head in the sand. She'd now told her friend Stacey as well as Dawn, and Stacey felt the same way;

she thought Brooke was mad, but, being her oldest friend, she wasn't going to tell Dean. She'd be an alibi, if necessary, until the day came where Brooke would finally reveal all and they'd all laugh about how long she'd managed to carry it off for.

Brooke shouted from the kitchen as she 'tried out' her latest imaginary day out with Paige. 'We went on a playground crawl.' She took a deep breath and walked back into the lounge. Paige seemed to get irritable at her mother's walking about, wanting her sat down where she could get some proper attention and began to give off all the signs that a screaming fit was waiting in the wings. As prepared as ever, Brooke whipped out a Chupa Chups from her jeans pocket and popped it into Paige's mouth.

Phew – just in time!

'Haha! That sounds cool! What was the favourite?' Dean asked innocently as he channel swapped.

Brooke'd known Dean would ask and she'd already decided what she'd say. 'Oh the one in Pilgrims Hatch. We visited loads; it was great fun. Definitely something I'd do again.' She was setting the foundations for using it many times as an excuse in the future.

Dean was delighted to hear that Brooke was doing something different and physical with their daughter as opposed to just shopping, the library or playing at Dawn's house. He even suggested that she should start a blog about playgrounds in the area. Brooke was secretly horrified. That wasn't anything she'd anticipated at all!

'Mmm, maybe,' she replied unenthusiastically.

Change the subject, change the subject.

'How d'ya fancy bathing Paige and telling her a bedtime story?'

Dean smiled a fake smile. 'Yeah, love to.' With that, he whipped the Chupa Chups out and waited for the screaming to begin. He didn't have to wait long.

8

Horse Tail Payment & An Unwilling Alibi

Once again, Brooke found herself at the gates of Ingatestone Hall. It was beginning to feel like re-visiting a favourite old holiday haunt. She made her way to the Reception, and, with newfound confidence asked to speak to Lord D'Arcy. She held her head high, didn't fiddle with her curls, didn't stutter and there wasn't a trace of red cheek in sight. Mrs Brompton smiled affectionately and didn't even ask her name or what business she had there. Instead, as Brooke wandered around the gift shop, she overheard Mrs Brompton inform Lord D'Arcy that Ms De'Ath was in reception to see him. Something about this made Brooke smile. She'd moved on and up in the eyes of the staff. They knew her!

Within a minute, the door to reception burst open with such force, it crashed into the wall, making everyone jump. 'Brooke, sweetheart, how marvellous to see you!' Lord D'Arcy held his arms out wide revealing a fashion crisis underneath.

'*Veni solver pro mea parte equus*[6]', she said confidently.

'*Gratias agimus tibi*[7]', he replied, again thrilled at his protégé's efforts in Latin. He rubbed his hands, a sure sign he was happy to see her. 'Come, come, let me get you a coffee.' He

6. I have come to pay for my share of the horse.
7. Thank you.

suddenly stopped and asked, 'You can stay a while, can't you? You're not going to run off straight away?'

Brooke laughed. 'No. I won't turn into a pumpkin for at least a couple of hours yet!'

As bold as brass, he grabbed her by the hand and pulled her in the direction of his private wing.

'Geoffrey, you really need to get shot of that cardie – it's completely threadbare at the elbows.' Brooke poked her fingers through the holes. 'Doesn't your wife inspect you before you go out in the morning? Is she here? It'd be nice to meet her.'

Lord D'Arcy roared and explained that sadly Lady D'Arcy was out with the Essex Brass Rubbing Society and that she'd given up trying to change his dress habits years ago. Poor woman had even managed to cajole him into going to Harrod's to see the personal shopper there. It'd been an unmitigated disaster, much to Lady D'Arcy's despair. His clothes were like old friends to him – rather like the furniture at his club – worn but familiar and therefore comfortable. Why would he want to change them for anything else? He didn't need to impress anyone. His Marks & Spencer cavalry tweeds, check shirt and Donegal jacket from seventeen years ago were perfectly adequate.

Brooke rolled her eyes as Lord D'Arcy continued marching towards his private wing and into the kitchen to make coffee. 'So... Miss Owner of a Racehorse Tail! How are you feeling about your little purchase in the cold light of day, eh?'

Brooke opened her handbag and pulled out a wad of notes held together with an elastic band. 'There's three and a half grand in cash right there.' She threw it on the table. 'That's how I'm feeling! Well chuffed!' She grinned.

'What did your husband say?'

Brooke bristled. Why did everyone always need to know what he thought? Why did they always assume that he would have some sort of say in it? Why couldn't they accept it was her money and she could do as she damn well liked with it?

'He doesn't know about it, if you must know.'

Lord D'Arcy's mouth dropped open, as though Brooke'd told him she'd just shot his wife or something.

'Shut your mouth, Geoffrey, there's a train coming,' she cackled.

Lord D'Arcy went on to lecture Brooke about the importance of keeping the man of the house informed about financial decisions and how Dean might feel somewhat emasculated by her actions.

Brooke listened, narked at his old-fashioned point of view, and then whipped her phone out and performed a lighting-quick search in front of Lord D'Arcy.

Emasculated; deprived of male role and identity. Mmm. Well I don't wanna make him feel like that.

Brooke screwed up her nose. 'He'd be seriously pissed off, that's for sure, but that's all the more reason not to tell him. If Turn The Paige wins any races, then I might. What's the chances, Geoffrey, d'ya think? Honestly?'

Lord D'Arcy struggled with her casual dismissal of Dean's involvement, but, regardless, went into 'teacher' mode about the risks and rewards in relation to syndicates and horse racing. He explained there were no guarantees, but that he was hopeful. This led on to educating her about some of the most famous races and race courses in the UK and Ireland.

'Oooh! Dean's gran's over in Ireland. Maybe we can race her there? She likes a bit of a flutter. What d'ya think?'

Lord D'Arcy gazed into Brooke's eyes as she spoke without heirs or graces; he was charmed by her enthusiasm and natural demeanour all over again.

'Well, we'd have to discuss it with the syndicate; if we start taking the horse out of the UK it begins to get expensive. I obviously spoke with our friends about your joining, by the way.'

'Oh god I forgot about that, what did they say? Were they hacked off?' Brooke suddenly frowned and bit her lip.

'Not in the slightest. We've been friends for a long time and they trust me. They thought it sounded great fun and can't wait to meet you.'

'Well who are they? I never even asked!' Brooke asked excitedly.

'Well, first there's Sir Blessington Staveley – he's a hotelier and a friend of mine. He owns a chain of around twenty-four boutique hotels and is president of The Independent Hotel Owners' Association. Then there's Antonia Dubarry OBE – she's a friend of Letitia's and sits on the board of several companies as a non-executive director. You'll meet them at some point.'

Brooke sighed and her shoulders drooped. When was she ever going to understand half of what was being said to her, without having to ask? She'd heard of an OBE but didn't know what it was and she certainly had no clue about non-executive directors. And she was meant to be meeting these people? She wasn't sure that this was a particularly sensible suggestion. It would surely expose her as a fraud and imposter amongst their class.

'Not sure about that Geoffrey; I'll only embarrass you. What is an OBE anyway? All I know is David Beckham's got one. And a non-executive director? What do they actually do?'

Lord D'Arcy looked at her sympathetically and patiently described in detail the criteria one has to meet to be awarded an OBE and then a non-executive director's responsibilities. He reeled through a list of five companies with whom Antonia Dubarry was a non-executive director: The Arts Council, Lloyds Of London, The Royal Opera House, Burberry, The Southbank Centre and Marks & Spencer.

Brooke jumped at the last name on the list. 'Wow! M&S? Does she get free knickers? Haha!'

Lord D'Arcy laughed. 'I don't think so, although I hear there's always a splendid free luncheon provided at their AGM.'

'AGM?'

A comprehensive explanation of annual general meetings was forthcoming, but Brooke's eyes glazed over as Lord D'Arcy attempted to hold her interest in share prices, dividends, strategic plans and corporate governance.

She blew out through pursed lips and looked a combination of weary and hopeless.

I'm useless. I don't know anything.

'Anyway, Geoffrey, we've gone off the subject a bit. When do I have to meet these people?'

'Well, it's not been arranged yet, but we should do it sooner rather than later. What days are you free?'

Brooke suggested a Tuesday or Thursday when she didn't work and Lord D'Arcy said he'd confirm when it would be. He then asked for her e-mail address, which she gave but was slightly nervous about doing so.

Brooke checked her watch and decided she ought to make a move. Lord D'Arcy escorted her out of his kitchen, across the grounds and out to her car. She knew what was coming next. He grabbed her firmly by the waist and pecked her on both cheeks.

'As always, an absolute pleasure to see you again, Brooke.' As he opened the door for her and she slid in elegantly, she thanked him for the coffee and said goodbye, leaving him gawping at her through the windscreen. She'd begun to pull away when she suddenly stopped, wound down the window and shouted.

'Hey! Geoffrey, you never counted the spondulix[8]!'

Lord D'Arcy smiled and dismissed both the suggestion, and her, with a wave of the hand. He then turned and strolled thoughtfully back.

***

Dean had agreed to a drink that evening with Martin, but had got so engrossed in the detail of the Disability Discrimination Act and ACAS advice on positive discrimination, he'd left the office later than planned. As soon as he realised the time, he shut everything down at lightning speed and ran down into Holborn underground.

By the time he'd arrived at Corney's in Canary Wharf, Martin had already downed four bottles of beer. He saw Dean pushing his way through the crowd of after-work drinkers – bankers, lawyers, traders and management consultants. After all, they were the only ones to be able to afford to drink at Corney's. Who else would pay £7.50 for a glass of wine? Or £4.50 for a bottle of cheap Japanese beer? Certainly no one in their Brentwood circle. Bottles of champagne were drunk

8. Money.

regularly here, but the men buying it had no idea what they were ordering – its sole purpose was to impress. The bar staff would regularly chuckle to themselves (and some weep) as they watched the mostly Essex-born traders pour orange juice into vintage Bollinger to make a Buck's Fizz.

Martin worked in the central services division of one of the banking firms and was a bit of a 'wannabe'; fascinated by the lives of those people in nearby offices who were in more meaningful jobs on the corporate ladder than he was. He was always trying to emulate them. Sometimes it worked, but most of the time his attempts turned out to be amusing entertainment for his colleagues. He lacked self-esteem and was quite insecure; Dean did find that a bit wearing on occasion. Martin did have other chums, but there was something about Dean that – as far as Martin was concerned – made him his 'best mate'. Dean was very non-judgemental as a rule and accepted him for what he was. Martin liked that and so Dean was his drinking mate of choice.

Dean wanted to broach the subject of Peregrine and to request that Martin backed up his story if Brooke happened to ask. Martin bought the first round and they moved to the only free high table they could find. It was packed, but Dean couldn't deny that the atmosphere was buzzy. They chatted about the football before Dean's thoughts moved suddenly to the fact that he'd told Brooke he'd be home at 9pm. Well it was already 8.30pm. There was no way he'd be on time, so he messaged her.

Will be more like 10pm babe – still in Canary Wharf with Martin.

At least that gave him a bit more time without having to rush.

'So…you done any more of them mystery visits then?' Martin asked.

'Yeah, a few.' Dean worried about how he would tell Martin about Peregrine.

'Oh! You need a partner in crime again?! I quite enjoyed that restaurant one I did with you as it goes.'

'Not exactly a partner in crime for another visit, but I do need a partner in crime for something else,' he ventured nervously.

'Sure, sock it to me!'

Dean was sure that Martin was not going to want this socked to him at all and he coughed nervously. 'Martin, do you know what a pomosexual is?'

Martin looked totally perplexed. 'What are you on about?'

'I'll take that as a "no" then. Well, a pomosexual is someone who "rejects sexuality labels or doesn't identify with any of them"'.

'Dean, I'm not bein' funny, mate, but what's this gotta do with me?' Martin was staring straight at him.

'I need you to pretend that you know a pomosexual called Peregrine and that you met him at the snooker hall in Billericay.'

Please don't complain, Martin.

'You what? You are kidding right?' Martin's eyes popped out on stalks.

Dean tried to explain the diversity challenge he had at work, how the SweatUbet assignment came up and how Brooke had caught him red-handed making an appointment with Peregrine; how he'd had to make something up – anything – just to get her off the scent of his secret mystery shopping. (He thought it was about time Angie at Sonny Global gave him another hotel visit.

The Royal Opera House might be very pleasant, but he needed an *overnight* break!)

Martin was dumbfounded. 'So, you're seriously telling me that Brooke thinks you went to the gym to interview a pomosexual called Peregrine for a job at TrussInUs? And that he's a mate of mine?'

'Well, yes, in a nutshell.'

'You're 'avin' a laugh. You gotta be. Not only do I not know any pommiesexuals or whatever they're called, but I'm not that way inclined. If Brooke thought for one minute I had a mate who was one, she'd never let me live it down. You know what she's like! And it wouldn't exactly bolster my reputation, would it? Besides, I bet there ain't any pommiesexuals in Billericay, anyway. It's just not that kinda town. It's an unrealistic story.'

'*Pomo*sexuals,' Dean said, correcting his pronunciation of the word. 'Martin, the whole fucking thing is an unrealistic story, but I haven't got any choice now. I'm bare-arsed[9] over a barrel.'

Martin's face was a picture. He didn't want to let his best mate down, but he didn't want to become known for fraternising with pomosexuals either. He was torn.

This was proving trickier than Dean had anticipated. 'Please, Martin. I owe you one. Next time I get a good mystery visit, I promise I'll ask you,' Dean implored.

But just not The Royal Opera House.

'Well alright, but I ain't 'appy about it, Dean,' Martin relented, gulping his beer.

Dean reassured him that unless Brooke mentioned it, nothing was likely to come of it anyway. Now it was Dean who

9. In a helpless situation.

wanted to change the subject.

'That's great. Thanks… I'm thinking of getting a puppy for Brooke.'

'You what? Why? Does she even like dogs? That girl's got you wrapped around her little finger she has. You're mad, you are.'

'Nah. It's my idea, not hers; she deserves it. She's a good girl and doesn't ask for that much as women go.'

Martin choked on his beer.

'It'd keep her company. I feel a bit sorry for her sometimes, to be honest. Stuck in the house all day with Paige screaming her head off. No wonder she goes shopping so much – she's probably bored stiff. Do you know how often she goes to the library with Paige?!' Dean looked intently and very seriously at Martin.

'Are you honestly telling me she's still going to the library? Having deep and meaningful discussions about Shakespeare with that Lady Townsley or whatever her name is?' Martin went into a fit of hysterics. Instead of joining in (even though Dean too had found it very funny at the time when Brooke had first told him), he felt a wave of protection come over him.

'What you laughing at? Why's that so funny?' Dean said it in rather an indignant tone.

'Brooke wouldn't recognise a book if one dropped in front of her!'

'That's a bit harsh. Just because she wasn't that great at school doesn't mean she doesn't want Paige to do better. She did get four GCSEs, remember. She had potential.'

'Yeah and spent the next ten years selling make-up!'

Dean was getting more cross and protective about his wife

and raised his voice slightly. 'It was for Clinique, as it happens – *the* best make-up company *and* in John Lewis – *they* don't take just anyone, you know.'

'Yeah, yeah, heard it all before. Yawn yawn. Why are you suddenly defending her anyway?' Martin had never seen or heard Dean defend his wife in this way and was taken aback. There was a tad of jealousy there too. Martin had no one to defend him; his shocking academic record, his fashion sense, his flabby body and his coarse ways.

'Right, I think it's time I went, Martin.' Dean looked stern as he got up. 'You coming?'

'No. You're alright. I'm staying for another beer.'

With that, Dean stared at Martin, took £15 out of his pocket and threw it on the table. 'Suit yourself. See you later.' And off he walked with a face like stone.

***

Dean arrived home to Brooke still up watching TV. He'd prepared to be scolded, as was her tendency when he'd been drinking with Martin. But she was so engrossed in the programme she barely glanced up.

Phew!

'Hiya, babe! What ya watching?'

'Some programme about The Royal Opera House; really interesting!'

Dean did a double-take before sitting down next to her and focusing his eyes on the TV.

Bloody hell, that's where I've gotta do my next mystery shop!

She'd only switched over to watch it because of what she'd

heard that day about Antonia Dubarry being a NED there. She thought she might learn something useful for when she finally met her. 'I don't think you'll be interested in it, Dean. It's about ballet and opera and stuff. You wouldn't make us a brew, would you?'

Dean frowned before strolling into the kitchen. Brooke's eyes didn't move from the TV.

'How do you know I wouldn't be interested in it? I might be,' he called out.

Brooke recalled their recent conversation where he'd boldly stated that they 'weren't interested in the theatre' which is why they'd never been. But she thought better of bringing all that up again. Dean realised he might be able to turn this situation to his advantage and take the stress out of deciding who to take on The Royal Opera House mystery visit. It would be so much easier to take Brooke – especially if she might actually enjoy it. It could even be a rare brownie point for him!

I managed to do the Wimpole Hall visit with her and Paige last year without her realising. I reckon I could do it again.

'So, why's it so interesting then?' Dean enquired with fake sincerity.

'I dunno; something different, I suppose.' Brooke shifted uncomfortably in her seat and tugged at her ringlets. "Those ballet dancers are unbelievable. You should see what they can do with their legs! I bet they're good in bed, hahaha! I've just seen some of those opera singers. God, those women have got massive boobs! And do you know, they can smash a glass if they sing a certain note?!'

'Well, you never know. One day I might be persuaded to go!' Dean said with just a hint of mystery.

About as likely as Dad deciding he's a pomosexual.

Brooke rolled her eyes as he brought her tea in, along with a thick wedge of bread smothered with peanut butter, for himself. 'What? I haven't eaten. I'm starving.'

Then the young couple spent the next thirty minutes next to each other on the sofa, glued to the TV in silence. It seemed as if their very souls were captured by the pas de deux in Swan Lake. Darcey Bussell and Zoltán Solymosi had seemingly fired something up inside both of them.

It was a sight to behold. Who would've thought it?!

9

Syndicate Meeting and SweatUBet Induction

Lady Townsend had summonsed Brooke from the library, where she'd been treating the antique leather chairs. Hugo had been asked to set Brooke up with her own desk and computer in there, so she could help Lady Townsend on tasks other than cleaning, much to Brooke's surprise and delight. Lady Townsend oozed elegance by the fireplace in the drawing room, rearranging some photographs while waiting.

When she finally appeared, Lady Townsend said, 'Well now, Brooke, we'll be meeting with our syndicate partners Antonia and Blessington next Wednesday. Geoffrey wants us all to go to lunch at Claridge's in London. Does that suit you?'

Oh my god, another one of those fancy places! Don't they ever eat anywhere normal?

Brooke was excited, despite finding these upmarket eating establishments a tad intimidating and stressful. 'Wow! That sounds fab!'

Lady Townsend raised her eyebrows and peered over her glasses. Brooke had gathered this was Lady Townsend's way of letting her know that she should find a better way of saying whatever it was she'd just said. Brooke growled quietly to herself. 'I mean, thank you, Mrs Townsend, that would be lovely. May I ask if I'm expected to work on that day?'

Yes, that sounded alright.

Lady Townsend smiled; alert to the smallest changes in Brooke's vocabulary and elocution, she could tell that she was making a real effort. 'No. I don't think that's wise. You can change your day and come on Thursday instead if you like.' After the unfortunate mishap at Tattersall's, Lady Townsend wanted to ensure there were no misunderstandings, so she added, 'Claridge's is a world-class hotel; very smart and very expensive, so you'll need to dress appropriately, dear.'

Brooke gulped.

Shit, am I gonna have to pay for my own lunch? How expensive is expensive?

She suddenly had visions of having to raid Paige's piggy bank as well as her secret stash. Her mind raced with all manner of things to do with the meeting. Would Dawn mind having Paige on Thursday as well as Wednesday? What excuse could she use if Dean got suspicious? Would they all travel together? What would she wear? What time would she get back? How should she address Mrs Townsend if this was a non-work situation and what about the other two syndicate partners? She fretted over the details but came to no conclusions.

'Of course I will, Mrs Townsend. I've heard of Claridge's as it goes. I saw something on telly about it once. Bono and Joan Collins go there. It's dead posh. I won't let you down or embarrass you this time. I promise.'

Bloody hell, there I go again! Putting myself down.

'I mean, I've not been there but I seem to remember it looked classy,' she added quickly.

'Brooke, you never embarrass me. You're on a journey, learning, no harm in that. Joan Collins is a regular, yes, but I've no idea who Bono is, I'm afraid.'

'No, I'm not surprised! What should I call the other two?'

'If you mean, how should you address them, I'm reasonably sure they'll expect you to use their first names, but I'll check so's not to make things awkward for you,' Lady Townsend replied. To Brooke's surprise – but relief – she followed up by saying, 'But I think you'd best still call me Mrs Townsend. We don't want to change the employer/employee status – not yet at least.'

It'd taken Brooke a long time to get used to calling her Mrs Townsend or Mrs T instead of Lady Townsend; the thought of calling her Letitia, well, she couldn't do it!

'What will they wanna know about me? I haven't really got much to say about myself, have I? Mind you, I did watch an amazing programme the other day about The Royal Opera House – I turned it on specially to see if Antonia Dubarry might be on it. Didn't see her, though,' Brooke said, tucking her shirt into her jeans.

Lady Townsend gave her another pep talk. She reminded Brooke of her own background – East End girl, rags to riches and all that. She spoke of their agreement to increase Brooke's hinterland and how her involvement in the syndicate would make a marvellous contribution to that end. She finished off by taking Brooke back into the library and pulling down a book on The Royal Opera House along with a couple of programmes; one for *Carmen* and the other for *Swan Lake*, plus the spring/summer programme of events.

'Take these home and have a browse. They should give you something to talk about, or ask about. As for Blessington, he's Geoffrey's friend. I've only met him a few times socially, so you'd best ask him.'

Brooke went on to explain to Lady Townsend that she'd also had a long conversation with Lord D'Arcy about NEDs and an array of topics to do with business when she'd gone to Ingatestone Hall to pay her syndicate money. Lady Townsend listened with interest and nodded her head in approval. 'That's excellent, Brooke. Well done! Now I must dash, I've got that meeting with the auctioneer shortly. Did you manage to catalogue all those items for him?' she asked.

Brooke nervously handed Lady Townsend an envelope. 'I hope I've done it right. I've never done anything like that before.'

'First time for everything, dear!' With that she marched out.

***

Dean had made an appointment for his SweatUBet 'induction' with 'Wayne', who'd first asked him to complete a medical questionnaire.

Please write something in your answers that would need to be followed up by the instructor doing your induction.

As Dean had suffered a groin strain playing football, he decided to put that down, whilst the agony of an overoptimistic tackle was still fresh in his memory. The rest was pretty standard. Inside the gym, Dean witnessed a plethora of men and women with toned biceps, six-packs and rippling quads that made him feel like a gangly year 7 student.

Why do they all look so orange?

Wayne talked to Dean about the importance of stretching before using any equipment. Before he'd barely got into his spiel, a young female instructor called Donna came over and told Wayne that he had an urgent call from a client and so she'd take over the induction. This was all done without asking Dean if he was happy with the arrangement.

Bloody cheek! Was your fitness instructor focussd on you and only you at all times? That's gotta be a 'No.'

Donna terrified him. She was small but fierce; her hair tied up in a tight ponytail, fully made up, including false eyelashes. Her Lycra leggings appeared to have been sprayed on. And what was that excuse of a top? It was barely more than a small piece of fabric cradling her enormous breasts, while keeping them firmly in place. Dean couldn't help but notice that when she turned around, he couldn't see them at all but, gosh, when she faced him, he got an eyeful which was jolly hard to ignore! His eyes sort of kept unwittingly wandering down to them.

I wonder what they do at night? If each tit falls outwards or whether they stay in place like weapons of mass destruction pointing to the sky?

Donna had taken the medical questionnaire from Wayne and was browsing through it as Dean was performing Wayne's calf stretch.

'So, what's the story with this groin strain then? Where exactly is it?'

Dean stopped what he was doing and repeated, 'Well, it's in me groin.'

'Yeah, I know, but which side?'

Dean gingerly pointed to the left region of his groin as Donna kneeled and looked directly into his crotch. 'Can you be more precise? Point to the exact spot?'

Dean could feel himself going red as he touched the spot and Donna leaned forward a little and asked him to do various movements with his left leg, checking which ones hurt, if at all.

As he gazed down at her, all he could see was the top of her head and her ample cleavage sticking out beyond that. This was all too much for Dean. His shorts were loose and he had no desire to inadvertently reveal what was going through his mind at that precise moment, so he suddenly brought his leg down and clasped his hands in front of him.

Did the instructor put you at your ease and make you feel comfortable? No, she bloody didn't.

Donna smiled. 'OK, well you'll just have to be careful.' She then asked him to do a hamstring stretch and showed him a bench where he could raise his leg and rest his foot. Dean hadn't done anything like that for a while and he struggled as he lifted his leg. Then it came. Without warning. Nothing the poor chap could do about it! A short but loud and violent fart emanated from between his buttocks.

Oh my god!

He froze on the spot, not knowing what to do for the best.

Shall I apologise? Or is it better to say nothing and pretend it didn't happen or that it wasn't me?

Before he'd had a chance to give it more than a second of thought, Donna said, rather more loudly than Dean would've liked, 'Better out than in, eh?' Dean wanted to crawl into a ball; thought he'd die of shame.

'Sorry!' he whispered. It's all he had.

The rest of the induction went reasonably well, with Donna doing most things required in between flirting with her regular customers, although her manner was rather forthright and somewhat rushed.

At the end of demonstrating the machines, suggesting how many reps he should do to start and how to record them each time he came into the gym, she said she'd let him go round on his own, tossing in casually at the end that she was there if he needed any help. She then went to talk to another member.

Did you see all the instructors constantly walking about talking to all the members?

Dean took this opportunity to pretend he was glugging from his water bottle as he scanned the gym, observing the instructors. There were four on the floor in total, all of whom were either leaning casually on a machine or sitting on a bench, chatting to people who looked suspiciously like they were their friends.

There was one older lady who appeared to be struggling to put some weights back, but the instructors were oblivious to her difficulties. Dean ran over, took them off her and put them back. She thanked him, but glanced over to Andy – the bulkiest of all the trainers in there –and coyly smoothed her baggy t-shirt over her chest, which had gradually shifted south over the years to go and retire near her waistline. Dean watched all this with fascination. He'd never belonged to a gym and was enjoying observing the dynamics play out between the various members and instructors. The place positively overflowed with sexual tension, narcissism and egos the size of the 20kg training plates the members lifted.

After a short rest, Dean moved to a chest press where a petite young woman in her early twenties was finishing. Dean recalled that Donna had advised him to lift only 20kg and to only do 10–12 reps to start to keep good form, but he double-checked his card.

Mmm. Wonder why she thought I couldn't do more?

Dean smiled at the young woman as she got off the machine,

noticing how tiny she was. He decided to double her weights, confident Donna was being overly cautious. He lay back and strained to push the bar up. Oh dear! It happened again! Only this one sounded terribly wet. And this time several people turned round and stared at Dean with a disdainful expression. He wanted to weep. Unable to do more than four reps, he suffered the humiliating experience of one of the Arnie wannabes (who was waiting to go on the machine) hovering over him and eventually having to help him complete the fourth rep.

Now I remember why I didn't ever join a gym.

He moved over to the running machines.

Did the instructor demonstrate how to use the monitors on the relevant pieces of equipment?

Well, he certainly remembered Donna showing him, but when he looked at it on his own, it seemed to have taken on the appearance and complexity of a spaceship dashboard – something out of *Star Wars* or James Bond. He rubbed his chin and strained to see all the features, as he didn't have his glasses on and hadn't brought them into the gym with him. He got on anyway, pressed the start button and then the button that dictated the speed. He didn't feel as though he'd pressed the + for long, but, within seconds, he was running at a pace he'd never run in his life – not even on a football pitch. He panicked and leaned forward to try and slow it down. Instead, he found himself running uphill at what seemed about 20mph. He looked around for assistance, but all the instructors were otherwise occupied or had their backs to him. He didn't want to make a fuss by shouting over, so carried on for a couple of minutes more, looking to others on the treadmills either side of him. They all ignored him and continued to run looking directly ahead of them, with earphones in listening to music. Beads of sweat began to pour off his brow and his face turned a remarkable shade of purple. His heart pumped so fast he was convinced a coronary artery was about to rupture. (He'd read all about that in The BMA *Home Medical Guide* and it wasn't very pleasant.) Then he could bear it no longer and resorted to stabbing rapidly and repeatedly at whatever buttons he could see through eyes now stinging with sweat. The machine began oscillating wildly, so he finally reached for the only button he recognised for sure – the power button. The machine stopped gradually, but Dean's legs felt so shaky that he fell off to one side and collapsed onto the floor, where he stayed simply to get his breath back and attempt to regain his composure.

Did you feel that the instructors were concerned for your safety and kept alert to misuse of equipment by members? NO! I nearly died! No fucker helped me at all!

After a few minutes Donna marched over. 'What are you doing lying down? You shouldn't overdo it your first time you know. I told you what to set the machine at.' Dean was still too breathless to explain. She glanced at the monitor and gasped. 'What the hell were you thinking? You had it on 10mph and a twenty-five per cent incline!'

Dean looked up at Donna and nodded subserviently as she thrust her hand down to help him up. Once on his feet, she laughed, patted him on his back and told him to take it easier next time, then wandered back to one of the many torture machines. Dean found a bench and sat down, with a hangdog expression, oblivious to other members looking over and nodding between themselves.

If you had any difficulties, was your instructor compassionate and did they give you alternative exercise solutions? NO! I could've had a heart attack!

Dean had had enough. He grabbed his towel and water bottle and made his way back to the changing rooms, where he had to complete his assessment by testing the showers, toilets and lockers. As there was no one in there, he took the opportunity to test out the locks on the lockers. He went round speedily locking and unlocking them at random. He got to one and discovered it had clothes in it, so quickly slammed it shut, only for a chap to burst in through the changing room doors at that very moment.

I don't fucking believe it! That could only happen to me.

'You looking for something?' the chap said in a sinister voice and with a look that reminded him of Brooke at her most scary. He walked towards Dean.

'Sorry, mate. Is this your locker? I forgot where mine is,' Dean replied in a most awkward manner.

The chap was clearly unconvinced and removed his paraphernalia without taking his eyes off Dean, before transferring everything to a nearby shower, seemingly unprepared to risk the opportunism of this petty thief. Dean took the chance to quickly open his locker and remove his Pears soap and Bulldog shampoo. He stepped into the shower cubicle and gave it the once-over, making a mental note of missing tiles, mouldy grout, the lack of even basic soap and the pubic hair gathered in a matted mess at the drain hole. He could not help notice how grey the hair seemed to be.

I wonder what the average age of the members is here?

He washed himself briskly, standing on the sides of his feet as much as possible to avoid catching something from this veritable playground for verrucas, making him look as though both his legs had been broken. His OCD kicked in and suddenly he couldn't wait to get out of the place. A quick visit to all the toilets proved no better, with broken seats, locks, more tiles missing and other 'things' on the floor that he analysed at a healthy distance, trying to fathom what they actually were.

His report for this gym was looking to be even worse than the one he'd done for the golf club the previous year. He hadn't thought it possible to get any worse than that, but here it was! He dried himself off, dreading having to come back one more time to attend the Boxercise class.

Hey babe, when u home? Got dinner here.

Hey babe. Be home in 20. Love ya.

OK. Has the pomo got the job?

10

Lunch at Claridge's

'Two days on the trot with Paige is enough to drive a sane woman nuts,' Dawn joked. 'Social services are on permanent alert from the O'Connors next door and pervy Doug and Jane tell me they've soundproofed their side of the house.'

Brooke squirmed. 'Oh, don't say that, pleeease! Life's difficult enough without worrying about that. Hasn't the screaming settled down at all?'

Dawn shook her head and looked very serious. 'So, where are you going for this meeting, then?' She looked Brooke up and down. 'You look gorgeous, by the way.'

Brooke smiled. She'd bought yet another outfit, this time from Minnie's Boutique in Brentwood; a pink pleated skirt with a cream silk camisole top and a navy-blue loose-fit blazer. 'Thanks, Dawn. Can you believe we're going to Claridge's?!' Brooke started to laugh.

'After what you've told me, I'd believe you if you said you were having lunch with the Prime Minister!' Dawn rolled her eyes.

'Nah. That's next week!'

They both giggled. Brooke explained that it wasn't her choice, that Lord D'Arcy had chosen it and that she was actually feeling sick with nerves at the thought of meeting the highly accomplished people in the syndicate. She'd been diligently reading the Royal Opera House brochure and had tracked down a couple of articles on the internet about Sir Blessington Staveley. She prayed she could remember it all. A wad of £200 in cash was stashed away in a secret compartment in her handbag. She'd reckoned the meal wouldn't come to more than that.

Dawn sat listening incredulously and declared that although she thought Brooke was wrong not to tell Dean, she couldn't help but admire her.

'You've got balls, girl, I'll give you that,' she'd said. 'I couldn't do it – 'anging around with people like that. They'd do my 'ead in. All that la-de-dah.' She brushed her finger up under her nose.

Brooke quickly came to the defence of both Lord D'Arcy and Lady Townsend. 'No. They're alright, Dawn. Honestly, they're decent people and they're lovely to me. God knows why. I think I'm a bit of an experiment to them. I've got to "increase my hinterland" apparently!' She put speech marks round the word with her fingers in the air. '"Common tart" to "lady" sort of thing!'

'You? A lady? Oh gawd 'elp us!' Dawn replied, guffawing. 'Don't you get all above your station. You're an Essex girl, remember – you belong in Brentwood!'

Brooke feigned a smile, a knot forming in her stomach as she let Dawn's remark go and extracted Paige from the bean bag in front of the TV.

'Give Mummy a kiss, darlin'', she implored. 'Mummy's going somewhere posh again today. I'll bring something back for you.' Brooke blew a raspberry on Paige's cheek while tickling her ribs, until she fell on the floor giggling uncontrollably.

'Thanks again, Dawn. I couldn't do any of this if it wasn't for you. I'll see you later. I should be back about 4.30pm, but Dean's playing footie after work so I don't have to panic about getting back, as long as you're OK?'

'What choice do I have? How else are you gonna get more hinterland?'

'You don't *get* hinterland, darling, you increase it!'

'Oooooh! Get you! Go on, bugger off and I'll see you later.'

With that they hugged and Brooke left for lunch at Claridge's.

***

Brooke arrived in town embarrassingly early. Lunch was at 1pm and it was only 11.30am. It was important to her that she wasn't late and that she looked perfect. For that, she needed to find a lavatory somewhere, where she could touch up her make-up beforehand. Having never been, she also needed to make sure she knew exactly where the hotel was.

Arriving at Bond Street, she knew that Fenwick's was close by. They had lavatories, so she'd touch up her make-up and walk to Claridge's from there. She enjoyed strolling down New Bond Street (even though her feet were already throbbing mercilessly in her Louboutins) soaking up the atmosphere of the upmarket shops and looking in the windows of Asprey and Ralph Lauren, as a pair of shoes, earrings or bag caught her eye. She made her way down Brook Street, past The Flyfisher's Club, which she remembered Lord D'Arcy had said he belonged to. She stood outside for a few moments, looking up at the building and contemplating what must go on in there.

How many clubs does a bloke need? What even is flyfishing?

Finally, she arrived outside Claridge's. It was still only 12.15pm. The exquisite warm red brick and art deco frontage beckoned. She was undecided about what to do, so walked around the building, down Davies Street and wandered into Brook's mews.

Haha, my name again! Destined to be here! Hahaha!

After enjoying pottering around the hotel's surrounding streets for about fifteen minutes soaking up the architecture, she decided she'd go in and wait in the lobby until either Lord D'Arcy or Lady Townsend arrived.

As she walked purposefully towards the imposing doors, the uniformed concierge opened a door for her with a little bow and nod. Brooke returned his smile and thanked him. On entering the lobby, she caught sight of what looked to be a small seating area around a black and white chequered tiled area, with sofas and armchairs by a large and inviting fireplace. There were a couple of people sitting there seemingly passing time as she wandered nervously up and down the corridor. A male member of staff carrying a tray with a smart-looking cocktail, passed her and smiled. Once she was confident she was permitted to sit there, she walked tentatively over and sat down on one of the large leather armchairs, legs firmly closed together and slanted to one side, Kate Middleton style. The gentleman sitting on the sofa looked up, smiled and said good afternoon. She replied with a simple hello. The lady who sat on one of the other armchairs glanced up from her phone briefly to see who had invaded the area, and promptly returned to her phone. She said nothing.

Snooty cow.

Brooke sat silently for a few minutes observing what was

going on; this was people-watching at its best. Some Chinese ladies stood close by, with armfuls of designer carrier bags. A group of American businessmen marched down towards the restaurant, talking in an animated fashion about some acquisition or another. An obviously supervisory female member of staff passed by, nodded at Brooke and said hello. She wore a plain tailored black suit, a crisp white shirt and a silk patterned scarf was elegantly styled around her neck. Her hair and make-up looked as though they might've been professionally done and she carried a black leather folder. Brooke mused that she had a managerial air about her and she felt a stab of envy.

Wow, she looks so sophisticated and she only works here.

Brooke smiled, nodded back and then checked her watch. She was thoroughly enjoying her people-watching, but was conscious she'd some time to go before lunch. She scrolled through Facebook; not because she was remotely interested in it at that moment, but because she felt compelled to appear busy for at least a few minutes. The black suit passed her three or four times over the next twenty minutes or so, each time noting that Brooke was still there and neither eating or drinking. The two other people who'd been sitting down had gone and she felt a little exposed. Guests came and went; couples, small groups, elderly individuals and even children passed to and fro.

Just before 1pm an older gentleman suddenly appeared at the end of the corridor and started walking towards her. He was sporting a particularly smart suit; dark navy with a red silk lining that flashed as he walked. He wore a serious facial expression as he stopped directly in front of Brooke and briefly looked her up and down, his eyes resting on her five-inch Louboutins.

'May I help you, madam?' he asked without smiling.

Why's he asking me that?

Brooke was rather taken aback. Her natural instinct was to stand to attention. The man instantly made her nervous. 'Er...no thanks. I'm fine,' she replied with a smile but a hint of suspicion in her voice.

'Would madam like a drink?' he asked with apparent hidden meaning.

'Er...no thanks, I'll be having lunch any minute now.' He stayed where he was and so Brooke felt forced to offer further explanation. 'I'm just waiting for a friend.'

The man showed no sign of leaving her alone and made her feel most uncomfortable as he bent over to speak to her. 'May I ask what time your lunch appointment is?'

'One o'clock. Why?' Brooke was perplexed.

'And may I enquire as to which restaurant you're dining in?'

God, this is like the bloody Spanish inquisition!

'I don't know as it goes. I didn't know there was more than one.'

'May I ask the name of the "friend" you're meeting?'

Brooke felt she had no choice but to tell this man, although she had absolutely no idea who he was. 'Well, there's a few of 'em actually. Lord Geoffrey D'Arcy, Lady Letitia Townsend, Antonia Dubarry OBE and Sir Blessington Staveley.'

Take that and stuff it up your jacksie[10]*!*

The man could barely contain his shock. He stood upright pretty sharpish.

'Oh, you're a friend of Lord D'Arcy? A very regular guest here. He'll almost certainly have booked The Reading Room.'

10. Between the buttocks.

The man's entire demeanour changed in a matter of seconds. He smiled, bowed a little and suggested he escort her to The Reading Room where she might be a little more comfortable as she waited for the rest of her party. Brooke stood up and did as she was told, tottering behind the man to a different comfortable chair in the restaurant.

'Please, allow me to get you a glass of champagne while you're waiting.' Brooke hesitated and the man immediately detected this. 'With our compliments.'

Ooh it's a freebie! Yay!

She suddenly remembered where she was and thought about her response.

'Thank you. That would be lovely.'

Just then, Lord D'Arcy walked into the restaurant, bang on the dot of 1pm.

'Brooke! How lovely to see you!' He greeted her as usual and she returned the greeting.

'Good afternoon, Lord D'Arcy, good to see you again,' the grand inquisitor said, holding out his hand to shake.

'Hello, Timothy! Brooke, this is Timothy Kitchener, the general manager of this marvellous and iconic institution; Timothy, this is a very dear friend, Brooke De'Ath, who's joining me for lunch. I've booked a table for five at one o' clock.'

Oooh, he did that the wrong way round. He should've introduced me to Timothy first. It says so in Debrett's. *And I've gone from being a friend to a very good friend! Haha!*

Brooke held out her hand and shook Timothy Kitchener's hand; particularly bone-crushing because she disliked the way he'd questioned her so much. Ten minutes later, Lady Townsend, Antonia Dubarry and Sir Blessington arrived and apologised for their tardiness.

All the introductions were got out the way and both Sir Blessington and Antonia confirmed their delight in meeting Brooke; said that they'd heard a lot about her and were very much looking forward to her joining their syndicate. Brooke's hands shook slightly as her champagne was given to her. Embarrassed that no one else had a drink, she apologised and explained that the manager had offered it to her 'with compliments'.

'Well, we've all got something to celebrate, haven't we, so let's have a bottle,' said Lord D'Arcy, rubbing his hands. He waved to the sommelier for the wine list, perused it for a few moments and then asked for a bottle of Billecart-Salmon 'Le Clos Saint-Hilaire' 1999. Lady Townsend and Antonia excused themselves to go to the powder room and left Lord D'Arcy and Sir Blessington to catch up; it had clearly been some time since they'd last met. Brooke took the opportunity to browse the wine list. Not that she was going to be choosing any (she was quite sure that was Lord D'Arcy's domain). Cocktails on the first page, followed by the champagnes.

Twenny-three quid? Oh that's not too bad.

'Geoffrey, which champagne are we having?' Brooke asked, eager to learn.

'Billecart-Salmon 'Le Clos Saint-Hilaire' 1999. Why?'

She turned over one more page and caught sight of the £590 price tag. She gasped audibly and clamped her hand over her mouth. The previous page had been champagne by the glass!

Shit! That's what I thought the whole meal would cost!

'Just curious,' she squeaked. How would she pay for her meal?

I've only brought two hundred quid!

Her fingers crept up towards her ringlets as she bit her lip.

'Claridge's has one of the best champagne lists in London!' Geoffrey boomed.

The ladies returned and the sommelier followed shortly with the bottle. He treated it with the same reverence as a museum piece. He showed the label to Lord D'Arcy, who nodded in approval. The sommelier then, with the utmost professionalism, poured out five glasses perfectly evenly. A fresh glass had been brought for Brooke, who by this time had quaffed her complimentary glass, much to her embarrassment.

'I would like to make a toast to our newest syndicate member – to Brooke!' Lord D'Arcy announced in that booming voice of his.

They all clinked glasses and looked towards Brooke in expectation of her saying something. She gulped and felt the inevitable fire move up her face.

C'mon, girl, say something! Anything! You have to!

Brooke's brain went into one of those spirals of manic thought from which there was no escape. The syndicate were silent, patient and calm, giving her all the time she needed to come up with something appropriate. After what seemed like an eternity, she finally took a deep breath and spoke with conscious and obvious effort.

'Thank you, Geoffrey. That's very kind. I'm most grateful to you, Mrs Townsend, Antonia and Blessington, that you've let someone…like me…' She swallowed hard and looked over to Lady Townsend, who raised her eyebrows. Brooke continued slowly and thoughtfully. 'I mean allowed me…to join your syndicate. I'm excited by this opportunity to do something…' Brooke was searching for the appropriate phrase that summed up her genuine thoughts about what she'd done. 'Well… something…something.' They were all willing her on. '…bloody amazing!' Jolly good effort. The entire table burst out laughing and clinked glasses again with a 'hear hear!' The ice had been well and truly broken. Brooke apologised for her language, but explained that this whole situation was almost too surreal for words.

They all nodded knowingly; they understood. At that moment Brooke scanned all their faces and realised she probably really was the experiment she had joked to Dawn about that morning.

The menus were brought and Brooke almost dreaded opening hers; she knew that there'd be a whole array of dishes that she'd never heard of that would require explanation. And, more to the point, beyond her price bracket. She'd almost certainly have to be guided. Everyone chose their food and Lord D'Arcy went through the menu with her, making suggestions.

I could murder a burger.

'I could murder a burger and chips!' Brooke joked. The whole table laughed out loud.

'Oh, my you're such a hoot! Not a problem, sweetheart,' replied Lord D'Arcy, immediately calling their waiter over, who asked how she'd like it done. Brooke's mouth dropped open; she'd not expected that at all. At that point she couldn't decide what to do for the best. She realised how stupid she'd been and kicked herself under the table.

I'm at bloody Claridge's, for god's sake! Idiot!

'I was only joking, Geoffrey,' she said awkwardly. Lord D'Arcy waved the man away and she looked again at the menu, selecting the cheapest hors d'oeuvre and cheapest main, totting it up in her head. 'I'll have the soup and the chicken please.'

Once the waiter had taken the order, the group discussed Turn The Paige. Geoffrey spelt out the syndicate's options, in terms of when and where the trainer believed she should be raced first. Mark had talked to him and run through some suggestions, after he'd witnessed some pretty remarkable galloping in her early training with him. He confirmed that she'd been a great buy and he was confident that with a few more weeks with him, she'd be ready to enter one of the more significant races.

Brooke had made a list of questions and asked if they minded if she ran through them. Nods of approval all round. She wanted to know everything from whether they could ask the jockey not to whip the horse because she considered it to be cruel, to whether she could choose what colours the jockey wore as she'd had some good ideas about this, through to how any winnings would be split and would she have to pay for entry to the course when Turn The Paige was running. Some of her questions were met with stunned silence, after which Lady Townsend would have the job of explaining the answers diplomatically. Others were met with amazement, revealing sharp, savvy and totally unexpected observations by this rookie syndicate member. A dark horse one, might say!

What you doing babe?

Brooke became almost paralysed as her phone went off. She apologised to the party as she took a quick peek and typed a response.

Eating.

Dean looked at his phone blankly and frowned.

Anything nice? I've got a Greggs sausage roll, you can't beat 'em!!

Brooke responded ***just a sarnie – gotta go*** before tucking into her lobster bisque. Without even thinking, she took a photo of it, leaving Antonia and Sir Blessington staring at her as though she'd performed some sort of stunning magic trick.

I'd love some knickers in this colour.

As she supped, she availed herself of a taste so rich and creamy that she made strange little humming noises as she slurped. Simply divine.

Wish me luck at footie we gotta beat those bastards 2nite or we're out the league.

By this time, Brooke'd switched her phone off. Dean waited in expectation of a response for the rest of his lunch break. None came and he felt wounded.

As lunch progressed, Brooke became more relaxed and even plucked up the courage to proactively ask Antonia about her role at The Royal Opera House. Antonia gathered she'd not been before, so preached about the joy of watching ballet and opera, positively encouraging Brooke to go. She listened intently to Antonia's description of the magic of Giselle and Swan Lake and Brooke mentioned she'd watched something on TV recently about The Royal Opera House and had been fascinated by it.

'Then you must go!' declared Antonia with the sort of determination that Brooke recognised. 'I'll arrange it. We'll go together. Letitia can come too; you'll come to the ballet with us, won't you, Letitia?'

'Oh absolutely, darling! *The Nutcracker*'s on at the moment, maybe we could go to that? I could manage next Friday. What do you think, Brooke?' Lady Townsend asked.

Oh my god, how the hell am I gonna manage this?

'Yeah, why not, it'll be like…a girls' night out!'

Lady Townsend and Antonia collapsed into a fit of laughter.

'Oh how marvellous! A girls' night out? I haven't been on one of those in years. And with someone who doesn't need to wear incontinence pads!' Lady Townsend almost screeched with delight.

'I mean…that would be wonderful. Thank you for thinking of me,' Brooke replied, not knowing quite what to say. 'I'd love to go to the ballet.'

By this time, the gentlemen were looking a tad alarmed at Brooke's effect on the older ladies and asked if everything was alright. The ladies simply giggled, having drunk far too much champagne, all encouraged by Brooke, who'd not only had far too much herself but had taken charge of the remainder of the bottle. She'd been most put out that the champagne they'd paid £590 for, wasn't even left on their table! They weren't even in charge of their own bottle! It'd been very carefully placed in an ice bucket on a stand at least two metres from their table. Well, Brooke was having none of that.

Bloody cheek! It's our booze!

She got up from the table and without fuss walked over to the ice bucket that housed their remaining champagne, grabbed the bottle and poured the remainder in everyone's glasses until the bottle was empty. The sommelier looked on aghast, ill-prepared for such an unorthodox move!

Conversation flowed and Brooke entertained the whole party with anecdotes about her social circle that had everyone in stitches. This'd been a lunch like no other Lady Townsend, Lord D'Arcy, Sir Blessington and Antonia had ever experienced.

By 3.30pm lunch was over and Lord D'Arcy summarised

what they'd agreed about Turn The Paige. Everyone nodded and Brooke was beyond excited.

The bill arrived and to Lord D'Arcy's horror, Brooke snatched it up, checked it, gasped inwardly at the £1500 figure, which included another couple of bottles of vintage Puligny Montrachet at well over £100 each, and without embarrassment, took the £200 wad of cash from her bag and handed it to him. 'There's a couple of tonnes there, Geoffrey,' she said. She explained that she'd not realised how expensive it would be but she'd pay him back the additional £100 she owed as soon as possible.

Lord D'Arcy was unable to compute what Brooke'd just done. He'd never in his entire life come across a woman who wanted to pay for her own meal and quite frankly, he didn't know how to respond.

'No. No! Brooke, this is my…er…this is on me… I'm paying for lunch. Please.' He looked crestfallen as he placed the palm of his hand firmly over hers. The rest of the table looked away, suddenly finding great interest in the artwork on the wall. Once the dirty little job of paying the bill was over, they all watched on in dismay as Brooke grabbed all the little branded wrapped chocolates and threw them into her handbag. Lady Townsend took a small but sharp intake of breath and closed her eyes momentarily.

Sir Blessington left first, for an appointment in Jermyn Street, Lady Townsend dashed straight to the British Museum and Antonia arranged a taxi to the Southbank, where she was meeting with the CEO. The only person who didn't have anywhere to go was Lord D'Arcy…and Brooke, of course; at least for a while.

'Would you like to have a coffee somewhere, Brooke, before you shoot off?' he asked in nervous anticipation. Brooke felt bad. She was so very fond of him, but had a feeling that this wouldn't be a good idea.

'Oh thanks, Geoffrey, that's very sweet, but I've gotta pick Paige up.'

Geoffrey's shoulders seemed to droop and his face came a close second, belying his words: 'Of course, sweetheart. No problem at all.'

He walked Brooke to Bond Street Station and as they stood outside, Brooke felt a slightly strange combination of anxious, tipsy, excited, energised and…what was it?

Ah yes…powerful. That was it.

***

On the train home, she turned her phone back on to see Dean's message about football and quickly typed a response.

Oh shit!

Good luck babe better late than never! Kick ass!

She arrived back, collected Paige from Dawn's and immediately gave her one of the Claridge's chocolates to appease her. Paige ripped the wrapper off the chocolate and clumsily found her mouth with it. Dawn had one too and Brooke kept a couple back for another time.

'So, how'd it go?' Dawn asked, waiting in eager anticipation for one of Brooke's now regular and hilarious rundowns of her day.

'Bloody hell, Dawn. The champagne was over a monkey!! And the whole bill for five came to one and a half grand!! I nearly died. I only took a couple of hundred quid. When I did try to pay my share I don't think Geoffrey was very happy, 'cause he wouldn't let me pay.'

'Fuck me, Brooke. Over a grand for five people? What did they feed you? Gold-plated fillet steak?'

They both laughed at the ridiculousness of it all and Dawn implored Brooke yet again to tell Dean what was going on. 'He's missing out, Brooke. He'd be so chuffed knowing you were doing all this stuff.'

Brooke buried her head firmly in the sand once more, gathered up Paige's things and made her way back to Elephant Close thinking about her up-and-coming trip to The Royal Opera House to see *The Nutcracker* with Lady Townsend and Antonia.

I can't ask Dawn again. I just can't.

She bit her lip and tugged at her curls.

11

Lies and Alibis

'Stacey, I need your help big time. I'm seriously in the shit.' Brooke held her mobile to her ear and whispered conspiratorially.

'What's up, babe? You sound well stressed.' Stacey was concerned and prepared herself for the worst.

'It's complicated. Very complicated. But… I'm going out next Friday and if Dean ever asks you, I need you to say I was with you.' Brooke put her right hand up to her forehead, unable to believe herself that this is what she was resorting to.

'You're not havin' an affair, are you, cause if you are, babe, I can't do this to Dean. He's a mate and a good bloke and he don't deserve it.' Stacey stood her ground.

'No, you daft cow! Course I'm not!' Brooke hesitated, knowing in her heart that Stacey simply wouldn't 'get it'. She pressed on regardless. 'I'm going to The Royal Opera House to see *The Nutcracker*.' Stacey fell silent. 'It's a ballet.'

'What the hell, Brooke?'

Brooke went on to explain that she'd been invited by Antonia Dubarry, OBE, who was a non-exec there, that she'd felt compelled to go (it was a freebie after all) and that she really was interested. Stacey was not convinced and reminded Brooke of her Essex roots; that people like them didn't go to places like that.

'I'll say we went on a girls' night out to The Sugar Hut or something. I just need an alibi for why I'm going out. I haven't done that since before Paige was born! I'll ask Dean to get back home early and I'll leave home about 5.30pm – to "get ready" with you girls. I'll bring all my stuff over to you and change at yours, if that's OK? I won't want Dean to see what I'm wearing. And I'll leave The Royal Opera House at about 11pm and get a taxi from Brentwood station at about midnight to take me home.' She'd clearly rehearsed her story.

'Well that ain't gonna work, we'd never get back home before at least 2am on any half decent night out!' Stacey roared laughing.

'Well, I'll have to say I wasn't feeling that great or something and I needed to get home.'

Stacey seemed undecided.

'Pleeeese!' implored Brooke.

'Fine. Whatever, Brooke. You're a mate, but you're on well dodgy ground if you ask me.'

Brooke breathed a sigh of relief and thanked her oldest friend.

***

While Brooke had been negotiating her alibi, Dean had his own challenges.

'Hi, Dean, it's Angie from Sonny Global. Pretty shitty reports for SweatUBet? Was it that bad?'

'Angie, I've never had such diabolical customer service. They're a joke. I'd have sacked the lot of them if I was their manager,' Dean replied.

'Mmm, well let's hope the Boxercise class is a bit better. Then you'll never have to go back there again. That's a promise! Anyway, I'm only ringing 'cause I wanted to check if you've made your booking for The Royal Opera House yet? It's gotta be done by next Sunday at the latest, but they've changed the brief to allow a weekend visit 'cause the performance isn't full. Thought you might wanna know that…just in case you were thinking of taking "her indoors". We hardly ever get offered weekend visits there, so they're pretty special.'

Dean agreed that was great news and told her he'd definitely book two tickets for next Saturday night. He was confident that he and Brooke weren't doing anything.

Dean got off the phone from Angie, still somewhat preoccupied with his current task. He chewed his pencil, anxiously studying his diversity challenge spreadsheet. He'd only managed to recruit one female Muslim so far. Her name was Jawaria; 'bringer of happiness', she'd helpfully informed him. 'Well, we could do with a bit of that around here,' he'd replied.

He'd questioned her in a roundabout way, to try and establish if she might have a disability of any kind too, maybe one that wasn't obvious; like six toes or something. He'd asked her what was one of the most challenging things for her at work and she'd replied 'my narcolepsy'. Dean hadn't the faintest idea what it was and asked her to explain. As he listened to her description, his excitement grew.

Jeez! Never heard of it! Falling asleep at random! Haha, who knew?

She'd reassured him it was usually mild and that as long as the team were made aware of it, it was usually quite manageable.

That's gotta be classed as a disability, surely?

He never checked its status and recruited her that day, without taking a reference, such was his desire and urgency to get the vacancies filled.

He decided he ought to book the tickets to The Royal Opera House in case the tickets ran out. He was both nervous and excited at the prospect of taking Brooke. Excited because he'd by mere chance discovered that she'd enjoyed the ballet on television – as had he, although he would never tell a soul for fear of mockery – and nervous, as he was going to have to come up with a reason why he had the tickets at all. The budget was £600 for two, including a three-course meal in the Balconies restaurant, and he knew that Brooke knew, there was no way on this side of the M25 that he would ever, ever spend that kind of money on anything, never mind two tickets for a ballet!

He went onto the website and had to navigate his way around the map of the theatre to establish what seats he wanted from the current availability. He'd never done this before. What was a stall, a grand tier? What was the circle and the grand circle? He decided they'd go as near to the front and in the middle as possible.

That's gotta be the best bet.

And so it was that Dean booked two tickets for the following Saturday's performance of *The Nutcracker* at 7.30pm.

Now, what the hell am I gonna say to Brooke? When am I even gonna tell her? She's gonna want at least some notice... I'll tell her on Saturday morning. Then she's got the whole day to get ready and get a new dress or whatever.

***

That week at work, Brooke thought about her 'girls' night out', smiling to herself one minute and feeling physically sick the next. She had to tell Dean she'd not be around on Friday night. Since they'd had Paige, their social lives had been reduced to a few evenings at friends' houses, taking Paige and either sleeping over so they could have a drink; or a meal at the pub where they also took Paige. This was going to be different; special and daunting. She considered what impression she'd made on Antonia and couldn't decide what she would've made of her. She'd amused her, that's for sure.

'Mrs Townsend,' Brooke said, as she was cleaning the large bronze sculpture of her husband Lord Townsend, as per the National Trust Conservation Guidelines. She took a deep breath. 'On Friday, at The Royal Opera House, what should I wear and is there anything I shouldn't say or do? I don't wanna make the same mistakes I did at Claridge's.'

Lady Townsend had sat her down at work the day after lunch at Claridge's and gently gone through the inappropriate things Brooke had said and done. Joking about 'murdering a burger', taking the champagne out the ice bucket and pouring it herself, taking a photograph of her soup, scooping up all the chocolates into her handbag, snatching up the bill that had clearly been given to Geoffrey as the host and then trying to pay her share of it. She hadn't been mean. It was all delivered in the way a science teacher might have told a class of year-ten boys about sexual intercourse; matter of factly.

'Just remember your hinterland. I wasn't persecuting you about Claridge's, my dear, merely showing you how to speak and behave with a little more decorum, that's all. And you will. I can see you're learning all the time.'

Brooke nodded as she looked down at her from her stepladder.

'But in answer to your question, smart and dressy.'

Brooke screwed up her little nose and frowned. 'But what does that even mean?'

'Think cocktail dress or even a ball gown, although I don't suppose you've got one of those.' Lady Townsend unintentionally sniffed a little and realised that was a faux pas on her part. She was always so careful not to offend Brooke. At that moment she'd wished they were similar sizes as she'd willingly have opened her wardrobe and let her choose something to wear for herself. After all, she had Dior, St Laurent, Catherine Walker, Valentino, to name but a few hanging in all their silk and chiffon glory in her wardrobe.

'Mmm. I might have to go on another little shopping trip. I haven't been anywhere fancy of an evening since Dean's Christmas work do at The Grange Hotel in London a couple of years back. That was before Paige was born and the dress I wore doesn't fit me now. Brooke cupped her breasts with both hands and jiggled them about as if to demonstrate. 'I'll have to have a think.'

'Well while you're thinking, can you tell me, did you manage to sort out the problem with the gardeners' holiday pay and if you've booked my hotel, flights and lectures in Florence next month?'

Brooke retrieved an envelope containing first-class flight tickets and a piece of paper from a pile which she showed to Lady Townsend. Brooke was at pains to say she hadn't quite finished and needed to check her figures first. It was a comprehensive calculation of the gardeners' holiday pay since 2012 and she'd found a number of errors, which meant old Jim Hughes had grumbled tiresomely about how he'd have to cut his holiday to Butlin's short. Brooke was reluctant to say so, but it appeared that Hugo'd been responsible for all the miscalculations, although she was quite sure it wasn't intentional.

Lady Townsend glanced at the calculations and raised her eyebrows. 'Well, that explains it then. Holiday pay has never been Hugo's strong point. How tiresome. But I'll wait until you've one hundred per cent checked it before I speak with the gardeners and Hugo. Well done though, Brooke. You're very savvy and remarkably alert.'

The two of them chatted a few minutes longer, before Lady Townsend glanced at her watch, said she was late for her golf lesson and walked out of the library.

Brooke took an executive decision to leave early and pop to TK Maxx to find a suitable dress for her night at the opera. Lady Townsend was incredibly generous and flexible, knowing that Brooke's home life with Paige was not easy.

***

Brooke collected Paige from Dawn's early, much to her surprise, but said she'd still pay her in full. It was her way of trying to demonstrate how much she appreciated her. Afterwards, she headed straight for TK Maxx in Basildon and within minutes honed in on an exquisite little black cocktail dress; knee-length, low cut-out back, feathered hem and three-quarter length sleeves. She wasn't ready to buy a full-length Tessa Daly-style gown. When would she ever wear anything like that again? No. She couldn't justify it, even though secretly she yearned to wear one. How would she possibly explain that away to Dean? No. Much as it pained her, knowing it would be the one and only time in her life she'd probably ever get the chance to wear one, she resisted taking any of them into the changing room. The only thing she took in there with her, was Paige; mercifully fast asleep in her buggy.

As Brooke swished open the changing room curtains, smoothing the dress over her athletic thighs as she walked and looking at herself in the mirror, several customers stood outside their booths, parading in front of partners for an opinion; their bra straps, ankle socks and greying underwear visible for all to see. Without exception, they all turned to stare at Brooke; an almost six-foot vision to behold in this rather dull part of Essex; Basildon's answer to Gisele Bünchden. Several people whispered amongst themselves, until one of the women could not hold herself back.

'Sorry, but I've just gotta tell you, you look absolutely gorgeous in that dress. Oh my god, you could easily be one of them catwalk models. Honestly.' Within seconds, they were all praising her and telling her how amazing she looked. Brooke flushed pink and focused on the floor, biting her lip and tugging her curls. The women fell silent, thinking they'd embarrassed her. Then Brooke thought about everything Lady Townsend had told her and looked up, head held high, hands on hips. Pure Essex sass.

'Thank you, ladies. Do you know what? I think you might be right. It does look rather bloody fantastic, doesn't it? I think I'm gonna take it!'

I shouldn't have said bloody.

They all burst out laughing and clapped excitedly, as a

bunch of girlfriends would do if one had just announced their engagement; several of them pawed her as though she were public property – a celebrity even – and lamented how they wished they had a figure like her.

Eventually Brooke made payment and walked past the long dress that she'd really wanted to buy; a chocolate brown, satin, tight-fitting, full-length dress with a halter neck, full-length sleeves and the most striking slit up to the top of the right thigh. She could only stare and imagine.

In my dreams, eh?

***

She drove back home and arrived minutes before Dean got back from work, stripping off and changing into joggers and a sweater.

The lounge looked far too tidy for a house that'd had Paige in it all day, so Brooke found herself doing the opposite of what she normally did; she quickly tipped up her entire toy box all over the lounge floor and kicked toys into all corners, throwing some on the stairs and in the kitchen, much to Paige's delight. Unfortunately, as was often the case, she chose to take her lead from her mother and Paige promptly emptied Brooke's handbag out and kicked the contents everywhere. Charlotte Tilbury was spread all over the floor…metaphorically speaking!

Brooke was making a cup of tea and smiled as she heard Paige rummaging through the mountain of toys and squealing, when Dean came through the front door.

'I'm home!' he shouted.

'In the kitchen!' Brooke replied.

Dean's face dropped as he noticed the state of the floor and navigated his way through the toy terrain to pick his daughter up. 'What are you like, eh? Couldn't find anything to play with, eh?!' He kissed her and threw her in the air, facilitating giggles galore as he wandered into the kitchen to greet his wife.

'Mmm, you smell gorgeous,' Dean said as he nuzzled Brooke's neck. 'How was your day?'

God, I've gotta tell him about Friday before he makes arrangements to play football.

Brooke turned around and started preparing Paige's tea. 'Yeah, same shit different day.'

God she's gonna be so excited when I tell her about the ballet. Maybe I should tell her now?

'Dean, before I forget, the girls are gonna have a night out on Friday and Stacey's asked me to come, so will you be alright staying in with Paige? I haven't been out with them for ages.' Her fingers shook as she sliced some apples and her heart pounded as she spoke.

Like bloody London buses. No nights out for months and then she gets two one after the other. Shame.

'That's a shame. I thought we might have a quiet night in.' He winked at her, hoping she might change her mind. She bristled and answered back rather too quickly.

'Dean, every night's a night in these days.'

Dean didn't want to risk spoiling anything so he immediately backed off.

'Yeah, you're right,' he lied. 'I'm pleased for you. You go and enjoy yourself,' he said with a forced smile.

'Thanks, babe. Can you get back from work 'bout five-ish, so I can go and get ready round Stacey's?' Inwardly Brooke breathed a sigh of relief and continued with her chopping.

Dean wandered back into the lounge and plonked Paige in the middle of her toy dump. 'D'ya realise Paige has emptied your bag all over the floor again?' Dean shouted. 'Don't worry, I'll clear it up.' As he diligently found everything from her bag amidst all the toys, he came across what looked to be a couple of small gold wrapped chocolates. He picked them up and turned them over.

Claridge's?

He frowned and jerked his head back.

'What you doing with fancy chocolates from Claridge's?' Dean shouted out.

Her immediate instinct was to run in and snatch them back, but it was too late for that. He'd already seen them. Instead, she froze on the spot, caught out yet again but with nothing prepared in her head to say back.

Damn, damn damn!

'Oh, er…one of the mums in the mum and toddler group brought them in. She's dead posh and said her husband had brought them back from some fancy dinner he went to. They all got a little box each.' Brooke crossed her fingers on both hands, shut her eyes and held her breath for a minute.

'Lucky you!' Dean shouted back, clearly falling for her little lie hook, line and sinker as he continued to clear up the lounge. Brooke's Latin book was thankfully zipped into a little compartment inside her bag.

Dean chuckled to himself.

I can do posh for my wife too, you know; just you wait!

12

Friday Night At The Ballet

On ballet Friday, Dean arrived home from work as Brooke was getting all her outfit together into a bag. 'Well, c'mon then, what's my favourite girl gonna be wearing tonight? Don't want all them blokes ogling at you too much!' Dean joked.

In a hurry and unable to think of a single excuse as to why she shouldn't show him, she very reluctantly pulled the little black number out and handed it to him. The whole point of him driving her to Stacey's to get changed was so he didn't see what she'd be wearing!

'No! Hold it up against you,' Dean complained.

Brooke rolled her eyes, tutted and did as she was told. Dean gawped like a prisoner who'd not seen a woman in years.

'Fuck me, Brooke, where d'ya get that? It must have cost a fortune.'

'TK Maxx of course, so no, it didn't!'

Dean stared at her so intently and longingly Brooke was unnerved. This wasn't Brooke's usual look at all. Her default style was sassy, sexy and revealing. This dress was another animal entirely and he was very unsure indeed what he felt about it.

'What's the matter? Why are you staring at me like that?' Brooke asked in a worried tone.

Please don't ask me where we're going.

'Nothing. It's just so…so not you. Gorgeous…but just not your normal style. Where are you girls going?' In the back of Dean's mind, he couldn't help thinking that she should be on the arm of Jude Law or some other rich, handsome man.

Brooke started putting the dress back as she spoke, nervously facing into the bag. 'Not sure. Probably just to The Sugar Hut.' Her heart was about to take a dive through her ribcage and run off to find somewhere to hide.

'Don't you look a bit overdressed for that? I mean…it's a bit…sophisticated, isn't it?'

Brooke laughed at his cheek. 'Charming! Are you saying I'm only allowed to dress in one way; the one to please you? What's wrong with looking a bit sophisticated every now and then?'

Dean laughed as they left the house and drove her to Stacey's, checking what time she'd be back.

'God knows. Knowing Stacey, it's bound to be early hours, but I'll get a taxi back so don't wait up.'

Dean kissed her and waved her goodbye as he dropped her off, with a slightly strange feeling in his gut that he couldn't quite identify.

***

'Oh my god, Brooke, you look amazing!' Stacey said as Brooke minced downstairs in her LBD. 'Are you sure you're not having an affair?'

'No! Can't a woman look good just for herself? Why does it have to be for a bloke?' Brooke scrutinised herself in the long mirror in the hallway.

I think it'll do.

'Dean only went and asked me to show him what I was wearing! So much for trying to hide it from him! Sorry, Stace, you probably didn't need to drive me in the end, but I couldn't change the plan.'

Stacey shrugged. 'Don't matter, babe.'

Brooke threw a cheap black pashmina over her shoulders and Stacey drove her furtively to Brentwood Station. Brooke felt like a criminal, which seemed a tad unfair given that she was only going to the ballet.

From the minute she got out of Stacey's car to the minute she arrived at Covent Garden station, to say she felt stared at, would be a grave understatement. People never even tried to hide the fact; in awe of her beauty.

It'd been agreed that they'd all meet inside the Bow Street entrance, where they'd then apparently be going on to eat in one of the restaurants inside. She made her way there and paused to admire the main entrance in all its glory; the world-famous Royal Opera House. She took a deep breath and walked purposefully through the beautiful old doors, looking out for Antonia and Lady Townsend.

'Brooke! Darling! It's so lovely to see you again! You look wonderful!' Antonia shouted loudly over a large crowd of elegantly dressed people. Brooke submitted to air kisses on both cheeks; Antonia seemed genuinely pleased to see her.

Antonia Dubarry, OBE, stood before Brooke in a Galliano full-length, dark-green velvet dress. She simply oozed old money and looked at least ten years' younger than Brooke knew her to be.

'Thank you, Antonia. You too.' Brooke felt slightly uncomfortable as she motioned her hands towards her own dress. 'It's just a TK Maxx jobbie, nothing to get excited about,' Brooke replied shrugging, pulling at the feathers and at a loss as to know what to say.

'No, Brooke. That's not right. Not right at all.' Antonia looked disappointed. Brooke panicked.

At that moment, Lady Townsend glided towards them in the lobby.

'Oh, Brooke dear, you look perfectly exquisite!' she cried, throwing both her arms out as if inviting the world to come and look. This was followed by another show of air-kissing and some small talk with Antonia.

Brooke had begun to feel confused and, as usual, Lady Townsend picked up on it. 'How are you feeling, my dear, and are you looking forward to the performance?'

Brooke couldn't hide her anxiety. 'Am I dressed… I mean, do I look…suitably dressed? Antonia gave me the impression that…it's only a TK Maxx jobbie. Only cost me twenny-five quid, but *I* thought it looked alright.'

Lady Townsend grimaced and took a deep breath. 'Brooke, dear, I don't need to know where you bought your dress, nor how much it cost. All I know is that you look wonderful. You don't need to make excuses or belittle what you're wearing. Say nothing. Enjoy the compliments. Mm?'

Brooke felt well and truly chastised and her head quite literally dropped at the response.

'Head up, dear. Head up, shoulders back,' Lady Townsend advised. Brooke did as she was told. 'So, are you looking forward to it?'

'Very much, thank you. In fact, I'm quite excited actually', she responded in a neutral tone. She'd been practising how to sound effortless and nonchalant, which she'd read in one of Mrs Townsend's *Tatler* magazines was a sign of the upper classes.

Antonia escorted them through to the champagne bar on the ground floor and clicked her fingers at one of the barmen, who caught sight of her and smiled.

'Three glasses of Laurent Perrier Rosé, please, Samir. Over by the piano, and three plates of smoked salmon sandwiches.' Samir nodded and the ladies glided over to the grand piano.

Brooke took a few minutes to absorb her surroundings: the stunning glass building with this huge and impressive circular bar in the centre seemingly serving only champagne, men dressed in evening suits, and as for the women…! Brooke had never encountered this sort of environment before.

Well this ain't no Sugar Hut, that's for sure.

Full-length evening dresses were abound and she listened to how the women spoke and watched how they behaved. They all seemed so confident and… Well, rather loud! Lots of laughter, smiling, hair flicking, air-kissing. Brooke couldn't decide if she felt an imposter or entirely at home. She still noticed the odd person glancing over at her, but they were more discreet about it than her fellow passengers on the 6.15pm from Brentwood.

Maybe I fit in better here than at home? Haha! That'll be the day!

She smiled wryly as she remembered Dawn's warning: 'Don't forget where you're from. You belong in Brentwood.' But Brooke was uncomfortable with that label and had to make a concerted effort to forget it. At least for this evening.

I'm damn well gonna have a good time tonight, before I turn into an Essex pumpkin at midnight! And I'm damn well gonna be a lady! I'll show the fuckers!

Samir brought over the sandwiches and champagne. Brooke noticed no one else was getting waiter service.

Guess that's what being a non-exec does for you. I thought we were going to a restaurant!

The ladies clinked their glasses and another toast was made, this time by Antonia. 'Here's to Brooke and another first for you. May it be the beginning of a life-long love of the ballet for you.' She apologised profusely for only having sandwiches, but even in her position she'd been unable to secure a table in either of the restaurants as they were already fully booked. Brooke didn't care.

'This building is stunning,' Brooke remarked as she pointed upwards to the white ornate ironwork and glass. Antonia gave a potted history explaining its past as the central place for a market selling flowers, fruit and vegetables. Suddenly a loud bell rang and there was movement in the crowds. Brooke looked confused.

What's happening? Where's everyone going?

'That means five minutes to go until the curtain rises' explained Lady Townsend.

They quickly finished their champagne and sandwiches, which Brooke realised Antonia hadn't even paid for. Antonia led the way, returning nods and hellos to at least a dozen people en route; some staff as well as others clearly there to see the ballet.

How nice to be recognised by all those people. I wonder how she knows them all?

Brooke observed Antonia's confidence and grace as she floated through the crowds and up the grand staircase, carpeted in deep red. Brooke followed suit as best she could as they all walked for what seemed an interminable length of time and finally arrived at a little door around a circular corridor.

Thank god, I could do with the loo.

On entering, the velvet chairs and incredible view of the stage put paid to that idea.

Oh my god, we're in one of them box things!

'Take a seat Letitia, Brooke,' Antonia invited them to sit as the bell rang a second time.

'I'm sorry, Antonia, but I desperately need the l…powder room.'

'That's fine. Turn right and it's a little further along on the left. Be quick though; you don't want to miss the beginning!'

Brooke remembered *Debrett's* advice about leaving a room without turning your back and felt this was a most appropriate time to put it into practice, so she proceeded to reverse out of the box, giving an elderly gentleman and his wife a shock as they came round the corridor to be confronted with Brooke's divine derrière slowly appearing in their path. Antonia and Letitia glanced knowingly at each other and smiled.

'She's a dear, isn't she, don't you think?' Letitia asked Antonia, taking the opportunity to discuss Brooke in her absence.

'Oh, she's quite a character – a real scream. Lacking breeding, of course, but nothing we can't help her with. She's really quite beautiful, isn't she? I simply adore her curiosity. It's so innocent…very endearing.'

'That's what made me want to encourage her to do something more with her life. You know, Antonia, I actually think she's very bright; she's done some marvellous work for me since I've started getting her involved in other aspects of my life apart from cleaning, but I fear her husband, Dean, holds her back somewhat. I've never met him, but I get the feeling from what she says that he's quite old fashioned and would rather she stayed at home. I think her toddler's a bit of a handful too. Screams for England apparently!'

Brooke found the ladies, thankfully with no queue. Nothing passed her by; she took in every last detail from the design of the taps to the brand of soap and the flattering mirrors, before trotting back. She almost, but not quite, allowed herself to flop down into the seat, but remembered where she was and who her companions were. With style and grace she took her seat slowly, elegantly and with her knees firmly clasped together. Antonia and Letitia watched her as she did so; satisfied with what they saw.

Suddenly the orchestra commenced and for the next forty-five minutes Brooke was totally captivated. Her body moved around slightly in her seat in time to the music and movements of the ballet dancers, lifting her head up as they leaped through the air, lifting her hands off her lap a little as the ballerinas moved their arms gracefully. It was impossible for her to not be moved physically as well as emotionally.

As the first few bars of 'Dance of The Mirlitons' played, Brooke sat bolt upright, seemingly straining to recall something. Then it dawned on her and she became very animated as she leaned towards Lady Townsend. 'Mrs Townsend,' she whispered excitedly, so as not to disturb Antonia's enjoyment, 'I know this song. I recognise it from somewhere, but I don't know where.' She was thrilled and clearly far more cultured than she'd realised. She actually knew the music. How marvellous!

Lady Townsend breathed deeply and leaned over slightly towards Brooke. 'It's not a song, dear, it's a piece. It was the theme of a chocolate bar advert, but we'll talk about it later.'

Brooke's face crumpled.

Course it was. Idiot. Cadbury's fruit and nut.

Lady Townsend realised she'd unintentionally belittled Brooke and immediately tried to make amends. 'But very well done for even recognising it!' Brooke managed a little smile.

The curtain came down for the interval and Antonia took them to the Crush Room. Elements of Brooks's Club came to mind yet again, as she looked up at the enormous chandelier. She felt she was imposing by accepting all this hospitality and decided it was her turn to buy a drink.

'Can I get everyone a drink?' she asked.

Antonia smiled at her and tilted her head to the side; a slightly condescending look, one might call it. 'No don't worry, darling, I pre-ordered our drinks; they're on that table over there.' She pointed and Brooke observed a table full of groups of drinks with receipts underneath.

Don't they all get nicked?!

Antonia went straight to the group with no receipt underneath. Another three glasses of champagne. After she'd picked them up, she quickly went to the bar and asked the barman for something to which he gave the thumbs up and indicated he'd bring 'it' over.

There was a small table in one corner which had a reserved sign and Antonia indicated they should sit there. Within minutes the barman had brought a selection of delicious miniature desserts and three forks. They were exquisite works of art in their own right, making Brooke clap her hands and giggle. 'Baby puddings!' She had to resist taking her phone out and photographing the food. Just then her phone buzzed.

Hows things? R U having fun? Send a pic.

Brooke practically had a meltdown on the spot. With only a split second of thinking, she turned her phone off and pretended to herself that she hadn't even seen it. She couldn't even bear to think about it; didn't want her evening ruined by guilt and worry. After tucking in to the delicious desserts, Brooke watched the people pour in from all over the theatre. They queued up waving notes and cards at the overworked bartenders, whose job it was to serve around two thousand people in a twenty-minute period.

This is worse than the bloody Sugar Hut!

The ladies discussed the performance as Brooke listened and took it all in. From time to time she turned around to see what was going on around her. It was noisy in that room, but the atmosphere was thrilling! Brooke felt as though she'd been beamed up to a strange faraway land for a quick snoop around, but had been so awestruck by what she'd discovered that she simply couldn't leave!

It felt like no time at all before the bell went, indicating they needed to get back to their seats again. Brooke was torn between wanting to stay and people watch in the Crush Room and wanting to watch the rest of the ballet. Antonia's demonstrative departure from the table gave her no choice in the matter and, before long, they were back in their box.

This eating in stages malarkey is definitely a bit weird.

Towards the end of the performance, the 'Dance of the Sugar Plum Fairy' played and Brooke recognised that too, but didn't know why. She wasn't going to say anything this time though. Mesmerised, she was transported to a world of pure escapism which she didn't want to end.

Why didn't Mum and Dad ever let me have ballet lessons?

The question kept going round and round in her head for the rest of the evening. If only she knew!

Why?

At the end of the performance, she stood up along with the rest of the audience. She clapped and cheered and, enraptured as she was, as naturally as blinking, put her thumb and forefinger between her lips and whistled. Very loudly. The Duke and Duchess of Wessex peered around one side of their box along with Sir Max Hastings and his wife peering round from the other.

Before Lady Townsend got a look in, Antonia turned around with a horrified look on her face and gently pulled Brooke's hand from her mouth. 'No whooping or whistling, darling. It's just not done.'

Shit! What was I thinking?

But in her 'pedagogue'-style relationship, Brooke was beginning to learn to take such comments on the chin. She was on a high; nothing could've ruined the evening for her at that moment. The tears flowed as Brooke watched the principal ballerina gather up the roses being thrown onto the stage for her, curtseying to the whole audience, reminding Brooke of her own inappropriate curtsies in the past. Lady Townsend offered her a tissue and gently rubbed her arm meaningfully for a moment, watching her intently. Brooke took it silently. The clapping seemed to go on for ever. Her hands hurt and her face ached from smiling so much.

That bloody curtain's worse than a whore's knickers!

Once the appreciation had finally died down and the final closing of the curtain had taken place, Antonia said she had a little treat in store. 'Follow me!' she said excitedly.

She escorted them down to the ground floor, through some back doors and corridors that were clearly not public and then quite suddenly they appeared in the orchestra pit! Brooke found herself surrounded by violinists, cellists and percussionists; many of the instruments she didn't even recognise.

'Good evening, ladies and gentlemen, I hope you don't mind but I've brought some friends to come and have a look and see where all that wonderful music was coming from,' Antonia said. As they were cleaning and putting their instruments away, the musicians said hello, waved or nodded and smiled over in Brooke's direction. Brooke noticed the man playing the celesta. Tall, dark, and handsome is the only way he could possibly be described. He motioned for Brooke to come over. After obtaining a nod from Mrs Townsend, Brooke sidled over and he invited her to have a play. She sat down and he demonstrated a few notes. She followed his instructions diligently and within a couple of minutes had played the first few bars of the third act of the Sugar Plum Fairy, pas de deux. She grinned as though she'd won Young Musician of The Year, laughing out loud as she stood up and thanked him. She was desperate to give him a hug, but was beginning to learn that that would almost certainly not be considered appropriate. He winked at her. She smiled back and caught up with Antonia and Lady Townsend, who were by now over the other side of the pit ready to leave. From there, they were taken to the restaurants and the upstairs bar and spent a few moments looking down onto the champagne bar they'd been in earlier.

'Do you have a little while longer or do you have to get back, darling?' asked Antonia.

'Well, I'm a little tired and wouldn't mind getting back but, Brooke, please do stay if you'd like to, dear,' said Mrs Townsend. Brooke felt guilty leaving her to get back home on her own, but was itching to see what Antonia'd got planned.

'Well as long as you don't mind, I'd love to see a bit more!' Brooke said with a grin on her face that couldn't hide her delight at what she was discovering. So, they said their goodbyes and Antonia then led Brooke through a rabbit warren of lifts until they arrived outside something called The Staff and Artists' restaurant. Next, they arrived at the wardrobe department. There were only a couple of ladies in there, who clearly knew Antonia well and called for her to come in. Antonia asked if they had a few minutes to show Brooke around. They were more than happy to oblige. Brooke gasped as she walked about; in awe of the glorious costumes. Pretty tutus made from netting, sequins and stretchy silk. And so tiny!

God, those waists are the size of one of my thighs!

Dresses, corsets, feathers, hats, ballet shoes, ribbons, wigs in every conceivable colour. The novelty, richness and luxury of it all was inescapable. Brooke asked the poor wardrobe ladies more questions in fifteen minutes than they normally received in a month of tours!

She had to be practically dragged out before being taken to a studio where some young dancers were finishing up. She and Antonia stayed outside and were able to watch through a large glass window as the dancers stretched and leaped and practiced their lifts. Seeing them up this close, made Brooke realise how graceful, flexible and supple these dancers were. She was envious and wrapped her pashmina around her body.

Finally, they went deep into the vast bowels of the Opera

House, where Brooke was shown the electronics behind each scene change. She was flabbergasted. She'd no idea that the ballet was so involved.

And there's me thinking it's just a few ballerinas prancing around a stage! Ha!

'There. I just wanted to give you a whirlwind tour, so you can see precisely how much is involved in the production of one ballet. Just imagine, every ballet and every opera has its own set changes, wardrobe and rehearsals. It's a massive industry all of its own.' Antonia had gone into 'non-executive and fundraising director' mode with abandon!

'Right, the restaurants and bars all shut after the performance, so people sadly can't get another drink before leaving...unless you happen to be a non-exec of course, in which case...bring on the champagne. Come on, darling, let's go up to the bar!' With that, they made their way up to the Amphitheatre bar and Antonia ordered yet another bottle of Laurent Perrier.

God, she can drink for an old girl!

They sat down at a table overlooking the champagne bar below and Antonia poured them both a glass.

'So, Brooke...tell me all about your husband. Dean, isn't it?'

Brooke's entire demeanour changed. It seemed that her 'turning into a pumpkin' vision had been brought forward an hour or so.

Back to her metaphorical floor scrubbing in her rags.

13

Between Performances

At about 1am, Brooke opened the front door as quietly as possible and tiptoed into the dimly lit lounge. Seeing the lamp on, she went to switch it off and discovered Dean fast asleep on the sofa, surrounded by beer bottles and a large Domino's pizza box.

Concern and relief overwhelmed her. Concern because Dean never left food and drink debris out. His desire for order and tidiness meant he couldn't be any other way, so this was something to worry about. Relief, because it meant she didn't have to suffer relaying an hour by hour run-down of her 'night out with the girls'.

Shall I wake him?

She chewed her lip and watched him for a minute or two, undecided. Then she pulled the duvet from the spare room and very gently placed it over him, praying he didn't wake up. She then switched the light off and crept upstairs to sleep alone.

***

'Morning.' Dean sat on the edge of the bed and placed a tray of tea and toast beside her. He watched as Brooke was roused from her sleep with a cat-like stretch, yawn and groan before opening her eyes.

'Thanks, babe! What happened to you last night? Drowning your sorrows?!' Brooke sat up and grabbed her mug of tea, a gnawing sensation in the pit of her stomach as she prepared for the inevitable chat that was coming. 'Mr Tidy Pants didn't even clean up after himself, but I couldn't bear to wake you.'

'I'm fine. Just had one beer too many. What happened to *you*, more the point?' Dean replied.

'What do you mean what happened to me? Nothing happened to me. Why?'

'You didn't reply to any of my messages. I asked for pictures of your night and you didn't respond at all.' Dean stared intently at her, looking deep into her eyes for some sort of explanation that he would be happy with. Brooke quickly grabbed a large piece of toast and bit a large mouthful, averting her eyes, disguising her speech and her facial expressions.

'Oh! Sorry, I didn't even look at my phone, never mind take any piccies. We were having such a laugh.' She gulped, her heart about take off like an Exocet missile.

'That's not like you.' Dean replied, not taking his eyes off her for one moment and making her extremely nervous as a result.

'Well, we haven't all been together for nearly a year. We had better things to do than spend all night taking selfies. Some of us have moved on, Dean.' She thought if she sounded stroppy, he would drop the MI5-style questioning. Dean hated it when she got like that and avoided it at all costs.

He didn't want to spoil the surprise he had for her, even though his suspicions had undeniably been raised. He'd left her to lie in as long as he dared, but knew she'd want to buy a new dress for the treat he had in store for her; she'd be mad if he didn't give her enough time, although he personally thought she should wear the one she'd worn the previous evening. Anyhow, he had to drop his concerns and focus on the day – and evening – ahead.

Here goes! Let's hope she likes it!

'Babe. I've got a little surprise for you!'

Thank god. Change of subject.

'What's that, then?' she replied, slurping her Twining's, trying to sound casual whilst feeling anything but. Dean's own heart was thumping like the drums in the Guiness advert! He handed her an envelope. She frowned, licked her fingers and opened it. Her heart sprouted legs and ran off.

What the hell? What is this? Shit. What's going on?

'Dean, what the hell is this?' she asked, tugging her curls and biting her lip. She fingered the two tickets and read them carefully.

The Nutcracker, 7.30pm, Saturday 3rd May 2014, The Royal Opera House, Covent Garden.

Holy mother of Gladys!

'So what d'ya think, babe?' Dean asked excitedly. He regurgitated his well-rehearsed explanation of how he'd come by this pair of £250 theatre tickets. He'd decided to tell her that he'd been given them as a thank-you by Kevin, CEO of their IT supplier.

Brooke could not talk; an unusual state of affairs for her. Words simply would not come as her brain went into paralysis mode. Dean stared hard into her eyes.

'Well? What d'ya think, babe? Crazy, huh?! You loved that programme the other day. I couldn't believe it when I was offered these.' He motioned to the tickets and stared at her, scanning her face for some crumb of comfort. He was reminded of the moment he'd told her when he'd got his company car; how he'd got it in banana yellow especially for her and how she still hadn't seemed pleased.

'I…I honestly don't know what to say, Dean.' Brooke had to work hard to keep a neutral face.

What in god's name am I meant to do?

'How about…thanks for thinking about me, Dean, it's gonna be great?!' he responded.

'Well…yes…it'd be great. It's just such a shock, that's all. Look at the price of these tickets.'

'I know. Crazy, huh? We'll have a right laugh!'

'Mmm. Not sure I'd call it a laugh. More like a cultural experience.'

'Like you would know!' he laughed.

If only you knew, Dean. If only you knew.

Brooke's paralysis meant she struggled to think on her feet. Not one plausible excuse came to her as to why she couldn't go. 'I'm a bit tired after last night, to be honest, babe.'

'What?! C'mon, babe, it's not a question of do you wanna go. We're going! And let's face it, when will we ever get the chance to go somewhere like this again in our lifetime? You were complaining only the other day about not ever *going* to the theatre.'

Brooke knew that in normal circumstances, Dean would correctly expect her to say yes to such an offer, faster than a ballerina's pirouette. To refuse wouldn't be her normal reaction.

'I was thinking you've got that gorgeous dress you wore last night. You could wear that. Kevin said it was dead posh and we'd have to dress up.'

Oh my giddy aunt. What if I'm recognised? All those staff I met last night? What if they're all there again tonight? What if Antonia's there again?! Oh shit!

Her mind went into overdrive. 'OK, we'll go, but I'm not wearing the same dress as last night, it stinks of sweat with all that dancing. I'll have to go buy something cause I haven't got anything suitable.' Dean gave a rather patronising smile and felt a bit sorry for his wife, for thinking she'd possibly know what would be suitable for such a place.

'Brilliant, babe! It's gonna be the dogs' bollocks! I promise.'

'What about eating? We'll have to eat before we leave or we'll have to wait until after the performance.'

'You mean show!'

Brooke took the safe option of saying nothing.

'I'm gonna treat us and we're gonna eat in the restaurant.' Dean automatically began mentally running through the visit brief for the restaurant.

'No, Dean. We can't afford it. Let's eat before we leave,' Brooke begged, recalling the menus she'd seen when Antonia had shown her around the restaurants. Of course Dean, knowing that he had to have a pre-dinner drink, three-course meal plus a bottle of wine, coffee and liquors, knew that eating before they left was simply not an option.

'No, Brooke. I've already booked us a table in the restaurant. We're gonna eat there.'

Without thinking, Brooke asked 'Which one?' As soon as the words had left her mouth, she realised her error.

Dean looked quite perplexed. 'Is there more than one? How d'ya know that?'

Oh blimey! THINK!

'Mmm...I dunno...mmm.'

'Don't tell me you read that somewhere,' Dean retorted suspiciously.

'No. I know...it was on that programme. Remember? Oh, maybe that bit was on before you got home. Yeah, I think it probably was.' She prayed silently that he'd accept her explanation. Thankfully he appeared to.

'I'll have to check my booking. I can't remember the name of it. Anyway, it'll be nice. We don't wanna spoil a special night out by having a Maccie D on the way, do we?!' he roared laughing. 'But we've gotta be at the table by five-thirty apparently. Seems a bit early to me, but they said something about not eating all the meal in one go? I didn't understand what they were on about to be honest, babe. I expect it'll make more sense when we get there.'

Of course Brooke knew exactly what was meant by it, having seen it for herself not twelve hours previously!

'Well, I guess I'd better get up and go find a new dress,' Brooke said in a resigned manner. Dean looked a tad deflated and Brooke knew she had to say or do something more in keeping with her usual self. She did the only thing she could think of to put Dean off the scent of anything odd.

'Where's Paige?' she asked.

'Having her morning nap. Why?'

'Well, I *have* just about got time to thank you properly... with some pre-theatre entertainment...if you're up for it?' Brooke gave him one of her seductive looks and pulled the duvet down to reveal her bare, curvaceous body. She adjusted her pose so it effectively said 'come and get me!'

Dean couldn't believe his luck – sex, ballet and a three-course meal all in one day.

***

Brooke's journey into town was speedy. As soon as she was out of the estate, she pulled over and rang Stacey. 'Oh my god, Stace!' she yelled down the phone 'you will not believe what's happened!'

'Try me,' Stacey replied with a 'seen it all' tone to her voice.

Brooke then went on to describe in detail what had gone on in the previous eighteen hours. Instead of gaining sympathy and compassion for her plight, Stacey became hysterical with laughter, much to Brooke's frustration.

'Stace!' Brooke screamed. 'You don't get it. I think Dean's suspicious. He doesn't believe I didn't take any pictures of our girls' night out.'

'Well that's cause you didn't! If I remember rightly...er...we didn't actually go on one!' she roared laughing even more.

'Listen, can you meet me in TK Maxx in twenty minutes?' Brooke pleaded.

'Well I ain't got anything else on, so yeah. You can tell me more about your cock-ups. See you in a bit.'

Stacey found Brooke wandering in the evening dress section, stole up quietly behind her and grabbed both her breasts from behind with an ''allo, darlin." Brooke yelped and turned round, ready to swipe the monster responsible but was relieved to see Stacey instead.

'You cow!' Brooke cried. 'Thanks for coming. Now, grab an evening dress to try on.'

'What? I'm not buying anything!' Stacey replied.

'Doesn't matter. Pick one you like so you can try it on.' Like Dean, Stacey knew Brooke's 'looks' and realised this wasn't a time to argue. She'd been friends with Brooke since primary school and there wasn't much she didn't know about her. She found an outfit she liked; very Stacey – brassy, blingy and bold.

Brooke had managed to find the chocolate brown satin one she'd had to discard a few days ago and was thrilled, although she kept wondering how else she might alter her appearance to avoid being recognised by any of the staff. She'd worn her hair down last night, so she thought she'd have an up do tonight and wear flats. Every time she thought about going back there, her stomach churned and she felt nauseous with stress.

I can't keep carrying on like this or I'm gonna get that atrial arrythmia the doc talked about.

They scuttled off to the changing rooms and changed into their outfits, all the while Brooke giving Stacey more detail about the evening and the heart-attack-inducing shock that Dean had given her that morning.

'I swear that could only happen to you, Brooke. You're unbelievable you are!' Predictably, Brooke looked stunning in her dress, Stacey – all seventeen stone of her – well let's just say a little less so; more like *Telly Tubbies* meets *Star Wars.*

Once Brooke was happy with her dress, Stacey, believing Brooke merely wanted some company whilst trying clothes on, started to remove hers, thinking they were all done. 'No, Stace, not yet,' Brooke whispered confidentially. 'There's something else I need you to help me with first.' She closed the curtains in the changing room, took out her LBD and changed into it with Stacey looking on, bemused.

'So, what's goin' on? What are we doin'?' Stacey asked, hands on hips.

'Now we need to find somewhere dark and you take a selfie

of us both on your phone so it looks like we're in a night club.'

'You *are* taking the Mick[11], Brooke?' Stacey responded in disbelief.

'No. Now, c'mon, there must be somewhere we can go.' With that, Brooke conducted a speedy reconnaissance around the changing rooms. There was nowhere at all suitable for her devious plan. However, she wasn't going to be beaten. Back in the changing room, Stacey was sitting in her playsuit messaging someone on her phone, waiting for Brooke's return. Brooke looked around helplessly. 'OK, Stace, get off your phone. Concentrate. How can we make it look a bit darker?'

Stacey looked up. 'Give us one of your heels,' she said sternly, motioning with her hand. Brooke frowned but removed one of her heels and handed it over, unable to imagine Stacey's strategy. Before Brooke could say a word, Stacey had heaved all seventeen stone of her rotund body onto the seat and with no warning, as decisively as an SAS killer, smashed the light bulb in the dressing room with the stiletto, rendering it dark in an instant. Brooke gasped at the audacity of the move, but took full advantage of the opportunity she'd created.

'Right, quick, let's go, take a couple now! And for god's sake look like you're having fun, Stace!' With that, they both posed for several shots, Brooke being forced to pull Stacey's fat lady pants down to induce laughter.

Customers in the other changing rooms could be heard questioning what on earth was going on in the end cubicle. Giggles, screams and demands of 'smile' and 'pull me pants back up, you bitch!' only led to more raised eyebrows.

After ten minutes, the pair came out trying their damnedest

---

11. Taking the Micky Bliss – piss.

not to laugh, with little success. Other customers followed them out with their eyes, tutting. There was no sales assistant in sight, thank goodness, so Brooke paid for her dress as Stacey put back her silver-sequinned playsuit on the rack.

They had a quick coffee in Caffè Nero where Brooke instructed Stacey to WhatsApp her the best images from their changing room antics sometime during the afternoon so she could 'show Dean' what a great time they'd had at The Sugar Hut, to appease any worries he may've been harbouring. Stacey reluctantly agreed, but warned her friend that this couldn't carry on and that she had to tell Dean about all this.

'Oh shut up, Stace! Not you too. You sound like Dawn. She's been banging on at me about it forever. I can't. At least not yet, anyway. I just can't.'

They parted with a hug and kiss and Stacey wished Brooke good luck, for what was surely going to be an even more memorable night than the previous one…but for all the wrong reasons!

***

By the time Brooke started to make her way home, she didn't have much time to get ready. She laughed silently to herself, shaking her head at the utterly idiotic nature of what she was about to do. She had to remind herself that she'd had the most wonderful time last night and that she should focus on what Dean had done for her and enjoy the performance for a second time. She was secretly thrilled they were eating in one of the restaurants, but alarmed because she knew the cost. Eating and drinking as little as possible would be her strategy.

Dean. Am passing McD – shall I get us both a meal deal, so we can keep our eating and drinking to a minimum at ROH?

Dean yelped. The mystery visit to The Royal Opera House was going to be not too dissimilar from his mystery visit to Nous Geraldine several months previously, where he and Martin had to eat and drink continually for about three hours. Dean's nerves kicked in. Could he actually manage to do this entire mystery assignment without Brooke realising? He was nervous, but significantly more experienced nowadays and as the afternoon wore on he'd become more confident in his ability to pull the whole thing off.

What? NO! just get chips, dont wanna spoil appetite!

Brooke sighed, but did as she was asked. She'd had no lunch and was hungry.

When she arrived home, her mother was already there, having agreed to babysit Paige. When Dean had told Jackie where he and Brooke were going, she was overwhelmed with excitement and pride.

'I reckon the day you get to see a ballet in one of them posh theatres in London is the day you've made it, Dean,' she'd said, almost tearful. 'I wanted Brooke to do ballet lessons when she was a tot, but when the teacher saw her, she took one look at her feet and said she couldn't do anything with 'em…or her and that she was sorry! She wouldn't even let her watch a class, poor little mite!' She explained to Dean in that 'entre nous' way, that she'd never told Brooke that particular story for fear it might psychologically damage her for life. Dean had nodded seriously in understanding and agreement.

Brooke and Dean scoffed down their chips and Brooke chose that moment to 'suddenly remember' to show Dean the photo Stacey had taken of them both 'in the nightclub'. Instead of glancing at it casually and returning to his chips as she'd hoped he would do, he put his glasses on, took the phone from her hands and examined the photograph thoroughly. Brooke felt sick.

'Where was that taken? It doesn't look like The Sugar Hut to me.'

'Oh just as we were leaving the ladies,' she offered hopefully.

'Of all the places in The Sugar Hut to take a photo and she took one there; she's weird.' Dean commented.

'I know. Daft cow! It's the only one we got all night,' she lied and moved swiftly on to finishing her chips and then clearing up the cartons. 'D'ya fancy a beer?'

All the while, Jackie was trying to play shopkeepers with Paige, who was more interested in jumping on her lap.

'Mum, she likes to have a hot chocolate in her bottle at half six and when you put her down, can you tell her a story and stroke her head until she falls asleep?' Brooke instructed. Her mother raised her eyebrows at the indulgent request.

'Yes, love. No problem,' she'd said unconvincingly.

When Brooke and Dean presented themselves to Jackie, she cried and lifted her arms up at them both causing Paige to fall on the floor. She didn't make a sound; merely lay there silently looking up at the ceiling for a moment before rolling over and toddling off, her nappy sagging in her batman leggings.

'Oh lordy lordy, Brooke. You look fantastic! I wish your Dad was 'ere. 'e'd have been so proud, but there's a big fight on the box tonight and he didn't wanna miss it.'

'No worries, Mum,' Brooke replied as she walked round the sofa to show her mother the dress from all angles. 'D'ya like my hair up like this?'

'Ooh yes, love, it looks very sophisticated. Just what you want in a place like that. Where's your heels?'

'Oh, my feet hurt from all that dancing last night so I'm wearing flats tonight.'

'What about me?' Dean asked, upset at being left out of the compliments.

'Oh yes, Dean. You look very smart. Shame you haven't got one of them tuxedo suits, but never mind. You've scrubbed up nicely,' Jackie said reassuringly.

Brooke and Dean gave Paige a huge 'kiss sandwich' followed by several minutes of extensive tickling and raspberry blowing on her tummy before finally handing her back to Jackie and leaving for the station.

Dean went to buy the train tickets while Brooke tried her best to stay in the background, taking an unhealthy interest in the Bakerloo line on the map. It was the same ticket clerk as the previous evening. He caught sight of Brooke and made some comment to Dean who joined Brooke and said, 'That bloke in the ticket office said you are "always so beautiful". Like he sees you every day or something!'

Brooke's heart sank.

Please don't tell me this is what I'm gonna have to put up with all evening.

14

Saturday Night At The Ballet

Theatreland was buzzing. As they walked down into Covent Garden, Dean spotted the Charlotte Tilbury shop and thoughtfully asked Brooke if she wanted to go in. She declined, worried the staff might see her and recall her looking through the windows the night before. Dean shrugged. 'Please yourself.'

Further down, a circus artist had caused a stir by falling off his large ball and falling into another artist who was attempting to remain statue like until someone paid him to move. The atmosphere was lively and fun and, for a few minutes, both Brooke and Dean forgot their respective challenges and enjoyed themselves, like any young couple in the West End.

Just before 5.30pm, Dean said they needed to go. Brooke went to walk towards Bow Street but Dean pulled her the opposite way, having been told he must go via the ticket hall to check the toilets and ask staff some questions to test their knowledge.

'I think you'll find it's in the corner, babe, over there.' He pointed to an inconspicuous entrance in the corner of the piazza, nothing like the grand entrance Brooke had used. Her face was a picture of confusion, but she didn't dare argue.

Just pretend it's completely new to me. Act like I've NEVER seen it before.

They entered the modern revolving doors. The immediate sight before them was of a white, clean and contemporary building. Brooke looked around, unable to grasp that this was the same building as she'd been in the previous night. Antonia hadn't shown her this part at all.

'I'm just going to the loo. Do you need to go?' Dean asked.

'No, I'll wait here.' Brooke strolled over to the area where brochures were stacked, picking one and browsing through it, keeping her face to the wall as much as possible. From time to time, she glanced around surreptitiously. Suddenly, out the corner of her eye, she spied Antonia Dubarry coming out of what looked like a small staff door, near the entrance.

I don't bloody well believe it!

Her stomach dropped and without giving any thought to the fact that Dean would be out in a minute, she dived into the nearby gift shop and made her way to the farthest corner. There, she proceeded to flick through the huge posters of Darcy Bussell, making sure her face was as far inside the display stand as was humanly possible.

Why's she here again?! Who goes to the ballet two nights in a row? Now I'll be spending the whole night trying to avoid her!

Dean came out the lavatory and looked around for Brooke. Scratching his head and frowning, he walked up and down the corridor but she was nowhere in sight. He came to the conclusion that she'd decided to go the lavatory after all, so he took the opportunity to visit the ticket office to test their knowledge. He walked slowly up to the next free ticket clerk, so he could observe their body language and name badge. 'Hi. Can you tell me what time the show finishes tonight please?' Rosie, according to her name badge, smiled.

'The performance finishes at 10pm, sir.'

Performance? Show? What's the bloody difference?

'And how long's the interval?'

'Twenty minutes, sir.'

God that's a bit quick!

'But a bloke can't eat a meal in twenty minutes!'

'Have you booked one of the restaurants, sir?'

'Yeah, The Balconies?'

'Well, you should make your way up there now, sir; you'll have your starter and main course pre-performance. During the interval you'll return and have dessert and coffee.'

'Right, thanks. What about afters?'

'Sorry, sir?' Rosie looked perplexed.

'You know. After the show's finished. Where can we have a drink after that?'

'Ah I'm sorry, sir, but the bar closes after the performance.'

You should make a complaint about some aspect of your visit to see how well the staff handle it.

Mmm. I might do that after the show. Go to the bar and complain we can't get a drink.

Brooke carefully exited the gift shop behaving like an undercover surveillance officer. She walked at pace over to Dean, with her head down.

'Where've you been? I thought you went to the loo.'

'Nah. Just popped in the gift shop.'

Ah. We've gotta visit the gift shop and make a small purchase.

'D'ya see anything you liked?' Dean enquired tactfully.

'There was a beautiful poster of a pair of red ballet shoes in there. Real classy.'

'C'mon, let's go and get it then!'

'What?! No! I didn't mean to buy; it was just nice to look at that's all.'

Dean took hold of Brooke's hand and became unusually demonstrative as he pulled her back into the gift shop, Brooke all the while looking out for Antonia. She showed Dean the poster, which was £20 –£10 more than his budget allowed.

'I don't like it that much, to be honest. Let's see if there's something else,' he said.

Were the display stands clean and well stocked?

Brooke wanted to sit down at the table as soon as possible, away from the busy public spaces and was frustrated at Dean's seeming insistence on buying her something. She followed him as he kept holding up a selection of little gift items, with raised eyebrows, to see what she thought and as only Dean could, kept running his fingers along the shelves complaining they were dusty and not very well stocked. Brooke tutted and rolled her eyes.

'Honestly, Dean, who cares? I'm not fussed. Let's go and sit down. I'm starving.'

Time was tight so he eventually decided on a keyring with a miniature pair of red pointe ballet shoes.

You must ask the staff a question to test their knowledge.

'Is this made in the UK, do you know?' Dean asked earnestly.

Brooke was jolted out of her nonchalance and stared at Dean in disbelief. 'What are you on about, Dean? What the hell does it matter where it's made?!'

'Sorry, sir, I'm not sure.'

No marks for you then.

He gave the keyring to Brooke, who tossed it into her bag. They left and made their way to the Balconies restaurant. On the way, the barman from the champagne bar the previous evening was walking towards them. Brooke caught his eye and looked away, but not quickly enough, as he nodded, smiled at her and said good evening in recognition.

'That's pretty impressive as it goes,' Dean remarked, nodding and making a mental note to put that in his report.

Brooke now recognised where she was and prayed that Antonia wasn't eating in the same restaurant, if indeed she was eating at all. She hadn't looked as glamorous as the previous evening and it occurred to Brooke that maybe she was 'working' – whatever that might involve.

They were shown to their table by a young man that Brooke thankfully didn't recognise. He asked if they'd like a drink or cocktail. Brooke said no thank you at exactly the same time as Dean said yes please.

'C'mon, love, have a cocktail.'

'Dean,' Brooke was leaning forward and whispering fiercely, 'we can't afford it. Have you seen the price of it?'

The waiter was waiting patiently for them to make up their mind, but in truth was anxious about the speed with which this couple were clearly going. André hated this type of table, these types of people, who didn't have a clue about what they were doing. After a couple of minutes, he stepped forward clearly expecting an order.

'Rubbish,' Dean declared. 'Two of them Kir Royals please.'

'Dean!'

He put his fingers up to his lips to shoosh her.

'Dean, you say it roy–al. French. Not "royal" like in the "royal family".'

Dean looked exasperated. 'Whatever! We're 'aving one!'

Brooke couldn't hide her confusion. This man who was always trying to avoid spending money was being extravagant in a way she'd not seen since he bought her the hot tub. This was a complete turnaround!

He's gone mad!

'Where's the menu?' Brooke asked as an excuse to conduct another scan of the restaurant.

'Well. It had to be ordered in advance and as I wanted to surprise you, I had to choose for you. I hope you don't mind, babe, but I think I've done alright.' With that he took out a copy of the pre-order he'd printed off. 'I chose different things for me and you, for starters, mains and pudding, so if you don't like yours you can have mine.'

'Three courses?! God, Dean, are you crazy? It's gonna cost a fortune!' Brooke was extremely concerned by now and reluctantly looked at the menu he'd selected for her. He'd ordered venison carpaccio, blood orange, rocket, hazelnut dressing to start followed by halibut, braised leeks, mussels, saffron sauce and chocolate, caramel tart, crème fraiche for dessert.

'Wow!' Brooke was staggered. He'd chosen well. She couldn't fault it.

But seventy-five quid? EACH?! Christ, that's a whole week's shopping at Aldi!

'But…'

'No buts. We're gonna enjoy tonight!' Their cocktails were brought and they clinked glasses.

'Cheers, babe!' Dean said.

'Would sir like to order any wine with your meal?'

'Yes please, can I see the wine list?' The waiter disappeared.

'Dean, what's the matter with you, this is gonna break the

bloody bank this is?' The sommelier arrived promptly at the table with the list and smiled at Brooke.

Oh fuck, that's the guy from the Crush Room last night.

'Nice to see you back again so soon, madam,' he said. Brooke inwardly crumpled and a nervous, high-pitched giggle tumbled from her mouth. Dean looked over to Brooke in confusion, who simply shrugged her shoulders and raised her eyebrows as if to say 'I don't know what he's on about.'

You must ask the waiter to recommend wine pairings for each course.

'What can you recommend?'

'Would sir like wine pairings or a bottle,'

'Oh I think pairings would be good.' He put on his best telephone voice, which made Brooke snort.

The sommelier went on to make three suggested pairings with in-depth descriptions, each one at over £10 a glass. Brooke's expression was one of utter amazement. Once again, she had no words.

Ask a question to test the sommelier's knowledge.

Dean had given this some thought and read up a little before they'd come out, about what sorts of things sommeliers are meant to know and discuss with customers. Dean nodded along, giving the distinct impression he was well versed in the best vintages. As if that were not enough, he then asked, 'Isn't that Burgundy a bit young to be served now?' Brooke could not contain herself and burst out laughing, humiliating Dean in the process.

'No, sir, the wine is perfect to be served now, I can assure you. Will that be everything?'

'Yep. All good,' said Dean. The sommelier left, chuckling to himself.

'Why did you laugh? And what did he mean "nice to see you back again so soon, madam?" Dean asked, genuinely confused.

'I haven't got a clue. He must've mistaken me for someone else,' Brooke said boldly and bluntly, her pulse taking on a life of its own.

'Mmm.'

'Anyway, what's with you and the wine? Since when do you know anything whatsoever about wine, Dean De'Ath?! That was so funny. I'm sorry but I had to laugh.'

'Well maybe I didn't want to embarrass you? Maybe I actually did a bit of research before we came here so I wouldn't come across like a complete dickhead? Now, maybe I've taught you a thing or two about wine, eh?' Dean offered provocatively. Brooke's shoulders dropped, feeling mean for laughing at his brave attempt to show himself – indeed both of them – in the best possible light. The real reason he'd researched remained, of course, a blissful secret.

'Aww sorry, babe. You were pretty impressive to be fair. I wouldn't have known any of that stuff,' she lied. Lord D'Arcy had been very diligent in his education of Brooke around the subject of fine wines and it had to be said that Brooks's Club had one of the finest wine lists in the world, worth millions.

At that moment, Brooke caught sight of Antonia gliding into the restaurant and making her way alongside the tables. Brooke completely panicked and suddenly buried her face into her linen napkin and began a fake coughing fit, which soon turned into a very real one, which thank heavens did not finish until Antonia had passed by their table. Dean, the waiter and the sommelier rushed to offer Brooke water. By the time she'd finished her coughing fit, her napkin had turned a bright shade of orange and was replaced without fuss by the waiter.

Once Dean had reassured himself his wife wasn't about to have a heart attack, they tucked into their starters then mains, in awe of the way the chefs had presented the food on their plates. They savoured every morsel and enjoyed discussing their dishes. To Brooke's horror, Dean leaned over at one point waving his fork and pierced a piece of her starter and shovelled it into his own mouth.

'Dean! Stop it! You can't do that in a place like this!'

Dean laughed. 'Who says?!'

Brooke found it highly amusing that Dean was taking such an obsessive interest in her food as well as his own. Endless questions about the taste, the temperature and all manner of other things were asked regularly throughout the dinner.

'You gonna write a review for Trip Advisor or something?' she teased.

If only you knew, babe!

This time, Brooke took photos. And lots of them! She couldn't wait to show her mother. Jackie would be so impressed! This food was every bit as superb as the lunches she'd had at Brooks's, Claridge's and The Jockey Club Rooms with Lord D'Arcy. Brooke revelled in the fact that this time, they weren't the guests of anyone. They were here doing it themselves.

Every so often her enjoyment was spoiled at the thought of how much it was all costing. She simply couldn't get her head around Dean's lavish spending. It was so unlike him. He was usually as 'tight as a duck's arse[12]', in Martin's words. In addition, she was on edge and constantly alert should she spot any more

12. Mean.

familiar faces to avoid.

'Has someone injected you with a spending drug?' she laughed.

'Only the best for my girl…the best girl ever,' he replied as he held her hand affectionately over the table and gave it a squeeze. By this time, the alcohol had begun to take effect and the two of them had relaxed and tried to put their stresses to the back of their mind. Dean was making the same schoolboy error he made at Nous Geraldine, i.e. enjoying himself to such a degree that he was forgetting what he was meant to be assessing. He suddenly asked Brooke, 'How long do you think it took for our starters and main courses to come?'

'You what?! What the hell, Dean! Why on earth does that matter? Just enjoy it. As you keep telling me!'

'Just curious, that's all. If you're paying the kind of money I'm paying, I was just thinking about how efficient the service is. There seems to be a helluva lot of rushing around. And we're gonna be chucked off the table soon I think to go and watch the show.' Dean's acting had improved immeasurably and Brooke was no wiser about his secret mission than she was before.

'Performance, Dean. It's a performance, not a show!'

'I reckon about five minutes for starter and ten for main – don't you think?'

'Whatever,' Brooke replied apathetically. Dean inputted the information in his phone, pretending he'd just got a message. As he did so, he realised he'd made very few actual written notes so far and was terrified of forgetting the detail, so said he needed the lavatory and rushed off to make some additional notes. He did not want a repeat performance of paper notes falling in a pool of urine as they'd done at Nous Geraldine, so he'd put the entire mystery customer questionnaire on his phone. He also checked what other questions he might've missed and so was gone for quite some time.

What in god's name is he doing in there? Building the bloody loos?

He finally appeared after nearly fifteen minutes and was ribbed mercilessly by Brooke for having such a weak bladder. Then the bell went and a young girl came over and informed them that they should make their way to their seats. 'And then we come back here for pudding in the interval, right?' Dean checked. The girl confirmed this. 'It's a bit weird all this eating at different times, don't you think? I feel like my pudding now,' Dean said.

'Well, it's the way they do it at theatres. There's no time to eat all of it before the performance and too late to eat after it,' Brooke explained.

They followed the signs to the stalls, with Brooke keeping her head down, but her almost six-foot frame was jolly hard to hide; even in flats she cut a striking figure. Along the way people turned their heads, including the staff designated to help guide people to their seats, two of whom recognised Brooke immediately so smiled and nodded. Dean noticed this. 'Babe, you look so gorgeous tonight. Have you noticed how many people are staring and smiling at you?' Dean remarked, feeling overwhelmed with love and pride at his beautiful wife.

As they took their seats, Dean looked around to assess how good their seats were and took a few photos. He was surprised that Brooke didn't seem more interested in this exquisite theatre. 'Babe! Look at them box things. I think that's the royal one where Queenie sits; it's got one of them crest things on it.

God, this place is dead posh. It looks even better in real life than it did on that telly programme.'

Brooke was terrified to look anywhere other than into her lap, but Dean persisted and even yanked her hand, pulling her up onto her feet. She very reluctantly looked up at the box but her eyes could not help shifting automatically to the box on the left, where she'd been the previous evening. She smiled to herself at the memory and at the ridiculousness of the situation she found herself in, but almost immediately caught sight of Antonia chatting to a party of people, presumably guests of hers again.

Blimey, what a life that woman must lead!

Feeling like a lighthouse, Brooke quickly sat down again but realised she needed to say something that would show Dean how excited she was, or he might suspect something. 'God, this is amazing, Dean. These seats are fab! Mind you, for two hundred and fifty quid, I would hope so! I can't believe we're actually doing this. It's so exciting!' She clapped her hands and Dean smiled a smug, satisfied smile.

The boy done good.

Dean took the opportunity while they were waiting for the curtain to rise, to make some more notes on his phone.

'Dean I wish you'd put your bloody phone away! Look, no one else is looking at their phones. Can't Martin live without your messages for five minutes?' Brooke complained. Dean did as he was told, but was struggling to remember some of the things he had to assess from his seat. He inspected the seats themselves, pushing them up and down a few times before sitting down and then scanning the floor and seats in front for any evidence of litter or lack of cleaning, much to Brooke's bemusement.

'Don't they have any of them binocular things?'

'Do you mean opera glasses?' Brooke replied. Antonia had brought a pair of her own along, which she'd lent Brooke at various points during the performance. 'I think you've gotta bring your own,' Brooke offered casually.

'And how would you know?!' Dean laughed. Brooke scanned the stalls rapidly and nodded over towards two or three other couples nearby who had their own. Dean appeared to accept the explanation.

Then the orchestra commenced, followed a few minutes later by the curtain rising and the wonderful and familiar (at least to Brooke!) scene of the party.

'Christ almighty, look at them geezers in those tights! Their balls look like they've been moulded into them!' Dean's mouth fell open as the male dancers leaped onto the stage showing off their athletic physique and superhuman strength.

Even Dean was able to appreciate the skills of these performers and so remained as fascinated at the spectacle before him, as he had been watching it on television. Brooke was delighted. It gave her real hope that maybe this was something they could do again together in the future; even if they couldn't afford £250 seats, there were clearly cheaper seats available.

They held hands for the whole of the first act. When it came to the 'Dance of The Merlitons,' Dean leaned over to Brooke. 'I know this tune! It's that music on that Cadbury's fruit and nut advert!' Dean exclaimed like a child who'd got a difficult test question correct.

'It's a piece, not a tune, Dean!' Brooke whispered back. Dean squeezed her hand and smiled without averting his eyes from the stage.

The interval came and they were gently swept along with the crowds back to their table in the restaurant. There was a sense of urgency to service, which Dean, who deplored being rushed, was very sensitive to.

'I don't like this feeling of being hurried,' he complained, before tucking into his panna cotta and raspberries with vigour, while Brooke tackled her chocolate tart. Dean stole a piece of it and received a sharp slap on the back of his hand, all noticed by the waiter, who tutted under his breath. The sommelier delivered their chilled glass of dessert wine; a delicious Muscat de Beaumes de Venise Cuvée Les Trois Fonts. By this time, they'd forgotten about their problems and about the cost of the meal and sipped this, their last glass of wine, before their evening ended.

'Oh my god, Dean. This is delicious. What is this stuff? I mean, what type of wine is it?' Even Brooke had not yet had the opportunity to try this exquisite amber liquid before. Dean tried to pronounce the name, but failed miserably, leading them both into a fit of giggles. They spoke in an animated fashion about the ballet and which parts were their favourite, before being recalled back inside the theatre for the second act.

When the opening bars of the dance of the Sugar Plum Fairy were played on the celeste, Brooke's whole body tingled and, without warning, her bottom lip trembled and tears gently flowed down her cheeks; at that moment, overwhelmed at the beauty of it, at the memory of her playing it in the orchestra pit, at the joyfulness of this unusual evening with her husband. She turned to Dean briefly, only to notice that he too looked emotional. She chose to ignore it and simply squeezed his hand. This was all most unexpected!

At the end of the ballet, they stood along with everyone else to clap and show their appreciation. Brooke was prepared for what she knew Dean would do and was already waiting to pounce on him as he put his fingers to his lips. She simply yanked his arm back down, held it there and shook her head with a serious look on her face. It reminded Dean of one of her 'don't even think about arguing' looks, so he resisted and shouted 'bravo' instead.

They left the auditorium and Dean, knowing they couldn't have a drink but needing to make his complaint, walked out via the Amphitheatre bar. As he went straight up to the barman who was washing glasses and tidying up, Brooke became nervous all over again.

'Dean, I don't think the bar's open after the performance.'

'I know and I'm gonna complain about it,' he replied, feeling pumped up and proud.

'What?! You can't. It's their policy. It's not the barman's fault.'

Dean ignored his wife's protestations. 'Scuse me, but can I order some drinks?' Brooke shifted uncomfortably from one foot to another as she kept a constant eye out for Antonia.

'I'm sorry, sir, but the bar is closed.'

'Well that's ridiculous!' he exclaimed loudly.

'Dean!' Brooke mouthed 'Leave it! We don't need another drink.'

Dean continued to take no notice of Brooke, knowing what he had to do.

How well did the staff member deal with your complaint?

The barman said that was the policy and would Dean like to talk to a manager about it? He confirmed that yes he did. Brooke became paranoid that Antonia would be called, although she believed she wouldn't get involved with minor issues like a customer complaint.

'José! Hey, José! Is the boss about? We've got a customer who wants to make a complaint.'

Oh my god, no. Please no!

'OK, I'll go get her,' José replied.

'Dean, I need the loo! Gotta go!' With that she sped off to the nearest ladies and remained seated on the toilet in a cubicle, biting her lip and tugging her curls for at least ten minutes, enough time she hoped for any possible unwanted meeting with Antonia to pass. She eventually came out, furtively looking around and over at Dean who was talking to a woman, who thankfully was not Antonia.

'I think it's crazy! You pay five hundred quid on tickets, another couple of hundred quid on dinner and then you stop people having a drink at the bar after the show! You take our money when it's easy for you, but when we wanna spend it, you don't let us!' Dean had raised his voice considerably by this time. Brooke was now pulling gently on Dean's sleeve and urging him not to worry about it; if he really wanted another drink, they could go somewhere else.

Well she's not doing much to appease me, so she's gonna get a no for handling a complaint well.

Dean waited a moment longer to check if Marie was going to back down. She didn't, so he grabbed Brooke's hand and declared they'd go elsewhere to spend their money. Brooke was embarrassed and so incredibly grateful that Antonia wasn't around to witness Dean's rant.

'I don't know what's got into you tonight. You're being even more anal than usual…and we were having such a nice time.'

'We still are, don't worry, let's forget about it and get home.' As far as Dean was concerned, the assignment was over and it was time to go.

'So you *don't* want another drink then?' Brooke enquired, exasperated at his seemingly fickle mood.

'Nah. Let's go home and have a nice cuppa tea.' Dean stopped in his tracks quite suddenly and turned to face Brooke. 'And, babe? You won't tell the lads about this, will you?'

15

Brooke Makes A Small Confession

On Monday morning, Brooke went into Operation 'OOAO' mode but with a growing unease at the constant lying. Dawn and Stacey both regularly gave her a hard time about it and were convinced that Dean would rather know about her fantastic double life than to be the proud 'keeper' of his wife. When Antonia had asked Brooke to tell her about Dean, Brooke ended up confiding in her; that she'd not told him about her job with Lady Townsend. Antonia was shocked, but understood her reticence. Brooke also revealed that even Mrs Townsend assumed Dean knew.

As Brooke drove to Purses, she tried to imagine what might happen if she revealed all to Dean. Would he get mad? Upset? Divorce her? Demand to know what she'd done with all her money?

He'd never understand in a million years why I'd wanna buy a racehorse – well, the tail anyway.

She sighed as she drove through the black iron gates and parked in the staff car park next to a car she didn't recognise. A beautiful black Porsche 911. She regarded it with curiosity before walking inside to work. Hugo came bounding out to meet her with a striking young woman by his side.

'Morning, Brooke. Let me introduce you to my girlfriend

Portia.' He was beaming. Portia remained where she was, her face an immovable, unfathomable, unemotional canvas. If she could've looked down her nose at Brooke, she'd clearly have done so. As it was, being almost thirty centimetres shorter, she was actually staring up into Brooke's nostrils. Brooke recognised the stylish £300 All Saints silk dress she was wearing, which led to Brooke smoothing down her own slightly creased shirt and jeans. Portia put her hand out for Brooke to shake, but Brooke had to walk over to her to do so. Portia managed a faint snarl rather than a smile.

Well she's got the worst resting bitch face ever.

Brooke did her now infamous bonecrushing handshake and Portia yelped.

That'll serve her right. Bitch.

'I'm guessing that's your car in the staff car park?' Brooke asked with a tad of envy in her voice.

'Yah,' was Portia's sole reply.

'Haha, Portia's got a Porsche!' Brooke exclaimed like a ten-year-old boy.

Hugo laughed out loud while Portia remained steadfastly unmoved facially or physically. She then threw a look over to Hugo. One of those 'does she belong to you?' type looks. Hugo, being a mere man, was incapable of picking up on the tension between the two of them and started explaining that Portia had come to stay with him for a bit. Brooke thought it polite to listen but actually just wanted to get on. Mrs Townsend had given her a big project which she needed to start; to take photographs and catalogue every book in her library and those in the attic for which there was no room.

At that moment Lady Townsend marched in. 'Portia! My

dear! How lovely to see you!' she cried. 'I didn't know you were coming over?' She proceeded to give her an air kiss and Portia's face finally cracked into a smile. For some inexplicable reason Brooke was overcome with jealousy. A feeling so strong she felt nauseous and humiliated, without understanding why.

'Portia, have you been introduced to my wonderful new assistant, Brooke?' Portia glanced over at Brooke and looked her up and down briefly – exactly as the Head Porter at Brooks's had done. Disdain was written all over her face.

'Yah.' Portia turned her back on Brooke and continued. 'Letitia, I've some glorious miniature oils I bought last week at Gagliardi's, which I wanted to show you. I'd simply love your opinion on them. Do you have a minute?'

'Of course. I'd love to see them,' Mrs Townsend replied and the two of them disappeared into the drawing room, leaving Hugo and Brooke alone.

'So what do you think, Brooke? Isn't she lovely?' asked Hugo excitedly. Brooke simply raised her eyebrows and said she had to crack on. As she walked away, her face became red and she could feel tears welling up inside.

Fucking bitch! Why was she like that? She doesn't even know me.

She tried cataloguing the books, but found her mind wandering and she was unable to work. She decided instead to get as far away from Portia as possible and attack the hall floor at the back of the house by the garden. The terracotta tiles were ancient and had apparently been imported from Italy. Like everything in Purses, it required specialist cleaning products. She gathered them together and as she knelt on a cushion to rub the cream in, she found herself thinking about Portia and those tiles got the best scrubbing of their lives! She'd been at it for almost an hour when she heard Mrs Townsend and Portia chatting and laughing coming in her direction.

'I'm just showing Portia the garden, the clematis is looking so marvellous at the moment,' Mrs Townsend said to Brooke as she approached. Lady Townsend opened the door behind Brooke and Portia stepped over her as though she was infected. Despite this, Portia managed to get some of the terracotta cream on her very expensive Jimmy Choo pumps and, with no qualms, asked Brooke, 'Can you wipe that off for me? I don't want to stain my hands.' The fire, rage and humiliation that rose to the surface was almost too much to bear and Brooke's face grew redder than it'd gone in her entire life. Lady Townsend's hawk eyes didn't miss a thing. With all the graciousness that only she could muster, she bent down, took off Portia's shoe, picked up one of the rags and brushes and gently removed the stain. 'There. I think that's done it. We can't have you walking around with orange feet now, can we?' Portia smirked at Brooke, put her shoe back on and walked out into the garden. As Mrs Townsend followed and shut the door behind her she looked at Brooke, gave her a knowing smile and winked! Brooke was stumped. What was all that about? Whatever it was, Mrs Townsend made her feel a tad better and she continued with her work, which was a much bigger job than she'd thought.

About forty-five minutes later, Portia and Lady Townsend came in from the garden. 'Oh, Brooke, you're doing a marvellous job. Those tiles haven't looked that good for years. Thank you so much. Portia, be a dear would you, I have to make a phone call – I'm a bit late as it is – would you please make Brooke a cup of tea? She's been working so hard, it's the least she deserves.'

Portia's robot face now turned to stone as she stuttered, unable to think of a reason why she couldn't do as she was asked. Before she had a chance to come up with one, Brooke smiled at Lady Townsend. 'Thank you.' She then turned to Portia. 'Twining's English Breakfast with milk and one sugar please.' Portia's eyes took on a sort of wild animal appearance before she shot off, suffering heart palpitations on the way at the sheer indignity of having to serve staff. Brooke giggled to herself and could not help wonder if Mrs Townsend knew exactly what she was doing.

That woman's a bloody legend she is.

Portia arrived with the tea, but refused to bend down, so Brooke stood up, took it and managed to be as gracious as Mrs Townsend had taught her to be. 'Thank you so much, Portia. That's very kind of you.' Portia turned round sharply without saying a word and stormed off.

Bitch. If that's what money and education does to you, I'd rather be poor and stupid.

Towards the end of the day, Lady Townsend came to find Brooke before she went home. She was at her computer in the library and so focused on what she was doing that she jumped when Mrs Townsend appeared by her side.

'Oh! You scared me. Sorry, I didn't even see you come in!' Brooke cried. Mrs Townsend sat on the edge of the leather sofa nearby.

'I just wanted to see you before you go, dear. I hope you're alright?'

'Why wouldn't I be?'

'Brooke. I'm not stupid. I'm a woman and an observant one at that. I can feel tension between people. That was not so much as being able to cut it with a knife as to feel a bomb was about to explode.'

'I'm sorry, Mrs T. But that girl is a f…not a very nice person.' Brooke was so very proud of her ability to control what came out of her mouth at that second!

'I know, dear. She's a stuck-up entitled, snob and I can't bear her.' Brooke's mouth fell open before she burst out laughing. 'Oh, Mrs T, you're so funny! You acted like she was a long-lost friend of yours!'

'I've met her a few times, but I'm only polite to her because she's Hugo's girlfriend. Otherwise, I wouldn't give her the time of day!' she replied.

'I don't know how you do it. I struggled to even thank her for the tea. Did you ask her to do that on purpose?' Brooke asked.

Lady Townsend took on a face of mock shock and surprise and said, 'I don't know what you mean!' and then winked again. Brooke giggled and it was as though a horrid black cloud had been lifted from her. She realised that her relationship with Mrs Townsend was turning into a slightly complicated one. Part boss, part mentor, part friend, part mother. All she knew is that she felt relieved. Any female competition for her time and affection had been demolished. She didn't even feel the same level of affection for her own mother and she pondered on why that might be.

All Mum cares about is that me and Paige look good. She's never actually…taught me anything. She's never done anything to develop me. She's probably the reason I haven't got any hinterland in the first place!

Lady Townsend looked at her affectionately and then said, 'I spoke to Antonia yesterday.' Brooke shifted uncomfortably in her chair.

'Oh, what did she say?' she asked nervously.

'She reiterated what a wonderful evening it was on Friday and how much she'd enjoyed your company again. She was thrilled you enjoyed it so much. She mentioned the…how shall I put it?…enlightening conversation you had about your husband Dean.' Brooke's face fell to the floor. 'I wish you'd have told me before that he didn't know you worked here. Heaven knows how you've managed to keep it secret all these months!'

'I'm so sorry, Mrs T. I didn't think you needed to know. I thought it might complicate things. I suffer from high blood pressure and have to be a bit careful, that's all, but he's really overprotective and doesn't want me to work because of it. I was worried you'd think I wouldn't be able to clean if I told you.'

'Well, you are a dark horse, young lady! You never cease to surprise me. But many people have high blood pressure and manage to work perfectly well.'

'Exactly! But he's terrified something'll happen to me, so he put his foot down. He does kind of worship the ground I walk on, if you know what I mean.'

'I can imagine. But where on earth does he think you go on the days you work here?'

'Oh god, I'm almost too embarrassed to tell you. I've told him so many lies. He obviously knows you exist, 'cause you sent that champagne for my birthday last year – that was so difficult to explain, so I told him we met in the library.'

'Well that's true, just not the town library!' Lady Townsend declared triumphantly.

'Hahaha! That's exactly what made me come out with it! So, anyway, he thinks I see you there and that we've become sort of…friends.' Brooke curled her toes up inside her shoes in shame. 'Most of the time he doesn't even ask what I've been doing or where I've been with Paige and when he does, I tell him shopping, or going to the park, or mum and toddler groups – anything really. He's only been suspicious a few times, but sometimes it's been really hard. Going to the ballet on Friday was so difficult, I can't tell you.'

'Well, it certainly explains why you can't get here any earlier and need to leave on time!'

Brooke's head dropped forward and she stared into her lap. Ashamed.

'I'm assuming he doesn't know about Turn The Paige either?'

'God, no! He'd think I'd gone nuts! He's a very…basic sort of bloke. He doesn't want much in life but to make me and Paige happy, but I've changed and he just doesn't get it. He can't understand why I suddenly seem to want more than he can give me. And I don't mean "stuff", I mean new experiences and learning about things; that's why I love coming here so much.'

Lady Townsend looked on sympathetically, but with an element of disquiet. She didn't approve of Brooke not telling Dean about her job, but on the other hand if by doing so, it meant that she might lose Brooke altogether, she didn't want that either. She too was now in a bit of a pickle.

There was only one thing for it. A nice glass of sherry for them both.

16

Dean's Boxercise Class

A couple of weeks or so after 'the ballet weekend', Brooke received an email from Lord D'Arcy. She sensed his excitement through the screen. It was all so very formal and...well...so very Geoffrey!

Dear Brooke,

It gives me great pleasure to inform you that Turn The Paige will be running in the Bunbury Cup on July 12th – that's Ladies Day – at 3pm at Newmarket on the July course! How wonderful that will be for you; to see her race where you joined our syndicate and bought her tail!

We will have a splendid day! We must meet soon to discuss the detail. I imagine Blessington, Letitia and Antonia will all want to be there. I'd like for us all to stay at The Jockey Club Rooms, so no one has to worry about not being able to have a drink or two and hurrying back home. Could you manage that, do you think? I'm jolly well hoping we'll be celebrating!

Such fun! Be in touch soon – just wanted to let you know the date ASAP.

Yours faithfully
Geoffrey

PS – Please don't forget you're welcome to visit Ingatestone Hall at any time.

Brooke cupped her hand over her mouth in a mix of shock and unbridled excitement and put the date and time in her diary. She immediately began the emotionally draining task of figuring out how she could pull this particularly challenging weekend off without Dean knowing. As she was thinking about it, her phone went. It was Dean. This time, she picked up, despite being at Purses. A first! And a nervous one at that.

What if he asks to speak to Paige?

'Hey, babe!' Brooke answered.

'Bloody hell, you actually answered! Just letting you know I'm gonna go back to the gym tonight to interview Peregrine again.' Dean's voice sounded odd. 'All this faffing about just to get a pomo on board. It's unbelievable. He'd better accept after all this.'

'Oh right. OK. God, it's so much hassle. I hope Dave's appreciating all this extra time and work you're putting in. We'll eat a bit later then. 'bout eight-ish?'

'Dave don't care. As far as he's concerned, I'm paid to do a job and it don't matter how long it takes. Yeah that's cool. Love ya, babe. See you later.'

There was something far less furtive about being able to actually answer her phone freely, now that Mrs Townsend knew and understood her little secret, instead of fumbling about with messages and trying to turn her phone off.

She went back to her library cataloguing, which she was thoroughly enjoying and learning a huge amount along the way. She'd derived particular pleasure from some of the titles she'd discovered in the attic. *The Female Eunch* looked interesting, along with *Bombproof your Horse*. *Outwitting Squirrels* she felt would be worth at least a cursory glance. She looked up the word eunuch: 'a castrated man placed in charge of a harem or employed as a chamberlain in a palace'.

Mmm, how can it be a female eunuch if a eunuch is a bloke? And when would you ever need to outwit a squirrel?

Such intellectual questions tested Brooke's powers of thinking to the limits, but she pushed on regardless and discovered many other arcane titles.

These are crazy! Who reads this stuff?

Every so often Newmarket came into her mind, making certain she could never entirely relax.

What am I gonna do?

***

Dean arrived at his compulsory SweatUBet Boxercise class with an instructor called Jo. This'd been one part of the mystery visit he'd not been looking forward to in the slightest. Boxing wasn't his thing and he'd certainly never have chosen to do it. Still, he'd already enjoyed the benefits of agreeing! His mind wandered back to the wonderful night he'd enjoyed with Brooke at the ballet. That report had taken him six hours to write up. He still hadn't heard anything back from Angie at Sonny Global about it, which worried him a little, because she almost always phoned him to thank him for his extensive reports. Maybe he'd gone too far with his complaint episode?

Anyhow, he arrived at the gym studio a few minutes early and was the first person there. He observed a female instructor setting up and immediately realised he must've gone to the wrong studio, so he walked into the one next door where another instructor appeared to be packing up. Dean shouted over, 'Scuse me, mate, which studio is the Boxercise class in?'

'Next door, mate. It's with Jo. She's just arrived, I think.'

'Oh. I assumed Jo was a bloke.'

'Nah, mate. Mind you, she punches like one!' the instructor said.

A woman?! Surely not? How will that work? That's gotta be dangerous, surely?

Dean moved back to outside studio two and peered through the small window watching Jo for a minute. He was horrified at the thought of being taught how to box by this diminutive woman. In fact, he palpitated as he found himself opening the door for a stream of women walking into the studio.

I thought this was for blokes!

He paced around nervously outside for a few minutes, dreading going in. It got to almost 6.30pm and he knew he had to get a grip and enter. As he did so, all the ladies turned around. He ignored them and marched up to Jo explaining that he thought it was a class for men. She responded saying it was a mixed class but often there were more women than men, but that it didn't matter; he was welcome whatever. She handed him a pair of pads and asked him to partner up, but there were odd numbers so she said she'd be his boxing partner on this occasion. Dean's face dropped.

How can I punch her? She's tiny!

Jo ignored the worried look on Dean's face and proceeded to instruct the class to warm up.

Before the class started, did the instructor ensure they asked you if you had any injuries or medical conditions?

Mmm, no.

Did the instructor give a thorough warm-up before beginning any boxing exercises?

The warm-up was wholly inadequate, being just a game of 'it'; like school children play in the playground. Even Dean knew from his football that one had to make sure all muscles were stretched. She didn't do any of that and, quite frankly, he was shocked, although given the less- than-satisfactory assessment he'd carried out of the induction, he shouldn't have been.

No wonder they want this one assessed.

Before long he found himself with his padded hands up in front of his face. Jo explained she wanted right hooks followed by left hooks for thirty seconds and then demonstrated, in case any newbies didn't know what that meant. Dean was almost literally gobsmacked as he staggered backwards while Jo was punching his pads. He had to put his entire body weight forward in order to stop himself falling back. They swapped and then it was his turn. He shuddered as he slid his hands into the wet gloves. He couldn't bring himself to go too hard so punched away pretty lightly.

Did the instructor speak professionally throughout the class?

'C'mon, you fucking fairy!' Jo screamed. 'PUNCH!' The ladies in the class roared laughing.

Absolutely not!

Dean was mortified, but decided it was more than his life was worth to disobey her. So he did his manly best and punched as if his life depended on it. Ten seconds of that and he was perspiring like he'd spent the day in Death Valley.

'C'mon another ten seconds, you lot, you can do it!' Jo laughed at the sweat pouring profusely down his face. 'If you can't manage another ten seconds, you'll have to do ten press-ups, you big girl's blouse!' Jo shouted at Dean. The ladies laughed again and Dean was propelled into action for another ten seconds but was feeling rather sick. He hadn't worked this hard physically in his entire life! Then, thank heavens – a thirty-second rest. This regime went on for several minutes until Dean could take no more and collapsed onto the floor. Football suddenly seemed like rambling. The class was stopped while Jo stood over him as a gladiator might, in a position of victory over his opponent. She laughed. 'OK, Dean, take five and then re-join. Just watch Dinah over there. You could pick up a few tips from her.' Dinah was a large black woman in her thirties who looked as mean as they come.

Dean watched Dinah pummel the living daylights out of the pads, which were held by Jane, a young feeble-looking girl with limbs like spaghetti who looked like she was allergic to everything. He got his breath back, drank some water and got back up, feeling somewhat shaky. The feeble girl then took the gloves and returned the compliment, remaining as white as photocopier paper.

How can she possibly stay white after that?

Dean mentally pulled himself together and stated he was ready to come back in. 'OK, Dean, you go with Dinah now and I'll go with Jane.' Dean gulped as he strolled towards Dinah, who was looking delighted at the prospect of destroying this imperfect male specimen. She reminded him a little of Brooke, but bigger…and blacker of course. But there was something about the glint in her eye and the smile on her face that made him feel that he was about to be decimated. She put her hands on her hips and cackled in that unique way - full of pure unadulterated joy! He nervously put on the gloves first and for thirty seconds performed upper cuts to the right and then to the left pads. Frank Bruno would've wept at his appalling form – stance square on instead of side on, head down instead of up, but Jo was too busy abusing spaghetti limbs to notice. A hippo would've been proud of Dean's purple broccoli face colouring and perspiration, and it spurred mean girl Dinah on to stand like an immovable statue, the punches to her pads barely registering. She cackled once more. Then the moment he was dreading; they swapped so he had the pads.

What's she gonna do to me?

Inside, he prayed to him upstairs that he would be saved. He was so nervous he kept shifting the pads to try and ensure he was as protected as possible.

'Keep your pads in the same place, man! Stop movin' them about!' Dinah shouted at him. As he made one last adjustment to his right pad position and ducked, Dinah had already swung and within a split second a loud thud reverberated around the class and Dean fell to the floor.

'That weren't my fault! 'e kept movin'!' Dinah screamed. For a few seconds Dean lay motionless; dazed and confused at what'd just happened. Jo rushed over.

'OK, big boy, let's sit you out. Ladies, please carry on for a few minutes with our usual exercises. Dinah, you use the bag.' Jo helped Dean to sit up and examined his eye. 'Oh gawd, that's gonna be a beauty in the morning!' she laughed.

If you had any difficulties in the class, was the instructor sympathetic and reassuring?

No, she damn well wasn't. Nil points!

'Well thanks for the information,' Dean replied sarcastically.

'Nah! You'll be alright. I've seen far worse.' She plucked a used tissue from her leggings and blotted the blood coming from a small, deep split under his right eye. She took a slightly closer look, but declared it wasn't deep enough to warrant stitches.

Did you see or experience first aid being administered appropriately?

The worst ever! She should be sacked on the spot!

'Right, Dean. Well, I gotta get on with the class. I think its best you don't re-join tonight. You can sit and watch if you like.' With that Jo got up and carried on the rest of the class. Rarely had Dean been so discombobulated. He looked up to see a dozen pair of female eyes on him. They all quickly averted their gaze as he did so and spaghetti limbs looked as if she were about to burst into tears. It occurred to Dean that maybe that's why she was there; to learn how to protect herself and assert her authority physically. He doubted it could ever work. She could've been steam-rollered by a sparrow. He couldn't decide what to do for the best. He knew in his heart he ought to just go home, but the humiliation of walking out was too much to bear. So, he stayed. And watched Dinah pummel away even more furiously than before. He feared for all her boxing partners. All the ladies expressed concern for him, said they hoped he'd be OK and that they'd hopefully see him next week.

Over my fucking dead body!

Jo packed up her bags, marched across the floor, offering a last bit of advice on the way out: 'Lots of ice, Dean – or bags of peas or sweetcorn on your eye. Get the swelling down.'

Did the instructor file a report in the accident report book if appropriate?

'Don't you have to report this in some sort of accident book?' Dean asked.

'Well, if you'd been knocked out or had to go to hospital I probably would've done, but nah, not much point. You'll be fine. Sorry, Dean, gotta go, I gotta date tonight. See you next week.' With that, she left.

Well fuck me.

***

Dean checked his eye in the mirror.

Shit! What the hell am I gonna tell Brooke?

He was meant to be interviewing someone. How can you get a black eye interviewing someone? He showered quickly, carrying out all his usual inspections for his report at lightning speed; damn pleased to never have to go back!

He rode home seething and in some pain. As he got closer to home, he slowed down; unable to decide what he was going to say to Brooke. He pulled over, took his helmet off and opened a small vanity mirror he carried in his rucksack and checked his eye again.

Bloody hell! It looks like I've been in a fight.

His eye had begun to close and the skin around it'd become red and swollen; it looked exactly like one Porno Gazza'd given him once after they'd had a heavy night in The Hungry Horse. Dean was mad enough to suggest that no woman would want to watch him in any porn film. Gazza had lashed out in a rage and punched him full-on. This eye was going the same way – black. He rode the rest of the way home slowly, becoming more and more panicky about Brooke's reaction. He unlocked the front door and walked gingerly into the lounge as Brooke came out of the kitchen.

'Oh my god, Dean! What the hell happened? Your eye! It looks terrible!'

'Don't even ask!' Dean said as he put up his hand, hoping naively to halt all conversation.

'So what happened?' she persisted. Dean stuttered, before coming out with the only thing he could think of under such intense pressure.

'He hit me.'

'Who hit you?'

'Peregrine.'

'What? The pomo you were interviewing? What the hell? Why?' Brooke asked, utterly shocked and bemused.

'Didn't like something I said, it seemed.'

Brooke didn't do half buckets of information. She wanted the whole kit and caboodle.

'Hang on a minute, let me get some ice and then you can tell me all about it,' she retorted. Dean groaned inwardly. More improvised fabrication required. Brooke came back with some ice cubes wrapped in a tea towel and gently placed it over his eye.

'So what on earth did you say that annoyed him so much?' Brooke asked while pressing the ice pack on his eye.

'I asked him…very nicely, if there was anything I needed to know, as his would be line manager, anything I might need to do or provide for…you know…someone like him.'

'And what did he say?'

'He just got up and said he wasn't some kind of freak and punched me across the table. Then he walked out.'

'No! You're kidding? I thought they were…you know…all fur and feathers – not fists and fighting!'

'Please do not tell anyone about this, Brooke. I could get into trouble if someone thinks I asked him a dodgy question.'

'Course, babe. I wouldn't. You poor thing! Are you gonna take it further?' Dean wanted the conversation to stop. He wished with all his might that he hadn't made up that particular lie, that he could've thought on his feet a bit quicker and come up with an explanation that would've been easier to draw a line under. But there it was. Brooke was suitably appalled and had one of those looks about her that convinced Dean she was about to go on one of her missions.

'I'd like to go round there myself and punch his lights out,' Brooke said, forgetting her language and decorum momentarily and returning to Essex girl fighting mode, whilst at the same time becoming so agitated that she pressed harder on Dean's eye, making him yelp.

'Anyway, I don't wanna talk about it. I'm well pissed off and I just wanna forget about it.'

'Where are you gonna get another pomo from though? There can't be too many of them about, I wouldn't have thought.'

'Dunno, but I've managed to get a Hindu with learning difficulties – Darpan; a bit of an odd bloke, but I thought there's bound to be something I can find for him to do. I might forget trying to get another pomosexual. I got three black people – or should I say people of colour, on one day! One from Canning Town – and he's one of them Evangelical Christians – wouldn't stop banging on about his church's gospel choir being on *X Factor*. The other two girls were friends from Notting Hill; they've done stuff for the Notting Hill Carnival – pretty cool as it goes. We ought to go there one year.' He was so relieved to get off the subject of Peregrine.

Brooke looked thoughtful and wiped away the ice-cold water dripping down Dean's face and onto his shirt.

'Well it sounds like you're doing a pretty good job without a pomo, so I'd forget about it if I were you.'

'Just did. Now, where's my tea, woman?!' Dean shouted in mock indignation.

'We'll eat on our laps tonight. Maybe a hot tub later?' she winked at him. 'Gotta take your mind off your injury somehow.'

Dean laughed and let out a slow, controlled breath as Brooke shimmied into the kitchen.

17

Brooke and Jackie's Day Out

A couple of weeks later, Brooke's mother arrived at Elephant Close for her and Brooke's weekly day out together. For the first time ever, Brooke had no desire to go shopping in Bluewater whatsoever. To do any shopping at all, in fact. She was much more interested in going somewhere a little more…how shall we say…cultural? Fear of being laughed at, along with possible outright rejection of the idea, prevented her from suggesting anything. But her mother knew her daughter well and sensed that she wasn't too keen.

'Well, we could go Lakeside instead if you like. I just thought you might wanna go somewhere different for a change.'

Brooke grasped the opportunity that had unwittingly been handed to her on a plate. 'Actually, Mum, I would like to go somewhere a bit different. But not shopping. How d'ya fancy going to a museum?'

Jackie's mouth fell open. Looking at her face, one would think she'd been asked to torture a small baby.

'What d'ya wanna go to a museum for?' It was posed in the same way as if Brooke had suggested she throw out all her nail varnishes; she looked genuinely perplexed. Brooke remained steadfast in her resolve not to be made to feel like it was a ludicrous idea.

'Like you said. Something different. There's a museum I've read about in Dedham, about an hour away; The Munning's Art museum. He painted a lot of horses, but there's other stuff there too apparently.'

Jackie continued to stare at Brooke like she'd just discovered she wasn't her daughter. 'But why?' Jackie asked, still highly confused.

'I'm getting the feeling you're not exactly keen, Mum,' Brooke said, feeling irritated.

Jackie picked up on it straight away and didn't want to spoil their day out together, so she swallowed hard and agreed, trying to sound chirpy.

'Well, if that's what you wanna do, love, we'll do it. Not sure it'll be my cup of tea and Paige might get a bit bored, but let's give it a go, eh?' she said. Paige'd had a quick nap and Brooke got her up and dressed while she screamed as though her mother was putting needles into her eyes. Brooke had recently bought some earplugs and had begun to use them for times such as this and as soon as Paige started, she thrust them in hard which had the immediate pleasant effect of dulling the noise.

'My god, that girl can scream, Brooke. Where's your Chupa Chups?' Jackie shouted, trying to hold her ears. Brooke had to remove one of her earplugs first, in order to hear her mother.

'Ah. Run out. Waiting for a box to be delivered. Let's hope madam behaves herself.' They finished getting ready and put Paige in the car. This simple act, which should take about ten seconds, had become increasingly difficult over the last few months. As Paige had got older, she behaved like a little Houdini. Not only had she developed a back arch as strong and unbendable as a titanium rod, but often, after she'd been strapped in, by the time her mother had got round to the front and belted up herself, the little devil had escaped and would crawl about in the footwell with the discarded crisp packets and old apple cores. It was exasperating.

'Mum, do us a favour, would you? You couldn't sit in the back with Paige and stop her getting out her car seat?' Brooke asked, becoming a tad irritated. Jackie did as she was asked and spent most of the car journey trying to distract Paige from being so fixated on escape. They played 'let's put lipstick on like Mummy' for which she used her own Avon 'rose pink'. Brooke and Jackie chatted away in the car and, before long, they'd arrived in Dedham and followed signposts to the museum.

They parked, then Paige was firmly strapped into her pushchair with a five point clasp, grasping a little colouring pad with some crayons to keep her occupied, so Brooke and Jackie could enjoy a stress-free visit. They made their way to the entrance.

It's the same banana yellow colour as the yellow room in Wimpole Hall and Flora!

'Blimey, twelve quid! That's a bit steep!' exclaimed Jackie when she saw the entrance fees. 'Just to look at a few pictures!' Brooke hadn't even thought to look at the prices. She'd only read about how wonderful the museum was and determined she'd go there, especially having now been to The Jockey Club Rooms and learned so much about the artwork there.

'They're paintings, Mum, not pictures.' Brooke corrected her.

'Whatever, it's a bit pricey, love.'

'Well, I'll pay. I don't mind,' Brooke retorted. It felt so good to know she actually had money of her own. It gave her a sense of power and control that she very rarely experienced.

'No, you can't do that, Brooke. You can't afford it and you know it. Here, let me.' And Jackie went to get her purse out her bag.

'Absolutely not!' Brooke cried, holding her hand up like a stop sign.

God, that sounded just like Mrs T!

'I can afford it, as it goes. I've got some savings now, so no, I'll pay and that's the end of it. It was my idea.' Brooke smiled as her mother looked on with a worried face when Brooke took out a large wad of notes from her new Mulberry handbag. (Unlike overflowing rubbish bins or smears on a wine glass, her handbag was simply not the sort of thing Dean would ever notice.) Jackie raised her eyebrows and frowned as Brooke flicked out forty pounds from the wad; plenty left over she observed, feeling slightly uneasy.

They were greeted, given a very brief overview, advice as to how to make their way around the museum and told about the cafe, which they decided they'd visit first. They ordered a pot of 'Good Old Breakfast Tea' for two and toasted teacakes. Jackie insisted on paying and Brooke graciously accepted.

'Well, this is nice, love!' Jackie said as she looked around the cafe. 'I've never been anywhere like this. In fact, I'd never even heard of it – or Alfie Munnings. How d'ya know about it?'

'It's Albert Munnings, Mum; Sir Albert Munnings,' Brooke corrected again.

'Oooh, just listen to you!' Jackie teased.

'You know I get *Country Homes and Gardens* sometimes? There was an article about it in there. It sounded interesting and there was something about the paintings of his horses that appealed to me. Dunno what, exactly,' she lied.

'Right, well I'll have to see then. I don't know nothing about horses, except people ride 'em!'

'And race 'em!' Brooke added naughtily, feeling a teeny bit thrilled as her secret knowledge was performing somersaults inside her!

They enjoyed their tea and Brooke fed Paige pieces of teacake, which she gobbled down messily then went back to her colouring. After their tea, they made their way into the first room. Brooke wandered off leaving her mother to push Paige, but Jackie didn't mind and every so often would point to a painting to show Paige.

'Look. Horsey! Say Horsey, Paige! Horsey! Horsey!'

'Hawseeeee!' Paige managed, creating delight on the face of her grandmother.

'Horse. Not horsey!' Brooke said casually. She was suddenly aware that was the third time she'd picked her mother up on the way she spoke. It was becoming a habit.

Jackie called Brooke over to a male nude, which seemed hidden in a small nook. 'Blimey, Brooke, come and look at this! I bet he makes the girls happy!' she cackled crudely. 'And have you noticed your Mr Munnings actually liked gypsies?! There's loads of paintings of 'em. Still, they never had a Dale Farm in those days, did they? Lucky them.'

Making their way up the wooden staircase, on the top floor, Brooke noticed a stuffed Pekingese in a glass cabinet and peered at it intensely. She was surprised to read that Lady Munnings had carried this dog with her absolutely everywhere, making her realise that the current trend for carrying chihuahuas in one's handbag was probably nothing new. *Oh my gawd, poor little thing!*

When they came to *Under Starter's Orders*, a detailed painting of horses preparing for the start of their race, they both examined the detail and even Jackie commented on how remarkable the work was. How lifelike it looked. She and Brooke picked out small details and discussed them; the silk fabric of the jockeys' shirts, the way the light caught the glimmering sweaty bodies of the horses and boots so shiny that one could almost feel the hard polished leather. As they talked, they could hear Paige happily chattering away to herself, but at one point Brooke became aware that the direction from where the chatter came had changed. She glanced over to the pushchair behind her, and, to her absolute horror, it was empty.

'Paige, where are you, you little devil?' Brooke shouted, oblivious to a couple close by in deep discourse over *Pigs in Great Thurlow*.

She ran into the room next door and there Paige stood, in front of a large painting: *Lady Seated in a Park*. Paige was looking terribly pleased with herself and Brooke went over to her and bent down.

'Did Paige like the pretty lady then?' Brooke asked her daughter in her 'Mummy' voice, endearingly trying to engage her in a chat about art. She turned to see which painting had taken her fancy and gasped loudly as she put her hand to her mouth, eyes bulging.

Oh fuck, fuck, fuck!

Paige pointed at the lady in the painting and gabbled excitedly, whilst pointing at her own lips 'listi, listi!'

The lady had taken on a rather different face to that which Sir Alfred had painted. Her lips were scrawled over with a red crayon making it look as though someone had taped over her mouth to keep it shut. Paige then pointed to her own eyes, 'Dada, Dada grasses, grasses' and then back to the painting. Brooke suddenly became aware that a chair was positioned – like a personal invitation to Paige to climb it – right next to one side of the painting. With one hand over her mouth, Brooke quickly stepped over to examine the canvas more closely.

Oh my god! She must have climbed up onto the chair!

There, super imposed on the lady's delicate eyes, were a rather bent and uneven pair of glasses in white crayon – faint but most definitely there.

'Paige! What have you done? You *naughty* girl! You're gonna go in the naughty corner when we get home!' Brooke pointed and stabbed her finger as she shouted at her, utterly beside herself, unable to control her anger and despair, her mother following close behind, scared and unsure how to react to this desecration, this act of vandalism by her two-year-old granddaughter. Brooke burst into tears, followed in quick succession by Paige.

'Brooke, calm down. I'm sure they'll understand. She's only a littlun. They must get things like this happen all the time! I'll go find someone.' Jackie dashed off into the distance.

Brooke roughly put Paige back in her pushchair and noticed the five point clasp still in place. The angelic-looking toddler must have squeezed and twisted her little body until she'd extricated herself. Brooke slumped onto the chair, head in hands and continued to sob, her stomach in knots. She was petrified. These paintings were worth tens or even hundreds of thousands.

Within a few minutes, Jackie was back in the room with

a rather stern-looking man in tow. He immediately reminded Brooke of the hotel manager at Claridge's, who'd assumed she was a prostitute plying her trade in the lobby – a common problem, Geoffrey had tried to reassure her.

'Good morning Mrs De'Ath. I'm John Smythe, director of the museum. I understand there's been an accident with one of our paintings. Perhaps you'd like to show me?'

Brooke gulped and stood up. Never before had she felt like such a naughty girl; one who was going to be given detention. She nervously pointed to the lady with the lipstick and glasses. John Smythe surveyed it, giving Brooke the impression that he required more precision from her as to where the issue was, so she pointed to the lips and then to the eyes.

'It was an accident, I'm so sorry. She managed to escape her pushchair and before I knew it, she'd done this. I don't know what to say.' Brooke was clearly distraught and spoke hurriedly but with sincerity.

'Yes, I can see clearly where the problem is,' he said. He moved closer to the painting and examined the affected areas for some minutes before licking his finger with his own spittle and gently rubbing the 'glasses'. All the while Jackie and Brooke were visibly holding their breath.

'Mmm,' he offered. He then did the same to the 'lipstick'. Brooke and Jackie shot a look at each other, frowning and mouths open. Paige sucked her thumb innocently, looking for all the world like one of those cherubs in church paintings the world over.

'Well, I'll have to get our conservator over to take a look, but I think you may be lucky. It looks as though the crayons your daughter used can be removed without damaging the painting, but I'll need that to be confirmed.'

'Oh, thank god for that!' Brooke wanted to hug him.

'Well, it's not guaranteed, but, in the meantime, I'll need to take your contact details and we'll get back to you to let you know the outcome.' Brooke could barely bring herself to ask the inevitable question.

'What if they say it won't come off?' Brooke asked, simply terrified of the financial implications.

'Let's cross that bridge when we come to it, mm? But whatever the outcome, I'm afraid I will have to ask you to pay for the conservator's visit,' he said, not unkindly. 'And may I suggest that if you bring a child into the museum again, that you do not bring colouring crayons in as an accompaniment?'

Brooke looked down in shame. Naughty girl!

It was a stupid idea. Didn't even think about it.

Brooke gave all her details to the director and they left the museum, tails between their legs, feeling shaken by the experience and Brooke absolutely worried sick about the consequences for her.

***

The next day at work, Brooke went about her business more quietly than usual, not engaging in conversation with Hugo and steering clear of Portia, who would insist on hanging around Purses instead of staying in Hugo's cottage. The last thing she needed was that wretched girl getting her all worked up. She continued to catalogue the books in the attic, where it was nice and quiet but she worked with a horrid foreboding continually present. She felt a bit sick and hadn't slept at all well the previous night. She'd told Dean about what happened at the museum and he'd gone into complete panic mode, pacing up and down the lounge, chastising her for being so stupid as to take colouring pens into an art museum.

He's only thinking about his bloody wallet!

Suddenly Mrs Townsend appeared at the bottom of the stairs to the attic and shouted up, as much as it was possible for Lady Townsend to shout. 'Brooke, dear, are you alright up there? You haven't been down all morning? Would you like a cup of tea?'

Brooke came down the stairs covered in dust, looking rather pale and dishevelled; not her usual groomed appearance.

'Are you alright, Brooke, you look very pale, dear?' Mrs Townsend asked her, looking concerned. She didn't expect what came next. Brooke burst into tears, sobbing into her hands, unable to speak for several minutes. Lady Townsend hadn't ever had to deal with anything like this and was rather stumped as to what the form was for such an occurrence. She gently put her arm around her back before asking very tenderly, 'Whatever is it, Brooke? What's happened?'

Brooke went on to tell her about the disastrous visit to the museum. Instead of embarking on a lecture about the dangers of Crayola in an art gallery, which Brooke had fully expected, Mrs Townsend simply asked, 'Did he say what the name of his conservator was?'

'No. Why?' Brooke managed to ask through her crying.

'Don't you worry about it dear. Leave it with me. Between Geoffrey and I, we know most of the conservators around here. I'll do a bit of research, but I'm sure it'll be fine. From what you said, he thinks its fixable and, even if it's not, they do have insurance for such matters.' Then, as an afterthought, she added, 'Poor little mite. She didn't know what she was doing was wrong, did she? She just saw a lady without lipstick and that wouldn't do, would it?!'

Brooke managed a laugh. 'I hadn't thought about it that way.'

Lady Townsend smiled and urged her again not to worry. Before she left, she asked 'Did you enjoy the museum by the way? It's one of my favourites.'

'Yes. It was great, although Mum didn't really get it I don't think, if you know what I mean. We normally go shopping. She looked at me like I had two heads when I said I wanted us to go to a museum for a change. It's hard, you know? I always feel like I've got to battle with everyone, explain to everyone – 'cept you of course – to be allowed to even *want* to do something apart from shopping!'

'Well done you! Stick to your guns! Increase that hinterland!' She punched her arm and fist in defiance like Nelson Mandela, and then left the room. It made Brooke laugh out loud. It was such an 'un-Lady Townsend like' thing to do!

The nasty grey thundercloud that had been hovering over her for the best part of eighteen hours suddenly disappeared. Lady Townsend had a way of always making Brooke feel reassured. Not like her mother, who'd regrettably spent the entire car journey home from the museum on her phone, trying to find out the value of the now-vandalised painting and informing her daughter that Dean wasn't going to be very happy about it. Lady Townsend was always so calm. So collected. So…in control and unflustered about everything.

I wish I could be like that.

She continued to beaver away in the attic when her phone went.

Heard from that conservatory geezer yet?

No. Conservator. Not conservatory! That's the bit on our house with all the glass in it!!!

Whatever. Felt sick 2 day. Couldnt even eat my sarni. Hope he rings today.

Me too. What makes you think it's a bloke?

Good point. Dunno. What you up to?

Brooke's familiar sense of fear rose again. She prayed he'd be too busy to pursue her for long and decided to change tack; a strategy she'd been taught to use with Paige by the nice ladies at the NCT mum and toddler group. Distraction.

Not much. Heard anything from the pomo?

Dean went cold all over, suddenly being forced to remember his worst lie to date. He now wanted to stop the messaging. Immediately.

No. Nothing. Gotta go. Got a meeting. C U later.

Brooke relaxed.

Phew!

At just before 4.30pm, Brooke packed up and went to leave Purses. As she pulled away in her car, she observed Lady Townsend walking quickly towards her, waving at her to stop. Brooke did so and got out the car.

'Is everything alright, Mrs T?'

'Yes, dear. I just wanted to let you know that Geoffrey's tracked down the conservator. He's pretty sure he's the same chap as he uses. He said he'd contact him and have a word and to tell you not to worry. Either way, he'll get back to you, hopefully by the end of the day. I hope you don't mind, but I gave him your mobile number. I just thought you'd want to know straight away.'

Oh god, I'm not sure that was a good idea.

'Of course not, Mrs Townsend. That's absolutely fine. Thank you.'

Shit! He'd better not try and make a pass at me again.

***

That evening, as Brooke and Dean had sat down to watch *Made in Chelsea NYC,* Brooke's mobile rang. She looked at the number and didn't recognise it, only that it was local and a landline. She was torn between answering it, in case it was Lord D'Arcy, and desperately wanting to know the outcome from the conservator. Dean urged her to pick up, praying it *was* the conservator!

'Hallo?'

'Brooke, sweetheart, I'm so glad I've caught you.' It was Geoffrey, booming as was his wont. Brooke felt her knees begin to tremble. Dean was watching her intensely, waiting to hear the news.

'Oh hello,' she replied without emotion.

'You'll be delighted to know that Joshua Crick, my conservator, is indeed the same chap they use at Munnings.' He waited for her to respond, but Brooke was trying to say as little as possible, knowing that Dean was thinking that it was the actual conservator she was talking to!

'And what does that mean?' Brooke replied. Dean frowned.

'Well, we've had a chat before he's even gone to see the damage and he's pretty sure that it's going to be fine. He gets plenty of work from me, so I've told him to ensure that it definitely *is* fine, if you know what I mean. Nod nod wink wink and all that, eh?!'

Brooke felt a mix of relief and concern that she'd seemingly forced a blackmail situation. 'Well that sounds positive.' Again, marvellously lacking in intonation, like she'd become a zombie.

Geoffrey was rather put out by Brooke's neutral tone. He'd assumed she'd be happy as Larry. 'Well, I must say, I thought you'd be a bit more enthusiastic about it. That painting is worth around £50,000, you know.'

'Oh my god!' Brooke couldn't contain herself and her face fell. It slipped out. Dean looked panic-stricken.

'What? Brooke! What is it?' Dean wailed loudly. Brooke put a finger in her free ear to drown out his noise.

'Who's that shouting?' Geoffrey asked.

'Oh that's my husband. Sorry he's a bit worried.'

'Well please tell Dean from me, not to be concerned. While you're on, are you able to come over to Ingatestone Hall next week? There's a few things I need to go through with you about Turn The Paige. What day would be best for you?' Brooke was stumped and, as usual, couldn't think on her feet fast enough.

'Mmm…mmm…OK then, why not, er…how about next Tuesday morning?' Brooke replied anxiously, her mind racing with all the possible ways Dean might be interpreting this. Dean's face was one of confusion. He continued to hang on Brooke's every word and watch her facial expressions for clues as to their financial liability. By this time, he'd taken on a very 'Brooke' mannerism, which was to shrug his shoulders with his palms facing upwards as if to say 'what the hell's going on?'

'Splendid. That suits me well. Now…make an old man happy, say something in Latin.'

Brooke's eyes widened in horror. 'No…er…I don't think so.' Brooke stammered.

'Go on! You know you want to! I won't take no for an answer sweetheart! No more nice lunches if not!' Lord D'Arcy teased.

Oh god, he's in one of those moods.

'*Oportet me ire instanter*[13]' she offered quickly and quietly… as though poor Dean might not hear!

'What the fuck are you saying, Brooke?!' Dean said, befuddled. 'What's he saying? How much are we gonna have to fork out?'

'Oh, sweetheart, you're getting very good at this! We must start corresponding in Latin soon. Learning to write Latin is also an art you know. Well, judging by the noise in the background, it sounds like you may have other things you need to attend to, so I'll say toodle pip and see you Tuesday morning.'

'OK. Bye and thank you very much for letting me know. See you then.'

'Bye then!' Lord D'Arcy pulled the phone away from his ear and stared into it, as though he'd had some sort of extra-terrestrial experience. Brooke was never that dull and joyless.

Brooke held the phone to her ear for a few moments more while she tried desperately to think of what she could say to Dean.

How the hell am I gonna explain that?!

As soon as she came off the call, she turned to Dean as she made her way to the stairs. 'Sorry, babe, gotta go to the loo, I'll tell you what he said in a minute, but it's gonna be OK.'

With that she dashed off to the lavatory, giving Dean no time to respond, and then sat on it, thinking. The moment she

13. I must go immediately.

reappeared at the bottom of the stairs, Dean cried out, 'What the hell did he say, Brooke? Can they sort it out? How much are we gonna have to pay?'

'He said not to worry and that everything's gonna be fine; we're not gonna have to pay for any damage. He can sort that apparently. He didn't mention his cost, so I don't know.'

'Thank god for that.' Dean made the sign of the cross and looked up to the heavens, hands clasped in prayer. 'And what was that weird thing you said to him?'

'He made a joke in Latin so I responded in Latin and that made him laugh.' She made the statement as though it was the most natural thing in the world.

'But how? You don't know Latin!' Dean exclaimed in disbelief.

'I can speak a bit. I found a book in the library, *Latin For Beginners*, so I've been giving it a go,' Brooke said nervously, tugging at her curls.

'You are absolutely unbelievable you are!' He was almost speechless. 'And why have you gotta go and see him on Tuesday? Is he trying to get into your knickers?'

'No!' Brooke gasped. 'He offered for me to come and watch him at work – you know, doing his actual conserving; getting rid of the marks, if I was interested. So I thought: why not? So I'm going over there next Tuesday.'

'Why on earth d'ya wanna go and watch some old geezer rub out a bit of crayon on a picture?'

'For a start, it's a painting, not a picture, secondly, I think it'll be a bit more involved than "rubbing out" and, finally, why *wouldn't* I want to go and watch?' Brooke remained very calm, with her legs crossed à la Kate Middleton, hands in lap and her face was as serious as Dean had ever seen her. It was as if she'd decided to nail her colours to the mast for the first time. 'Tell me that, Dean. Why wouldn't I? Do you really think that all I care about is Charlotte Tilbury lipsticks, East Enders and drooling over Cheryl Cole?'

Dean was flabbergasted. All he could muster was a shake of his head to indicate a 'no'. He was often crushed when confronted by one of her 'looks'. She had many of these for different types of arguments, one for DIY disagreements, one for dealing with Paige tiffs, one about her wine consumption and so on and so forth. But this was a new look. One he'd never encountered before, and being the mere man that he was, he couldn't immediately fathom what it meant. He traced her face with his eyes, hoping to get a glimpse of what the unspoken message or messages were lurking in what she'd just said. Poor chap was clueless; body language and facial expressions completely defeating him.

'Now, I'm going to get a glass of wine, would you like a beer?' she asked firmly. Dean nodded without saying a word.

With that, she marched off into the kitchen returning with a Becks and a large glass of Chardonnay. She sat back on the sofa, took a deep breath, unzipped the secret compartment in her handbag, pulled out her Latin book and commenced the chapter on second conjugation verbs.

18

Diversity Challenge Update and Close Shaves

'So, what have we got so far, Dean?' Dave asked, flicking over some reports on his desk.

'Well, I would just like to start by saying, Dave, that this is not an easy task you've set me here. I don't think you realise how complex it is,' Dean began.

'I'm sure it's tough, but what's the bottom line? How many have you recruited?' Dave asked, clearly disinterested in Dean's problems.

'Well, bottom line is that, as of today, we've got one Jewish lady called Ruth. Turns out Brooke's got a Jewish mate called Stacey and her mum knew someone who was looking for a job. She seemed very nice, she'll be good with the more difficult customers I think, a Hindu bloke whose got learning difficulties... Darpan. I'm sure we can get him on data processing or something basic. He's alright he is.'

'Oh that's a good one, Dean, very good!' Dave said excitedly.

'Then I managed to get three black people – sorry, people of colour – all in one day. Dennis from Canning Town – he's one of them Evangelical Christians in a gospel choir. He's got a diploma in Computer Science, so I'm sure that'll come in handy. The other two are girls, Charmaine and Alyssa. They're mates from Notting Hill. They were friendly and very chatty;

they'll be good on the phones.'

'Well that all sounds very promising, Dean. What about people with different sexual and gender identities? I think we'll be judged harshly if we haven't got a few of those in the mix somewhere.'

'I know, but I'm struggling to be honest, Dave. Especially with pomosexuals. The very nature of what they are means you can't tell and they don't wanna say. But I'm working on it.'

'That's a shame, Dean, a real shame. I really want one of them on the team.'

Dean sighed. 'I know. I'm interviewing a woman next week who I think might be a lesbian, but I'm not one hundred per cent sure.'

Dave rubbed his hands with glee. 'Hey hey hey! Bingo!' Dave leaned forward conspiratorially. 'That could be very interesting, Dean, if you know what I mean.' He winked.

Dean, being the slight prude that he was, didn't know what he meant at all. 'What makes you think she is one?'

'Dunno, just a few little clues in her CV. Like she helped to organise Pride last year in London. Not saying that means she is, but maybe makes it a bit more likely, don't you think?'

'I do, Dean, yeah.' Dave's brain seemed to have gone into overdrive.

'But, Dave, I think we're gonna have to have some white people of no particular identity, race, disability or religion, or we might not be able to fill all twenty-three roles. It's been bloody hard work getting this lot. It's taking up all my brain space. So, for example, I could get this girl who's just finished a degree at Oxford University of all places. She doesn't know what she wants to do as a career yet; just wants a temporary job until she decides. Her CV looks bloody brilliant, but she won't help us get the diversity award.' Dean was unsure how Dave would respond, to what was a subtle way of asking him if he'd done enough and could he go back to recruiting like he normally did?

Dave stood up and pulled his trousers up hard by the waistband so they rested on top of his pot belly rather than lay under it. 'Well, just keep on going till the last minute. The Gala Dinner isn't for several weeks yet, so don't give up. The girl from Oxford might actually be good though – posh totty… shows that we'll have entitled toffs as well as the under-represented lot. You know, shows a bit of balance in the team. Not all minorities. And don't forget we must have someone who's pregnant and a refugee – not fussed about which country they come from. Now you'll have to excuse me, Dean, I've gotta go. I'm playing golf at Sunningdale this afternoon.' With that he picked up his jacket, patted Dean on the back on his way out the door and left the office for the rest of the day.

Dean sat and thought about it for a few minutes before venturing back out onto the floor for a walkabout. Not like Brian used to – to check up on people's toilet breaks, but to talk to his team, make them feel he cared and was ready to listen to whatever they wanted or needed to talk to him about. He tried jolly hard to be a better man manager than his predecessor.

As he was mulling over the office's lack of left-handed scissors, Angie from Sonny Global rang.

'Hi, Dean. Angie here.'

'Hi, Angie.'

'How's your eye? Blimey, that report on SweatUBet was pretty brutal. You're sure you want it to be sent to the client as it is? I think they might want a more detailed conversation with you. What that instructor did was a sackable offence.'

'The eye's fine now, thanks very much, and yeah, I do want that report to go as is. They deserve it. They're absolute shite, Angie!' Dean bristled thinking about it.

'Right, well OK then. Just wanted to check. The Opera House was very pleased with your report by the way. They've only ever had a couple of paragraphs in the free text comments box before. Yours ran onto four pages of A4!'

'Well, we had a great night and they treated my wife particularly well for some reason. She was made to feel like a million dollars, so thanks for the visit, Angie. Wasn't sure it was going to be my bag, to be honest, but we both really enjoyed it.'

'OK, well we've got a few more visits coming up. How d'ya fancy doing a pub?' she enquired, guessing his answer before Dean even responded.

'Now that's right up my street. As long as it's not too complicated, 'cause I've got a lot on at work at the moment.'

'Well, the pub's The White Hart in Roydon for a three-course meal, drink and coffee. Gotta be done on a Saturday lunchtime in July.'

'Roydon? That's near that go-karting track Lewis Hamilton went to as a kid! Definitely do that one. We can go karting after.'

'I've no idea, Dean. Not a racing fan myself, so couldn't tell you. So, is it a yes?'

'Yes. Could be fun. I'm assuming I can take a mate?'

'Yep, the visit's for two people. I'll send you all the details nearer the time.'

'Brilliant. Thanks, Angie. Speak soon.'

Dean had a warm glow about him. Go-karting in the

morning, lunch at the pub and maybe he could make it a lads' day out and drive a bit further up the M11 to that war museum with all the planes? He'd always wanted to go there. What tremendous fun this was going to be! He just had to think of a way to tell Brooke he was going on a lads' day out. He checked his diary and the only Saturday he could do was 12th July. He messaged Martin.

Hey mate! Are you free on 12th July?

Yeah. Why?

Another mystery visit to a pub. Wanna make it a lads' day out though – go-karting and war museum as well.

Def yes. Count me in.

Great. Talk more detail soon. Lets go for a pint next week.

***

The following weekend, Dean and Brooke were shopping in Brentwood High Street, Brooke trying to pull Dean over to the Mark Wilkinson Kitchen Showroom and take him through the advantages of a central granite island with boiling water tap. Meanwhile, Dean was more interested in hose pipe fittings. Paige simply sat in her pushchair and decided this was the day she'd discover the joys of throwing her toys out onto the pavement; she'd worked out that this is how she got the attention of not just her parents, but an array of new and interesting orange people she'd never seen before, stopping to pick them up and give them back to her. It took the family fifteen minutes to walk 200 metres.

At one point, a young woman stopped to give Paige her fluffy white rabbit back, no longer white or fluffy in fact. She bent down and said a few words to Paige before looking up at the parents. Dean's eyes met hers and suddenly he felt sick.

'YOU! It's YOU! You BASTARD! You made me lose my job!' the tiny young woman screamed out while stabbing the air with her forefinger.

'I…I…' Dean was floored. Jo from SweatUBet's boxercise class stood up and glowered at him, observing the remnants of the black eye Dinah had given him.

'You want the other one sorting out, you fucking fairy?' she screamed and went to punch Dean, who at least had learned how to defend himself. He held his arms across his face and body and she caught him on the radius. 'That'll teach you!' she roared out and stormed off, shouting at Brooke along the way 'I feel sorry for you, love, if that's your husband. Spincless douchebag!'

It all happened so fast Brooke couldn't gather herself together fast enough to think straight. She stood there with her mouth open, speechless. A rare occurrence indeed. The only thing she could manage to retort was, 'Piss off you little hobbit, or I'll shove that rabbit right up where the sun don't shine!' which she immediately regretted, furtively looking around in case she saw anyone she knew.

Oh god, if Mrs Townsend heard me say that she'd have killed me.

'Dean. What the hell was all that about? Who was that woman?' Brooke demanded.

Dean too was speechless, but knew he couldn't afford to be for very long, or there'd be trouble. 'I've got absolutely no idea! I've never seen her before in my life!'

'You must know her! She clearly knows you!' Brooke said

suspiciously.

'I'm telling you I don't! I promise! She must've thought I was someone else.'

'That's twice in the last week you've been punched by strangers! What's happening, Dean? Is there something you're not telling me? Are you getting in with the wrong people again?' Brooke pursued, remembering the time he'd befriended a bunch of fairground gypsies as a teenager and got involved in all manner of dodgy dealings; it only ended when his mother had been round to the site and walloped the main man with her handbag and lectured him about 'real Catholics'.

'No! I'm not. Nothing's happening!' Dean retorted.

Brooke looked decidedly dissatisfied with his answer and felt sure he was keeping something from her. Suddenly, both Brooke and Dean became painfully aware of a number of people standing around in the background, watching and listening to their public row. Voices had been raised. One woman eating a sausage roll sitting on a bench looked particularly familiar. She stopped eating and walked towards Dean and Brooke.

Oh fuck!

Oh shit!

'Hey, guys! I see you've not lost your taste for fighting, Brooke De'Ath. How are you? Not seen you in a while.'

That's all I need, Karen bloody 'punch me outside the Sugar Hut' Diamond.

Dean had that rabbit caught in a headlight look and was also alarmed in the extreme at this shocking revelation that his wife was apparently a prize fighter.

Oh god, please don't mention what that bloody ruckus you saw you in Pret! That sodding M.O.T. card!

Brooke had to use every ounce of graciousness and decorum she could muster so's not to lose her dignity in this most uncomfortable and unfortunate situation. She tilted her head up slightly 'à la Lady Townsend' and smiled.

'Hello, Karen. I'm fine, thank you. I think there was a bit of a misunderstanding there. We don't know who that woman was. A case of mistaken identity, I think. Anyway, lovely to see you. How are you?'

'Yeah. I'm all good, thanks. Did Dean tell you I saw him in Pret the other day, causing all sorts of havoc it looked like; cheering and clapping and all sorts?' she said innocently enough.

Brooke looked over to Dean and squinted her eyes slightly before turning back to Karen, sounding entirely measured and calm. 'No, he didn't mention it actually, but he's so busy at work at the moment aren't you, babe?' She turned back to Dean momentarily with a fake smile. 'He forgets to tell me all sorts of things. Never mind unimportant ones.' Ouch! What a comeback! One all! 'He's been promoted, you know, and it's quite stressful for him having to deal with some very complicated HR issues at the moment, so I'm not surprised.'

That'll teach her, the bitch!

Dean was beginning to perspire and found himself yet again in a situation where he wanted to vanish as fast as was humanly possible. 'Like I said at the time, Karen, that was nothing to do with me. I don't know what they were all cheering and clapping about.' He tried to laugh it off, but it came out as unconvincing. 'It was something the manager said, not me. Anyway, it's great to see you again, but we've gotta go, it's taken us forever to get down the high street, 'cause madam here keeps throwing toys out her pushchair.'

'OK. No worries! Well, nice to see you both and little Paige – see you around! Bye!' And off Karen trotted, waving at Paige and stuffing her sausage roll back into her mouth again.

Dean and Brooke both said goodbye and waved her off in the opposite direction. The atmosphere crackled as they glanced at each other, but neither wanted to be the first to start trying to unravel what had come out in that conversation. They pushed Paige along silently for a while, having removed all her toys. Dean carried the white fluffy rabbit and the yellow rubber duck while Brooke carried the miniature tool box and crane and they silently made their way back to the car.

When they arrived home, Dean could hold back no more.

'Brooke, I'm sorry but I've gotta ask, what was Karen talking about you fighting? I can't believe you ever fought. You're far too beautiful for fighting.'

Brooke didn't want to tell Dean about her past unladylike fracas outside The Sugar Hut, but she knew she couldn't get away without saying anything. 'It was nothing, Dean. Just one stupid incident years ago, which as usual Karen's blown up out of all proportion. I don't wanna talk about it, OK?'

That look again. The new one. Dean shrugged, but was clearly unhappy with the answer.

'What was she talking about in Pret, Dean?' Brooke asked in a most straightforward manner.

'Nothing! I was in Pret and bumped into Karen just outside. I had to go back in 'cause I'd forgotten my umbrella. While I was in there collecting it from the counter, something went on between the manager and staff – I don't know what it was all about, but they all started cheering and clapping. Karen is trying to convince herself it had something to do with me, but it didn't. That's it!'

'Mmm. And I still can't get over that little dwarf hitting you like that. It's just too weird if you ask me,' Brooke carried on.

'I notice you're not interested in the fact that she actually hurt me! I'm badly injured! She might've broken my arm, Brooke, and all you care about is *why* she hit me!' Dean tried playing the sympathy card, in the hope Brooke would forget all about it.

She mellowed for a few minutes as she looked at his arm. There was indeed a bruise coming up. 'Well let's get another ice pack on it. I've still got some peas left.'

They both tried normal conversation that evening, but it was undeniably stilted. It had to get back to normal soon because there was too much at stake and too much that needed organising that required coordination; on both their sides.

In bed later, Dean lay there, staring at the ceiling, thinking.

Two punches from strangers in one week. She's right. What's happening to my life? I'm gonna have to talk to her soon about the lads' day out as well. Make sure I get the car on that day. 12th July's a way off though, so should be fine.

Brooke lay there mulling over what had happened that afternoon. She couldn't pinpoint it, but she felt increasingly uneasy.

And I've gotta find a way of telling Dean I need the car for Newmarket. Still, 12th July's a way off yet so should be fine. God knows what I can tell him I'm doing.

19

A McDonald's Visit, A Fright and The Gallops

First thing on the Tuesday, Brooke made her way to allegedly 'watch the conservator' repair the damage to the painting; as far as Dean was concerned anyway. In fact, she'd driven to Ingatestone Hall to talk with Lord D'Arcy about the syndicate and the upcoming race. He'd told the other syndicate members that he'd take responsibility for educating Brooke in things horse-racing related and all plans for racing Turn The Paige.

Going on one of her days off meant she could take her time and not have the stress of trying to get back home before Dean. She arrived at reception, who now treated her as an old friend of Lord D'Arcy's, which still gave Brooke a warm glow. Paige, unfortunately, was in tow but so far behaving herself.

Lord D'Arcy came to collect them straight away, excited as ever at Brooke's mere presence, and walked alongside her as they made their way to his private wing. She thanked him profusely for his help with the conservator, who'd managed to repair the damage for under a hundred pounds. Paige toddled along, gabbling away long sentences that couldn't be deciphered, but she seemed happy enough. Every so often she'd stop and point at an object of interest or touch something and on more than one occasion she attempted to climb a tree or a wall along the way, stopped only in the nick of time by Brooke's lightning reactions, which she'd begun to develop ever since she and Dean discovered Paige could climb out of her cot unaided. Over recent weeks Brooke had found her inside the washing machine, standing on top of the dining table and trying to climb into Dean's compost bin at the bottom of the garden. She was a climber, a real tomboy Brooke was discovering; much to her despair. She'd wanted a glittery, sparkly, pink girlie girl, not a Spiderman, puddle-splashing, mud-throwing overactive tomboy.

They sat at the table in his kitchen and Brooke watched Lord D'Arcy fuss about making tea with a teapot, loose leaves, a tea strainer and a tea cosy, as well as cups and saucers.

'So, is Lady D'Arcy in today?' Brooke enquired casually.

'Ah no, Brooke. You've missed her again, I'm afraid. She's out playing bridge.' Brooke was increasingly feeling Lady D'Arcy was a figment of Lord D'Arcy's imagination!

'What's that then? Remind me.' Brooke was curious. She'd heard about bridge, but couldn't pinpoint where.

'It's a card game, which one could describe as intellectually and socially stimulating. Not for everyone, it has to be said.'

'Definitely not for me then! I remember now, that's what they play at Brooks's. They even had a special room for it!' Brooke laughed.

'There you go again. Putting yourself down. You're perfectly capable of learning bridge if you want to,' Lord D'Arcy replied looking over his spectacles as a headmaster would to an unruly child.

'Now don't get me started on anything else, Geoffrey! I'm still trying to get to grips with basic Latin. I'm on me second conjugation verbs at the moment,' Brooke joked. She then went through the ones she'd learned to date, like a child reciting times tables to her parents.

As she spoke, Lord D'Arcy was beguiled, staring at her long slender legs, wishing they were wrapped around him and imagining what it must be like to make love to this glorious creature. He and Lady D'Arcy regrettably slept in separate beds. Had done for years. The last time he tried to institute foreplay even, she'd waved her legs about frantically, claiming dispensation due to the contraption around both her feet, designed to stop her bunions getting any worse and to help straighten her big toes. Not the most seductive device on the planet and, as far as Lady D'Arcy was concerned, certainly not conducive to any hanky-panky!

Brooke waved her hands in front of his eyes. 'Geoffrey, you're miles away! Let's talk about Turn The Paige.'

Geoffrey was reluctantly jolted out of his daydream before beginning to explain the other costs involved in running a syndicate. The training, stabling, legal and vets fees, entering races etc. etc. Brooke was a tad alarmed, as she hadn't known any of this before she rashly offered to join. She'd naively thought she had to pay her share and that was it! Poor girl! Lord D'Arcy picked up on her concern and told her not to be worried about it for now. Hopefully, if Turn The Paige was placed on 12th July she could pay some of the extras from the winnings.

'So, what's the trainer bloke said about her? Does he think she could win?' Brooke asked.

'A little too early to be that confident, sweetheart. It's unheard of for a filly to be entered into The Bunbury Cup, they're almost always geldings, but Mark has said she was a sound purchase and that she's responding very well to him.' Geoffrey's eyes lit up suddenly. 'You could come with me to see her on the gallops if you like. I made an appointment for a stable visit this afternoon,' Geoffrey offered, as a means of getting Brooke on her own once more. Not that he realistically thought anything would happen. No, he merely enjoyed her 'joie de vivre'. She made him feel young again and more in touch with the real world as opposed to the peculiar one he inhabited.

'Oh that could be fun!' Brooke said, when a message came through on her phone from Dean.

Hows it going babe? Whats the damage?

Brooke went cold.

Yeah all good. Gonna be under £100!

Thank Christ for that!

Send a pic of it after its been done.

Brooke went even colder.

I'll try. Not sure allowed to use camera here.

'Geoffrey, I know this is a strange question but have you got a picture anywhere of that painting that Paige damaged?'

'Mmm. I'm sure I have somewhere. Come with me to the library and we can take a look. Why do you need one?'

'A long story, Geoffrey. A long story,' Brooke said wearily. Geoffrey knew when not to ask questions, so dutifully went into the library and found a book on Sir Alfred Munnings' work. Flicking through the book, on page 47 they came across *A Lady Seated in a Park*. Brooke sat Paige on her lap and pointed it out to her. She became very animated, waving both hands emphatically, pointing at the lips and eyes on the photograph, her face contorting in all manner of ways as she spoke.

'Hawseeeees! Listi! Listi! Garsees dada! Paige nawteee corn. Mameee cos.' Her face turned to Brooke, mouth turned down and eyes lowered, like a puppy in an advert designed to elicit sympathy.

It was obvious Paige remembered the day at the museum and how cross her mother had been. Brooke recalled her outburst and Lady Townsend's words: 'she just saw a lady without lipstick!' Brooke hugged her and assured her that Mummy wasn't cross any more. She put her on the floor and carefully took a photo of *A Lady Seated in a Park* on her phone and sent it to Dean, while Lord D'Arcy took the opportunity to flick through the book, saying he'd not looked at it for a long time. Before she knew it, Paige had disappeared from her peripheral vision. Brooke suddenly whisked around to see her standing, waving at the top of the library ladder at around three metres high. Brooke's phone buzzed.

Haha I wonder what made Paige choose that one to draw on!

Oh my giddy aunt!

'Paige! Hold tight!' Brooke spoke firmly but carefully, as she didn't want to panic her daughter by screeching at her, even though that is precisely what she wanted to do. Like a shot, Brooke legged it over to the ladder and climbed up it at speed, as Paige simply let go when she turned around to look down at her mother. It took every ounce of strength and flexibility Brooke possessed to stop Paige from falling off the ladder and Brooke inadvertently yelled out at the difficulty of the move to grab and keep hold of her. Her phone buzzed again.

How long did it take him to clean it up?

'Brooke, are you alright?' Lord D'Arcy shouted as he ran over and quickly held the bottom of the ladder, giving him the most marvellous view of Brooke's bottom. He had to mentally tell himself off for thinking such irreverent thoughts in a crisis.

Brooke climbed down slowly, holding Paige tight under her right arm. She was visibly shaking at what'd almost happened. When they arrived on solid ground, Brooke hugged her tightly for several minutes with alternate feelings of relief and anger. Paige appeared bemused. More phone buzzing.

We should buy a copy somewhere and hang it in her bedroom – just for the mems!

Brooke quickly checked her phone, read the messages and put it back in her pocket.

For god's sake, Dean.

'Well, she's a little devil this one, isn't she?' Lord D'Arcy said, not knowing entirely what to do with himself at this point. 'She was probably bored. I think we should leave for the stable visit right now. It'll be more interesting for her to see some horses.'

Brooke was torn. She was irritated by Dean's annoying messages during the stepladder crisis and part of her was so unnerved by Paige's near-miss, yet another part of her was asking herself why not? She'd nothing else on and thought it could be fun and something different for Paige – real horses! Not paintings of horses! She dithered for a few minutes, and finally said, 'I'm not sure, Geoffrey, I think she might get irritable and, trust me, that'll make things very unenjoyable!'

'I know! Why don't I ask if Mrs Dodsley, my housekeeper, would be prepared to mind her for the afternoon? She's got twelve grandchildren, so she's certainly experienced and she's looked after ours from time to time. I'm sure she wouldn't mind. Let me go and ask her.' He was desperate to keep Brooke with him. Brooke ummed and ahhhed and before she had any choice in the matter as Mrs Dodsley had been yanked away from polishing the brass boot rack and presented to Brooke as a potential way out of her predicament.

'I'd be delighted to, my lovely. She looks a right little poppet.' Mrs Dodsley looked as close to Mary Poppins as it was possible to look, without actually being Mary Poppins.

Oh my god, if only she knew.

'She can help me with me jobs can't you, Paige? We'll do some cleaning and polishing and sweeping, won't we?' She held out her hand to Paige who had on her best celestial face and doe eyes. Paige took her hand willingly, along with the bright yellow duster Mrs Dodsley had in her hands and garbled something to her, looking very happy.

'Well, are you sure, Mrs Dodsley? She can be quite a handful. You'll need to keep your eye on her a hundred per cent of the time. She climbed the library ladder just now, without us even noticing, and she almost fell from the top. Honestly, you can't let her out of your sight for one minute. And she's not had anything to eat yet.'

'Don't you worry, my lovely. You go out and see your horse. I'll sort her out and I'll see you when you get back.' Brooke picked Paige up, squeezed her tightly, pecked her cheek and gave Mrs Dodsley three Chupa Chups in case of emergency. She then waved her daughter off; delighted she was able to potentially be left with someone other than Dawn but slightly alarmed at the ease with which she walked off with a complete stranger!

Geoffrey made a quick call to the trainer, who confirmed the visit and by 11am they were off. Brooke was hungry and wanted a McDonald's on the way. 'Now, Geoffrey, I'm probably gonna regret asking this, but have you ever had a McDonald's?'

'No. I'm afraid I haven't.'

'What, not even with your grandkids?!'

'Absolutely not! Clare, my daughter, forbids it!'

'Right, well you're gonna have one today!'

'We could always eat at The Jockey Club Rooms again?'

'No. I'm putting my foot down this time. I always go where you want. Now it's my turn and you've gotta eat lunch where I want!' Today she was clearly not to be messed with. 'Besides, it'll increase your hinterland! It works both ways, you know!' She burst out laughing. Geoffrey couldn't help himself and joined in, slapping the steering wheel with his right hand at the same time.

'Oh, Brooke, you're such a hoot! You really are an absolute scream!'

'Be prepared to be educated in the ways of burgers, chips and milkshakes!'

'Oh bloody hell! What fun this is going to be!' Geoffrey roared his mighty loud roar, almost deafening Brooke in the process.

I've already got one screamer, please don't let me get a shouter as well.

When they got to the Harlow junction on the M11, Brooke instructed Geoffrey to turn off and they were soon at the McDonald's near the roundabout. Geoffrey parked and as they got out, it occurred to Brooke that he was going to stick out like a sore thumb. On this particular day he was sporting red trousers that were now so washed-out they were actually pink, a blue button-down Oxford shirt with two buttons undone and a brown paisley cravat around his neck, topped off with a navy-blue blazer with gold buttons and his ubiquitous brown brogues. In fact, Brooke had never seen him wear any other shoes ever. He even wore them to Claridge's without cleaning the mud off them first.

Mmm, well this is gonna be interesting.

'Lead the way, young lady! This is very exciting!' Geoffrey rubbed his hands and grinned from ear to ear at the prospect of this American delicacy. As they made their way around the car park to find the main entrance doors, Geoffrey stopped and looked at everything, as though he'd arrived on the moon and was wanting to explore every centimetre of it, in case he never got the chance again. As soon as they walked through the doors, a couple of youths came crashing through in the opposite direction and barged Geoffrey out the way. No apology. Nothing.

'I say, chaps! Go easy! You nearly knocked me over there!' Geoffrey called at them.

'Fuck off, Grandad!' came the reply.

'Well I never!' he exclaimed. Brooke patted him on the arm sympathetically.

'Ignore 'em, Geoffrey. Ignorant pigs.' She tutted and led Geoffrey past the self-ordering screens.

'Hang on, Brooke, what are those?'

'Oh, you can use them to order and pay by touchscreen instead of talking to a human if you like, then, when your number comes up you just go over there and pick your order up.'

'Good heavens! That's incredible! But what's wrong with giving your order to a person?'

He went over to one of the screens and started pressing various parts of it, like a child would when being given a new toy and finding out how it worked. 'This is extraordinary,

Brooke.' He was mesmerised as he then stood back watching various young people tap their order in at lightning speed, flash something at the screen and walk off to the collection counter.

'No, Geoffrey. It isn't. It's called modern technology!'

'What did he just do with his card? He didn't even put it into one of those machines to pay?' Geoffrey was clearly perplexed. Brooke smiled.

'It's called contactless Geoffrey. There's a chip in bank cards that means you can just show it to the machine, it bleeps, reads your card and takes the money out of your account automatically.'

'But surely that's dangerous? What if I dropped mine in the street? Any Tom, Dick or Harry could pick it up and use it if you don't have to enter your number?'

'Well the banks say they'll cover that to a certain degree as long as you report it.'

'Well I never!' Geoffrey removed his card from his wallet and Brooke showed him the sign on it that indicated it was set up for contactless transactions. Then she slapped him on the back of his hand playfully. 'Now leave it alone, or we'll be finding you've ordered ten veggie burgers or something.' She walked him to near the front counter, where there were queues at several tills and she pointed up to the picture boards that showed all the options available.

'Golly there's quite a choice. What do you normally have?' he asked.

'Varies, to be honest. Depends what I'm in the mood for. Sometimes I like a quarter pounder with cheese and other times I could kill for a filet-o-fish and an apple pie. Always chips and always a milkshake though. Chocolate.'

Geoffrey stood in the way for several minutes trying to decide. He was taken with the idea of a burger of some sort as he was aware that McDonald's was famous for their burgers and he felt compelled to try their chips. He thought it probably wasn't the done thing to order a burger without them. He didn't eat chips at home as Lady D'Arcy never made them or bought them. It was always potatoes from their own vegetable patch, dug up shortly before they were required. They'd inadvertently joined a queue and, before he knew it, they were at the front. 'Good morning, young man!' Lord D'Arcy bellowed.

The lad behind the counter, (Barry on his name badge) stared at Geoffrey, wide-eyed, absorbing the mode of attire in front of him, with which he was not familiar. Harlow was neither a big user nor purveyor of cravats and blazers. He nodded as a means of acknowledgment, raised his eyebrows and asked, 'What can I get you?'

'Well…there's so much choice, quite frankly, I'm having a little difficulty in deciding.' Geoffrey continued to scan the picture board menu above. Barry rolled his eyes and leaned impatiently against his till…waiting.

Brooke moved forward 'Well while you're deciding, I'll have a Big Mac, large fries, chocolate milkshake and a McFlurry. I'm starving.' Barry inputted the order and then turned again to Geoffrey.

'What can you recommend, young man? It all looks positively delicious!' Geffrey boomed and rubbed his hands in anticipation of a suggestion. Barry looked over to Brooke blankly.

'They don't suggest things, Geoffrey. You just have to pick.'

'Oh. Well you'll have to help me. I think I want a burger, but which one? I'm not overly hungry. What's that Big Mac you're having?'

'Nah. You don't want that then. How about a quarter pounder? D'ya like cheese?'

'Mmm. I've not had a burger with cheese before. Yes, I'll try that but, young man, please can you ensure it's well done? I don't like it pink.'

'Geoffrey, there's no choice, you can't tell 'em how to cook your burger. It's all done the same. Now, d'ya want chips?'

'Oh yes, rather. Never have chips at home.'

'Right, that's a quarter pounder with cheese and regular fries.'

Barry turned to Geoffrey and asked 'Do ya want that as a meal?'

'Well of course I want it as a meal. That's what I'm here for. A meal.'

'No, Geoffrey, what he means is: do you want a drink with it?'

'Oh, right…erm yes, well why didn't he say so? I'll try one of those milkshakes – strawberry, please, and I see you have apple pie. I'll take one of those and I'd like mine with custard please.'

Brooke couldn't help but giggle. 'No, Geoffrey, they don't do custard!'

'Well one can't possibly eat an apple pie without custard! The very idea!'

'Rubbish, we'll have it with strawberry milkshake and apple pie – without custard,' Brooke instructed Barry. She winked at him, smiled and rolled her eyes in sympathy.

Barry entered Geoffrey's order. 'Ten pounds fifty please.'

'Good god, is that all?' Geoffrey turned to Brooke and

whispered conspiratorially, 'I think he's made an error!' Brooke smiled and waved her card at the machine; all the while showing Geoffrey how contactless worked. Geoffrey shook his head in amazement and then watched with fascination as the server went to several different steel chutes and picked the order quickly and efficiently into two large brown bags. He was rather perturbed at the amount of shouting going on between the staff and wondered if it was strictly necessary. 'They're not terribly civil to each other, are they?'

'That's the way it is at Maccie D!' Brooke responded.

Barry returned and with the same level of disinterest as he'd shown the rest of the time asked, 'Sauces?'

'Oh yes please. Do you have fig and onion relish? It's a splendid combination,' Geoffrey asked, rubbing his hands and looking over in anticipation behind Barry for evidence of his chosen sauce in a jar somewhere.

'Nah. Ketchup, mayo and BBQ. That's it.'

Geoffrey looked most disappointed, now needing guidance as to his choice of condiments.

'Just give us two of everything, mate' Brooke said, falling back into her old Essex speak and very aware of a rather large queue building up behind them along with mutters of: 'prick, knobhead and wanker.'

Oh god, I said mate! What'll Geoffrey think?!

Once they'd picked up their order, Barry's eyes followed them as they walked away, mouth gaping and wondering if he needed to pinch himself. Brooke asked Geoffrey if he wanted to eat in or eat it in the car as they drove along.

'Oh, eat in definitely! It's so interesting! I don't think I've ever had such a cheap lunch in my life!'

Brooke continued to giggle quietly to herself as she watched Geoffrey tuck a paper napkin into his cravat and remove his items from the bag one by one, inspecting each in turn. He had a rather clever way of holding the burger Brooke observed, using his little fingers to squash the back, which meant the filling didn't fall out. He watched Brooke pick up one of her chips and dip it into her chocolate milkshake.

'What are you doing?' Geoffrey asked, aghast at her action.

'Tastes nice,' was the simple response. 'Go on, try it.'

Geoffrey tentatively dipped a chip into his strawberry milkshake. 'Mmm. Not too bad. Not too bad at all. Well I never,' he mumbled to himself. This was turning out to be quite a culinary education for Lord D'Arcy. Every so often, he looked up from his munching, only to discover a number of people staring at him. One chap appeared to be wearing a full leather biking outfit and more earrings than Lady D'Arcy owned and his girlfriend wore a tiger-print onesie. The front part of her hair was also in curlers, which Geoffrey couldn't fathom at all. It put him on edge rather and Brooke picked up on it.

'Now you know what it feels like,' she said meaningfully.

'What?'

'Not fitting in. Having people staring at you the whole time.'

'Yes, I suppose so,' was all he would say and went back to eating his chips and sucking his milkshake. When it came to his apple pie, he took it out the bag and held it, staring as if it were a strange unidentified object he'd found on this planet he'd landed on. He turned it over, unsure how this was apple pie. Brooke took it from him, opened the end and pushed the pie up.

'There. That's how you eat it, holding it between your fingers.'

'Who on earth eats apple pie like that? Surely there must be plates and spoons available?' Geoffrey asked in horror.

'Ordinary people who come to McDonald's, Geoffrey! And no. There's no plates or spoons,' Brooke retorted. 'Now get that down your Gregory!' How easy it was to slip back into her old way of speaking when back in a familiar environment. He did as he was told but yelped out as the piping hot filling spurted into his mouth.

'Look, read the packet! It says WARNING! HOT FILLING!' Brooke cried impatiently.

Geoffrey looked wounded and finished the pie in silence, licking his lips and fingers enthusiastically afterwards. He was staggered at the sheer volume of food that Brooke managed to eat. He liked to see a girl with a healthy appetite; liked girls with some meat on the bones as it were! Within ten minutes they'd finished everything.

'Well, Brooke, I must say, that was rather delicious. A most pleasant surprise! I'll have to tell Clare she should at least try one. I'm sure the twins Tarquin and Tobias would be thrilled. Now, do they have lavatories here, do you know?'

Brooke pointed and left him to it as she put their rubbish into the bin and waited…and waited… eventually going over to check if he'd found them. He was still standing outside, looking like a fish out of water.

'Blimey there must have been a long queue. You're still here!'

'Well actually, there was only one other person when I arrived, but several ladies joined the queue, so it was only right to let them go first.'

'Oh my gawd, Geoffrey, what are you like? This is Harlow. Dog eat dog. Every man for himself. You'll be here all day if you do that! Now, come on, we haven't got all day, have we?'

'Oh I couldn't possibly go while there were ladies queuing outside.' Just then the lavatory became free and Brooke pushed him into it and turned round, arms folded in a 'don't mess with me' style to face the queue. After he came out, they crossed in front of the counter where they'd been served and Lord D'Arcy waved at Barry and boomed 'Goodbye, young man, goodbye. Thank you so much! Wonderful meal!'

'Geoffrey, your flies are undone,' Brooke quietly mentioned. He rushed to rearrange himself as they walked into the car park. As always, he opened the car door for Brooke and watched as she slid her long slim legs into the car.

***

In under an hour they'd arrived at the training yard; Mark was already getting their horse ready. Geoffrey made the introductions and Brooke immediately asked if she could stroke Turn The Paige. This'd been the first time she'd seen her since the auction and she was excited but nervous and didn't want to say or do the wrong thing. Mark laughed.

'You been round horses before?' he asked, knowing from Brooke's demeanour around Turn The Paige, that she hadn't.

'No. I would've loved a pony as a kid, but Mum and Dad could never have afforded it. I couldn't even have lessons. Probably a bit old to start now!'

Mark (who'd been secretly briefed by Lord D'Arcy) showed her how to approach the horse safely and stroke and pat her. Without Brooke asking, he told her about some of the most important qualities a good racehorse must have; calm, relaxed yet alert. He pointed out various things about the horse's bone structure, muscle tone, balance, coat, ears and back that made her a good racehorse. He told her what to look out for when she watched her on the gallops. Brooke's now infamous questioning made Mark smile and want to educate her even more. And not just in the way of horses, it has to be said! He was an attractive older man and Brooke found herself looking at him earnestly as he talked to her.

Eventually, they went off to the gallops and Brooke experienced a thrill unlike anything else she'd ever done. It wasn't just excitement. It was much more than that. She tried to figure out this new emotion she was feeling, as she watched Turn The Paige gallop past at great pace. On this fresh, bright day, she and Geoffrey rested their arms on the white posts and used Lord D'Arcy's binoculars to watch their horse as she galloped further away, Brooke trying to remember what Mark had taught her to look out for.

Is she covering the ground with ease and does she have a lengthy stride?

Her heart pumped so fast and so loud she felt sure Geoffrey could hear it.

'Isn't she wonderful, Brooke?' he shouted as the horse galloped past.

Brooke didn't know how to put into words how she felt. She was breathless as she spoke. 'She's…it's…the whole thing is so amazing, Geoffrey. I can't believe I actually own a part of her! I can't wait to see her race. I've got a good feeling about her, I really have. I feel so…I can't explain what I feel!' She laughed and threw her hands up in the air in frustration at being unable to express herself.

Geoffrey smiled and ventured further than he had before by putting his arm around her shoulders, giving her a squeeze and saying, 'I know, I know. I think the word you're looking for, if I may say… is proud. And I also think you're a natural risk-taker. Risk is dangerous and therefore exciting.'

Brooke thought about this for a minute and decided he was correct. She was proud she'd earned the money to pay for the tail, proud she'd asserted her wishes and made it happen, proud that it'd all been her own doing and she felt sure she'd be proud when Turn The Paige would at least be placed, if not win. But he was right about the other thing too.

She gave Mark and Geoffrey a run-down of what she'd seen and any comments she had and Mark nodded, clearly impressed.

'Can she win, Mark?' Brooke asked in a hopeful tone.

'Unlikely, if I'm honest. We're taking a big risk entering her into the Bunbury Cup at all. It's all geldings. She'll be the only filly running. But she's quite an extraordinary horse, in my opinion and I've trained hundreds; her temperament's well suited to that sort of race and I do think it'll be worth a shot. Looking at the other horses running, I'd hope she'll at least be placed.'

Brooke felt a pang of disappointment. She'd wanted unequivocal confirmation that Turn The Paige could win.

They had a quick cup of tea together and, shortly after, Brooke and Lord D'Arcy sped back to Ingatestone Hall. On the way back, Brooke's mind went from thinking about Turn The Paige to just Paige! Had she destroyed Ingatestone Hall? Had she given Mrs Dodsley a heart attack? Had she jumped into the hot tub and drowned?

By the time they'd arrived back at 3.30pm, Brooke had convinced herself that Mrs Dodsley would never babysit Paige ever again. Imagine her surprise when they entered the kitchen and Paige was happily helping Mrs Dodsley bring the vegetables in from the garden, for supper that evening. Brooke saw Paige was in only a nappy and nervously asked how she'd been.

'Oh, she's been a delight she has. That little girl's a clever one if you ask me. We've done all sorts together, we 'ave.' She pinched the little girl's cheeks affectionately and Paige beamed. 'Haven't we, poppet?'

'Did she have any screaming fits?' Brooke enquired, dreading the answer; this was all seeming too good to be true.

'No, my lovely. I didn't need them lollipops neither. She needs to get rid of her energy and a bit more attention, that's all. It's all bottled up. She needs more exercise, that's all it is, I'm sure. Forget the lollipops. Just chuck her out in the garden with a ball if she screams again.'

'Why's she only got her nappy on?' Brooke asked, not wanting to appear ungrateful, but genuinely perplexed.

'Oh that! She discovered my make-up in my handbag. I've not got much in there, to be honest, but she was determined to have all of it out and me Rimmel powder went all over that little dress of hers, which *by the way*, she kept trying to take off, so I had to wash it. It's in the tumble drier now. Probably ready.' She disappeared off to fetch it.

Paige ran over to her mother with arms up, gabbling away and looking flushed. Brooke picked her up, swung her around and kissed her on the top of her head. She smelled of freshly dug potatoes and brass polish.

Brooke said her thank-yous and goodbyes and Lord D'Arcy

escorted her to her car. Once Paige was strapped in – *without fuss for the first time in forever* – Brooke observed, Lord D'Arcy was waiting to say his own more personal goodbye. Brooke couldn't – didn't want to – stop him from what she knew was coming. She was too fond of him. He put his arms around her waist, yanked her towards him and pecked her hard on both cheeks.

'Sweetheart, I've so enjoyed today. You're a first-class student, you know. You listen, you digest, you learn, you understand and if you don't, you ask with no fear. It's pure joy!'

'Thanks, Geoffrey,' she replied, slightly embarrassed. 'And you were right, you know. What I feel right now is proud. And it's all down to you and Mrs Townsend. Also, I think you're right about being a risk-taker. The thrill *is* in the danger. Roll on July 12th, eh?!'

***

As soon as Brooke arrived home, she threw Paige's toys all over the lounge floor and ran upstairs to change into her 'at home all day' clothes. This was followed quickly by bathing Paige in order to get rid of the potato smell. It was while she was conducting this operation that Dean arrived home.

'So how did it go with the conservatory man? You never replied to my messages!' Dean shouted as he walked through the front door.

'I'm up here!' Brooke shouted. Dean bounded up the stairs two at a time and into the bathroom.

'Yeah it went fine. You got the photo though?'

'Yeah. She's gonna be trouble this one!' he bent down and

kissed Paige on the belly followed by a big, loud, long raspberry. 'What the hell's she been doing? This water's filthy!'

Oh shit!

'Oh she ran off into the gardens of the museum when I was talking to the conservator. By the time I'd got to her she'd found a nice big puddle.'

Let's hope that'll do.

'I was trying to sort her out and forgot to reply. Yeah a poster of the painting could be a bit of a laugh!'

'How did it go, anyway? Interesting as you thought?' Dean asked.

Brooke thought back to Paige's terrifying ladder incident, the farcical lunch with Geoffrey at McDonald's and the mad dash to the gallops at Newmarket. Unable to stop it, a beam spread across her face followed by a chuckle.

God, if you only knew!

Then with a hint of mystery and still smiling she replied, 'Yeah. Let's just say it was…most interesting!'

20

Challenges, Up the Duff and Brooke's Whopper

'Babe, I forgot to mention it the other day, but just to let you know I need the car on the twelfth. It's a Saturday. It's a lads' day out and we're going go-karting and then onto The War Museum to go see the war planes.' Dean was lying in bed facing the ceiling as he tried to control his breathing and sound as natural as possible.

Brooke sat bolt upright. She hadn't yet thought about what she was going to say *she* was doing on twelfth, so was ill prepared to have this particular conversation at that moment.

Shit! How the hell am I gonna get to Newmarket without a car?

All she could manage was: 'Oh. I wish you'd have told me sooner. What if I'm going out on that day?'

Maybe I can cadge a lift with Mrs T or Geoffrey? I bet they're staying up there the night before, though.

'What?! You've got every other day of the week free and the car every day! I've only got it at the weekend. And just like you had your girls' night out, I haven't had a boys' day out for months and I wanna go,' he complained.

'Since when've you been interested in war planes anyway?'

'Martin's organised it.' Dean made a mental note to inform Martin that he'd been the one to organise the day.

'When will Martin ever learn to drive? He's always scrounging lifts off everyone else,' Brooke complained, still trying to calculate whether she'd any chance of persuading Dean to change his mind.

'Will you leave that poor bloke alone?! I know you don't like him, but he's my mate! I'm gonna go and you're just gonna have to do whatever you wanna do on another day. You've got plenty of others to choose from. I haven't.' This was a very rare moment of both defending his friend and of the worm turning. He threw back the duvet and stomped off to make a cup of tea, feeling slightly resentful at having to justify why he should have the car on that day.

'Doesn't sound like I've got much choice, does it?' she shouted at him like a sulking teenager might, fell back down in bed again and blew out hard and slow; she too was feeling slightly resentful.

Why should his wants always come before mine? Why should he always expect me to fit in with whatever he's organised? I'm gonna have to talk to Mrs T and Geoffrey. There's no way I'm missing Turn The Paige. No way.

Dean brought her up a cup of tea a few minutes later and in the spirit of trying to keep the peace, he kissed her on the top of her head. 'Love ya,' he offered with a face like a child craving love.

'Love you too,' she responded in a sulky fashion.

To try and get her out of her mood, he changed the subject. Smart move! He'd learned from the master (or mistress, to be more precise!). 'Wish me luck. I've got a massive day of interviewing today. It's the last hurdle. I've almost filled all the roles for the second call centre, you know,' Dean stated proudly.

Brooke looked up, unable to hide her genuine surprise and pleasure. Dean's tactic had worked; clever chap! 'Blimey, that's good news. It doesn't feel like that long ago you were struggling to get anyone at all.'

'I know. It's been bloody hard, but I'm nearly there. I still haven't found a pomosexual or a pregnant woman yet, so I'm focusing on that now. But guess what? Last week I found this great website – The Refugee Council – and I managed to find a Syrian refugee through them. Faisal. He's only a bloody architect. Dead clever. So he's gonna be a team leader. I felt a bit sorry for him to be honest, having to take a shitty job in a call centre, but he says he can't get a job here as an architect.'

'Blimey, that's a bit of a come down, poor bloke. As for pregnant women, well that's a turnaround, Dean De'Ath! You said you didn't *ever* want to employ a pregnant woman a few weeks ago!'

'Yeah, well Dave's said I've got to. No choice. Talking of that, make sure you're not doing anything on 26th July. That's the Chamber of Commerce Gala Dinner in London. The diversity award's gonna be given out that night and Dave's booked us a few company tables. Partners of senior managers are invited too. Chance for you to dress up. Who knows, we might win the award?' As he'd anticipated, Brooke appeared thrilled and immediately began talking about what might be a suitable dress for the occasion.

However, as soon as Dean left for work and the front door slammed, Brooke messaged Lady Townsend and Lord D'Arcy to explain her predicament and ask for a lift on 12th July from either of them. They both responded as she'd expected by saying that, regrettably, they were staying up the night before, so were unable to give her a lift. Lord D'Arcy, however, told her not to worry and that he'd sort something out for her.

Brooke threw her phone on the bed and prayed that he could.

***

Later on that day at work, Dean's interviewing continued apace. One after the other, a wide assortment of individuals of every skin colour, every religion, every sexual identity and disability paraded in and out of his office, much to the fascination and amusement of the rest of the team, who'd no idea of the diversity challenge Dean'd been set. He'd feared a revolt amongst them and thought the best course of action was to tell them nothing and present them with a fait accompli.

At the end of his stream of interviews, Chloe appeared at Dean's office door and knocked timidly. That was immediately cause for concern, as Chloe was about as timid as Donald Trump talking to a *Washington Post* reporter. Dean's relationship with Chloe was different to anyone else's in the office. He liked her and especially her refreshing attitude towards men: almost anti-feminist. They'd enjoyed many conversations over the years, some quite sensitive and private and she'd always given him the heads up if something was afoot among the team; she was like the MI5 spy of the office. Chloe had always fancied Dean and her flirting with him did his ego so much good, he never stopped her.

'Dean, you gotta minute?'

'Sure, come in.' He motioned to the chair in front of his desk for her to sit down, but she remained standing. He watched her face. 'Hope it's nothing serious. I've had helluva morning,' he joked.

'Well, that depends on what you call serious,' she responded. Dean didn't like the sound of that one little bit. He waited for her to speak, but nothing was forthcoming. She stood poker-faced, staring down at her folded hands, seemingly struggling for the right words.

'So, what is it? What d'ya wanna talk about?' Dean asked nervously.

'I don't know how to say this, so I'll just come out with it, Dean. I'm pregnant.' Chloe looked up, apparently anxious about what Dean would say. After a nanosecond of letting the news sink in, Dean stood up.

'Oh my god, Chloe!' He rushed around the desk and all but flung himself at her, as though he'd just discovered she was a long-lost relative. 'You've saved the day!' Chloe's face exprcssed confusion, shock and relief all rolled into one. 'Oh, Chloe, you've no idea what fantastic news that is. Music to my ears, I can tell you.'

'Dean, what are you talking about? I thought you'd be mad! 'No pregnant women in my business and all that!'

'No! Not at all! Quite the opposite.' It dawned on him that he might need to give an explanation for his rather overexcited and unexpected reaction. 'Sit down and I'll explain.' Dean went on to give a detailed account of the task he'd been set by Dave, the beauty parade that the whole office had probably witnessed going in and out of the office for the last few weeks, and also about the diversity award. He finished off by admitting: 'And all I needed was a woman who had a bun in the oven[14]. And now I've got one. You!' He held her at arms' length and looked at her belly, a bit swollen he now realised, although one would

14. Pregnant.

never know she was pregnant; she'd just look a bit tubby to most people. He moved back to his chair rubbing his hands excitedly and almost as an aside said, 'Congratulations, by the way. I didn't even know you had a boyfriend. How far gone are you?'

'Thirty-two weeks.' And I haven't got a boyfriend.'

'What is it then, the Immaculate Conception?' Dean laughed out loud and looked very indiscreetly at her stomach. 'Bloody hell, Chloe, you don't even look pregnant.'

'Ha ha. No, Dean, it's called a one-night stand and a big, big mistake.'

'Oh god, Chloe. Sorry. Shouldn't have joked about that.' Dean was rather stumped as to what to say next.

Is she happy about it?

'No worries. I couldn't decide whether to keep it or not and, by the time I had, it was too late to do anything about it anyway.'

'Bloody hell, that's a bit rough. I'm really sorry.'

'But about my having conveniently filled your quota of pregnant people, I don't think I'm gonna be able to help you out there. I'm moving to Doncaster to live with Mum and Dad, so they can help out with the baby. So… I'm also handing in my resignation. You'll only have to put up with me for one more week!' She put an envelope on his desk. Well, she may as well've got out a crossbow and fired an arrow straight through Dean's heart, if his reaction was anything to go by.

'No! You can't! I mean…not yet! Don't resign yet. Please. Can you possibly wait until after 26th July?'

'Why? What's happening on 26th July?'

'That's when the Gala Dinner is and when the diversity award will be given out. We're really hoping to win. It'd be great if you could be there. You know…still employed by us…still part of our team… and still pregnant.' Dean looked at her in high anticipation.

'Well, my due date's 15th August but they say I could drop anytime from thirty-seven weeks', which is…' Chloe checked the calendar on her phone. 'Eighteenth July – the week before the dinner, so I don't think that's gonna work, to be honest.' But Dean wasn't going to take no for an answer.

'We'll make it work, Chloe, don't worry. If we win it, I want you to be up on that stage with me collecting the award. We'll even invite your mum, so she can be with you…just in case!'

They debated the sticking points: She wouldn't be allowed to drink alcohol at the ceremony, she didn't have an evening dress for a nine months' pregnant woman, her mum had a tiny car she wasn't sure she could even get into, what if her waters broke and might she simply be too exhausted by that point?

'I dunno, Dean, it seems a bit too risky to me, but let me have a think and I'll come back to you.'

They left it at that for the time being, but, in truth, Dean had already convinced himself that Chloe would hang on in there for him. He'd done her many favours over the years, now he wanted this tiny one back in return. He mulled it over.

Not too unreasonable an ask, is it?

***

Back at Purses, Brooke continued working on a vast array of projects that Mrs Townsend had deemed her capable of undertaking. And she did not disappoint. In fact, her cleaning and housekeeping duties were decreasing almost daily. The silver was polished less frequently, the floors mopped more quickly and tasks that she'd done on a very regular basis when she'd first arrived at Purses were no longer done at all! Brooke fretted about it, but Lady Townsend dismissed her concerns with a regal wave of the hand. Lady Townsend continued to challenge her, giving her tasks that Brooke believed were way beyond her ability. But in every case, albeit sometimes with a little guidance, she rose to the challenge, much to Lady Townsend's delight. And they'd had many amusing moments along the way.

She'd forced her to have meetings with the auctioneer and sent her to buy antiques on her behalf. She even asked her to choose her entire new spring and summer wardrobe from Harvey Nichols with a budget of £10,000. Well golly, she thought she'd died and gone to heaven on that particular day! She'd never had so much fun in her life! She'd also had to prepare notes and presentations for various talks and lectures that Lady Townsend would be giving, and writing up minutes from a wide array of trustees' meetings.

As the day to Newmarket drew closer, Brooke became more and more excited. She and Lady Townsend had told Hugo about Brooke's sudden and surprising involvement in the syndicate. He'd found it highly amusing. Brooke would spend a considerable time talking about Turn The Paige to Hugo, who knew a lot about 'form'. It turned out that not only was his father an avid racehorse fan but – and it should've come as no surprise to her – Portia's father also apparently owned one outright. No syndicate for him. As each revelation came about, Brooke realised that what was so special, incredible and exciting in her life, was just people going about their daily business in Lady Townsend's world. Nothing to write home about. All just taken in their stride.

Brooke spoke to Lord D'Arcy on several occasions about the 12th July. She was becoming anxious at not having a firm offer of a lift to Newmarket and Geoffrey was always so vague about it. She also had to think of an excuse to go out for the day *and* stay overnight. And she had to ask her mother if she'd have Paige for that weekend as well. Brooke buried her head in her hands and let out a little scream. The stress of it was enough to give her palpitations. Her mother had always found Paige a bit of a handful, but it was too much to expect Dawn to take her for the whole weekend. Whenever Brooke went to collect Paige on a Friday afternoon, Dawn was practically waiting to open a bottle of Magner's.

Brooke was struggling with such deceit this time. Where on earth could she say she was going that required her to stay overnight? But she was desperate to experience the luxury of The Jockey Club Rooms and to practice her conversational skills and to implement *Debrett's Guide To Etiquette* with the horseracing fraternity. The thought of declining the offer was unbearable to her. She'd rather give up Charlotte Tilbury lipsticks. So, she did what any self-respecting Essex girl did when faced with such a dilemma; she reached for a large glass of Chardonnay to help her with the imminent choices she faced.

One engagement that she'd recently had to arrange for Mrs Townsend was tickets and accommodation for The Indie Literary festival in Bristol, which was going on from 10th July to 20th July. Mrs Townsend would be attending the second weekend. Given that Dean had only ever associated this Lady Townsend with books, reading and the library, Brooke was mulling around in her mind the vague possibility of telling Dean that she'd been invited to the book festival by Lady Townsend on 12th and 13th July and that they would stay at a local hotel. The five-star Bristol Harbour Hotel and Spa was the one she'd actually booked for Lady Townsend, so she wouldn't tell him that of course. The cheap Holiday Inn Express would create less argument. The more she thought about it, the better the idea seemed. She already had various booklets and brochures about the festival sent to Mrs Townsend and so could talk in detail about the speakers and events she'd read about. As was often the way, Brooke found herself becoming intrigued with this new found thing called a 'literary festival' and decided one day she'd like to go to one for real.

It took her a few days to finetune her story in her mind. She'd considered telling Mrs Townsend what she was going to say to Dean, but then felt dreadful about dragging her into her web of lies, so decided against it. She had to own it.

Even without meeting her, Dean had taken an instant dislike to Lady Townsend, due to the seemingly extraordinary changes she'd been effecting in his wife. He liked the blond and ditsy woman he married and was rather vocal about what he saw as the negative influence this woman was having on her; from Brooke's dress sense, which had gradually gone from tight-fitting and sexy to modest and elegant, from reading *OK!* magazine to *National Geographic* and from watching *Big Brother* to being captivated by *University Challenge* of all things! Brooke wasn't at all sure how Dean would react to her 'going off on a jolly weekend' with her.

***

One day the week before race day, after agonising over it for hours, Brooke determined she'd finally tell Dean about her 'going away to the Indie Literary Festival' that weekend. She was more nervous than she'd ever been about this particular lie. It was such a whopper! Could she hold her nerve? What would he say?

Maybe he won't even let me go!

Brooke considered that thought and bristled at the mere concept of Dean having any sort of control over her anymore. He wouldn't see it as control, of course; he would see it as protecting her, looking out for her, keeping her safe – and almost certainly out of the hands of any other lecherous men. She had to couch this in such a way that he'd not feel threatened, that she was in 'safe' hands and that she wouldn't be doing anything remotely stressful, physically demanding or expensive. Maybe she'd say she felt sorry for Lady Townsend? Maybe she could say that because her friend let her down at the last minute and she didn't want to go alone, that none of her other friends were available? Maybe Lady Townsend could have high blood pressure too, therefore would completely understand the need to be cautious? Then he might see this as Brooke doing a good deed for an old lady.

Yes, that'd work I think!

The sound of Dean's moped rumbling outside snapped her out of her thoughts. Her mouth became dry, her cheeks flushed and her heart was galloping as if trying to reach its personal best. His key turned in the lock and he shouted, 'Home!'

'Hey, babe!' She swallowed hard, but more saliva flooded into her mouth as fast as she'd swallowed it. Before Dean had even put his helmet in its special place, Brooke rushed out to greet him in what appeared to be a flurry of excitement. 'Guess what?' she asked excitedly.

'You've bought another hot tub?' he joked.

'No. Don't be daft! I just got invited by Lady Townsend to go to the Indie Literary Festival in Bristol on 12th July weekend! How about that?'

'What's that, then?' Dean asked, in what can only be described as a measured tone.

'Turns out it's pretty famous. It's like, days of author events, book readings and speakers, that kinda stuff!' She tried her best to come across as casual but excited.

'What's she wanna go with you for? Surely she's got some other old fogies who'd be more interested in that stuff?' he responded after a moment of hesitation. 'And, more to the point, why d'*you* wanna go with *her*?'

'Well, for a start, the friend she was meant to be going with let her down and none of her other friends are available and, secondly, I'd love to go with her. Like I tried to tell you before, she's a lovely old lady and we've developed quite a bit of a friendship as it goes. We love talking about books and she thought it might be a nice, like, opportunity for me. So sweet! And I've never been to Bristol.' She glanced casually over to Dean as she plumped cushions on the sofa.

'That's the weekend I've got my lads' day out.'

'So…what difference does that make?' she enquired whilst quietly hyperventilating.

'Well, I'll have the car. We already agreed that and who'd have Paige? Can't see your mum agreeing to that somehow; she can't even handle a two-hour stint, never mind two days.'

'But you're only going out on the Saturday, aren't you? You

could have Paige on the Sunday?' She was pushing hard.

'Well, to be honest, I was hoping to have the whole weekend off. No responsibilities at all. Just be free to do what I want with the lads for a change.'

'Oh. Right. Fair do's'

I'm gonna have to play this very carefully.

'Well, I can get a lift, so I don't need the car. I'll talk to Dad first and make sure he can be around. It's only when Mum's on her own that she finds it difficult to cope. In fact I'm sure she'd be pleased to see me getting out a bit more; especially to somewhere like that. And with a lady! She'll be dead impressed!' Brooke said hopefully, punching the cushions in an increasingly frenetic fashion.

Dean was about as enthusiastic as when he was forced to play 'Let's Go To Lakeside Shopping' with Paige.

I'll never hear the end of it.

He could hear Jackie now putting on her best telephone voice,

'Oh well of course my daughter is friends with Lady Townsend.' Oh my god it makes me wanna puke.

'You don't look very happy about it, Dean. I thought you'd be pleased for me that I was going away on a nice weekend. I was so excited and now you're making me feel like there's something wrong with it.' She was now pummelling the cushions.

'Well, I just think it's a bit weird, that's all.' Dean felt uncomfortable, but couldn't realistically think of a reason to say no without coming across as some sort of evil jailer. 'You'd have to take your blood pressure machine with you and you'd have to tell her about it in case anything happened.'

'Dean, we're reading and hearing about bloody books! Not

chopping the trees down to make 'em! As it happens, Lady Townsend suffers with high blood pressure too, so she's well aware of the situation.' The lies were coming thick and fast now. It was almost as if Brooke actually believed what she was saying.

'Blimey, you two are pally pally.' He threw his arms up in defeat. 'Well, I suppose I don't see why not.' Deep down though, there were about a thousand reasons why he wasn't happy about it. Not least, was she really going away with Lady Townsend?

'Great. That's that then!' She wanted to hug Dean and give him a big kiss given how utterly relieved she was, but when she thought about his reaction, it narked her.

Why shouldn't I go away for the weekend with a friend? What's he so suspicious about? Where does he think I'm going?

As she decimated the last of the cushions, Brooke failed to see the irony.

Why on earth doesn't he trust me?

21

What To Wear

'Oh my good god!' exclaimed Jackie. 'Two days? I dunno, Brooke. She's quite a handful you know. Where are you going that you can't take her with you?'

Brooke crossed her fingers and screwed her eyes shut, as if it might help the guilt go away, as she told her mother that she was going to the Indie Literary Festival with Lady Townsend, 'the woman she'd met in Brentwood library'.

'Blimey, Brooke! Well, I can't say no to that then, can I? My daughter going to a book festival with a lady! Oh my gawd! I'll have to tell Maeve about this. She'll be dead impressed. Anyway, I'll have to ask your dad first. I don't want him stressing. His diabetes is bad enough. I dunno how he'd cope with Paige for that long.' What she really meant is that she didn't know how *she'd* cope with Paige for that long! ''ang on a minute...' Jackie placed her palm over the mouthpiece of the phone and mouthed dramatically to Rick, who was engrossed in the sports pages of the *Daily Mirror*, 'Rick! Rick! She only wants us to have Paige for two days – overnight!' Her eyes were wide open with horror. 'But she's going to some book thing... with this Lady Townsend woman!' She gave him one of those looks that implied they should all feel very privileged about it.

Rick was much more laidback than Jackie. Nothing

fazed him. She could've told him Brooke had been invited to Buckingham Palace and he wouldn't have batted an eyelid. He was one of those world-weary black cab drivers who'd seen it all. He looked up from his newspaper and smiled. 'It'll be fine, love, don't worry about it. Poor doll needs a break from that kid. We'll manage. Say – he would say tell her yes. But tell her from me not to start getting any fancy ideas from her lady friend. She's my favourite Essex girl, don't forget.'

Jackie relayed the good news to Brooke, who, on the other end of the phone, punched the air and mouthed 'YESSS!!'

'Thanks, Mum, you're a star.'

'Mmm. A glutton for punishment, more like. Just tell her to be on her best behaviour and make sure you send her with plenty of them Chupa Chups lollies. And Dad says not to start getting any fancy ideas, 'cause you're his favourite Essex girl.'

There it was again. First, she'd had it from Dean, then from Dawn, then from Stacey and now from her own father.

What is it with people? Why do they wanna keep holding me down? Holding me back? Determined to not let me forget I'm Essex? I'm sick of it.

She had to hide her anger and frustration at that last comment. She needed them more than they needed to see their granddaughter right now. So, she graciously thanked her mother and arranged for them to pick Paige up at 10am on 12th July. She still hadn't heard details from Geoffrey how he was going to get her to Newmarket, but she didn't imagine it would be earlier than ten.

The days leading up to the big day were almost unbearable for Brooke. She had to keep reminding herself what she'd told Dean, what she'd told her Mum and Dad and what she'd told

Lady Townsend. She'd started to make notes about her story so she didn't get muddled up. Such deceit could induce a heart attack! Her mind shifted yet again to what she was going to wear to the races. Lady Townsend had instructed her on smart dress and a hat if she wanted as they would be in the members area of the Grandstand, where there was a dress code – and it was Ladies Day after all.

Never worn a hat in me life! Don't think I'm gonna start now somehow. Maybe I could borrow something from Antonia? I wonder if Mrs T could ask her for me?

She soon plucked up the courage to ask her. On the Wednesday before the big day, Brooke arrived at work as usual. It was hard to believe that Dean, poor chap, still had no idea that she was off to work three times a week and had been for almost a year! It probably said more about him than her! As Brooke walked into the hall, Hugo came out to greet her with a smile on his face.

'Morning, Brooke. There's a large delivery waiting for you in the Blue Bedroom upstairs. Mrs Townsend said she'll see you up there when you arrive. Who's a lucky girl, then?'

'What d'ya mean?' Brooke asked, confused.

'The delivery's from Antonia Dubarry; it looks like a bunch of rather nice dresses to me.'

Brooke's face lit up and she squealed and ran up the stairs two at a time. She spent the next two hours trying on numerous dresses and suits. However, it was the Dolce & Gabbana dress and jacket that won the day; a 1950s-style, white heavy silk dress with navy polka dots, matching jacket, little white gloves and a wide-rimmed navy straw boater with a ribbon and bow at the back. She stared intently at her own reflection in the long mirror. Now it was *her* turn to look herself up and down. Ruthless self-assessment instead of being judged by others. Her eyes rested on her own face and she scanned it, looking for fault. Was she good enough? Her scrutinising moved down to her body, sharply sculpted by the boned bodice of the dress. Was she worthy enough? She considered her belted slender waist, holding in all that fakery. Would people realise she was actually an imposter? A fraud. Didn't belong. A woman of *no* substance. Depressing working class pretending to be upper class. Was she merely entertainment for the syndicate? She burst into tears.

I wish Dean was here and I wish Mum could see me dressed up like this.

A few minutes later, Mrs Townsend walked briskly into the bedroom. When she saw Brooke, she gasped audibly at this vision of beauty in front of her. Then she noticed Brooke's tears and her face fell. 'Brooke, what on earth's the matter? Why are you crying?' Lady Townsend was genuinely taken aback.

Brooke could not answer her because Brooke didn't know.

'I dunno… I mean *I don't know*, Mrs T. It feels all wrong and yet so…so…exactly right. I'm feeling all confused. It must be my hormones or something.' She went to wipe her nose on her sleeve, but was caught as quick as a flash by Mrs Townsend who thrust her own hand forward to stop her.

'No! Don't do that, dear! Here's a tissue.'

Brooke realised her faux pas and cried some more. 'See, if you hadn't been here, Antonia's dress would be covered in my snot! I'm not safe to be released into polite society.'

'Now don't speak like that, Brooke, dear. We're trying to improve your hinterland…and your vocabulary, remember. "Snot" is not a word that should be in it. Ever. Mmm?' She looked at Brooke over her spectacles. Brooke wiped her nose on the tissue and sniffed hard. 'My guess is that it's all been rather overwhelming for you of late. Perhaps you'd prefer to leave the races or even leave the syndicate?'

'Oh god, no! Please! I can't wait to go. I'm so excited I wanna burst.' Mrs Townsend was relieved. 'I love how I look and how it makes me feel, but it frightens me at the same time. It's like I'm a sort of modern-day Cinderella. I'll go to the ball, wear this beautiful dress, have the most fantastic day and then have to go back to the reality and grind of life at home with Dean, who thinks I'm only fit to stay at home and get his tea.'

Lady Townsend regarded her as she might a piece of fine and complex artwork. 'I do understand that, Brooke; never forget where I came from. My advice to you right now is to take full advantage of all the opportunities being presented to you. Enjoy them. Let the people you've met help you, broaden your horizons and educate you. Who knows what you could become? And don't forget, it's not a one-way street either, dear. We learn things from you as well – Geoffrey especially! I don't know what you two find to talk about, but he's utterly intrigued by you and your life.'

Brooke laughed as she remembered their recent trip. 'Did he tell you about our little detour to McDonald's the other day?'

Lady Townsend looked shocked. 'No! Geoffrey went to *McDonald's*? With *you*?'

'Yep. Can you believe he asked for custard and a plate and fork for his apple pie?! I can't remember when I laughed so much!'

Lady Townsend shook her head in disbelief and laughed heartily. This small exchange lifted Brooke's spirits and she thought about Lady Townsend's remark: 'Who knows what you could become?'

She's the only one who thinks I can become anything. And maybe Geoffrey. Why doesn't anyone else? My own family and friends, who've known me way longer? And why do I feel like I'm betraying them for even trying?

Brooke looked one more time at herself in the mirror. She'd not wanted to wear a hat, convinced she'd feel too conspicuous, so she was pleasantly surprised at how she felt with one on top of her head now. There was something about it that actually made her feel *less* conspicuous; the rim was extremely wide so, depending on how it was positioned, she could partially hide her eyes, which somehow made her feel a little more comfortable.

Instructed by Lady Townsend, she walked elegantly and confidently around the Blue Bedroom on tiptoe, *Sense & Sensibility* placed strategically on her head by Lady Townsend, who assessed her walk, as a ballet teacher might her pupil. Brooke's head was held high; she pulled her shoulders back and slowly, gradually a beautiful, broad smile appeared.

'I think we've nailed it, Mrs T!' Brooke went back to the mirror one last time before removing the outfit and tilted her chin upwards. As she absorbed her reflection, she pinned down that feeling that'd escaped her earlier.

An increasingly present, steely determination, to overcome whatever barriers she faced in her life, in order to be successful.

22

A Day At The Races

The day before race day, Brooke finally received the information she'd been waiting for via a text from Geoffrey.

Someone will come to pick you up at 11am, take you to Purses, wait for you to change and bring you to Newmarket. Ring me when you arrive and I'll come and find you. G

About bloody time, Geoffrey!

At last, she could relax. She'd been on tenterhooks for days because Lord D'Arcy had been busy and unusually uncommunicative. At just before 10am on race day, Jackie and Rick came to pick Paige up. Dean was on his way out to pick up his chums for their lads' day out – and his mystery assessment, of course. He greeted his in-laws quickly but warmly and gave Paige an affectionate kiss on her head and a quick cuddle. He turned to Brooke with a feeling of unease. Holding her at arms' length he looked her straight in the eye and in a measured tone said 'You too have a nice weekend - with your new friend.'

'She does have a name you know. Lady Townsend.'

'Mmm. Yeah. Whatever. Enjoy your books and I'll see you Sunday. What time will you be back?'

'Not sure, but I'll get a lift home so no worries. I'll let you know what time I think I'll be back.' It didn't go unnoticed by Dean or Brooke's parents that she couldn't look him in the eye as she said this and her voice sounded different. Dean gave her a hug and long, lingering kiss on her lips. Rick rolled his eyes.

'I love you, Mrs De'Ath, and I'm so happy you're my wife.' Then he wheelspan away in Flora.

What the hell does he mean by that?

Before she had much of a chance to think about it, Paige let out one of her screams. She'd got her hair caught in the zip of her Spiderman outfit she was trying to pull on. Jackie tried to extract her hair, while Rick tried to stop her screaming and Brooke found a Chupa Chups. Jackie confessed to feeling very nervous about having her for two days and went through an outrageous list of scenarios that might occur: she has an accident, won't go to sleep, refuses food, screams and won't stop (their biggest fear), won't get into her car seat, climbs a tree and can't get down etc. and what would Brooke want them to do if any of them actually happened?'

Internally Brooke panicked in case her mother talked herself into changing her mind. Once Paige had stopped screaming, Brooke ran upstairs to get her bag of things and a huge box of toys and chivvied them all out the door before it was too late. Once the front door had shut, she leaned against it and let out a huge sigh of relief. At last, she could focus on herself. She checked her watch. She had under an hour and with experienced military precision and organisation, she packed her own overnight bag with everything she thought she'd need. She finished tidying up and checked the house was in good order for Dean, so that he didn't have anything to complain about. Her mind went back to his departing words and a knot of pure, unadulterated guilt tied itself up in her stomach and failed to dispel.

On the dot of 11am, as Brooke sat waiting for her lift, a monster-like SUV with blacked-out windows turned into Elephant Close and gradually drew slowly up outside her house. An enormous man, Middle Eastern in appearance, in a suit and dark glasses, knocked at the door. She leaped up eagerly and left the house, banging the front door behind her. As Murphy's Law would have it, her nosy neighbour Mikey watched on with interest as he pretended to hose down his car in his drive. He became positively intrigued, if not downright alarmed, when the big man yawned and stretched his arms out, revealing a Glock 17 in a holster, under his suit jacket. Mikey dropped the hose and gawped, quite unable to speak. He knew those two next door were up to no good. They were obviously into drug-dealing. Brooke pretended she hadn't seen him and allowed the big man to open the back door of the car for her. Meanwhile, Mikey ran inside to share what he'd witnessed, with his wife. They discussed the gun, the fact Brooke had a large bag and debated whether to phone the police. Instead, they twitched behind the curtains.

As soon as she got in, Brooke leaned forward. 'So who are you then? I'm assuming Geoffrey… I mean Lord D'Arcy sent you?'

'No, my boss… he send me,' the man replied starchily.

'Well, who's your boss then?' Brooke asked somewhat alarmed.

'Sheikh Mohammed Bin Halem. He say I must pick you up, take you to Purses? Wait, then drive you back to Newmarket.'

Brooke's mouth dropped open and she burst out laughing.

OH… MY… GOD!

She sat in the back of the SUV chuckling away to herself,

trying to imagine the conversation that must have gone on between Geoffrey and the sheikh. When they arrived at Purses, she invited the man to come inside for a cup of tea while she got changed. He looked at her as though she were mad.

'No. I stay here.'

'Please yourself, mate. I won't be long.'

She dashed inside and bumped straight into Hugo. 'Sorry, Hugo, gotta dash. Got better fish to fry today!' They both laughed as she bounded upstairs to the Blue Bedroom to get changed. She'd already done her hair and make-up. In the full-length mirror, she examined herself carefully, made a few adjustments, pulled on her gloves and placed her boater at the correct angle on her head. One more look followed by a broad smile. As she elegantly made her way down the steps, Hugo was at the bottom of the staircase. She felt as though she were in a film, like this was not really happening at all. A most unexpected sound emanated from Hugo in the form of a wolf whistle.

'Oh my god, Hugo, who knew you could wolf whistle?' Brooke cackled coarsely, rather smashing the illusion of sophistication.

'Wow, Brooke! I mean just…wow! You look utterly gorgeous. Or should I say, you scrub up quite nicely?' He leaned against the wall, folded his arms and made no bones about staring. He couldn't take his eyes off her. Brooke's immediate response was to crack a self-deprecating joke, but she stopped herself in time, remembering Mrs Townsend's words: 'you must learn how to take a compliment graciously'.

'Well thank you so much, Hugo. I rather think that I look like the bees' knees too!' she retorted with an exaggerated plummy voice.

Hugo couldn't help himself. He walked up to her and gently gave her a kiss on the cheek. 'Seriously, Brooke, I don't know what to say.' He began to have the same unholy thoughts that Lord D'Arcy frequently had in Brooke's presence and had to banish them out of his brain fearing he may no longer be responsible for his actions. 'Just have a wonderful day – and I hope she wins. I've got a hundred pounds on her each way.' He winked.

Course you have.

'I will, Hugo, and thanks for the compliment – it's good for a girl like me! I won't be a minute, I've just gotta get some stuff from the library.' She dashed off and grabbed all the literature on her desk about the Indie Literary Festival before returning and saying goodbye to a still mesmerised Hugo. And with that, she walked out and towards the car. The big man got out and even his stern poker face cracked into a little smile as he opened the door for her, with a small nod of the head.

By 12.30pm they'd arrived at The July Course, where Turn The Paige would be running in a few hours and where she was about to meet the syndicate for lunch. The pressure she felt was purely self-inflicted. She agonised over how she looked, what she'd say, what food she'd choose and how she'd eat it, how she should behave during the race, how much she should bet, if indeed she should bet at all, what she should do if their horse won and what if she lost? The complexities of the multiple decisions she had to make for the entire day going forward were a nightmare. She rang Lord D'Arcy.

'I'm at the entrance. Can you come and get me?' she asked, feeling totally out of her depth. She began to drag her overnight bag out the car and wondered where she could put it, before the big man noticed and stopped her.

'No! No! You leave in car. I take to Jockey Club now. They put in room!' he shouted, alarmed at this strange woman's even stranger actions.

'On my way, sweetheart!' Geoffrey roared with obvious pleasure, over background sounds of people chatting and laughing loudly. Brooke smiled. He was like the warm, all-encompassing arms of a protective father when she needed it the most.

She could not help but giggle as Lord D'Arcy bounded towards her like a youthful, untrained puppy but in a crumpled linen suit and panama. Lord D'Arcy stood before her and was without words; he simply gestured towards her. He gave her an owners' entrance badge, grabbed her hand and gently pulled her along and into the members' area of the Grandstand. As she was entering, she recognised a group of rather crudely dressed young girls hanging around outside, the same ones who'd sneered at her at Tattersall's. She took a deep breath while they gawped at her. As she passed them, she smiled and managed a nod and a 'Good afternoon, ladies!' in her very best telephone voice, before walking past with her head held high.

Take that, bitches!

One can take the girl out of Essex but one cannot take Essex out of the girl! She knew she looked striking and was in the mood to take advantage of it. Within a few minutes she was in the company of Lady Townsend, Antonia, Sir Blessington and Lord D'Arcy of course. They all seemed delighted to see her again and were quick to engage in conversation about all manner of things. She'd read the *Daily Telegraph* every day leading up to this day. In addition, to familiarise herself with the terminology, she'd forced herself to read the *Racing Post*, but had fallen asleep in bed with it, causing Dean much angst. What was his wife going to do next?

Lunch was a set menu, which relieved her of the stress of choosing her food, so she was able to actually enjoy it, along with champagne that flowed. Her party were clearly in a separate part of the complex to the 'ordinary folk'. She observed an actual physical barrier between the two areas, where the brigade that had paid £65 (being dressed in smart suits, fancy frocks and hats) were separated from those that had only paid £12 (being dressed in jeans, t-shirts and trainers.) For some reason this bothered her out of all proportion and she found herself continually staring at the people on the other side of the fence, who in turn were quite clearly staring at the people on her side of the fence. At one point a man on the 'other side' made some sort of sexual gesture at her and guffawed. Brooke was shocked and could think of nothing else to do but poke her tongue out and walk away.

Perv.

The atmosphere crackled with anticipation, as the jockeys prepared their horses for the first race and Lady Townsend came and sat with Brooke at the end of their lunch, to share in the excitement. Antonia joined them and left Lord D'Arcy and Sir Blessington to chat. Both ladies complimented Brooke on how she looked. Antonia especially seemed so excited that she'd made Brooke's day even more special by loaning her D&G. Brooke didn't understand what she'd done to deserve it and she was oblivious at that moment to how many people – especially men – in the grandstand – the Jockey Club capitalise this word on their website, were literally dribbling at the very sight of her.

The noise and building excitement were palpable and Brooke took the opportunity to ask Geoffrey how she could place a bet on Turn The Paige.

'Oh, sweetheart, of course! I'm so sorry! I forgot you haven't had the chance! We already placed our bets earlier. Come with me and we'll get that sorted straight away. Then we'll watch the weigh out and see her being paraded around the ring before the race.' With that, he grabbed her hand again and escorted her to the betting area. There and back, heads turned and Geoffrey was clearly relishing being seen with this beautiful young filly on his arm! Brooke had to work on keeping her mouth closed as she absorbed the atmosphere; the immaculately dressed women, the colour, noise and the money changing hands at the betting booths.

'How much do you want to bet?' Lord D'Arcy asked.

'God. I dunno. I've never bet on a horse before. Only in a sweepstake with my old workmates. The Grand National, I think it was.' Brooke was feeling invincible, helped by rather too much champagne and multiple compliments. 'I dunno, how about a monkey? Or maybe a grand?'

Geoffrey looked quite confused. 'A monkey?'

'Yeah. You know. Five hundred quid,' Brooke replied.

'Is that Essex speak?' he teased.

Brooke realised that Geoffrey would almost certainly not know any slang, so amongst the shouting and general noise she went on to loudly explain the basic numbers, slurring her words as she did so. 'You've got your "deep-sea diver" – a fiver. You know, five quid. Then there's a "score". Twenny quid. A "Pony's" twenny-five quid. A "Bullseye's" fifty quid. Then there's a "ton" which is a hundred and a grand's a thousand pounds.'

'Oh I know that last one,' he retorted, feeling rather pleased with himself. 'Right…well then… a monkey it is. Do you want that each way, placed or to win?'

'Actually, I'm feeling very lucky today, Geoffrey. I checked out the form of all the other horses in the *Racing Post* and I can't see why Turn The Paige can't win! So d'ya know what?' She swayed slightly. 'I'm gonna put *two* grand on her to win!' She stabbed the air as she spoke, still slurring.

Lord D'Arcy didn't want to burst her bubble, but he did feel compelled to urge caution. 'Sweetheart, one should never bet more than one can afford to lose. That's an awful lot of money for a first-time bet. Remember what Mark said – she's the only filly and unlikely to win. Maybe you could bet on her being placed, mm?'

Bloody cheek!

'Who says I can't afford to lose a couple of grand? I've got savings, you know!' she shouted back annoyed, swaying slightly and waving her finger at him. 'Two grand to win!'

'Alright, sweetheart, as you wish.' He held up both his hands in the surrender position. Brooke removed a wad of cash from her handbag and counted out the notes, asking Geoffrey to watch and make sure she didn't miscount. Even she realised she'd had a tad too much to drink.

'Will you come with me and make sure I say it right?' she asked in a helpless voice.

'I've got an account with the Tote so I can do it for you if you like?' Lord D'Arcy offered.

'Nah. I'll do it myself. Gotta learn, Geoffrey. Gotta learn! Thanks anyway.' She didn't understand the Tote, so asked if she could please go to the William Hill booth. She'd heard of

William Hill. Geoffrey smiled and stood right by her as she placed her bet.

£2000 at 20:1 on Turn The Paige to win in the Bunbury Cup at 3pm. The cashier handed Brooke the ticket. She squealed and clapped her hands wildly; her trademark reaction to an exciting moment. It was topped off by catching their jockey Darren O'Hearne being weighed in. Brooke gave him a wave and thumbs up and he waved back with a full-on Irish smile. They then made their way to the parade ring. Geoffrey pointed out her pricked up ears and confident, almost cocky stride; Turn The Paige looked relaxed and content. If a horse could look cheeky, this filly did! Brooke gave another wave to Darren as they were led away to the starting gate.

She looks so good. She's gonna win, I can feel it!

They made their way back through the crowds and Brooke found herself grinning at everyone as she held on to her hat after a gust of wind threatened to blow it off her head. She wanted to tell the world what she'd done and for them to be as excited for her as she was. To the other racegoers she appeared to be just one of the many very tipsy upper-class twits with more money than sense.

There were two races before Turn The Paige and four afterwards. Even though Brooke hadn't placed any bets on any other horses, she decided she'd secretly choose one in each race, based purely on whether she liked the jockey's colours or the name of the horse. Her heart raced as the thunderous sound of galloping horses' hooves on grass reverberated everywhere and the crowd cheered, shouted and screamed for their own horse. There appeared to be no holding back and so she too began cheering for Cleaning Lady in the first race. It came a respectable fourth and she surprised herself at how she'd got so animated. She selected the next horse based on the jockey's red and green stripes – Dean's favourite jelly baby colours.

At about 2.45pm, the syndicate made their way to the front of the grandstand to get the best possible view of the race. Brooke genuinely felt her heart was about to burst and she became quite concerned. Within a few minutes she'd pulled her new 'wrist watch-style' mobile blood pressure device out of her bag and as discreetly as possible conducted a quick test. It was up quite a bit, so she took a minute to sit down, shut her eyes and take a few deep breaths. The rest of the syndicate were so preoccupied they didn't even notice as the jockeys coaxed their horses into the stalls. Lord D'Arcy looked around for Brooke and was alarmed to see her in an apparently meditative state.

'Brooke, sweetheart! Are you alright? The race is about to start. Quick!' he shouted. She stood up to join him. Mrs Townsend stood on the other side of her. Then, after a few more moments in a state of high anticipation, the stalls banged open and they were off! Turn The Paige's colours were pink and black diamonds – a colour combination Brooke had highly approved of. She could see the horse clearly from where she was standing and from the off Brooke screamed as though she was being tortured, her arms flailed and she shouted, punched the air and jumped up and down. 'C'mon, girl…you can do it, COME ON! COME ON! TURN THE PAIGE… YOU CAN DO IT!' She had completely forgotten anything about decorum and screamed with every fibre of her being. Both Lord D'Arcy and Lady Townsend occasionally turned to watch her and exchanged a knowing smile. Their own support was somewhat more muted. Turn The Paige was running in the back third at about half way, so as if it were even possible, Brooke turned up the volume and the speed of her support until she was screeching and at serious risk of damaging her vocal chords! As the pack moved around and with another four furlongs to go, it was as if Turn The Paige suddenly realised she was in a race and she stepped up her speed and began to overtake the front third of the pack one by one. Brooke was as good as out of control, as she saw her horse get closer and closer to the front. The roar from the syndicate was getting louder around her and Brooke thought her eardrums might explode – worse than Paige! At one furlong to go, Turn The Page was running in second place and yet again, she got a second wind and suddenly shot off, came alongside and then overtook the leader, Mummy's Boy. Brooke let out one almighty long scream as she punched the air with both hands continually for the last ten seconds of the race after which her world went into a weird kind of slow motion as she watched Turn The Paige cross the finishing line in first place. Brooke could not contain herself and threw her arms around Geoffrey first whilst continuing to scream in his ear. She then turned to Mrs Townsend, who was laughing, clapping and looking quite flushed. Brooke thrust her arms around her and picked her up off her feet yelling 'We won! We Won! Turn The Paige won! I knew she'd win! I knew She wouldn't let us down!'

'Brooke, let me down dear, please!' Lady Townsend was ill prepared for such a move and her Tena Lady Silhouette pants suddenly came into their own.

'Thank you thank you so, so much for letting me in to your syndicate!' she yelled out throwing her arms open wide towards the group. Sir Blessington and Antonia were clapping and cheering in a dignified way and found Brooke's reaction highly amusing but endearing nevertheless. All of a sudden, Brooke felt very dizzy and her head pounded. She knew it was blood pressure-related and it was dangerous to ignore the symptoms, so, not caring about what anyone thought, she once again put her BP device on her wrist and measured. It was alarmingly high at 148/96. So, without any fuss, warning or explanation to anyone, she simply lay down completely horizontal, right where she was across the empty seats while everyone else remained standing. On catching sight of her, the rest of the syndicate immediately bent over her and Lord D'Arcy demanded someone get a paramedic from the first-aid tent. With her eyes still closed, Brooke held up her hand – the one with the BP device on it – and formed her hand into a 'STOP' position. Lady Townsend noticed the device on her wrist and remembered Brooke had told her that she had blood pressure issues. She knelt down by Brooke's head and whispered in her ear very gently, 'It's alright, dear, someone's coming to help. Just keep calm, breathe slowly and don't worry about anything else at all. We'll look after you.' She took Brooke's hat off, stroked her hair and held her hand.

A paramedic was there within a few minutes and cleared the area of people. He asked Brooke a few questions to gauge how she was, which she answered clearly but with her eyes still shut. He saw the blood pressure device and looked at it, by which time her blood pressure had already gone down. He took his own reading, which was higher than Brooke's. He repeated it five minutes later and it'd gone down again. Then he requested someone get some water as he took her pulse and conducted an ECG on the spot, as he felt there was a mild risk of heart attack, given her answers to his questions. He then pricked her finger to test her blood sugar levels. Having consumed at least one bottle of champagne, possibly even two, there were no problems on that front! Then she opened her eyes to see Lord D'Arcy wide-eyed and scared, Antonia looking mortified, Sir Blessington looking at his racing programme and Lady Townsend tending to her.

Brooke smiled weakly at them all. 'I'm fine. Honestly, people, I'm fine. I just had a funny turn. It's my blood pressure, that's all. I just needed to lie down.' With that she sat up slowly and put her hat back on. They helped her get back into a sitting position and the paramedic declared she didn't need an ambulance or to go to hospital, but highly recommended that she came back to the first-aid tent to lie down for a bit.

'But I want to lead Turn The Paige into the parade ring! Please?! You can't not let me. Not now!'

They all looked at the paramedic and waited with bated breath for his reply.

'OK, but only if I come with you, you walk slowly and afterwards you come and lie down.'

'That's a good compromise, dear, I think we must take this good man's advice. We'll be right by your side. And I wonder if we shouldn't phone your husband, dear?' Mrs Townsend offered. The rest of the syndicate all nodded and mumbled their agreement with the plan.

'Do not call Dean under any circumstances – please. He doesn't even know I'm here! You'll send my blood pressure through the roof again if you do!' she pleaded. They reluctantly agreed, but said if she got any worse or had to go to A&E, they would have to.

Lord D'Arcy was so concerned about telling Brooke what she'd won, fearing another onset of symptoms that he decided to keep quiet about it until a time he felt her delicate heart could take the shock. Very slowly Brooke was helped to her feet and with Lord D'Arcy on one arm and the paramedic on the other, followed by the two ladies and Sir Blessington, they made their way very carefully down to the ring and congratulated the jockey. Brooke patted the horse on the side of her head and whispered 'The girl done good…girl done good!' Then she took the lead and walked alongside as they paraded their winning horse to the world. Well, Newmarket anyway. Brooke couldn't remember any time in her life when she'd felt such a thrill.

Although reluctant to keep her end of the bargain, Brooke did as she was told and went back with the paramedic to the first-aid tent, where he made her lie down in a peaceful room on her own. The others thought it best not to go with her, that she should have no distractions, no one to talk to, just to lie down and rest for an hour or so. Lady Townsend agreed to come back and collect her before the last race if she was deemed to be fit and well enough to watch it and maybe they could persuade the directors to delay their post-match congratulatory drink until Brooke was with them all. She shut her eyes but could not stop smiling as she replayed the last half an hour or so through in her mind again and again. She lay there, clothing loosened, looking for all the world as though she'd been deflowered!

Crikey, my throat hurts… I've never screamed so much in my life… My god, she won! She actually won! I can't believe it! I wonder how much I've won?

Brooke never was any good at maths and she certainly didn't understand odds, no matter how much Geoffrey had tried to explain to her. So, she was quite clueless as to the size of her win. In the back of her mind, she secretly hoped she might double her money. As she lay there in the warm tent with a significant amount of champagne on board, her blood pressure beginning to decrease and the pounding in her head beginning to fade, she succumbed to sleep.

***

'Brooke, dear. Brooke? How are you feeling?' Mrs Townsend was gently stroking Brooke's hand and talking quietly, not wanting to shock her. Brooke stirred and opened her eyes, saw Mrs Townsend and smiled.

'I didn't dream all that did I, Mrs T? Turn The Paige did win, didn't she?'

'Yes, dear, she did indeed. How are you feeling?'

Brooke sat up slowly and while Mrs Townsend watched, Brooke measured her own blood pressure – the irony of her doing that in a first-aid tent completely passing her by! It was back to normal.

'Hey, Johnny?!' Brooke shouted through to the other side of the tent. 'My BP's back to 120/80, can I go now?' Johnny came through and conducted his own reading: 130/76.

'Mmm. Well as long as you're feeling OK. But I strongly suggest you don't do anything more stressful today' he advised.

'OK, well I won't pick a horse for the last race then!' The simplicity of her argument made him chuckle. She had a sudden thought and asked if she could take a selfie with him and Lady Townsend. They both looked somewhat perplexed, but agreed anyway. Brooke was careful to get a headshot only – no clothes could be seen – of her and Mrs Townsend at any rate. She'd tried to take a few selfies earlier, but the background was always a giveaway.

Then they joined the rest of the syndicate back in the grandstand just in time for the last race. Lord D'Arcy welcomed her back as though she'd been gone forever, fussing over her, insisting she sat down and getting her a glass of water. Brooke remained seated and Sir Blessington bullied anyone who dared to try and stand in front of her, so she could still see the race. She felt like a princess! This enforced position meant that the decorum seriously lacking earlier, was most definitely present now. For a few moments Brooke De'Ath looked the epitome of elegance and class. Once the race had finished, Geoffrey deemed her fit enough to break the news.

'Brooke. Sweetheart. You need to collect your winnings. Are you aware of how much you've won?'

'No, not really. A couple of grand? Something like that?'

'Brooke, I want you to put that machine thing back on your wrist again before I tell you.'

She laughed, assuming he was joking.

'I mean it, Brooke. Seriously. Please put it on now.'

'Alright, Geoffrey, don't get your knickers in a twist[15]!' Brooke obeyed and showed him the perfectly normal result.

He took a deep breath before announcing, 'Brooke. You have won forty thousand pounds.' Lord D'Arcy picked up her wrist and checked the number again – status unchanged.

'Hahaha, Geoffrey. And the rest. Come on, tell me. What did I win?' He maintained his serious face and tone of voice, which worried her.

He repeated, 'Brooke. You have just won forty thousand pounds.' He looked straight into her eyes and then again at the

15. Don't panic.

device and this time the number was up. 'Now, Brooke, please, breathe slowly, take it easy, do you want to lie down again?'

Brooke's face was unreadable; almost vacant. Eyes staring straight ahead, hands dangling down by her side, brain a fog. No words would come out. The rest of the syndicate looked at her as though she were a caged animal in a zoo, who'd suddenly decided to stop entertaining the visitors. Brooke's eyes suddenly shifted to theirs and the sight made her giggle. The giggle became a chuckle, the chuckle became a laugh, the laugh became a wail and the wail became the sort of sobbing laugh of a near hysterical woman, with tears flowing freely down her cheeks.

'Now let's get you seated up at the bar. The course directors kindly delayed our winners' drinks until you were feeling better!' Lord D'Arcy explained.

'Winners' drinks? Never mind about winners' drinks! 'What the hell am I gonna tell Dean?'

***

While all these shenanigans were going on in Newmarket, over in Roydon, Dean and his chums spent the morning go-karting and eating lunch in the less-than-desirable pub he'd been requested to mystery visit. His friends were decidedly unimpressed and gave him untold grief for insisting they ate there. They were, of course, oblivious as to Dean's secret mission and as he was driving they'd no choice but to do what he wanted. He became extremely perplexed about the assignment, because many questions he had to answer simply didn't make sense in the context of this pub. Early afternoon was spent drinking at a local pub in Duxford and then on to the Imperial War Museum where they all suitably embarrassed themselves singing the theme tune to the *Dam Busters* film with the ubiquitous pretend binoculars up at their eyes.

When they got back to Brentwood around 7pm, they spent the rest of the evening in Wetherspoons Dairyman, drinking yet more beer and eating burgers and chips, before getting back home around 11pm. Dean crashed out in front of the TV for half an hour, but before he went to bed, to satisfy himself, he pulled the hard copy of the mystery shopper questionnaire for The White Horse in Roydon, out of his man-bag. As he looked carefully at the front cover, where the venue name, address and contact details were, his mouth fell open.

The White Horse, Roydon, IP22 6DS

Shit! That's not a Hertfordshire postcode. I think I've just mystery shopped the wrong fucking pub!

23

Celebration Time

Brooke'd finally come out of her dazed state and allowed herself to be treated like a china doll and driven back to The Jockey Club Rooms. The syndicate were not going to meet up again for dinner until 8pm so everyone went to their rooms. Brooke noticed the manager Christopher in the entrance hall as she arrived. He greeted her warmly and asked if she'd had a good day at the races. She wasn't quite sure how to answer that.

A win, forty grand and a near-miss heart attack! How can I explain all that?!

'Yes, lovely. Thank you, Christopher. I'm not sure where my room is or my bag. The man who brought me to Newmarket said he'd bring it here.'

'Ah yes, Sheikh Mohammed's bodyguard.'

'Oh, so that's what he was! I did wonder.'

'Your bag's been taken to your room. Follow me.' With that he escorted her to a room on the first floor, chatting as they went. He opened the door for her and watched her face. A vibrant floral cover was thrown over the huge, high bed. A small sofa, armchair and table were positioned in the corner of the room overlooking the lawn. Christopher explained how everything in the room worked.

'Blimey! This is gorgeous. I've never stayed anywhere this

posh!' Brooke exclaimed, neither embarrassed or ashamed. No airs or graces there! Christopher smiled and beckoned her over to the window where he pointed to the bronze statue of the horse; *Sariska* by Philip Blacker, and gave her a little history lesson about it, as well as about the famous statue of one of the greatest racehorses in the world – *Hyperion* – the one that could be seen from the High Street. Brooke listened with interest and Christopher stayed for some time patiently answering her many questions about the club and its members.

'Oh my god, Clare Balding's a member here? Are you serious? Holy Moly!'

After some time, Chrisopher discreetly looked at his watch and said he'd have to go, but that she should contact him if she needed anything at all. He sensed that this was not her normal environment and wanted to make her feel as comfortable as possible.

Once on her own, she went back into the bathroom and picked up the toiletries one by one, sniffing as she went. She examined everything. Especially the paintings – of horses, naturally – on the bedroom wall. The tea and coffee-making facilities could not be wasted, she decided, so she made herself a cup of tea, sat down on the comfy chair and stared out the window at some race-goers who were taking a stroll around the gardens.

From her handbag, she pulled out her cheque from William Hill and stared at it.

What on earth am I gonna do with it?

All the money she'd ever earned with Lady Townsend was in cash. She and Dean had never had separate bank accounts; they'd only ever needed a joint one. To say that a cheque for forty thousand pounds being deposited would cause a stir, was an understatement.

Maybe I'll have to open a bank account of my own?

Something made her think that Dean wouldn't be comfortable about that. Her resourceful brain went into overdrive trying to think of creative ways to get to her winnings without opening a bank account. Maybe she'd talk to Geoffrey. He seemed good with money and might be able to advise her.

Maybe he could invest it for me? He's always banging on about his portfolio, whatever that is.

However she ended up accessing the money, the bigger question was what on earth would she spend it on? They could go on a fabulous holiday to the Caribbean – she'd always wanted to go there, ever since she'd heard it was a favourite haunt of Beyoncé. She could buy a whole new wardrobe of designer clothes or a second car – a little Porsche, maybe? Second-hand, of course, but that wouldn't matter. Maybe it could go towards moving to a bigger house, now Dean was earning more? Hutton Mount in Brentwood – a private estate. That's where she really wanted to live. Even Google's street cars weren't allowed down there. All of those things were possibilities, except Dean might just notice them!

Maybe she'd have to spill the beans now? Brooke went round and round in circles in her head, eventually deciding to run a relaxing bath. No problem is so big that it can't be solved by a warm bath with plenty of bubbles. She'd brought a second outfit of her own to wear down to dinner; a jumpsuit with wide leg trousers and a flattering halter neck in a vibrant red and a large black chiffon shawl to wrap around her shoulders.

As she lay in the bath, surrounded by the smell of jasmine

and patchouli, her mind wandered to Dean. Instead of the happy warm thoughts she normally had when she thought of him, her mood became low and it worried her. Was it guilt? Was she depressed at the thought of leaving here and going back to normal life? Was she worried about him finding out about the money? Was she falling out of love with him? She dismissed the last thought as quickly as it had come. She knew it wasn't that, but something in her gut didn't feel right. She continued with her bath regardless and relaxed as best she could, occasionally giggling when she actually thought about where she was and what she was doing.

An hour later, Brooke strolled into the dining room to see Antonia sitting at a table. She walked over to her and realised she was in the same dress she'd been in all day. Brooke quickly scanned the room and came to the conclusion she was the only person who'd changed. Antonia read her mind.

'Don't worry, darling. You look fabulous. We're all a lazy bunch who can't be bothered to change!' A waiter pulled the chair out for Brooke and she sat down elegantly.

'Oh I wish someone would've told me I shouldn't have changed. I just assumed everybody would' Brooke responded in a rather mournful tone as she looked down at her attire.

'Please don't worry. What a day it's been!' Antonia said.

'I know, it's been unbelievable. I still can't get my head around it to be honest. I haven't had the chance but I must thank you for lending me that dress. I felt like a million dollars in it! And them gloves! I mean *those* gloves! It's all in a bag for you to take back if that's OK?'

'Brooke, nothing gave me more pleasure today than seeing you in that dress.'

Soon, the rest of the syndicate arrived and Geoffrey immediately ordered more champagne. A bottle of Vintage Krug was brought to the table, followed shortly by another. Despite desperately wanting to, Brooke resisted looking at the price list, for fear she'd start calculating the price per sip. Sir Blessington proposed a toast to Turn The Paige and her first ever win.

Hahaha! Making a toast to a horse – that's cool, that is!

Brooke had the lobster on Geoffrey's recommendation and looked alarmingly at the array of tools that came with it, more reminiscent of the dentist's than a smart restaurant. A nutcracker-looking device and a tortuous-looking long, thin rod with two prongs at the end of it rested menacingly on her plate. She gawped, as the rest of the table chatted away easily.

Why did I have to go with lobster? How on earth am I meant to eat this?

She felt that all-too-familiar fire rise up into her cheeks and tears began to form behind her eyes.

Get a grip, Brooke. It's only food.

Then, suddenly, she remembered *Debrett's* guide to challenging foods, where she'd read about the correct way to eat an apple! It took all her mental energy to try and recall what it had said about how to eat a lobster. She smiled to herself as she recalled the procedure for cracking the legs and using the fork to dig deep into the claws in order to retrieve the delicious white flesh. She looked over at Geoffrey's dozen oysters.

'Can I try one of your oysters, Geoffrey?' Brooke had never eaten oysters and only ever seen them being eaten in films.

'Of course you can, sweetheart!' And he wasted no time in showing her how to squeeze fresh lemon juice on, ensure the flesh is pulled away completely from the shell and then with the wider part of the shell against the lips, slurping it all down in one.

'Mmm. Very salty! But delicious!'

'Here. Have another one.' This time he let her prepare the oyster herself, which she did perfectly but then proceeded to miss her mouth completely, so the ice-cold oyster slid straight down into her ample cleavage (although decidedly less ample now that she'd stopped breastfeeding!).

'Aaaagh!' she wailed as she stood up and leaned forward (much to Geoffrey's delight) scooping the wretched thing out with her fingers from between her breasts. She wasn't sure what the correct form was at this point, but not wanting to waste what she knew to be almost five pounds' worth of oyster, she threw it into her mouth as one might a piece of popcorn. Then, with a little shrug of the shoulders, said, 'Sorry, but waste not want not. That's what my mum always says.'

'Too damn right. Bloody good advice from your mother!' bellowed Sir Blessington, at which point they all chuckled. Brooke felt relieved and the rest of the meal went without a hitch and a good time was had by all.

Before Brooke climbed into bed, she messaged Dean, who was still reeling from his error and wondering how on earth he was going to manage to do his mystery visit – but to the correct pub in Norfolk. His phone pinged with a message from Brooke.

Having a wonderful time, a really great day!

Good. Glad to hear it.

How was yours? Fun?

Yeah good thanks. No reply to earlier message?? When will you be back?

Oh sorry, just seen it. Been full-on. I think about 3 or 4 ish? Not sure. xxx

OK. CU tomorrow some time. X

Why only one kiss?

Brooke lay her head on the pillow and fell asleep slowly with a deep, gnawing feeling in the pit of her stomach.

24

A Stressful Sunday

The next morning, Brooke awoke in her luxurious room and absolutely did not want to get up, never mind leave. She lay there imagining what it must be like to be someone like Kate Moss and living like this permanently. She closed her eyes again and allowed herself to pretend…just for a minute or two, before crawling to the edge of the bed and sitting forlornly in her Primark pink sheep pyjamas.

Dean urgently had to find a lunch companion to go with him to The White Horse in Roydon, *Norfolk*. Not easy for a chap, with virtually no notice for people. In the end, out of sheer desperation and because Chloe knew Dean was a mystery shopper, he asked her. She was not only free, but over the moon to be going out with Dean on his own, for a leisurely, free Sunday lunch. He'd declined to mention that it would need to be done at lightning speed. Chloe lived in Chelmsford, which was en route, so he agreed to pick her up from Chelmsford station. Despite her pregnant body, she went to town making herself look as sexy as humanly possible. It was irrelevant to her that Dean was a married man and so she allowed her mind to run wild with possibilities of what else they might do in Roydon apart from eat lunch. She was ready for some fun. The last this pregnant woman was likely to be having for some time!

It was not a good start to the day for either of them.

Brooke decided to send Dean a message and the photo of her with Lady Townsend and the paramedic. Maybe that would reassure him that she was genuinely with Lady Townsend, if that was what he needed.

Look who had a BP moment and had to go to first aid?

Well, it's partly true.

WTF Brooke?! R U OK?

Overwhelmed with anxiety all of a sudden, Dean temporarily abandoned his mystery shopping problem and made a video call. She leaped out of bed and frantically searched for the most blank background she could find, which meant standing on top of the toilet seat; a plain white wall behind.

'Hiya, babe? You OK?' Brooke asked, trying not to sound too alarmed.

'Where are you? Are you alright? What were you doing in first aid, for god's sake? I told you to be careful. I knew you shouldn't have gone!' Dean barely paused for breath.

Brooke gulped. 'It's fine. I'm fine. I had a funny turn that's all and Lady Townsend thought it best to play safe and marched me to the first-aid tent. But honestly, Dean, it was nothing and it went down quickly. Just thought I should let you know. I'm back in the hotel now.' She suddenly regretted sending the photo.

Dean breathed a huge sigh of relief. His overprotective tendencies had kicked in with a vengeance. 'If you say so, but I can't help worrying about you, babe. You're just so precious to me. How's the book thing gone anyway? And what's your room like – let's have a gander!'

Oh bloody hell!

'Er, that's a bit tricky. I'm on the loo!' she lied.

'What?! You answered your phone in the bog?!'

'Yes, but it's a bloody Holiday Inn Express; so not exactly The Hempel Hotel,' she said as she glanced at the positively palatial bathroom. 'I can't chat or I'm gonna miss breakfast. Then we're off to listen to…she racked her brain to try and recall who was speaking at the festival that afternoon…I dunno, some geezer who wrote a book backwards or something.'

'Yeah, right. Sounds fascinating,' Dean replied sarcastically. 'One of these days I'm gonna take you to The Hempel and then you'll understand what real luxury is.'

God, Dean De'Ath, if only you knew!

'Just let me know what time you're leaving, so I can be here when you get back,' he continued.

'What are you all up to today then?' she asked innocently.

'I dunno, haven't decided, as yet,' was all he could say. 'Your mum said I didn't have to pick Paige up till later this afternoon, so I thought I'd make the most of having some time to myself.'

'OK, but don't forget I haven't got my keys with me. Right, well, enjoy and I'll see you later.' They said their goodbyes and blew kisses to each other for a few moments.

Phew!

Brooke stood down from the toilet seat.

Phew!

Dean had forgotten she didn't have her keys. He blew a raspberry and dashed upstairs to get dressed. He needed to leave at 10am to be on the safe side to get to the pub by midday. That would leave him an hour to do the visit and another couple of hours to get back, pick Paige up and be home before Brooke. This was going to be very tight indeed!

***

Brooke returned to lay on the bed, knowing she should be on her way down to breakfast, but reflecting that this was probably the last time she'd ever come to the Jockey Club Rooms. She considered once more her options regarding telling Dean about her job, Turn The Paige and the winnings. It simply sent her into a spiral of arguments for and against. In the end she showered and joined the syndicate for breakfast, her dilemma unresolved. They'd already nearly finished their kippers and Eggs Benedict, much to her embarrassment. She'd fancied the traditional full English Breakfast with local Powter Newmarket sausages, but reluctantly went for their continental buffet. The syndicate was most concerned about her, and fussed about pulling out her chair and offering to get her breakfast for her.

'People! I'm fine! Please stop fussing!' It came out rather more loudly and filled with exasperation than she'd intended.

'Of course, sweetheart. You're strong as an ox! We're just worried about you, that's all,' Geoffrey said tenderly.

'The only thing I need to worry about is how on earth I'm gonna hide forty grand from my husband!' she joked. They all gawped at her as she tucked into her smoked salmon and cream cheese bagel.

'Do you mean he doesn't know?' Sir Blessington asked incredulously.

'Afraid not. He doesn't even know I've got a job, never mind a race horse or now an extra forty grand. I haven't even got my own bank account! I don't know what I'm gonna do with that bloody cheque!' She quickly covered her mouth, realising her swearing.

'Good heavens! You're going to have to sort that out right away, young lady,' he responded with a look of horror. 'You can't keep things like that from your husband. It's just not done.'

Brooke laughed at his traditional views, and, taking a big risk, replied, 'Oh don't *you* start! I get enough of that from my mate… I mean my friend Dawn. I'm a strong, modern woman and have every right to be independent.' Whilst not an entirely accurate statement – yet, she tilted her chin in the air and feigned serious offence as she struggled with the rather odd-looking glass jar and lid in which her strawberry yoghurt was resisting being eaten. Geoffrey saw her struggling with it, gently took it from her hands and prised open the mini kiln jar for her. Oh the irony!

'Good for you, Brooke, you tell him!' laughed Antonia.

'I've said exactly the same, Blessington' said Geoffrey, in cahoots with his like-minded friend. 'It won't do a chap any good knowing his wife's keeping important financial information from him you know. He needs to be part of it.'

'Well, what *will* you do with the money dear?' asked Mrs Townsend gently.

'Dunno. I thought I might have a chat with you about that, Geoffrey. You're into all that investing stuff. Maybe you could invest it for me? Put me in one of them hedge fund things. That'll give me plenty of time to think about what I can spend it on!' Brooke replied.

All Geoffrey could think about is that such an arrangement would mean many more visits by Brooke to Ingatestone Hall! Barely able to hold back his excitement at the prospect, he immediately responded. 'I'm quite sure I could help you with that. In fact, I'd be delighted to help. There are some excellent opportunities to be had on the stock market at the moment.'

'Maybe you could put it into an educational trust fund for Paige, dear?' Lady Townsend intervened rather quickly, keen that Brooke didn't fritter it away on a Chanel handbag and a crate of vintage champagne. 'That would help to pay for an excellent private education.' Brooke stopped eating for a moment and thought about the suggestion. She'd come to realise that so much of why the people she was with now, were like they were, was due to where they'd been educated. Their hinterland all began with a top-notch education.

'That…is not a bad idea at all as it goes.' She chewed her lip and chopped up her apple as per *Debrett's*. 'Would never've thought of that.'

'There's an excellent private school near me – Elizabeth Fry Prep. You might have passed it. It has an excellent reputation,' Lady Townsend offered.

Geoffrey, keen not to destroy his chances of getting Brooke over to his private wing again, suggested that this was probably not the time to discuss it and that maybe Brooke could come over next week to discuss her options. They all agreed.

***

Dean picked Chloe up as agreed and was rather alarmed at her appearance, considering she was pregnant. She was wearing a rather short and revealing skirt, high-heeled boots and strappy vest top. He hadn't thought to tell her to wear something so she'd blend into the background – a must for mystery shoppers. As she slid into the passenger seat, her thighs came into full view. Dean found it most challenging to avert his eyes. Every so often he'd take a sneak peek sideways at her lean, muscular quads and sigh nostalgically as he changed gear.

Brooke don't wear skirts like that anymore.

Suddenly he put his foot down hard on the accelerator, knowing he had minimal time, forcing Chloe back into the car seat.

'Hey, Dean, slow down! What's the rush?'

'The table's booked for twelve so we can't hang around,' he replied, still not thinking to explain that he needed to be back by 3pm.

Chloe shamelessly flirted with Dean for the entire duration of the journey, and, unable to escape, he had little option but to go with the flow. She frequently crossed and uncrossed her legs and leaned forward every so often to look in the passenger mirror to check her make-up, revealing the growing bosom of a woman in her third trimester. She made a pretence of pulling her skirt back down, but her subtle smile showed that in reality it was a most half-hearted effort! At one point, Dean put his Ray-Bans on, as though this would make her go away; like a child does in hide and seek.

On arrival at the pub, Dean went into full-on focused mystery shopper mode. 'Chloe, can you check the plants outside, while I check the tables and chairs?'

'Check 'em for what?' Chloe replied, somewhat peeved that she was being set to work instead of seduced.

'You know, plant health. Green leaves, watered, nice flowers – that sort of stuff.' Dean immediately walked around the beer garden, which was in front of the pub, glancing casually at the tables, chairs and umbrellas.

Chloe reluctantly walked up to one of the hanging baskets

and made a superficial attempt to check it over. Some bikers outside with a pint, stared at her and mumbled something between themselves. She moved onto the next one and looked around self-consciously, noticing that the bikers were still staring at her.

'Nice pansies!' she exclaimed, semi-giggling, feeling compelled to explain her hanging basket fetish.

'They ain't pansies, love, they're begonias,' responded the long-haired bearded chap sporting the Harley Davidson jacket. 'Pansies are annuals. Begonias are perennials,' he offered by way of further explanation.

'Chloe – come on, we haven't got all day!' Dean shouted over from the front door stabbing his watch with his forefinger. Chloe abandoned any further plant examination and followed Dean inside the pub.

They walked round to the restaurant entrance and were greeted by a chatty, friendly waitress. She escorted them to their table and left them with menus. No sooner had they sat down than Dean piped up. 'Chloe, can you go to the loo please? Check toilet rolls, soap, hand towels and that every loo is clean and smells nice?'

'What? I thought we were gonna have a nice lunch together?' she asked, her voice oozing with disappointment.

'We are, but we still need to do everything in the brief; it's still a mystery visit, don't forget!' Dean explained through clenched teeth and in an exaggerated whisper.

Chloe reluctantly got up and checked out the ladies. Having arrived at the pub a matter of minutes after it opened, the lavatories clearly hadn't even been used so she went into both toilets and in a perfunctory manner lifted the toilet seats in each. On returning to the table, Dean was peering at the menu. Chloe gave the lavatories the thumbs up and Dean noted her comments as she scanned the rather extensive menu. Dean mentally reminded himself of what they had to order.

You and your guest must both have a drink, different starters, main courses, desserts and coffee.

When the waitress returned to take their order, for speed, Dean ordered a bowl of olives and a steak while Chloe picked double-baked souffle and wild mushroom risotto for her main course. The waitress announced, 'Just to let you know the souffle will take about twenty minutes and the risotto is made from scratch and will take thirty minutes, will that be alright?'

'Yeah, no worries, I'm not that hungry yet anyway. Bit early for me,' Chloe replied.

'No. You can't have that, Chloe. Please can you choose something else?' Dean pressed with a sense of urgency in his voice. Chloe and the waitress both turned to Dean together in wide-eyed indignation.

'You are joking?' Chloe asked.

'No.' Dean ignored Chloe and turned to the waitress. 'She'll have the pea soup and chicken Caesar salad.'

'But I don't want salad!' Chloe exclaimed, realising that this was not going to be quite the leisurely foodie lunch she'd envisioned.

'Don't worry about her, love. She doesn't know what she wants half the time. You know what pregnant women are like.' He patted Chloe's small bump. 'She'll have the pea soup and salad.' Dean gave Chloe a look that was not to be argued with.

Ask a question about the menu to test the waiting staff's knowledge

'Can you tell me where the olives are from?' Dean asked.

'Booker Cash 'n' Carry,' the waitress replied.

'I mean which country?'

'Oh. I'll have to check.' She gave Dean a withering look.

The waitress looked at Chloe helplessly and not without some concern and left.

'I can't believe you made me have a salad! All that lovely food and I've gotta eat bleedin' rabbit food.'

'Sorry, Chloe, but most of those other dishes are gonna take way too long.'

'Why can't we just relax and enjoy ourselves? We've got all the time in the world!'

''cause I've gotta get back home by three, that's why!'

'Well why didn't you tell me that when you asked me?! I wouldn't have bothered if I'd known that!' Chloe's voice was raised and the waitress glanced over, wondering what the relationship was between these two. Chloe folded her arms and rested them on her bump and her demeanour took on that of an annoyed teenager.

Dean ignored her and discreetly made some notes on his phone. He glanced around the pub to assess the state of the tables, the decor, and the bar. He observed that the cruets, cutlery and paper napkins had been placed haphazardly on each table.

Inconsistency. Humph. The enemy of TQM.

He also noticed that even from where he was sitting, the shelf and bottles of Amaretto, Crème de Menthe and apricot brandy were covered in dust.

Who even drinks that stuff anyway?

'I hope you're better at housework than whoever cleans this

place!' Dean joked. 'Just look at it!' He nodded towards the bar.

'You're unbelievable you are, Dean. I'm beginning to feel sorry for Brooke. It must be like being married to a tax inspector. Always trying to find a mistake.'

The waitress arrived with the soup and olives. 'The olives are from Greenland.'

Dean frowned. 'Are you positive? Surely Greenland's way too cold to grow olives? They need a sub-tropical climate.'

'Well, that's what chef said.' She shrugged her shoulders and left them to it.

'Well, I don't think the product knowledge is very good here.' Dean tutted and made another note on his phone before scoffing the green stuffed olives down in under a minute. Chloe's pea soup was a beautiful colour and piping hot. After not really wanting it, she found herself actually looking forward to it. It was as delicious as it looked. She took a few spoonfuls, then Dean surreptitiously glanced at his watch and called the waitress over.

'We've finished thanks, you can clear now.'

Chloe was halfway through taking her fourth spoonful and looked up, but again Dean's facial expression made her almost throw her spoon back down in her bowl, which was then removed by the waitress, who'd come to the conclusion that he was one of those men who exerts coercive control over their partners and is likely to dump her after she's had the baby.

What kind of husband doesn't let his wife finish her pea soup?

'Was your soup attractively presented, hot and tasty, would you say?' Dean questioned her with extreme seriousness. Chloe answered with equal extreme seriousness.

'What I had of it, I estimate it to have been approximately

ninety degrees, the green was an excellent match to pantone green #00ad43 and from 1–10 on a tastiness scale, I'd give it an eight.'

'Excellent. Thank you. That's the helpful kind of answer that the clients love.' Dean's face was a picture of satisfaction.

Chloe burst out laughing. 'Dean, I'm joking. I hope you're not seriously gonna put that in your report! Just say it was very nice!'

Main courses came quickly and again Dean checked his watch and waited for the waitress to leave them before saying, 'C'mon, Chloe, you've gotta get a move on. You've only got ten minutes to eat your salad.'

Dean always ate quickly. In fact, Brooke despaired at the speed he would shovel food into his mouth. It was so very undignified and she'd noticed it even more recently. And he still used his fork the wrong way to eat his peas. Was there any hope?! Chloe watched Dean demolish his steak after giving it the onceover to assess its presentation. She stared at her salad despondently. She'd so wanted the wild mushroom risotto.

'Come on, Chloe. Hurry up!'

'Aaargh!' she replied, furious that she'd given up a precious Sunday for this farcical lunch date. With that, she grabbed her knife and fork and all but snarled at him while not taking her eyes off him for a moment, in the same way that boxers do to each other at the pre-match weigh in. She mirrored Dean by purposefully shovelling her salad into her mouth until the iceberg lettuce and shredded pieces of chicken hung outside her mouth and dropped onto the table.

'That's my girl. Get it down your Gregory!' Dean said, satisfied that Chloe was now making efforts to eat quickly.

The waitress furtively watched Chloe from behind the bar. She felt very sorry for her and could only imagine being married to a man who seemed to enjoy watching his wife be forced to consume food in such a manner. Especially as she'd made it clear she wasn't even that hungry. The moment Dean had cleared his plate, the waitress knew the score and came over to remove the plates again, even though Chloe hadn't quite finished. She dithered about offering dessert, not wanting to make the poor girl eat any more, but Dean waved to her for the menus. She dutifully but reluctantly brought them. Dean asked her to wait as they both looked at the list of delicious desserts on offer: lemon meringue pie, clementine cheesecake, chocolate caramel tart and raspberry surprise pudding. Chloe had her eye on the lemon meringue pie, but before she had a chance to say anything, Dean spoke with some urgency.

Only got seven minutes to get out of here.

'We'll both have ice cream – I'll have the chocolate, she'll have the strawberry, coffee and the bill as soon as possible please.' Chloe's mouth dropped open as Dean took the menu from Chloe, shut it and handed it back to the waitress with a smile.

The ice cream and coffees were brought to the table and before Dean had a chance to say anything, Chloe swapped her strawberry ice cream for his chocolate, much to Dean's chagrin. His phone buzzed.

Leaving now, should be home by 3pm. Missed you xxx

Oh shit! Think think!

OK see you later. Should be back but gotta pick Paige up first.

You'll have to be home. I haven't got a key remember!

Oh Christ

OK

'Right, Chloe, you need to—'

'I know, I know! Hurry up. You shouldn't eat ice cream too quickly you know, it can give you brain freeze.' Chloe tried to heap her chocolate ice cream in as speedily as possible, like Dean, but it hurt her teeth and gave her a headache, as well as making her look vaguely bulimic.

'Too bad. We've gotta get going.' Dean took one more glance at his watch, ate a couple of spoonfuls of his ice cream, slurped his coffee and slipped his card in the bill wallet on the table. Whilst he waited impatiently for the waitress to appear and for Chloe to finish her coffee, he took the opportunity to check his crockery, cutlery and beer glass for chips or dirt of any kind and also take one more look at other tables and how efficiently other customers were being served.

'I need a slash and to check the men's loos. Be back in a minute.'

The waitress watched as Dean shot off to the lavatories, then took the opportunity to go over to Chloe. 'Are you alright, love?' she asked her, looking gravely concerned for Chloe's wellbeing. Chloe, who had chocolate ice cream drips either side of her mouth and on her chin, was a bit taken aback.

'Yeah, fine thanks.'

The waitress quickly looked around to make sure Dean wasn't about to come out of the lavatory, leaned forward and spoke in hushed tones. 'I know all about men like that. You know there are other options. Here.' She took one further look around and then pulled a piece of paper discreetly out of her apron pocket, slid it across the table, patted Chloe's arm and walked away. Chloe turned the scrap of paper over and saw a phone number scrawled on it. Underneath it said *Women's Aid.* After Dean paid the bill, they left. As they did, Dean looked around for their waitress.

Did any member of waiting staff ask you if you enjoyed your meal and say goodbye?

His eyes met hers behind the bar, but instead of a warm thank you and parting greeting, she merely stared at him with a look of contempt. He smiled back anyway, wondering why she looked so miserable and unfriendly.

Outside, Chloe burst out laughing and showed him the handwritten slip. 'She only thinks you're a wife beater!' Dean was appalled. He couldn't hit a fly, never mind his wife, or even someone pretending to be his wife. He badly wanted to go straight back in there and put her right, but he knew that would be unprofessional for a mystery shopper, so he drove all the way home, angry, resentful and horribly misunderstood.

God knows what I'll put in the report. I don't want anyone thinking I slap my wife around.

Chloe couldn't get him to talk about anything else, so in the end she turned the radio on, shut her eyes and had a little nap. Dean took advantage of the fact and put his foot down, driving well over the speed limit most of the way back. As he dropped Chloe off at her house, she leaned her unmissable chest through his window with a twinkle in her eye. 'Are you sure you wouldn't like to come in for a coffee?'

'No. You're alright. Thanks for coming, Chloe. You've helped me out of a hole.' Chloe's shoulders dropped and her smile disappeared.

Yeah, and there was me hoping I could get you into one.

Dean waved cheerily as he sped off into the distance, totally oblivious to Chloe's disappointment.

Right, Chelmsford to Romford.

He looked at his watch.

That's about half an hour. Should be fine if I give it a bit of welly.[16]

As he drove, he thought for the first time in a couple of days about his daughter. All the worse-case scenarios about her behaviour and screaming whilst with his in-laws, suddenly came to the forefront of his mind. He groaned inwardly at the grief he was bound to get from Jackie about how much hassle she'd been. Their steady lives would undoubtedly have been thrown into disarray by the tiny little wrecking ball called Paige. That girl knew how to cause havoc, how to make grown adults feel permanently on edge and how to create an atmosphere of constant potential mayhem. He wasn't looking forward to picking her up.

***

At 2.45pm, Brooke arrived back in Brentwood, brought home by Lady Townsend. Despite everything, she still couldn't bear the thought of her seeing where she lived, so as she'd done when she was very first offered a lift home by her, she asked to be dropped off in Brentwood High Street, so that she could 'pick up a few bits and pieces'. Lady Townsend obliged and Brooke, knowing that Dean would wonder why she'd not been dropped off at home, messaged him to say she needed to pick up some 'lady bits' and she'd be home by 3pm.

At just before 3pm, Brooke arrived home but there was

16. To put one's foot down on the accelerator.

no sign of Dean. She checked her watch and looked around at her neighbours' gardens feeling somewhat exposed and uncomfortable at being unable to get into her own home. Mikey the neighbour tutted to himself and brought his wife over to the window again to have a good look. 'See, look at her, she looks guilty as hell. I'm telling you that woman's up to no good.' His wife folded her arms, tilted her head and nodded in agreement. Within seconds, Dean screeched into Elephant Close, making Brooke visibly jump. The car was parked, Dean got out and marched purposefully towards his wife and embraced her. She kissed him back. Whilst all this lovey-dovey behaviour was going on, they failed to notice that their daughter had found her way out of the car, over to Mikey's drive and onto his sprinkler system, soaking herself into the bargain. Mikey came running out, more convinced than ever that he was living next door to the next big Essex criminal family.

'Oi, Dean, get your kid off our sprinkler system!' Mikey shouted.

'Oh get a life, Mikey – she's just a kid! She's not gonna do any damage!' With that he pulled her away by her hand, gave her a kiss and demonstrated that she was as harmless as marshmallow.

'Right, you little sod…get inside right now!' Dean whispered to Paige up close, not in the mood for disobedience.

For the rest of the afternoon, Dean and Brooke did their best to avoid eye contact with each other and little Paige was used as a shield against their guilt: playing with her, cooking her tea, bathing her, telling her a bedtime story, putting her to bed. It was so much easier to lie when one didn't have to physically face the person one was lying to! Keeping busy and in a different room for as long as possible was the best cover and all giveaway signs of deceit were avoided. No eye contact, use distraction, change the subject, ask questions, rather than try to account for questions asked of you. That was the way to deal with this sort of a situation.

'Yer mum said Paige was pretty good; kept taking a ball into the garden every time she tried to give her a lolly apparently!' Dean said at one point trying to break the atmosphere. Brooke recalled Mrs Dodsley's strategy; how she'd told her that Paige didn't need lollipops but that she just needed to expend all her energy by chucking her out into the garden with a ball.

When Paige had finally fallen sleep, Dean stomped down the stairs slowly and wearily, feeling ill at ease about lying to Brooke about his day and equally awkward asking her about her weekend. Unbeknown to him, she was feeling exactly the same way.

Why is that? Why am I frightened about asking my wife about her weekend?!

Brooke recognised his discomfort. She was an amateur psychologist of the highest order and strutted over to him assertively, oozing sex, lust and desire. Her last resort strategy.

He'll forget everything if I can get him into bed.

She was right, of course. The inevitable followed and – suitably distracted – Dean actually spoke little of his Saturday; an odd comment here and there about go-karting or war planes. And poor Martin had been used as an alibi without his knowledge or permission; apparently, he and Dean had just spent all day Sunday playing golf!

Brooke's strategy was to blind Dean with science. She hoped that by not letting him get a word in edgeways and talking at length about the fascinating process authors use to write a book, that she'd bore him to death. It worked. After a few minutes, she rolled over to find Dean dead to the world.

Phew!

25

Posh Schools and Progress

The next morning Dean went to work leaving Brooke in bed as usual. The atmosphere was muted, but not as strange as it had been the night before. A good dose of hanky panky had eliminated most of that, although Brooke's mind was elsewhere for the entire duration: move house? Foreign holiday? New clothes? Porsche? Or private schooling for Paige? It was a wonder the act was able to be completed at all, given her total disinterest at the time. But she knew that wasn't so terribly odd. She'd had numerous conversations with girlfriends over the years about how the female species are notoriously good at putting on an act, when the harsh truth is that they'd so often rather be getting through that pile of ironing or rearranging the kitchen cupboards.

As soon as Dean had gone, Brooke searched for Elizabeth Fry Prep on her laptop. She scrolled through the photos of the young girls in their brown and blue stripy uniform and little brown hats. She thought back to her own primary school uniform at Parklands – no blazers or hats for them, just polo shirts, sweatshirts and plain grey skirt.

I wonder if it actually makes a difference…what they wear?

After a few minutes, she clicked on 'fees.' £3000 per term.

Holy moly!

A rapid calculation delivered the astounding revelation that to put her daughter through primary school would cost £45,000.

Just think what I could buy with that?!

She didn't have time to dillydally, being due at work at 9.30am. She hadn't been in contact with Dawn since the win and couldn't decide how she'd break the news. She vaguely considered not telling her at all, but soon dismissed that notion as unworkable. If she hadn't had Dawn to offload her dilemmas onto, she believed wholeheartedly that she'd have had a nervous breakdown by now.

Operation OOAO commenced and they'd left by 8.45am, fifteen minutes earlier than normal, to give her time to have a chat with Dawn. On arrival at Woodman Close, Brooke discovered, to her horror, that Paige had already unstrapped herself from the car seat and was playing with her crane in the footwell of the passenger side. She snatched her out quickly.

Dawn opened the door in her dressing gown, coffee mug in hand and leaned on the door frame. 'You're early. Everything alright?' Paige ran in and plonked herself down on the bean bag in front of the TV, as Dawn put on one of the hundreds of kiddies' DVDs she had stacked up in the corner. They were very useful when she needed to get on and Paige needed to be kept occupied. For the first time since leaving Paige with Dawn, instead of smiling as she watched her daughter enjoying the antics of Peppa Pig, Brooke felt a pang of concern.

I wonder how often she puts her in front of the telly like that?

'You got a minute, Dawn?' Brooke asked tentatively, pulling her ringlets and biting her lip.

'Yeah, sure. You alright? You got time for a cuppa?' Dawn

knew Brooke well and could sense something important was coming.

'No, I'm fine thanks.'

'Good weekend?'

'Well, that's what I wanted to talk to you about.' She sat on her hands and shuffled about on the sofa.

'Well spit it out then!' Dawn said, impatient to hear the latest in the Brooke De'Ath saga.

'You know I bought that racehorse? Well, the tail anyway!'

Dawn rolled her eyes as she collapsed onto an armchair. 'Not exactly information you can forget, babe.'

Brooke giggled nervously. 'Well. She raced at the weekend… and she won.'

'Wow! You lucky cow! So what was the prize?'

'Well the prize was thirty-five thousand guineas and my share of it was three thousand guineas.'

'Oh bloody hell, Brooke! Better than a kick up the backside, eh?!' Dawn cackled and slurped her coffee.

'But that's not the main thing.' Dawn was all ears now. 'I put a bet on her as well… And I won the bet.'

'Hahahaha! Only you, babe! Only you!' Dawn slapped her thigh with her free hand as she cackled all the more loudly. 'How much d'ya win?' Brooke gulped and took a deep breath.

'So I put two grand on her to win.'

Dawn sat bolt upright and her face went a sort of ashen grey.

'I was a bit tipsy.'

'Two grand? What odds?' she asked as quick as a flash.

'20-1. I've just won forty grand, Dawn.' Brooke's face was more neutral than Dawn had ever seen it.

'You're 'aving me on.'

'No. But they gave me the winnings in a cheque so I can't cash it!'

Dawn's mouth fell open, her eyes bulged like a frog and she shook her head from side to side before standing up and pacing up and down like a maniac.

'You've just won forty grand and you're telling me all you're worried about is how to cash the bloody cheque? I'm assuming you've told Dean this time?'

'No. I haven't and now I'm royally screwed. I dunno what to do. I can't do anything with it that wouldn't make Dean suspicious.'

The next twenty minutes were taken up arguing about the rights and wrongs of telling Dean, after which Brooke checked her watch and explained she had to go. Before she left, she dug around in her oversize tote bag, pulled out an envelope in which she'd put £200 and handed it over to Dawn. 'This is for you. Just wanted to say a massive thanks for everything you've done. I couldn't have done any of it without you.'

Dawn opened the envelope and took the money out. 'Blimey, Brooke. Two hundred quid. You don't have to, you know.' Dawn suddenly felt bad about chastising her. 'Mind you, it's a bit like blood money!'

'We'll talk more when I pick Paige up. See you later.'

With that, the women hugged and Brooke left for work. She had a busy day ahead: French polisher, landscape gardener, the groundsmen about pinning pornographic images up in their shed and an order with Fortnum & Mason. And she must make an appointment with her hairdresser for Dean's gala dinner on 26th. She always loved going to see her stylist, Chris, in Saffron

Walden; a good excuse for some like-minded conversation. An unusual gentleman, it has to be said!

***

Dean wrote up his report of The White Horse on the train into work and was able to get it to Angie at Sonny Global first thing. She'd made several calls to him during the course of the morning to check on what he'd written. She'd found it a most amusing report but was not sure the client would think the same. Dean confessed to her that he'd originally gone to the wrong pub.

'You're not the first and you won't be the last,' she said, matter of factly. 'The worst one we had was a bloke who was meant to visit a hotel in Acton in Cheshire, but he went to a hotel with the same name in Acton in Dorset instead. When the client got the report, they informed us that they don't have al fresco dining or any staff called Wayne or Margaret. That was dead embarrassing. Now I know why teachers were always banging on about "read the instructions carefully first". You'd be amazed at how many assessors don't bother.'

Angie made Dean feel a little more reassured, but he still felt an idiot and was concerned that he may have blotted his copy book. He fretted about it all morning. Such a worrier! In addition, the poor chap was perplexed by Chloe's seemingly stand-offish demeanour towards him that morning. Although he knew it had been a tad rushed, he expected at least a thank you for the free lunch, but alas such a gesture was not forthcoming.

Women, eh? Never understand 'em.

He looked forlornly at her little bump, thinking that despite being in her third trimester, she didn't actually look terribly pregnant.

I wouldn't be surprised if the diversity awards panel don't even believe she is pregnant.

Dean messaged Brooke.

Babe how big were you when you were seven months pregnant?

Brooke glanced at her mobile, which lay on her desk in front of her, as she was speaking to Fortnum & Mason on Lady Townsend's landline about Beluga and Ossetra caviar.

Wtf Dean?! Why?

Chloe doesn't look that big. People might not believe she's pregnant.

Dean we're all different! Leave the poor girl alone! Why the hell does it matter anyway?

I'm not sure I believe her now. That bump is so small.

Brooke had listened to Lady Townsend and Hugo often enough on the phone to Fortnum's and she'd learned to sound more confident, assertive and to use the language they would use. Little did she know that when Purses phone number came up on their display that it was immediately transferred to their VIP team who'd made notes on Lady Townsend's file. '*Watch her assistant, Ms De'Ath. She can be very demanding.*'

Dean. It's perfectly normal. Sorry. Gotta go!

The doorbell rang as she was getting off the phone.

Why? Where to?

Oh not this again!

She thought for a moment as she made her way across the hall.

Someone at the door.

Well it was partly true – just not their door!

OK CU tonight. KFC?

Brooke opened the door to the award-winning garden designer, Julie Foxton, whom she had been introduced to by Lady Townsend a few weeks prior at The Chelsea Flower Show. They embraced and kissed one another on each cheek as though they were old friends.

'Good morning, Julia, how lovely to see you again. Please, come out into the garden. I've arranged lunch outside as it's such a beautiful day. I hope that's alright with you. We can discuss Mrs Townsend's plans while we're eating.' Appalled at her own desire for comfort food, Brooke found herself craving KFC whilst tucking into her poached salmon and asparagus with hollandaise sauce.

***

Meanwhile, Dean was spending an inordinate amount of time putting together TrussInUs's nomination for the diversity award. He went to great pains to provide detailed backgrounds and photographs of all his team. That proved a very challenging morning. He got cross with Ruth because she wouldn't undo her blouse one more button to reveal her Star of David pendant and he struggled to get a decent full-length shot of Jawaria in her burqa (although he quickly realised he could have just used a photo from the internet). He'd brought a can of Guinness for Patrick to hold and insisted he wore a lapel pin of the Guinness harp he'd found online. Patrick had complained he felt like 'Michael O' fucking Leary'. In addition, Dean thoroughly annoyed Chloe by asking her to stick her stomach out, so she looked 'a bit more pregnant'.

His final appointment had been a transexual called Linda – his proudest moment and his trump card. At 5ft 11" with a build like an NBL player, she struck an intimidating figure, albeit one dressed nicely in a John Lewis own-brand wrap dress and comfy Gabor shoes. Her CV was chequered to say the least, but by the time Dean had found her, he didn't care. He was sure she'd be good at something. He'd simply have to find a relevant skill and use it. Trying to get them all together in a group photograph proved difficult and stressful. He'd insisted on 'directing' the shot and continually kept moving people to try and 'show' their uniqueness, while the customer support phones rang in the background.

Finally, at 7pm, he finished his nomination. He rarely left the office late, because Brooke gave him such a hard time if he wasn't back to bathe Paige, but, on this occasion, he'd rung her and said he wouldn't make it. He left the office and went to Staples round the corner to professionally print and bind his nomination. The front cover had a photograph of the entire team grinning like toothpaste models, underneath the TrussInUs logo made out of rainbow colours and with the strap line '*supporting you from every angle*'. He took one last look through it, before placing it reverently in a large padded envelope and posting it, followed by the sign of the cross and a glance upwards.

I deserve to win this award. I'm gonna win!

26

Advice from Lord D'Arcy

The following day, after offloading Paige with her mother for the morning, Brooke paid a visit to Elizabeth Fry Prep. She'd made an appointment to have a look around, after talking with the school secretary on the telephone.

Having never set foot inside a private school in her life and so not knowing what to expect, she looked and felt out of place. Prior to her arrival, all she could envisage was an 'Eton like' establishment, which she'd once seen on a documentary and which created feelings of amazement, envy and laughter.

She'd been greeted by the deputy head, Miss Satchell, who was exactly the gracious sort of woman Brooke had hoped to find. She explained the school's Quaker ethos and values and took her around a variety of different classes, letting the lessons and the children's behaviour speak for themselves. Brooke got a brief glimpse of drama, sport, science and music. Inexplicably, her lip quivered as she witnessed a five-year-old girl attempting to play the violin, an eleven year old recite a poem off by heart on a huge stage in front of her whole class, a seven year old run so fast in a race on the playing field that she vomited at the finishing line and a girl of around nine answering a question in the fully equipped science lab about osmosis.

What's osmosis?

She was particularly intrigued by one group of pupils who sat in a circle in the middle of the assembly hall in complete silence, for no apparent reason whatsoever. She couldn't imagine an education or environment so utterly different from her own schooling in Romford. The more she thought about it, the more she knew that their local state primary school was never going to be good enough for her little girl. She'd learned too much about what it took in life to get on and it started here. An excellent education.

It was impossible to escape the sense of calm, desire to achieve, high expectation, impeccable behaviour and tiny class sizes. Each time she walked into a class with Miss Satchell and was introduced as Mrs De'Ath, the girls would respond in that long drawn-out way only primary school children can and in unison, 'Gooood…mooorning…Mrs Deeeee…Ath.' Brooke laughed and gave them all an enthusiastic wave. The girls giggled in return.

Visiting the school in person was one of the worst (or best) things she could've done. In just two hours she was sold and could no longer imagine Paige going to school anywhere else. She took away a prospectus and told Miss Satchell that she'd be in touch in due course.

She went straight from there to visit Lord D'Arcy. The cheque from William Hill was burning a hole in her pocket and she'd regularly take it out, as if to check it was still there and still real. Did it have a deadline by when it could be cashed? She simply didn't know.

She no longer had to park down in the field of Ingatestone Hall with the visitors; she was permitted to park up near Geoffrey's private residence. She also no longer had to report to Reception, but went straight to his front door and knocked. Having visited Elizabeth Fry Prep, she was excited to a chat about it with the ever-reassuring Lord D'Arcy. Not like her own father whose negativity had often resulted in Brooke being paralysed by indecision as a youngster and internally lacking in confidence. As she reflected upon the difference between her own father and Geoffrey, the door opened and a strange woman answered. This threw Brooke completely; apart from Mrs Dodsley, no one else'd ever been there when she'd visited.

'Can I help you?' asked Lady D'Arcy, looking and sounding decidedly suspicious and glancing over Brooke's shoulder towards her car and back again.

'Oh hello! I've come to see Geoffrey.' She stood rather awkwardly, as though she were collecting for The Red Cross or something.

'And you are?' replied Lady D'Arcy coldly, looking Brooke up and down as she rearranged one of the curlers nestled in her rather thinning grey hair. Brooke immediately observed her support stockings wrinkled at the ankles, her tweed skirt, and a no-nonsense cotton shirt, done up almost to the very top and with every stitch doing its job! It was clear she was sporting one of those twenty-four-hour panty girdles that distributes fat evenly across the body, giving her silhouette an unnatural quality.

Brooke shrank to around six inches and her face turned the colour of one of Mrs Townsend's Jubilee strawberries. It was that *Pretty Woman* moment again. The same feeling she had when arriving in the porter's hall at Brooks's and on meeting Portia. Brooke bit her lip and yanked at her curls. 'I'm Brooke.'

Should I say I'm friends with Geoffrey? Maybe she won't like that?

'Brooke De'Ath. I'm…er…I'm in the syndicate with Geoffrey…er Lord D'Arcy.'

'Oh *you're* Brooke!' she said in a very long, drawn-out and plummy voice. '*Finally*, we meet. Humph! Well, he talks more about you than anyone else he knows. Turn around. Let me see you properly,' she barked.

Brooke was speechless, but, without argument, slowly turned around on the spot outside on the doorstep, head bowed.

'Lift your head up, girl!' she boomed. 'What are you looking at the floor for?!'

'I…I—'

'Stop gibbering like an idiot and come in,' she demanded, rendering Brooke completely terrified. 'GEOFFREY! GEOFFREY! SOMEONE TO SEE YOU!' Lady D'Arcy hollered up the stairs like a sergeant major. They must've heard her in Mountnessing a couple of miles away!

From upstairs, Brooke heard, 'Coming, dear!' and Geoffrey bolted down the stairs, seeing Brooke as he reached the bottom. 'Brooke! I'm so glad you've come!' He walked towards her and, much to Brooke's surprise, did his usual waist grab and kiss on both cheeks. Lady D'Arcy didn't bat an eyelid.

'Darling, let me introduce you to Brooke. Brooke, this is my wife Lady D'Arcy – or we all call her Yorky.'

Brooke went to shake her hand and, for the first time, she met her match in the bone-crushing stakes. Lady D'Arcy squashed her fingers until Brooke yelped. She couldn't help feel there was an element of cruelty in the action, as she watched Lady D'Arcy's menacing smile creep across her face. There was absolutely no way that Brooke felt able to call her Yorky after that.

What stupid kind of name is that?

She almost curtsied, but managed to stop herself in time. 'Good morning, Lady D'Arcy. Delighted to meet you.' At least she thought she would be, but it turned out that she wasn't delighted to meet her at all. Under normal social conventions, one could an expect an 'Oh please do call me Yorky!' But Lady D'Arcy didn't, ensuring that Brooke would never call her anything else but Lady D'Arcy.

'Have you offered Brooke a cup of tea, dear?' Lord D'Arcy looked eagerly over to his wife, who merely raised her eyebrows at the suggestion.

'No, dear, I'll leave that to you. I'm going to my club. I'll see you later.' With that she nodded curtly at Brooke and trotted off upstairs to remove her curlers. Lord D'Arcy motioned for Brooke to come into the kitchen while he made her tea.

'So, the women have got clubs as well as the blokes?' Brooke asked realising she'd still so much more to learn about these people.

'Well, she's a member of The Special Forces Club in Knightsbridge. It's mixed.'

'So what d'ya have to do to get into that club then?'

'You have to have killed someone with your bare hands,' Geoffrey replied with not a hint of humour.

That'd explain it then – a sort of female terminator!

'What and Lady D'Arcy's done that, has she?' Brooke enquired, wide-eyed and half thinking it was a tongue in cheek statement.

'The less said about it, the better. Now, let's talk about your winnings!' Geoffrey subtly moved the subject on, leaving Brooke's imagination to go into overdrive as she pictured Lady

D'Arcy strangling some poor unsuspecting fellow.

Brooke spent the next four hours listening to Lord D'Arcy talk through a range of options for investing her money. ISAs, stocks, bonds etc. Most she didn't understand but she did quite fancy the idea of investing in a vineyard. As long as it produced Chardonnay, she'd told him, she wouldn't be averse to it. Each time she thought she might go for one of his suggestions, she thought of Paige in a little brown, and yellow striped blazer and adorable brown hat. She almost felt as though she'd be letting Lady Townsend down if she didn't take up her suggestion. Would Dean even approve of Paige attending private school? It'd never come up in conversation before – unsurprisingly. Although Paige wouldn't go for some time yet, it was inevitable that, by that point, Brooke would have to tell him about this double life she'd been leading. One isn't suddenly able to afford five years of private school fees!

After much debate, they came to a compromise. Geoffrey suggested that half was put towards an educational trust fund straight away and the other half was invested. If his investments went well, it could mean that he made enough for her to put Paige through private secondary school as well.

'Blimey, Geoffrey. I wasn't thinking that far ahead!' she cried.

'Well, my dear, you ought to. It's not always easy to get children into the best public schools, you know. Benenden, for example – a splendid all-girls boarding school where my Clare went – you have to apply four years in advance in order to get a place there!'

'Boarding school?! I don't think I could ever send my kids away to a boarding school. That's well cruel, that is. Besides, it's gonna cost a fortune just to send her to the local private school; I bet those posh secondary boarding schools cost a bomb. I can't see me ever being able to afford any of them – unless you're an investing legend, Geoffrey!'

'Oh, Brooke, sweetheart, you still have so much to learn,' Geoffrey responded in an unintentionally patronising manner. 'Are you aware that schools like that have scholarships and bursaries?'

'What's a bursary, then?'

'It's a means of helping students who would otherwise be disadvantaged by lack of financial means.'

Brooke laughed out loud. 'You mean free cash for poor buggers like the De'Ath family?!' Brooke retorted sharply. 'I'm not into handouts, Geoffrey. I can earn my own money, thank you very much.'

'I wouldn't look at it like that, sweetheart. It's Paige's education you need to be thinking about. Not your pride.' Geoffrey spoke kindly but firmly, making Brooke regret her comment.

Humph, I'd definitely need to think about that.

'Does Paige have any special talents? She could get in that way,' Geoffrey enquired; the fact that she was only two years old completely passing him by.

'Well, she's a bit too young to tell at the moment, to be fair. But I would say screaming is definitely up there.' Geoffrey laughed. Brooke thought about his question for a minute. 'Well, she's completely fearless. As you know, she's a climber and really flexible. I just started taking her to Tumble Tots at that church up Doddinghurst Road and she's like a ninja warrior. She'll make a brilliant little gymnast one day. That's what Danusha

Makelove said, anyway.'

'Who's Danusha Makelove?'

'The Tumble Tots lady. She used to be a gymnast herself, so she should know.' Brooke stood up. 'Anyway, I gotta go, Geoffrey. Thanks so much for all your advice. It's been really helpful. I think your idea's a good shout – half investing and half on education. I think Mrs Townsend's gonna be chuffed. I still can't get my head around all this, to be honest. It feels like I'm living in another world.'

'But, Brooke, in terms of cashing this cheque, if I may say, it would be sensible to have your own bank account. Then cashing it'll be easy and it'll come in very useful in the future, I'm sure. Carrying cash around and only ever being able to pay for things with notes is very um… very…well you know.' Geoffrey shifted around awkwardly on his feet and looked at the floor.

'Common! I know. But I wouldn't dare, Geoffrey. If Dean found out, he'd go ballistic.'

'Mmm. Well… I can ask my bank and see if there's a possibility that I can get it cashed for you there. I've always banked with Coutts so I can't see them saying no.'

'Thanks, Geoffrey. Just let me know, 'cause I really don't wanna open a bank account. It'll be nothing but grief trying to hide it from Dean. I can always find hiding places for notes!'

'Alright, sweetheart.' Lord D'Arcy looked at her with something resembling pity and escorted her to the front door.

'And one last thing.' She reverted to her desire to please and not upset. 'Can I keep back just a bit, to buy myself a new suit for work? Mrs Townsend's got me going to loads of meetings with a bunch of important people up town soon and I haven't really got anything suitable to wear.'

Geoffrey laughed. 'It's your money, sweetheart! One posh suit it is.'

27

The Hairdresser and The Gala Dinner

Brooke pulled into the car park on Saffron Walden Common, as she had done every three months for the past five years. She only ever went there to get her hair cut. Or at least that's what she told Dean and, ostensibly and superficially, this was true. But a visit to Law's salon to see Chris was so much more than that and she'd been so busy for the past nine months that she'd skipped one of her appointments. Unheard of! She'd visited her old school friend Amber, soon after she'd moved to the town and she'd dragged Brooke along to sit and talk to her while Chris cut her hair. The like-minded soul that he was, they clicked and Brooke decided there and then that he simply had to cut her hair. Their unusual relationship had subsequently grown over the years, even though Amber had long since moved elsewhere.

As she walked through the market square, it dawned on her what a delightful little market town Saffron Walden was. Elegant, sophisticated and a cut above your average town.

As she arrived in the salon, Chris spotted her, from where he was deep in foils with Janey Smythe's ash-blonde highlights. At a volume that ensured all customers in the salon turned around, Chris yelled, 'Aaaaaaaaah! Oh my god, Brooke De'Ath! Where have you been, my love? Salve! Salve!' Janey Smythe's highlights were abandoned, gloves were ripped off, foils dropped and brushes dumped as he strode across the salon, his heavily tattooed arms open wide. 'Come here, my love, and give us a hug!'

Janey Smythe sighed and raised her eyebrows at another customer.

'Salve, Chris!' Brooke replied enthusiastically, but at the same time conscious that the entire salon had come to a grinding halt. She hugged as requested.

'*Ego quidem omnes vos desiderabat*[17],' Brooke said as she stroked his back.

'*Vos desiderabat: ego quoque. Desiderans te videre ingredere*[18]*!*' Chris replied, looking over dramatically despondent.

'*Et ideo bene amhere modo possumus loqui*[19],' Brooke smiled reassuringly.

Vicky Bray-Rivers – the Queen Bee of the Saffron Walden 'ladies who lunch' set, glanced discreetly over to this unknown competitor and sniffed snootily before returning to an article on *Pilates For Your Pooch*.

Becky, the young new apprentice, stopped sweeping the floor and gawped at Chris, as though he'd sprouted a second head or something. Chris instructed Becky to show Brooke to a chair and make her a tea.

'I'm just finishing Janey's highlights and I'll be with you. I've got *so* much to talk to you about!' Chris trotted back to Janey and apologised for the interruption, going on to explain his and Brooke's special relationship. Janey listened while Chris talked, barely pausing for breath. The more he talked, the more

17. I have missed you.
18. I have missed you too. I yearn for you to walk through the door.
19. Well I'm here now so we can talk.

she became intrigued about this woman Brooke and she found herself craning her neck to check her out.

Finally, Chris finished Janey's highlights and gathered the staff over to admire them. 'Doesn't she look gorgeous?' Chris asked. It was a rhetorical question but they all nodded, prodded, poked and stroked at various places signifying agreement. Chris and Janey made a big play of air-kissing several times and Chris wished her luck with her job interview, declaring boldly that with hair like that she'd nail it.

Once the preamble about what he was going to be doing with her hair was over and after she'd had it washed by Becky, Brooke's trip to Law's began in earnest.

'So, what've you been doing with yourself? What's the latest with that crazy job of yours with that old lady? I've been dying to know! I've so missed you! Our chats!' Chris exclaimed.

Brooke went on to give a brief summary of everything that'd happened since her last visit six months previously.

'Oh my god, Brooke. What are you like? Well don't you dare stop coming here just 'cause you've come into money!' he joked.

'Never. Where else can I get my fix of Greek and Roman history?! Absolutely no one else "gets" me, if you know what I mean,' she replied.

'Well, your Latin's improved since your last visit!' Chris responded.

'I'm trying to get my head round first declension nouns at the moment – bloody nightmare.'

'Oh I sympathise! They're tough!' Chris pulled her hair in various directions and clipped up sections of it as he talked. 'Now, I've been dying to ask...did you see Mary Beard's documentary about Caligula?'

'Oh my god, I was like, how can someone so off his marbles rule anything?'

Sarah Barnsley pretended not to be listening, but her eyes shifted to the mirror to her left, so she could lipread above the noise of the hairdryers. Chris held the ends of Brooke's hair up to show her where he planned to cut.

'I reckon you need a good two or three centimetres off, OK? The guy was completely unhinged. He must be one of the earliest examples of cross-dressing in history, no?'

Luella Bates giggled in her chair as she earwigged the conversation.

'Yeah three centimetres is perfect – to my T2 vertebrae. What I don't understand is what kind of message he thought he was giving to the common people, when he built a house for his bloody horse from marble and ivory!'

Snip, snip, snip.

Becky the apprentice gawped, making no bones about the fact that she was finding the discussion absolutely fascinating.

Snip, snip, snip.

'Tilt your head forward for me, my love.'

Snip, snip, snip.

'He was so wasteful, wasn't he? I can't believe he made them build a bridge across the sea, just so him and his bloody horse could keep galloping across it for fun. What was all that about?'

Snip, snip, snip.

'Well he just didn't care, did he? No wonder he felt entitled to have it off with his sisters.'

Snip, snip, snip.

'What a complete perv. All that business about it being an offence to mention goats in his presence just because he was a hairy bugger himself.'

They both fell into a fit of very loud giggles as Chris picked up some of Brooke's hair off the floor and put it up against his chest, gurning to resemble the ugly Caligula.

Chris's brother Steve looked over to him and mouthed, 'Shut the hell up, Chris!' He was used to Chris and his unorthodox ways, but not everyone was and it would take some getting used to for many ladies, coming in to get their hair cut and being subject to such…well let's just call them curious conversations! For many, where they were going on holiday and how their children were doing, was as deep a conversation as one expected from the hairdressing community. But not in Law's Salon. It provided so much more than superficial conversation. It was pure theatre and entertainment, all for the price of a haircut!

Chris poked his tongue out, threw the hair down and continued unabated. 'And he was a two-faced sod! Can you stand up, my love, so I can brush the hair off you?' Brooke stood up and allowed herself to be swept all over. Conversation ceased for a while as he blow-dried her hair to within an inch of its life. 'So, what's this special dinner you're going to?' Chris asked as he put the finishing touches to his styling.

'Dean's company's going for an award from the Chamber of Commerce. He's done so much work, bless him; trying to recruit the most "diverse workforce".' Brooke put quote marks around the phrase as she said it. 'It's been well hard, but he reckons they've got a good chance of winning. I'm looking forward to it! Never been to anything like that before.'

'He needs a Caligula,' retorted Chris, as sharp as a pin. They burst into another loud fit of giggles at the till. 'Now, Brooke De'Ath, you need your highlights doing again. You shouldn't leave it so long! And now I've just become a member of the 'L'Oreal Artistic ID team,' Chris coughed and put on a display of mock superiority, 'you'll be getting the best. They don't take on just anybody, you know!'

'Oh blimey. Well done. I can't believe you didn't mention it earlier; most unlike you!'

'Well Caligula and Agrippina won the day, didn't they, my love'?' he joked.

'You doing anything nice at the weekend?' Brooke enquired.

'I am, as it goes! Me and Steve are going to a charity event at Peterborough United's ground tonight; it's gonna be great!'

'Bully for you! Enjoy!'

They gave each other a final goodbye hug and Brooke left, feeling like a million dollars as well as her appetite for Classics talk sated.

***

When she got back home, Dean was rehearsing an acceptance speech, in case they won the award. She let him get on with it so that she could spend time getting ready. He spoke to an empty room.

'I am honoured to be here this evening with my beautiful wife...'

No. That don't sound right. Brooke's got nothing to do with it.

'I am honoured to be here this evening with my fantastic team, who've been so supportive of my efforts to ensure TrussInUs has the most diverse workforce in our industry. In return, as our strapline says, 'we'll support you from every angle'. We've learned a lot along the way and I think it's safe to say that we all have a better understanding of diversity than we had before. Never again will I say BLT. No more will I wonder what's under a hijab or think that all Muslims are terrorists. And I've come to realise that women's brains don't drop out just because they're pregnant, as you'll see from our very own gorgeous, sexy Chloe! I'd like to invite her and the whole team up on stage to show off our very own "variety box!" Come on up, guys!'

Mmm. Not sure about that...maybe it should be ***our*** *efforts?*

As Brooke walked in, Dean looked up and wolf-whistled at her. 'You look bloody amazing!' he said.

'Thanks, babe. All for you. Don't wanna let you down on your special evening.'

'You'll never let me down, babe. Look at you. You're beautiful.' With that, he stood up and gave her an enormous squeeze and nuzzled into her neck. 'You smell gorgeous. How d'ya fancy a bit of slap and tickle[20] before we leave?! Paige is in her playpen.' He winked at her followed by wide-eyed anticipation and the cheekiest of grins.

'Dean De'Ath, I've just had me hair done. It'll get ruined!' Brooke retorted in alarm.

Dean let her go and shrugged, knowing no sane man would even attempt to overturn such female logic. He quickly returned to his speech and read it out loud to Brooke. 'What d'ya think?'

'Oh, babe. That's really beautiful. God, I hope you win after all this!'

***

20. Sex.

By 6pm, they were both dressed up to the nines. Dean had even hired an evening suit and bow tie and put it on expenses. Brooke decided she didn't need to buy another dress. She could wear the LBD she wore to the Royal Opera House (first time round).

They'd decided not to ask Jackie to babysit again and so, for the first time, they used a local girl – a near neighbour's teenage daughter called Poppy, who'd come recommended by Katie Mellor. 'She's a little diamond' was all she kept saying about her. 'Just feed her pizza and chips, four pound an hour – no more or you'll make it hell for the rest of us – and she'll be happy as Larry.' Brooke did as instructed and, sure enough, as soon as she arrived, she seemed very content and played nicely with Paige.

Suddenly Dean's phone rang.

'Dean, it's me, Chloe. I'm really sorry, but I'm not gonna be able to make it tonight. I've been having twinges on and off all day. I think it's too risky, so me and Mum are gonna stay at home.'

Dean fell onto the sofa in despair.

'No, Chloe! Please don't do this to me! Not now! I'll do anything to get you to come.'

Brooke listened to Dean's end of the conversation for the next few minutes, wondering what on earth was going on.

'I tell you what, Chloe. I'll give you a £500 bonus if you make it – as a special thank you!' Dean sounded absolutely desperate. 'What d'ya say?'

Chloe thought about the very generous offer and what she could buy for the baby with that money and quickly reversed her decision not to come, but made it clear she'd be leaving the minute she could. Dean breathed a sigh of relief followed by an internal groan as he thought about having to tell Dave why he'd paid Chloe an extra £500 that month.

It felt odd to Dean making a train journey in such fancy clothes. He kept tweaking his bow tie and complaining that his dress shirt was too tight and uncomfortable. Brooke sat with her legs crossed, looking elegant but feeling as though they ought to be sitting in First Class. She glanced into the first-class seating area and a fellow passenger noticed her and joked, 'Don't look at what you can't afford.' Brooke was mortified and turned to look out the window.

How dare he?! How does he know what we can and can't afford? Tosser.

As was often the way, Brooke wasn't quick enough to come up with a suitable response, so she smiled smugly and thought of her winnings.

If only you knew, mate. If only you knew!

By 7pm they'd arrived at Conway Hall, which was already buzzing with a huge crowd guzzling pre-dinner drinks and wolfing down canapes; the crowd was much larger than Dean had expected. There must've been several hundred people there. Dean's face dropped when he realised how many businesses they were up against, but tried to keep a stiff upper lip for the sake of his team. Heads turned the minute they began making their way through the crowd. Women stopped talking to observe this heavenly looking creature and men dribbled into their drinks pretending not to notice her. Dean suddenly caught sight of Chloe and her mother. Brooke chatted comfortably with them both, congratulated Chloe and hoped that everything went well for her. Dean gave her an insensitive squeeze and thanked her profusely for making the effort to come.

By 7.30pm the crowd were instructed to go into dinner. Led

by Dean, who checked out the table plan and directed his team accordingly, the staff took their places at the various tables that'd been placed close together so they could talk to one another.

Before the dinner was served, Dean excused himself and went to speak to Chloe. He pulled her away from her table as surreptitiously as possible, looking extremely serious and concerned.

'Look, Chloe, I know you're nearly there, but I still think you don't look very pregnant. You could just be a bit fat! I'm worried they'll think I've made it up just to win the award. Can you make sure that if we win and I invite you up onto stage that you stick that belly out and make it as obvious as possible that you are actually pregnant?'

'For god's sake, Dean! You're lucky I'm here at all! I could've not bothered and left weeks ago to go and live with Mum and Dad. I've done the mother of all favours for you by staying on until today!' She could barely comprehend what he was asking her!

'I know, I know, but you know how much this means to me, Chloe. You know how I've struggled. Please?' Dean pleaded.

'Alright alright, keep your hair on! I'll do my best, OK?' Chloe waddled back to her chair and sat down.

Throughout dinner, Dean kept asking his colleagues if they thought the presentation of their meal was good, if they thought the staff were efficient and if anyone came back from the lavatory, they couldn't escape Dean's heavy questioning about toilet rolls and soap. He'd got to the point in his mystery shopping career whereby he simply couldn't switch off when he was out. The staff put it down to his well-known OCD behaviour at work.

At 9pm the award ceremony began. There were awards for every imaginable facet of running a business: best training programme, lowest carbon footprint…

That'll be me next year if Dave's got anything to do with it.

…most profitable company, best manager, fastest-growing business, top exporter, company with most female managers, most creative product, best contributor to local community. The list went on and on. It got to about 9.45pm and the chairman announced the next award.

'The next award is one particularly close to my heart. As the parent of a gay son and a disabled wife, I've seen for myself the prejudice they've suffered over the years and so it gives me great pleasure to present this award to a company who've clearly gone the extra mile in ensuring that their workforce is representative of British society today. They've truly grasped the Diversity Challenge and risen to it. It gives me great pleasure to announce the winner as… TrussInUs!'

Dean bounced up, turned around to his team and punched the air as he shouted 'YESSS!' Brooke let out a little yelp and flung her arms around him. Dave high-fived him and his team started clapping and cheering along with the rest of the crowd in the hall. Dean felt his heart was going to leap through his rib cage with pride and joy. He fiddled about with his bow tie and pulled his trousers up by the waistband before making his way through the tables and onto the stage to collect the award.

He went on to make the speech he'd prepared earlier. He had a copy of it in his pocket, typed in Arial font size 14, double-spaced for easy reading and stapled in the corner in case he dropped it. Although he had it in front of him, he knew it off by heart and he delivered it well with only a few pauses and a couple of minor fumbles.

'I am honoured to be here this evening with my fantastic team, who've been so supportive of my…*our* efforts to ensure TrussInUs has the most diverse workforce in our industry. In return, as our strapline says, '*we'll support you from every angle*'. We've learned a lot along the way and I think it's safe to say that we all have a better understanding of diversity than we had before. Never again will I say BLT. No more, will I wonder what's under a hijab or think that all Muslims are terrorists. And I've come to realise that women's brains don't drop out just because they're pregnant, as you'll see from our very own gorgeous, sexy Chloe! I'd like to invite her and the whole team up on stage to show off our very own "variety box". Come on up, guys!'

The crowd, at a loss how to react to such a speech, forced Dave to start the clapping off and after encouraging other tables to start clapping too, the staff from TrussInUs clumsily made their way up onto stage. Linda led the pack, dressed from top to toe in a long red satin number with very high matching heels. Dean had instructed all the team to use the evening to show their 'uniqueness'. So next up was Dennis, who had shaved a cross into the back of his head to please his boss. He didn't mind; it was his idea. Darpan hadn't done anything special and looked around in awe as he enjoyed his moment of fame. Charmaine and Alyssa, who were carrying enough gold between them to make Missy Elliot look underdressed, strutted with sass all the way to the stage, punching the air and screeching with laughter as they got onto the stage. Patrick lolled about behind with pint of Guinness in hand clinking glasses with people on the tables as he went. Ruth marched on after them and organised everyone on the stage, followed by Faisal who appeared totally bemused by the entire event, although he did sneak in a quick selfie and immediately send it to his wife in Damascus.

Where's Jawaria?

Back at the table Jawaria was asleep (aka having a narcoleptic moment). Dave and Jules decided they ought probably to leave her be as they weren't sure how she'd react if they shook her awake. Being the bosses, none of the rest of the staff felt they should intervene, so they left her there.

Where's Chloe?

Somewhere in the middle of the hall Chloe could faintly be seen from the stage, bent over and holding the back of someone's chair. She looked up towards Dean with an expression of sheer terror. Dean motioned to her to come to the stage. As the clapping subsided, she very, very slowly walked towards the stage steps, holding her belly and looking decidedly unwell. A woman on one of the tables asked her if she was OK.

'Fine thanks. Just pregnant!' She stopped again and began to hyperventilate.

The woman looked aghast. Dean held up his hand to the audience and shouted, 'Hang on a minute. I'll be right back.' The audience started to murmur and talk amongst themselves as Dean ran down the steps and straight over to Chloe. He whispered through gritted teeth, 'Come on, Chloe. You can do it! Just a few more steps and a couple of minutes of speech and then your mum can take you off.'

'AAAAAAGH!' she suddenly screamed out, making several people noticeably jump in their chairs and look at Dean with suspicion. 'I knew I shouldn't have come, Dean. Big, big mistake!' she managed to get out from between clenched teeth. He took her hand and all but dragged her up onto the stage while one of the organisers quickly grabbed a chair and invited her to sit on it. Dean carried on.

'This is our beautiful Chloe Babblecock – expecting… and er…about to drop any minute I think…hahaha! So I'll be quick…'

'AAAAGH!' Chloe bent over and let Charmaine and Alyssa rub her back as she let out an almighty groan.

'She's been a stalwart throughout her time with TrussInUs and we very much hope that she'll return at some point in the…'

'AAAAAAGH!' The hall gasped, haunted by Chloe's wail; all eyes moved to the figure slumped over a chair. Several women at tables stood up and looked around helplessly.

'Future. I…'

'AAAAAGH…me waters have broken! I can feel it! Get Mum!' she wailed.

Oh shit! That's all I need!

Dean put his hand up above his eyes to shield them from the bright lights, looked out into the hall and shouted to Chloe's mother, 'Scarlett, can you come up and help? Can someone call an ambulance?' Another of the organisers found some spare tablecloths and threw them onto the stage where Chloe's waters were seeping slowly towards the edge. Scarlett was already navigating her way through the tables towards her daughter. In the meantime, the whole team had crowded around Chloe to protect her from being gawped at by the audience. Dennis fell to his knees praying. Finally, Scarlett got to her daughter and wrapped her arms around her.

'C'mon, love, the ambulance is on its way, let's move you off this stage.' Dean smiled at Scarlett from the other side of the stage and gave her the thumbs up. Scarlett mumbled something under her breath and shook her head at Dean.

With the help of Dennis, Chloe was carefully walked off the stage, where a staff member had managed to find a wheelchair. Chloe's pale blue, comfortable maternity dress was now sporting a large dark stain on her bottom. She fell into the wheelchair with another loud groan and was wheeled away by Dennis to the foyer of Conway Hall, where she continued having contractions every few minutes.

As none of the organisers had yet come up onto the stage to guide Dean as to what he should do, he was unsure how to play things from here, so he merely held up the award and shouted above (what was by this time) a very noisy hall of people, all discussing the pros and cons of having come to an award ceremony so close to the birth. 'Thanks for this. I dedicate it to Chloe Babblecock! Good luck, Chloe!'

Just then Archie Wright, the current president of the Chamber of Commerce, bounced up onto the stage and practically pushed Dean out the way as he grabbed the microphone.

'Er...well that's a first! Thanks everyone for your patience and sorry for the mess and such an erm...unforeseen event! I think Chloe's in good hands now though, so, unless anyone has any wild objections, I think we should continue with the rest of the ceremony. We still have a few awards to give out.'

He turned to Dean and asked him to get his team off the stage pronto as they were now running behind. Dean ushered them all back to their seats, like children at the end of a school nativity play, thanking them profusely as he did so.

Where the fuck are Dave and Jules?

'What's all the commotion?' asked Jawaria, suddenly coming

out of her narcoleptic episode and noticing the movement and noise all around her. The team laughed in amazement.

'Go back to sleep, Jawaria! You only missed us winning the award and Chloe's waters breaking on stage!' shouted Charmaine. Jawaria was horrified and started apologising profusely to the team that she hadn't been up there with them to help.

When Dean sat back down, he noticed a handwritten note next to his coffee.

'Sorry, Dean. Had to go. Well done! See you Monday.' It was signed by Dave. No explanation. Nothing!

WTF? I don't believe it!

He didn't have too much time to dwell on why they'd had to go. Brooke was nowhere to be seen and Dean felt he couldn't leave the team at this particular time. Maybe they were traumatised? Maybe they would need counselling at what they'd witnessed? His diversity notes had also spoken about people with mental health conditions and how easily some people got PTSD. He looked over with concern at Darpan, who seemed fine on the surface hoovering up everyone else's dessert with glee and licking his fingers loudly; but what if he was supressing suicidal thoughts after witnessing such a traumatic event, that he himself didn't even realise he was suffering?

Back at the tables, the team swung from chatting about their concern for Chloe's wellbeing, wondering whether it would be a boy or girl, what name she'd give it and delight that they'd won the award. Patrick started taking bets as to how much the baby would weigh.

Brooke had gone to stay with Chloe until the ambulance arrived and did her best to placate Scarlett Babblecock who complained that Dean had pressurised her daughter into going to the dinner when she should've been at home. As Brooke watched Chloe in agony, writhing around on the wheelchair, her mind turned momentarily to Dean's desperation for another baby. It made the hair on the back of her neck stand up in terror and she stroked Chloe's hair as much to calm herself down as Chloe.

'Don't worry, babe. Won't be long now,' Brooke said sympathetically.

Once the ambulance had taken Chloe and her mother away, Brooke returned to the hall, by which time the award ceremony had finished. She went straight over to Dean and embraced him.

'Poor you, babe! Of all the things to happen! She was a few weeks early though, right?'

'God, I know! Crazy huh? Not one hundred per cent sure she told me the entire truth about her due date, to be honest.' The fact was that he'd not told *Brooke* the entire truth about Chloe's due date, as he'd a feeling that Brooke would've given him hassle. 'I hope she's alright. Her mum didn't look too happy.' He took a large glug of beer. 'D'ya think my speech went alright?'

'I think everyone was stunned, babe; it was just so beautiful. Well done. I'm so proud of you!' She pecked him on the cheek. 'Who needed a pomosexual, anyway?' They both laughed. Gradually the evening came to a close and people started making their way out of the hall and home. Before his own team left, Dean gathered them all round his table and one last time thanked them profusely for coming to the dinner, for all their help in winning the award and for their help with Chloe. He said he hoped they'd all had an enjoyable night. They all seemed touched and said they'd see him Monday.

Brooke and Dean waited until they'd all left before they too made their way home, reflecting on the general success of the evening – Chloe's waters aside. As they pulled in to Brentwood station, a message came through on Dean's phone.

'Apple' born 11.15pm 6Lb 2oz. Mum and baby doing OK. No thanks to you Dean De'Ath!

'Chloe's had a girl!' Dean declared joyfully.

'Yay!' Brooke cheered.

'Bloody stupid name though – Apple. Only a bit better than banana.'

'Aww that's so cute. That's Gwyneth Paltrow's kid's name. What did she weigh?'

'That's the best news of all. 6lb 2oz.'

'Why's that the best news?'

'Patrick was taking bets as to who'd guess the closest to the weight of the baby. I've just won twenny quid! If you wanna place a bet and guarantee winnings – I'm your man! Hahahahah!'

Brooke chuckled away to herself as they climbed into a cab and Dean fell into a smug, self-satisfied sleep on the way home.

At number 6 Elephant Close, Poppy was perched on the edge of the sofa, waiting for Dean and Brooke, coat on, clutching her little handbag with a somewhat vacant/terrified expression. The second she heard the front door, she was up like a shot. 'Gotta go, Brooke, sorry. Pay me tomorrow. Hope you had a nice time.'

With that, she ran off to number 32, at the end of the road, as if her life depended on it. Brooke waited until she'd seen her get inside her house before closing her own front door.

'Wonder what that was all about? I'm gonna check on Paige.'

Brooke crept up into Paige's bedroom and peered into her

cot. Unfortunately, there was no sign of Paige and her room looked as though World War Three had taken place in there.

Oh shit!

'Dean! We've got a problem, Paige isn't in her cot!' she shouted loudly down the stairs. Brooke immediately checked the bathroom, while Dean leaped up the stairs two at a time and ran straight into their bedroom. Occasionally Paige had found her way into their bed during the night, so he assumed she'd done that this evening. She was, however, not there. He whisked around maniacally and noticed the bottom drawer of their large chest of drawers was open. He dashed over and there, inside, all curled up in her West Ham babygro was Paige, snuggled up in between Brooke's collection of M&S cashmere jumpers.

28

Post Award Glow and Agonising Dilemmas

The Monday morning after the gala dinner, Dean had an unusual spring in his step as he got ready for work. Setting up the ironing board, he ironed his shirt with his usual military precision. In Dean's book, crease-free shirts were not merely desirable but essential. There's no way he'd leave it to Brooke, who was capable of scorching anything within seconds of it hitting the ironing board. His mind went back to Friday evening. He'd won the award! What a night! (Except Dave and Jules inexplicably deserting poor Jawaria, left nodding off into her tiramisu.) He was now ready to leverage all the power and influence this award might give him.

Brooke felt a bit groggy, but was itching to tell Mrs Townsend about Dean winning the award. Unfortunately, she was forced to stay in bed for longer than normal while Dean was faffing about, polishing his shoes. Once finished, he bounded up the stairs and presented himself to his wife. 'What d'ya think, babe?'

'Very nice, but aren't you gonna be late?' she said slightly too impatiently.

'Maybe. But I'm the boss, and after Friday night there's no harm in reminding them of that,' he said as he repositioned his tie in front of the mirror. 'I meant to say, you were fabulous on Friday night. I was dead chuffed that you're my wife. It does a man no end of good having someone as gorgeous as you to take along to an evening like that.'

'Aww thanks, babe!' Although the words came out naturally enough, for some reason she felt ill at ease with his 'compliment'.

Does he think I'm just one of them 'trophy wives?'

'So what you doing today?' Dean asked innocently. Brooke was taken by surprise and said she didn't know. It was fully accepted by Dean, who finally said goodbye and left for work.

The second the door slammed, Brooke was up like a shot, sweeping from room to room like a tornado, getting Paige ready first and enabling her to eat her mashed-up Weetabix by herself, by leaving her tied to her high chair with silk rope. Dean had learned from his granddad, who had been in the Navy, that a figure of eight knot was difficult to undo, so he thought it would be safe as well as educational for Paige. Lately, tying her in like this had afforded Brooke a little more uninterrupted time to put her make-up on, although it was clear from the amount of gloopy Weetabix on the rope that Paige had certainly attempted her Houdini act; merely not succeeded yet.

Brooke didn't fancy breakfast, so left a tad earlier than normal, arriving at Dawn's just after 9am. Dawn opened the door, yawning and munching on a slice of toast.

'So…did he get the award?' Dawn asked, having patiently listened to Brooke for weeks, relaying the challenges of finding a pomosexual and the ins and outs of the Refugee Council.

'Yes! He did! Oh, Dawn, I was dead chuffed. He looked so important! Up on that stage with everyone. But you'll never guess what happened?'

Dawn had got to the point that absolutely nothing would surprise her about her friend anymore and with blank face said,

'I'm sure you're gonna tell me.' She picked Paige up and plonked her on the beanbag in front of the TV.

'Chloe's waters broke on stage! It kind of messed up Dean's speech but she was alright in the end and had a baby girl a couple of hours later in hospital!'

Dawn shook her head and rolled her eyes. 'You got time for a cuppa?' she asked.

'No thanks, I feel a bit icky this morning – too much booze and tiramisu at the weekend!'

'You decided what you're gonna do about your winnings yet?' Dawn asked casually.

Brooke was hesitant to say. A knot quickly appeared in the pit of her stomach.

She won't approve of Paige going to Elizabeth Fry. I just know it.

'Well?' Dawn asked, wide-eyed.

'Well… I haven't exactly decided yet,' Brooke lied.

I'll suss her out first.

'But I spoke to Lady Townsend and Geoffrey and they've got some really good ideas,' she continued.

'Like what?' Dawn asked.

Brooke gulped. 'Well… I think I'm gonna put some of it in an education fund for Paige to go to Elizabeth Fry and the rest Geoffrey is gonna invest for me in stocks and shares.'

'You are fucking joking?'

'Dawn! Shh – no swearing in front of Paige!' Brooke put her fingers up to her lips.

'You can't send her there –stuck-up little snobs – that's what they are. And that's just the kids! You should hear the mums – ugh – completely up themselves in their fucking Range Rovers and Pilates classes.' There was disapproval and then there was vitriol. This rant definitely fell into the latter.

'I didn't think you'd approve somehow. But I haven't completely made up my mind yet,' she lied, resenting the way she was being made to feel about doing something so good.

'Don't turn her into something she ain't, Brooke, just 'cause you've had your head turned by that Lady Townsend woman,' Dawn retorted, scratching her bottom.

'Dawn, she's a good person and she's taught me a lot – not least that I'm capable of so much more than I'd ever thought. I wanna make sure Paige fulfils her potential.'

'Oh my giddy aunt, just listen to you. Yeah, well that may be, but you don't wanna turn her into one of them snooty, entitled kids that pour out those gates every day.'

'I think I'd better go, Dawn, before I say something I regret,' Brooke said with tears rising and her cheeks becoming flushed with anger. 'See you later.'

With that she pecked Paige on the cheek (whose eyes did not move from the TV) as she walked out.

Dawn shrugged. 'Whatever.'

As Brooke drove to Purses, her mind churned with Dawn's words. Did she have a point? Would Paige turn into the sort of child that her friends and family would despise? Why would she? The girls she'd met at the school were charming and beautifully behaved. They wore sensible shoes and still played hand-clapping games in the playground! And what's wrong with Pilates anyway? Before she realised, she was at Purses.

I'll talk to Mrs T. She'll know what to do.

She walked in through the staff entrance and immediately noticed the house was unusually quiet. The drawing room door was shut, also unusual at this time of day.

She must be in a meeting.

Brooke made a tea and took it into the library. She opened the pile of post on her desk straight away: an invitation to a gallery opening in New Bond Street, an invoice from the French polisher, draft landscape drawings from Julia Foxton, a begging letter from the WWF and a catalogue from Fortnum & Mason. As she considered what to do with it all, she sipped her tea, then grimaced.

God, that's disgusting!

She turned on her computer and quickly paid the polisher, replied yes to the gallery invitation and threw the begging letters in the bin.

Poor Mrs T. They've really got their claws into her.

Then she briefly browsed the Fortnum's catalogue. When she reached the page entitled 'Biscuits', her mouth watered, particularly when she read the description of their delicious *Piccadilly lemon curd* ones. How she fancied one of them right now! She flicked through the pages but returned to the biscuit page, biting her lip as she stared at pictures of the smooth, crispy little mounds of delicious, lemony yumminess. She reluctantly put the brochure down and moved onto the drawings for the Japanese garden, but couldn't focus. Her mind kept wandering from bamboo screening and red lacquer bridges to the wretched biscuits! Saliva filled her mouth until she could bear it no longer. In a moment of rashness, she picked up the phone and ordered a couple of tins to be delivered to Purses ASAP.

'Of course, Ms De'Ath. We'll get onto it straight away,' the sycophantic girl from Fortnum's replied.

How things have changed! Sixteen quid for some biccies! Obscene!

Once the order had been placed, she relaxed and was able to look at the drawings with a calmer disposition. She made notes to discuss with Lady Townsend later.

The wooden floor on the other side of the library suddenly came into view when the sun shone through the window. She gasped when she noticed how filthy it was. Without another thought, she fetched the floor polishing wax and cloths and set to straight away on her hands and knees rubbing and buffing. She inwardly chastised herself for letting it get so bad and forgetting her priorities. Mrs Townsend kept reassuring her that she wasn't overly concerned if the cleaning didn't get done quite as regularly as it used to, but Brooke kept noticing things that had been left too long. She decided that today she'd assess the entire house, make a comprehensive list of outstanding cleaning tasks and work out a rota for completing them; not easy between all the other jobs that Mrs Townsend now ensured filled her days. It took her two hours to compile a list of over a hundred tasks. This concerned her; she didn't want Mrs Townsend to stop involving her in the more interesting things, so she decided to keep quiet and just work her way through it.

Where is she anyway? And where's Hugo? I've not seen them all morning.

As she went to make herself another cup of tea, she passed the drawing room and the door swung open. Out came Hugo.

'Morning, Brooke! I was just going to come and find you,' he said cheerily and with a strange look on his face that Brooke couldn't quite fathom.

'Where've you both been all morning? The house has been like a morgue!' Brooke complained.

'Ah! In deep conversation with the old girl – she wants to

see you,' he whispered and nodded his head and eyes in the direction of the drawing room. Brooke's stomach fell to the floor, convinced she must have done something wrong. Mrs Townsend rarely asked for her like that. If she wanted to talk to her, she'd always come and find her.

'What for? What have I done?' Brooke's face was a picture; terror, innocence and panic all rolled into one. Hugo had to laugh. 'Don't laugh! Tell me, Eton boy!'

Hugo patted her on the arm and said, 'Don't worry, it'll be fine!' He then pushed her towards the drawing room. All this made her very nervous and unsure of what she was about to face. She tentatively poked her head around the door.

'Morning, Mrs Townsend. Hugo said you wanted to see me.'

'Oh, that was quick, dear. He's only just left. Come in and sit down.' She patted the sofa next to her. Brooke's stomach dropped even further. By this point, she'd convinced herself that Lady Townsend, too, had noticed the gradual decline in the cleanliness and general state of Purses.

'First things first, how did the awards dinner go on Friday night?' Lady Townsend sat down in the armchair opposite, all ears.

Oh my god, she actually remembered!

'Oh!' Brooke was pleasantly surprised and so she momentarily forgot her worries. 'Dean won the diversity award, Mrs T! He actually won! But one of his team – Chloe Babblecock – she was pregnant and her waters broke on the stage and we had to call an ambulance!'

'Good heavens! The poor girl! What was she doing there so late in her pregnancy?'

'God knows. I don't think Dean realised how far gone she

was and then she went into labour a bit early. Anyways, she had a baby girl called Apple a couple of hours later and so it's fine.' Brooke seemed anxious to get that part of the conversation out the way and move on. 'So… I think I know what you want to talk to me about and, before you say anything, can I just say that I've been round the whole house this morning and made an up-to-date list of all the outstanding jobs that need doing and I've worked out a rota for when I'll fit them in around all the other stuff you've given me.' She barely paused for breath before saying in a panic, 'I know I've probably got me priorities a bit wrong lately.'

'"My" priorities, dear – not "me" priorities.'

'Sorry, yes. Anyway, I'll get back on track, Mrs T, I promise.' Brooke spoke at lightning speed.

'Brooke. I don't want you cleaning another thing. Ever. Do you understand?' Lady Townsend looked and sounded very firm and did that looking over her glasses thing. The colour in Brooke's cheeks turned to the same shade of red as her lipstick. Tears welled up in her eyes again for the second time that morning. She looked like a rabbit from *Watership Down.*

I've been sacked. I can't believe it, she's sacked me!

'But, Mrs Townsend… I—'

'Brooke, listen to me. Hugo has just resigned. He's moving to London with Portia and taking up a new position with the Duke and Duchess of Portland.'

Brooke was dumbfounded. 'Oh my god, no! That's terrible. What on earth are you gonna do? You won't be able to cope without him – especially if I've gotta go too.'

'What *are* you talking about? You're not going anywhere, young lady. I'm promoting you to take over from Hugo.'

Brooke's mouth dropped open as though she'd suddenly been told that Mrs Townsend wore fake pearls.

'Close your mouth, dear, you'll swallow a fly.'

'I... I just don't know what to say.' Brooke stared at the floor, hands in lap, overwhelmed with emotion and feeling thoroughly sick.

'Yes would be a good start, dear,' Lady Townsend responded nonchalantly as she sat with her legs crossed, eyes piercing as she observed Brooke's face. 'But...you would have to work full time. We could be flexible about the hours, but I'm going to need you throughout the week – and even the occasional weekend. I'm offering £30,000 per year and we'd have to be all above board with that. Now, I know that your husband's been kept in the dark thus far, but I urge you to talk to him, Brooke, and tell him about this job offer. I think it's for the best.'

THIRTY GRAND?! What about Paige? And Dawn?

'I thought you'd just sacked me!' Brooke cried.

THIRTY GRAND?!

'Only from cleaning, dear! Your first job will be to recruit a new cleaner. She can start with your new jobs list!'

THIRTY GRAND?! I can't believe I'm worth thirty grand.

'Oh my giddy aunt! I'm flabbergasted, to be honest, Mrs T. Are you sure about this? I'm no Eton girl, you know.'

'No, well you couldn't be, dear, it's an all-boys school. Of course I'm sure. You've proven yourself ten-fold and between Geoffrey, Antonia and me, I think we've successfully increased your hinterland to a level where we can let you loose on polite society!' Lady Townsend burst out laughing and Brooke joined in until the tears flowed. Again.

'I wanna say yes, but I need to think about how I'm gonna

approach Dean. I think it'll be as much about *what* I'm doing. He's bound to think it'll be too much pressure. He always said he'd never see me get ill like his mum 'cause she had to work like mad just to keep the kids fed and clothed and he had five sisters as well and so, like, he wants me and our kids to have an easier time of it. I think it might make him feel a bit threatened, too.' It all tumbled out, one word after another like a pre-recorded message.

'Children, dear. Not kids. Kids are baby goats.'

'Sorry, children! You can see what I mean.'

'I can, Brooke, but I want you to think very carefully about that before saying yes.' At that moment Hugo came in with a tray of tea and biscuits. *Piccadilly lemon curd* biscuits. Brooke's eyes lit up and she breathed in quickly.

'Where d'ya get them biscuits?' she asked accusingly, clapping her hands in delight and grabbing the plate without being offered. She scoffed several down as though she hadn't eaten for a week.

'I've got a secret stash down in the stables,' Hugo replied.

'You two are so funny. I shall miss listening to the banter between you.'

'So? Are you going to take the job?' Hugo looked at Brooke in anticipation.

'Probably, but I need to work out what I'm gonna say to Dean. And my childminder Dawn, I've got a bit of a problem there, I think.'

'Won't she be happy to have more hours?' asked Lady Townsend, naively.

'No, it's not that. I haven't had a chance to tell you yet, Mrs T, but I went to see Geoffrey about investing my winnings and we came to the decision to put half away in an education fund for Paige so she can go to Elizabeth Fry Prep and invest the other half. I went to see the school and I just loved it. I can't imagine her going anywhere else now. Those little brown hats are so cute!'

'Well, I'm delighted, Brooke, you've made a very wise decision.'

'Thing is, Dawn's a bit…a bit Essex…if you know what I mean? A rough diamond and very down to earth.' *The irony of it,* thought Lady Townsend! 'When I told her I was thinking of sending Paige to that school, she went on a complete rant. It's obvious she doesn't approve.'

'Socialist, is she, dear?' Lady Townsend asked.

'Dunno. But I'm beginning to think I might have to find someone else to look after Paige. I've gotta think about who else could do it.' She held her stomach.

Uggh! Too many biccies.

Lady Townsend accepted that Brooke needed time to consider and said she didn't need an answer for a while. Hugo smiled and mouthed 'See? No need to worry!' Brooke left the drawing room in a daze. Her life was turning into one very complicated series of events.

***

That afternoon, Brooke picked Paige up at the usual time. The atmosphere was tense and she tried to pretend that nothing had happened that morning. Dawn had gone into 'silent mode'. She was apparently 'fine' when Brooke asked, as was Paige.

She returned home, plonked Paige straight into her playpen, went into the toilet and threw up. There she stayed for the next half an hour until she heard Dean come in through the front door. She sat on the toilet, her head buried in her hands. The same hands that were holding a white stick with two red lines as clear as day bang in the centre.

'Babe? I'm home!' Dean sounded unusually excited.

Brooke managed a strained shout from the lavatory, 'I'm in the loo!'

For another ten minutes, lips were bitten, ringlets pulled, chin quivered, tears flowed and stomach churned. Dean paced around outside the lavatory door, itching for her to come out.

'You alright in there, love? Paige's nappy's so full she's trying to take it off herself!'

Brooke eventually came out the lavatory looking somewhat dishevelled but looked Dean straight in the eye. Dean stood tall with both his arms out of sight and a grin as wide as the Amazon, barely able to contain his excitement. From behind his back he slowly produced what he'd decided was *exactly* what Brooke needed at this time.

'For you, babe.'

Brooke opened the basket lid to discover six inches of shiny, silky cream fur, aka a French bulldog. Dean watched Brooke's face intently and hopefully, as she absorbed what he'd done. Her face was unreadable as she watched the eight-week-old puppy curled up asleep.

'Well say something then!' Dean implored.

Non iterum[21]*!*

'Dean... I think we need to have a little chat... There's something I need to talk to you about.'

21. Not this again.

Thank you for reading and I hope you enjoyed the story! If you could spare a moment or two to leave an honest review on Amazon using the link below, it would be much very much appreciated.

https://www.amazon.co.uk/review/create-review/?ie=UTF8&channel=glance-detail&asin=183826924X

You can sign up to receive occasional and funny 'behind the scenes' information about my stories and advanced notification of new releases.

www.helenefield.com

The first book in the De'Ath Family Antics Series,
The Mystery Shopper & The Hot Tub is available here:
www.amazon.co.uk/dp/1838269231/

Acknowledgements

I would like to thank Teri Hampton, Leah Held, Alexander Merrow and Steve Johnson for their feedback, which was so incredibly helpful in ensuring this novel worked; also to Nicky Lovick for her editing and proofreading duties.

I must also thank Christopher Tregoning, Honorary Trustee of The Newmarket Horse Racing Museum, for generously giving up his time to advise and help with everything to do with Tattersall's, owning a race horse and racing at Newmarket.

I am most grateful to Jessie Burlinson for acting as consultant midwife and medical advisor extraordinaire!

Thanks must also go to Christopher Ogston, General Manager of The Jockey Club Rooms for his wonderful tour and for imparting so much knowledge about the paintings and objects d'art.

The Law brothers, Chris and Steve, also deserve a mention for agreeing to feature not only their hairdressing salon, Law's in Saffron Walden, but to play cameo roles in the story!

In addition, Jenny Hand, Director of Albert Munnings Art Museum must be acknowledged for her advice about conserving paintings; procedure and protocol.

Finally, I must pay tribute to my wonderful husband, Nic, yet again; he has helped me on many occasions and contributed in a number of ways to the story.

Printed in Dunstable, United Kingdom

66688885R00221